## LET THE PUNISHMENT
## FIT THE CRIME . . .

The noble spat in Gawaine's direction: "We are not done with you, *horseboy*. Stand up and come here."

"He is not your property, or anyone's," Naitachal said very softly. "If I were you, I would leave him alone."

*Property.* Gawaine's hands clenched the edge of the table as the Bard's foot crunched into his shin; he pulled his legs under him and ignored the warning. One of the nobles nudged the other and laughed loudly. "Hey. Lookit the horseboy. He din't like what you said."

"Awww," another chimed in. "Poor li'l thing, is it angry?"

"Awww!" added the first.

"Enough!" Their leader shouted over the laughter. "I said stand up, horseboy. Take what's coming to you."

Gawaine launched himself up and out, but his fists and nose came into abrupt contact with an unseen barrier. "Damn all, let me at them!"

"Sit down. Be still." Naitachal spoke so quietly that Gawaine should not have been able to hear him. But the words echoed between his ears, and knocked the legs from under him. He fell, a boneless bundle, and only by luck came squarely down on the chair.

Naitachal, the Dark Elf, flowed to his feet. As one, the four young blades stepped back—but there seemed to be some barrier behind them as well as before. The Bard who had been a Necromancer smiled and raised his arms. For a moment all was still. His lips moved soundlessly in echoing silence.

Finally the silence was broken by the innkeeper's frightened wail: *"What have you done to them?"*

## ALSO IN THIS SERIES
Castle of Deception, *Mercedes Lackey & Josepha Sherman*
Prison of Souls, *Mercedes Lackey & Mark Shepherd* (forthcoming)

## Baen Books By Mercedes Lackey
Bardic Voices: The Lark & The Wren
The Ship Who Searched (*with Anne McCaffrey*)
Reap the Whirlwind (*with C.J. Cherryh*)
Wing Commander: Freedom Flight (*with Ellen Guon*)

*Urban Fantasies*
Knight of Ghosts and Shadows (*with Ellen Guon*)
Summoned to Tourney (*with Ellen Guon*)
Born to Run (*with Larry Dixon*)
Wheels of Fire (*with Mark Shepherd*)
When the Bough Breaks (*with Holly Lisle*)

# THE BARD'S TALE
# FORTRESS of FROST and FIRE

# MERCEDES LACKEY
# &
# RU EMERSON

BAEN

Baen Publishing Enterprises
P.O. Box 1403
Riverdale, NY 10471

ISBN: 0-671-72162-3

Cover art by Larry Elmore

First Printing, April 1993

Distributed by Simon & Schuster
1230 Avenue of the Americas
New York, NY 10020

Printed in the United States of America

For Doug (of course)

And to my very dear friends, the Amarylidaceae

--Ru Emerson

# Chapter I

For the first time in many days, the west wind died away with sunset. It was fairly warm and very quiet along the edge of the Whispering Woods. Quiet enough in the stable that the human boy grooming two travel-worn horses could easily make out individual voices from the Moonstone Inn, some distance to the west—and upwind—across a neatly tended courtyard. Mostly dry or downright sarcastic elven voices, but of course, the Moonstone was owned by White Elves. An occasional, coarser human voice rose above the rest.

Gawaine sighed and freed a hand from his present task to push long, loose carrot-colored curls back under the edge of the cloth band, then went back to currying the horses. His master would wonder where he was, why it was taking him so long to finish such a simple task. *But I like being in a stable*, Gawaine thought. *Even after four years, I feel like I've come home, tending to the horses, breathing the smell of horses and hay*. A loud burst of laughter from the inn made him jump; his gray stepped back nervously and he automatically rubbed the heavy neck muscles, reassuringly. "It's all right, Thunder; sorry I startled you," he said softly. "They startled me, though. Somehow you don't expect that kind of raucous noise from an inn full of White Elves."

Probably that had been some of the humans.

Though Gawaine had had to reevaluate his notions of White Elves when Naitachal brought him into elven country. "I thought they would be — well, look at them, tall and beautiful, so long-lived! You'd think they would all have beautiful souls, too; that anyone with so much time would be more spiritual. It's just like everything else, Thunder," he mumbled gloomily. "Things used to be so simple." Thunder — named partly for his storm-cloud color, mostly for the heavy way he set his feet down — leaned against him and lipped his hair. Gawaine chuckled softly, gave him a shove so he could get past him into the open, and patted his rump on the way by.

Across the aisle, there were at least a dozen elven horses. He smiled and sighed happily. Thunder was his own horse, and he dearly loved the cobby dapple gray, but those beauties . . . they made him warm and shivery all over. "Look at those long legs, at that golden tail, and you," he murmured as he wandered down the aisle. "Oh, you love." The horse in question turned its head to give him a long look from under thick lashes, then turned back to its feed. Gawaine sighed again and turned back to take care of his Master's black, Star. *What an insipid name for such a nice-looking fellow*, he thought. From another point of view, he'd been named by his Master after one of the heroic steeds from an epic verse — which was *really* silly when you got to know the phlegmatic, unexciteable Star.

Star munched while Gawaine rubbed, ignoring both the boy and Thunder, whose jealousy made an hour like this difficult. Thunder caught hold of Gawaine's tunic and tugged, and when Gawaine turned his head to free the garment, lipped at his hair again, catching hold of the band and pulling it off his young master's head. Thick, copper-colored curls fell across his face and Gawaine had to shove them back and hold them with one hand while he snatched at the cloth band. He finally caught it, slid it over his forehead and smacked Thunder's neck. "Stop that. Behave yourself." Thunder simply looked at him. Gawaine scowled as he shoved the last of his hair off his forehead and out of his eyes, and moved around to Star's other side to finish his grooming.

Another burst of laughter from the inn; someone was telling lamp-wick jokes in there, from the sound of things: ". . . only one, but the wick has to *want* to change!" And a cutting retort topping the laughter, "How dreadfully witty the entertainment is tonight!"

*Change.* Gawaine stopped rubbing and let his chin rest on Star's back. Four years of change for him — four years that sometimes felt more like a full lifetime. It was increasingly difficult for him to remember that boy who had been one of Squire Tombly's horseboys. "Sixteen and looking for all the world like twelve," he murmured. Star laid back one ear and Thunder turned to look at him curiously. Not that it was much better now; at twenty, he still found that most of those around him looked at the carroty hair, the slender build, and those wretched freckles and thought, "Fifteen, at most." It had been worse, though: he had been short to boot, back then, smaller than anyone else on the squire's land save the *genuine* children.

Fortunately, he hadn't been the twelve he'd looked, because before his voice broke, he hadn't been able to sing two notes in tune together. "I would probably have still been stuck in that foul-smelling little cell where Naitachal found me — if the squire hadn't simply executed me."

Unpleasant thought. For five years — six? — his whole life had revolved around caring for the squire's horses. Life had been hard, of course, especially for the smallest horseboy, and particularly for one who looked like he did — the only pale, freckly redhead, half the size of the others, and especially for someone as serious as he normally had been, even then. It had been even harder once he had shown so much of a gift for dealing with horses and had come to the personal attention of the squire's horsemaster. Standing out for size and looks had been one thing; standing out because he was good at what he did had caused no end of trouble, with first one and then another of the other horseboys finding ways to make life miserable for him.

All the same, it hadn't been a bad life. He'd been cared for, well fed, and there was a simplicity to things he looked back at with longing. In that life, a boy performed his tasks and did them well, obeyed orders, kept to his place and got on with the other boys in the stable — or at least, didn't fight with them enough to bring himself to the attention of the horsemaster. That was Right; anything else was Wrong. There weren't any complications, none of these moral dilemmas one tripped over constantly in the Real World. No shades of gray anywhere.

Gawaine sighed, righted himself, and applied the brush to Star's dusty flanks. Probably that had only been a boy's view of matters, or what Naitachal called "looking back with one blind eye." Things couldn't have been quite as simple as all that, however they looked from a distance of four years and a lot of miles.

They had certainly gotten complicated with a vengeance when the squire's prize stallion had vanished — and Gawaine, as the horse's groomer and the only one of the stableboys who dared approach the brute, had been accused of its theft.

"So stupid," he mumbled, and Star shifted to look back at him. "The horse vanished from his *stall*, it was so *obvious* that magic had to be involved — and back then, what had I ever done that someone could think I had the least bit of magic? Besides, if I'd been able to create Darkness all around the stable, even at night, and then send the stallion elsewhere, wouldn't everyone been aware I had that kind of Power?" He looked at Star and shrugged; the horse blinked and went back to his feed. "Anyway, what was a mere stableboy supposed to do with a horse like Firestorm?" *Sell it, and at a very high price*, they'd said. Yes, and how was a mere horseboy supposed to account for such sudden wealth? That had been most conveniently glossed over — everyone ignoring the fact that Gawaine hadn't disappeared with the horse, or shown any signs of having a personal supply of coin. The mage the squire hired to examine the entire stable and all the staff hadn't been able to locate a cache of coin or find any trace in Gawaine's mind of having cached anything — except the wooden top he had hidden, years before, to keep one of the older and larger boys from taking it.

Gawaine grinned, remembering the look on that mage's face — and on the squire's — when the compost heap had been excavated and they had found, not a bag of silver and gold, but a rotting bit of fashioned oak. At the time, he had found that episode almost more embarrassing than being put on trial for horse thievery.

There was no doubt the squire had been deeply embarrassed, too: bellowing all those orders, up to his knees in the hole, waiting for evidence to be pulled from the hot, reeking mess only to find . . . That moment had ended Gawaine's public trial; Squire Tombly had tromped off, shouting furiously, and his final order had resulted in his erstwhile horseboy being chucked into a cell.

Magic. "Who would ever have thought?" Gawaine

murmured. He hadn't ever given it any thought himself; so far as he knew, neither had anyone on that entire vast estate. If it hadn't been for someone saying what so many thought, that the stallion could only have been spirited out of the stable by magic . . . Gawaine patted Star's neck, ran his fingers through the long mane to comb free several thorny seed-pods. That had been the real cause of all his troubles: magic. He had only been a minor suspect in the matter until that mage showed up. Tottery, white-haired, half senile, the mage had gone down the line of horseboys and come back twice before stopping in front of Gawaine and leveling a trembly, liver-spotted hand at his nose. And on the strength of his word that there was "something about this boy" — and no other evidence whatever — the squire had named Gawaine horse thief, and turned him over to the guard.

Gawaine leaned against the back wall of the stable and stared into space; he could almost see — and smell — that nasty little dirt-floored chamber, right next to the goat sheds. Almost as if they had known how very much he loathed the smell of goat and wanted to get in a little subtle torture. Not Squire Tombly, of course: the squire wasn't a subtle man at any time, and he had no doubt been heating irons and consulting with his by-the-day rent-a-mage, to see what would hurt the most — even if the first application of pain got a response to the whereabouts of his stallion. Between the two — the reality and the possibilities — Gawaine's spirits had been very low indeed.

"If I'd been squawking in a boy's soprano, I'll wager Master Naitachal would have gone right by — probably at double step," Gawaine added to himself, and grinned. He'd been singing, partly to pass the time and mostly to keep his spirits up, and the Dark Elf — once Necromancer, now a full Bard — later claimed he had been stopped in his tracks by the underlying Power he felt in that voice. There wasn't any doubt Naitachal had been impressed enough by Gawaine's singing, and his potential; as proof of that, he had immediately gone to the manor house to find out who the singer was, and, when he had gotten that far, discovering what such a singer had done to deserve such a fate. Learning that much, he had somehow convinced the squire to keep the hot irons in the firepit and off his horseboy, and had talked long and hard enough to — well, not convince the man of Gawaine's innocence, but at least to let Naitachal investigate the matter on his own.

Of course, who would dare argue with a Bard? Naysay him, and Squire Tombly would have been cringing for the rest of his life as his name was bandied across the kingdom in truly hilarious, eminently singable, and extremely unflattering song.

Something tugged at his hair, Gawaine started back into the present and looked up to see Thunder, his long gray head resting on Star's back, gazing mournfully into his face. Gawaine laughed, freed his hair and gave Thunder a shove. "Stop that, you fool," he said. "You look so silly when you do that. And Star has carried enough weight today!" Thunder shook his head, spraying grain fragments across Star's back; Gawaine gave him another shove, this one hard enough the gelding gave him a reproachful look before pulling back into his own stall.

"Naitachal," Gawaine mumbled, and sighed heavily. Oh, the Bard had gotten him released from that gruesome, reeking little box of a cell. He'd found the horse and — unfortunately — also found the thief: the squire's own son. "At least he took me with him when he left — and at least he left quickly." The squire hadn't been wildly pleased to learn his spoiled son had gone from being merely spoiled to becoming actively involved with the wrong kind; Gawaine was glad his new Master not only knew all the stories and songs about the fate of messengers with ill news, he'd had the sense to act on that knowledge — and to ask as his reward the services of the boy he'd rescued. "I wonder how long I would have lasted, if I had remained there." Not a very good thing to think about.

He looked up, brought back to the present once more as several men came into the stable, two of them noticeably weaving. One of these latter was at the stage of too much drink that he'd become maudlin; his companions were trying to shush him, get their horses together, and get free of the inn and surrounding country before full dark fell.

"Wretched, snotty elves," one of them whined. "Tell a few jokes, try to get people laughing, and wha'd they do? They kick us out!" He turned to one of his companions and clutched his tunic. "Did you ever see such a dull crowd?"

"Well, all right, not recently," the second man allowed. "Come on, Robyun, time we went home." But Robyun had seen the boy at the far end of the stables; he pulled free of his friend and came down the aisle. He wasn't so drunk he couldn't see Thunder edging a few steps back into the open, or the shift in the gelding's withers; he halted two stalls short of Thunder's and asked cheerily, "Hey, boy! Carrots! How many Mystics does it take to change a lamp-wick?"

"Sir?" Gawaine asked. He couldn't manage any more than that, without adding something truly abusive. Carrots, indeed!

The man laughed raucously; his friend came up and started to drag him away, and the drunk shouted out, "Two! One to change the wick, and one to *not* change the wick!"

" — and three to make loud fools of themselves," came a sardonic remark from the front of the stable. The men halted so abruptly their joke-telling friend fell flat on his face. Gawaine sent his eyes sideways to see a long, lean, silver-haired figure propped indolently against the doorframe, arms folded across his chest. "Are you not gone yet?" he asked pointedly.

"We're just going." One of the standing men spoke quickly and loudly, covering whatever the fallen one was trying to say. They pulled him to his feet and hurried down to the horses waiting there — still saddled, poor creatures, Gawaine saw with irritation. Without a backward glance or remark, the three mounted — the joke-teller had to be pulled up by one arm and the neck of his coarse-woven shirt — and rode out the back way. As they vanished into the darkness, though, a loud voice slurred out, "Hey! How many White Elves does it — " The voice was cut off abruptly, and the only further sound was that of hooves moving quickly into the distance.

*As if things weren't complicated enough, just being in elven territory — in the company of a Dark Elf,* Gawaine thought tiredly. He went back into the stall to check that Star had enough to eat and that the bucket was full and knelt to collect the saddlebags Naitachal had left for him to bring — as usual, all the heavy stuff, but that was one of the perquisites of being a Master — then staggered back to his feet. He was watching the bags as he juggled them into better position, paying no attention to anything else, as he put a shoulder into Star's withers to get past him. A low sound, someone clearing his throat, and the sound of a pair of long shoes not two steps away.

Gawaine let out an airless squawk and dropped everything. He had forgotten all about the White Elf who had followed the drunks out to the stable, assuming he'd gone back inside once they'd left. Apparently not.

"My. Jumpy, aren't we?" the elf asked dryly. He ran a practiced eye over the bardling's travel-stained shirt and breeches, ending at the scuffed boots, then looked rather pointedly, Gawaine thought, at the pile of leather bags between them. His stomach tried to fall into those boots. *Don't let him see how badly he did scare you,* he thought. He squared his shoulders and drew his eyebrows together.

"You weren't exactly making your presence known, and I was busy," he replied shortly.

"Did you expect me to tromp like a three-legged cow, or a human?" the elf replied. "And are you going inside with those?"

"Why? Are you trying to say I'm stealing them?"

Impass. The elf bared his teeth in what could have been a smile except that it didn't move beyond his lips.

"Why would I? Or why should I care if one human steals the goods of another human?" He took a step forward; Gawaine held his ground as the elf looked in both directions, then leaned close to his ear to murmur, "Or those of a Dark Elf, hmmm?" He tilted his head to one side, waited for some reaction. Gawaine raised one eyebrow, something he knew many found very irritating, and waited. "A Necromancer?" the elf added, in case this fool of a human boy didn't understand. "The Necromancer Naitachal?" he added helpfully.

"You mean, the Bard — my Master?" Gawaine asked with a lips-only smile of his own.

The elf tipped his head to the other side and studied him for a very long moment. He raised one eyebrow himself then. "You — know what he is, then? And who?"

"If you want to know, if I know his name, I have for the past four years. And if I know the meanings of those terribly long words," Gawaine replied dryly, "the answer is yes. If you have nothing important to say, the *Bard*, my Master Naitachal, who *was* a Necromancer but no longer is, is waiting for his bags."

For a moment, he wondered if he might not have pushed his luck; the elf narrowed his eyes and looked genuinely dangerous. Suddenly, he laughed, jumped back and gave the bardling a sweeping bow, then turned and left the stable. Gawaine blotted a damp forehead with his sleeve, gathered up the bags, and practically ran for the inn.

"What, does that make three of them now?" he grumbled as he had to slow for a very poorly lit section of path. "Three White Elves with my best interests at heart and a very low impression of human ability to tell nonhumans apart."

Even if he hadn't been able to tell White from Dark Elves — he would have to be blind or babe-witted to not see that — it didn't matter. Because one of the first things Naitachal had done — even before he had let Gawaine swear the oaths that would bind him as apprentice to Master — was to set the boy down and explain who and what he was, and what he had been. *He didn't really have to tell me, not then; he could have let it go until I'd learned to trust him for what he was.* But that had never been Naitachal's way; the Dark Elf had always been totally honest with him, and however much his Master irritated him by shunting aside his questions about matters mystical and the greater truths, Gawaine had to admire his honesty. After all, most people — most beings — went out of their way to avoid Necromancers. All Dark Elves, really, since it was said they all practiced that black art.

At least *this* elf had given up after a few moments of verbal fencing: The one who had accosted him at the door had been maddeningly persistent. "He used to practice necromancy, do you know what that is? What it means? Why would he have given it up, entirely? His kind don't, you know." And on and on, halfway to the stables after a tight-lipped Gawaine. Getting no response, he had finally made a very rude remark about his young companion's parentage and relative intelligence, and left him.

Oh, well. Gawaine juggled off-balance bags, muttered a curse under his breath as one of them fell, and bent down to pick it up, dropping the other two in the process. "Could be worse," he reminded himself. "You could have been inside the whole time, sitting with Naitachal and having to cut your way through the atmosphere in there to get up to the bar for more ale." There had been plenty of other times since they'd crossed into elven territory that the elves had gone out of their way to make it clear their absence would be cause for celebration; here, things had been downright frosty from the first.

Except for the innkeeper, of course; like most innkeepers, he was willing to put up with just about any clientele, so long as the coin they carried was honest and the guest showed some sign of reasonable behavior. Coin they had, but then, Naitachal had done very well as far as bringing in coin with his singing, at the last three towns they had visited. And though Gawaine had a sneaking hunch his Master minded the cold shoulder he invariably got from his White cousins, he dealt with those at the inn much as he did anyone else — elven, human, or otherwise — who used the word "dark" like a curse: with dry, cutting humor at least the equal of any White Elf's.

The path was lit near the inn, the inn and the doorway lit as well, but Gawaine had the bags clasped high in his arms and couldn't see his feet at all. He tripped up the single step; men and elves at half a dozen tables close to the open door turned to stare. He righted himself against the doorframe, sent his eyes briefly skyward, and walked into the close, dark room.

He had to cross the entire common room; Naitachal, as usual, had taken a table in the farthest and darkest corner of the whole place. And between the sooty black of his garb and the near-ebony of the Bard's visible skin, there wasn't much to see of him but startlingly intense blue eyes. Gawaine got a grip on the bags, and walked over to join him, trying to show the same cool exterior his master did. Not easy, with so many elves casting sidelong, narrowed looks into the corner, watching this most recent arrival with the same suspicious glances.

"Master?"

"Hmmm? Ah. Good, you brought them. Keep them by your chair, will you? There's a good boy." Naitachal waved him to one of the empty chairs. Gawaine felt around cautiously with his foot for the bag that held his harp and the other that contained their shared lute, then set the saddlebags on the floor, pulled the chair around so his back was to the door — and all those speculative and unpleasant looks — and dropped down with a sigh. He had been on his feet longer than he'd thought; the backs of his knees and the soles of his feet ached.

After that one rather abstracted remark, Naitachal went back to his companion. Gawaine scooted his chair forward and planted his elbows on the edge of the table so he could listen to the low conversation. The third at the table paused, eyeing Gawaine sidelong, then staring openly at the bright red hair. Gawaine scowled, the man blinked as though suddenly aware he'd been caught staring — and probably about to make some remark about fires, or carrots, or something else equally infuriating — and turned hastily away.

The Bard stretched, looked up as the innkeeper appeared between him and the human with a pitcher and an extra cup for the new arrival. "Gawaine, this is Herrick, a trader from the north. Herrick, my apprentice, the bardling Gawaine. Herrick has been telling me about the lands he's passed through recently, and he has the most interesting story about — well, if you don't mind telling it once more, master trader?"

Herrick shrugged, drew his cup close and poured, sucked the foam off the rim before it could run over the edge, then drank down half the contents. Gawaine watched him and fought a sigh; he suddenly felt tired all over. *I know full well what this means. I know that look. Master Naitachal has found another detour on the road to the Druids. Another wretched Adventure, when all I really want is Truth. And after all he had promised, after these last three side trips — ! It's not fair. He's been around for so long, he's seen and done so much, but when I ask for answers, he can't or won't help me, and he — well, he doesn't laugh, but he might as well. And then, when I ask to go somewhere where I might learn what I want to know, he does this. Again!*

Well, there wasn't any use fighting it; only one of them was Master, and it certainly wasn't Gawaine. He filled his cup, leaned back in his chair, and tried to make himself look interested in the man's story.

# Chapter II

If Gawaine had to force himself to look attentive at first, he became genuinely interested as time passed: Herrick had been plenty of places and had an ear for a good story; better, he could tell one himself. One couldn't readily separate truth from tall tale, but Gawaine didn't mind that: As a bardling, he knew quite a few tall tales of his own — most of his being set to a tune, of course — and he liked a good one. The one Herrick had just finished, about the lake full of drowned men who rose to the surface at the full moon and crept ashore to lure village women — well, that just begged to be set to music; Gawaine's eyes glazed over as he considered a variation on an old, minor-key tune that might fit the tale's mood.

He came back to the present with a start as Naitachal kicked his shin under the table. Herrick had moved on to another story and the Master's eyes were bright. *Pay attention.* Gawaine leaned forward and nodded once, warily drawing his feet back under the chair in case the Bard decided to make certain he was with them once more.

"Now, some of these things I've told you were told to me, young master," Herrick said as he turned from Naitachal to Gawaine. "Though I know well the men who told them, and don't doubt their veracity. This I am about to tell you I can swear is solemn truth, for I have seen this place with my own eyes, as I swore to the Bard here." He lifted his cup and tipped his head back to drain it, let Naitachal fill it for him once again, and slid down in the chair until he looked no taller than a dwarf.

"To the north of here, many days journey above Portsmith and not a little east, there is a broad, rolling land where the peasants are rosy-cheeked, their sheep and goats fat, the babies plump, and the grain grows very tall and thick — surprisingly to my mind, for the winters are long and there are many days to each side of the shortest when the sun barely peers above the southern mountains before it sets again. Then, the local people say, the snows come and lie deep in the valleys and dells, wind blows it into sharp-edged peaks, and lakes freeze to a great depth so that a man who would take fish must spend a long time indeed hacking his way through ice. The men sit around such holes, they say, drinking the clear, oily and viciously strong liquor they distill from tubers, safe from the wind in tents which they bring onto the lakes, and they fish and smoke, and tell tall tales. The bears which come down from the northern mountains are very large, and there are men who swear to me they have seen white bears in particularly cold years.

"The women spend the cold season spinning and weaving a truly splendid wool, some of which I carry with me even now, in hopes of trading it to seamen who sail in chill northern waters — for the stuff is waterproof, thick, and keeps out the worst of winter."

Naitachal stirred; this corner was dark even compared to the rest of the poorly lit common room, but his eyes gleamed, and Gawaine bit back another sigh. "Yes, but my dear Herrick, all this of winter is interesting, but surely no one would go there in winter." Herrick laughed, and the elves at the next table who had been scowling at the three off and on for some time made a great show of getting up and moving. The Bard turned a hand over and smiled faintly as the laughter died on the trader's lips. "Pay no heed; if we were out of line, the innkeeper would say so. They are simply paying guests, like us." His voice had risen a little on the last words; one of the elves turned to glare at him and Naitachal gave him a cheerfully, toothy grin.

"Well — what was I saying?" Herrick asked, and supplied his own answer before either of his companions could. "Oh, yes — winter. No, no one would go there in winter — or try to; he would never reach his destination, between wild animals, creatures that prefer night to day and don't mind the chill, and the roads are impassible in any event. Certainly no one would go and stay over the winter, who wasn't used to such a climate; imagine a hundred days or more with nothing but a little twilight once a day! I myself would go mad and slay the first man who laughed within reach of my knife!"

"So would I," Gawaine said, with a meaningful look at the Dark Elf across from him. Naitachal merely grinned once more and waved the trader to continue.

"However, it is a pleasant enough country once the snow melts. But that is not the amazing part of the tale, young bardling. Not far from that land, to the north, there is a valley where summer *never* comes."

Herrick paused dramatically. Gawaine shrugged, adding when it became clear the man was waiting for some response, "Well, yes, I have learned some of the songs myself, about the land well to the north where there is ice all year round and not even twilight once a day during winter."

"You mistake me," Herrick said. "This is near to that northern clime, but no more so than that where the peasants grow their grain and some of the most enormous cabbages I have ever seen. There are seasons — ordinary seasons — all around the valley, but in the valley itself, there is never a spring, never a summer. Snow and ice cover the ground there, even when the peasants not a league away have sheared their sheep and planted their corn."

He paused again. Gawaine looked at him. "Oh." There didn't seem anything else to say. His Master's eyes were very bright. The trader turned from apprentice to Master and spread his arms wide, nearly knocking over his cup.

"Well. Anyway, there you have it."

Naitachal caught the cup, set it upright and refilled it. "And you saw this place, this valley, with your own eyes?"

"Well — " the trader temporized. "Well, I spoke with the natives. They don't actually go *near* it, you understand; after all, what could cause something like that but a terrible curse or something" — he lowered his voice dramatically — "something even worse than that?"

Gawaine shifted impatiently, snagged the pitcher, and poured himself what was left of the ale; it wasn't much and the jug had long since lost its chill. *Flat, too, probably*, he thought gloomily, and sipped at it. "Worse," he said finally. "Such as?"

"Now, lad, don't badger the poor man," Naitachal said cheerfully.

"No, sir."

"It's all right, sir," the trader said. He drank down the last of the ale, wiped his lips on his sleeve, and set the cup down with a loud click. "As for what caused it — well, they wouldn't say, and my experience with the kinds of nasty critters that like cold is limited. Avoid them, if you see what I mean. But I did find one young man willing to take me to a place where I could look out over it — not that he'd go up onto that hill himself, mind! — and though it was a goodly distance, I could see what looked like a tower of some kind and definitely plenty of white surrounding it."

"White," Gawaine echoed. "Well, but early enough in the year, that could be snow that hadn't melted yet, couldn't it? Or, maybe salt, or a glacier . . ." His voice trailed away; the trader was shaking his head gravely.

"It was high summer when I was there, not spring, lad; there wasn't snow anywhere but on the high peaks. If what I saw was that much salt, the peasants would know about it. According to them, there was a time that valley was simply another place for their great grandsires to hunt in the summer, and ice-fish in winter. So, no massive salt bed, no lake — and unless someone has come up with a way to create a glacier overnight and fill a valley with it for no good reason, not a glacier, either."

Silence for several long moments. The innkeeper came with another pitcher of ale, collected the empty pitcher and departed. Naitachal stirred finally. "Quite a mystery," he said softly. "And all within — what would you say? — the last sixty years?"

"Perhaps that. They seem to be a long-lived people."

"I — see." His eyes hooded, the Bard sat in silence for a while, lips moving; his companions watched him. "And they know this for certain, that summer never comes there?"

"So they tell me." Another long silence. The trader poured for all three, then asked, "Sir, you'll forgive my curiosity, but — if you are Naitachal, aren't you the Dark Elf who traveled with Count Kevin, some years back?"

"You know Count Kevin?" the Bard countered.

"Well enough." The trader shrugged modestly. "I go that way once or twice a year and he always has me to dinner, so I've heard a great deal about how he came to be count, and — if you are indeed Naitachal — how much of his present situation he owes to you."

Naitachal smiled faintly. "Well — I doubt I was as

much good to him as I fear he says; he took fairly good care of himself, you know, and he was as responsible as anyone for reverting Carlotta to the fairy form that was properly hers. If it hadn't been for him taking on his full Bardic powers just then, I am quite certain I would not be here talking to you just now."

"I hadn't heard about that part," the trader said. "At least — bits and pieces from some of those around him, particularly that amazon warrior Lydia who captains his guard."

"Ah, Lydia. How is she, these days?"

"Impressive," the trader said shortly. He seemed disinclined to talk further about her. He took a swallow of ale, looked around the inn. "I was going to ask, since you are the Bard Naitachal, if you plan on performing tonight?"

*Oh, wonderful,* Gawaine thought. A human bardling and a Dark Elf Bard, performing in this particular inn. But his Master was already leaning back in his chair to look the room over. Gawaine shifted to look behind him and along the far wall. Not surprisingly, the place was jammed, but there were nearly as many humans as elves at the moment, and over near the windows by the door that led to the road, a few shadows that were neither elven nor — quite — human.

The Bard straightened up, glanced at his apprentice, and gave a small shrug. "Perhaps." He grinned suddenly, and his eyes gleamed with brief, amused malice. "No one looks *quite* ready to feed me to the wolves at the moment, anyway! More likely, I will let my apprentice do the singing for this evening; this would be a good place for him to perform, and increase his reputation."

"If they don't feed *me* to the wolves," Gawaine mumbled under his breath, but the Bard kicked his shins once again and he fell silent, bending down to pick up the mandolin case while his Master went over to have a word with the innkeeper.

By the time he returned, Gawaine had the mandolin out and was bent over it, fine-tuning the lower strings. Naitachal leaned across his shoulder to murmur, "He says the entertainment will be welcome, and assures me that no one in the neighborhood has sold overripe fruit of late." Gawaine glanced up sharply, and his Master gave him a positively evil grin. "A *joke*, apprentice mine."

"Oh. Of course." And probably meant to get him loosened up to sing and play comfortably; Gawaine could feel his throat tightening the way it still did, now and again.

"Start with something about warfare," the Bard went on thoughtfully. "To get their attention. Maybe the new one you wrote about the sea battle, Amazons against pirates, and that dragon?"

"It's not really finished — " Gawaine began doubtfully. Naitachal cleared his throat ominously and he added with haste, "Yes, of course."

"From there, you can probably go to one or two of the classic love ballads, maybe another heroic or adventure song — nothing too long, mind, I don't think at this hour you'll find much of an attention span out there!" The Bard stood listening as his apprentice finished tuning the mandolin, and finally shrugged. "If anyone has any requests, use your own judgment. Finish with something humorous, always best to leave them laughing."

"Yes." Gawaine shoved the chair back and got to his feet. Silence from the tables around them, rapidly spreading across the room.

He sang the sea-battle song first — even though it made him uncomfortable, performing something he wasn't ready to share with the outside world yet. But

when he finished, the room was very still; the silence
was followed by long and loud applause and even a
few scattered bravos. He stood, bowed to the room;
back in his corner, he could see the Bard giving him
that look that said, "Told you so." He kept the smile in
place somehow, sat back down and the room went
quiet as he touched the strings.

Love songs — he sang one of the truly tragic ones,
followed by a humorous tale of lovers parted by a pair
of snooty fathers, reunited only after a series of wild
adventures involving disguises, misunderstood letters
and passwords, and counter-disguises. Midway
through, he executed a rather complex run on the
mandolin, and when he dared look up once more, he
could see that a few of the nearby elves were paying
close attention and — he would have sworn — even
smiling, while most of the humans were clapping or
tapping the table.

He finished with "The Maiden, the Mage and the
Blue Earring." It was an ancient piece, and as far as
Gawaine was concerned, extremely silly — the vain
and arrogant young woman who covets something
she's never seen, the supposedly rare and wondrous
blue earring, and the young lovelorn mage who deliv-
ers it: a gold-colored circlet that turns her ear blue,
and a smack alongside the head that makes it ring. . . .
Well, he might consider it silly, but his audience didn't.
Quite clearly some of them had heard it before and
others hadn't, but all of them laughed so much he had
to pick a repeat phrase on the mandolin at the end of
nearly every verse until the room was quiet enough for
him to go on with the next one.

He sang one very short song after that, a soft little
ballad that mothers used to put their children to sleep
— a sweet song that quieted the room and let him
escape before his throat went dry. He scooped up the

few coins from the floor before his chair — dropped there by some of the men nearby, he noticed, though he hadn't expected any of the locals to part with cash for the apprentice of a Dark Elf, no matter how well he entertained them — and went back over to the corner table. Somewhat to his surprise, there was a new round of applause out in the room, and someone cried out, "More!" Gawaine stood behind his chair and took the full cup the trader had poured for him, but before he could even raise it to his lips, Naitachal was on his feet, the harp in his long-fingered hands.

As the Bard settled on the stool in the middle of the inn's common room, there was silence — an expectant hush on the part of the humans and some of the others present, a wary, tight-lipped and glowering stillness on the part of the nearest White Elves.

Naitachal ignored them all, ran his fingers over the harp strings a few times, then began a pleasant, if rather sad, song about a sailor's widow. He followed this with an instrumental, one his apprentice hadn't heard before, and he listened as breathlessly as anyone else present. The Bard continued to play very quietly under the applause as the song ended, then broke into a rousing run.

The bardling's jaw dropped and he stared. *He wouldn't dare sing "Althiorian's Last Charge" — in the Moonstone?* But that was exactly what his Master was doing, and astonishingly enough, everyone in the room, including the White Elves, was listening intently, and with every sign of pleasure as the epic wound up to the great battle and then down to the moment when the great elven hero killed the last of his undead enemy. Gawaine could feel his heart beating faster, the blood warming his cheeks.

And then it was over; Naitachal ran his fingers down the harp strings, stood and bowed. Deathly, total silence, followed by thunderous applause and the ring of coins. The Bard bowed once more, smiled as he straightened, and turned to take in the entire audience. He was still smiling as he returned to the table, and as he brushed by his apprentice, he murmured, "Just go and pick up the take, will you?"

Gawaine scowled. "You would take money from those who have been looking at you like *that* all evening?"

"Why not?" The Master clapped him on the back. "It spends as well as friendlier coin, don't you think?"

"Hypocrites," the bardling grumbled, but Naitachal merely laughed, clapped him on the back again — this time with enough weight behind the gesture to shove him away from the table — and went to resume his seat and repack the harp.

# Chapter III

Naitachal leaned back in his chair and shoved his long legs out before him as Gawaine settled into his first song and the common room of the Moonstone went quiet. He sent his eyes sideways toward the trader, watched thoughtfully for a moment or two. The man was impressed by the boy's skill with that mandolin, and by his voice, no doubt of that — partly, the Bard decided, because he had placed Gawaine somewhere around 15 and couldn't believe someone that age would have so much honed talent. A glance the other direction assured the Bard that his apprentice had the attention of most of those in the room; even the innkeeper had stopped washing cups and carrying ale, and had propped his elbows on the bar so he could rest his chin in his hands and pay heed to the tale.

*Very nice. Very — technically correct.* The Bard slid a hand off the table to surreptitiously scratch his ribs. If his bardling had been doing a *real* job of it, he would have been able to kick off his boots and scratch his feet; no one nearby would have paid the least attention.

But Gawaine's music, for all the flawless technique, the constant practice, the voice that never broke or slipped from a high note — his music was about as exciting as an accountant's columns. This thing he'd just written, now: Naitachal repressed a sigh. He himself could find half a dozen places in the first few lines where he would be able to send men's blood beating and have them flocking to some lord's banner — three or four others in those same lines where he'd have them all weeping, or cowering under a bench.

*Who would have thought two young humans could be so very different?* Kevin — now Count Kevin, of course — had been the same sixteen years Gawaine was when his Master found him and pulled him from a very tricky situation. They'd both had red hair, both had obvious talent and that undercurrent of magic buried deep down that was enough to make any Bard say, "Aha!" and grab the boy before another did.

But the similarity ended right there. Of course, Kevin had been old Aidan's bardling — his loose cannon, when Naitachal met him, because the Master had sent his apprentice out on his own. To copy manuscripts. Kevin, mad for adventure and with a distinct propensity for calling down all manner of bad luck, had managed to get himself in hot water right up to his neck from the first. *Imagine, a bardling wanting to fight with a sword. Worse, with his fists!* Well, one good punch with his right had cured young Kevin of that particular notion; so far as Naitachal was aware, that first punch had been his last.

The real problem was that Kevin had been so insecure, unsure of himself in so many ways — though he did a good job of hiding from most of his companions that he'd never done anything more dangerous than sit at his Master's feet and learn bardry. Naitachal grinned and settled even lower in his chair as the first song ended and the room erupted in applause. *Couldn't hide the truth from a Dark Elf, though.*

Unlike Kevin, Gawaine had not had all that early training in voice and lute; Gawaine had spent his childhood years feeding and currying horses, and his musical talents had been very much undeveloped — raw talent, no skill — when Naitachal found him.

Still, both boys had grown up in backwaters, neither had actually been inside a city in all his childhood. Unworldly, both. A personal attribute, Naitachal feared, Gawaine clung to as much as Kevin had wanted to shed it. And there was a passion in Kevin that was sorely lacking in Gawaine; Kevin had wanted full power — even though it had frightened him so much when it finally came that he'd nearly backed away from it. Gawaine, on the other hand: Gawaine *had* the power, Naitachal thought gloomily. Whether he'd ever bring it to the surface was another thing entirely. Gawaine would much rather sit at the feet of some holy man and suck down Ultimate Truth. *Poor little thing; to think he actually once thought he'd get that from me.* On sober thought, Naitachal wasn't exactly certain Gawaine had stopped believing his Master had the answers.

Laughter all around the room; the Bard roused himself to check what his apprentice was doing now, then rubbed his shoulders against the chair, leaned his head into the hard, carved wood and settled back into his thoughts *Maybe I've been pressing the kid too hard in one direction — too much practice might be what's keeping him at this level.* What with Gawaine longing to go in search of Ultimate Truth — and his Master, older by far and much more sensible about such things, doing his best to keep him focused on what counted — maybe that was the whole problem.

A little excitement, a little adventure, something to take the bardling's mind off Druids and other mystics, magical sites where a man sat all night and came away with all the answers . . .

Get him out of the cities anyway, out of the populated areas where con men posed as holy anchorites and fleeced the unwary for everything they had. Force-feed him a little *real* life, warts and all, and with a little luck and some hard work on the part of his Master, peel a little of that rosy veneer off his eyes and his mind. To say nothing of his soul.

"Besides," Naitachal mumbled to himself as the laughter rose around him, "I could use a little adventure myself, a bit of travel, see some new people and sights, maybe pick up some new songs or some odd instruments." Like that long-necked gourdish thing with four strings he'd bought out in Silver City a few years ago, *that* was supposed to be from somewhere well to the north. Pity he'd never been able to work out how it was properly tuned. Or strung.

The mere thought raised his spirits, more than he would have thought possible — as though he hadn't realized himself what a rut they'd gotten into lately until the consideration of new lands and a little travel came into his mind. When Gawaine came back to the table with a few bits of silver and copper coin and a flushed face, Naitachal even felt pleased enough with himself and the situation in general to take on a tough audience.

The money the tough audience gave him was enough to pay for a proper meal and a good room at the Moonstone, and two nights at a decent inn on the edge of Portsmith.

The road between the Moonstone and Portsmith was a clean, broad and well-tended one; unlike some places they'd traveled, Gawaine knew he didn't need to worry about their being jumped by bandits anywhere along the journey, or attacked by unpleasant beings. Between the White Elves and the King's men, such instances were rare indeed.

His stomach had hurt the entire day, and he had to keep rubbing damp hands down his breeches. *Portsmith. Of all the places I would really rather* not *go!* Besides this northern valley, of course. Unfortunately, so long as he was the bardling and Naitachal the Bard, he didn't really have any choice.

Oh, leave his Master and strike out on his own — maybe. Gawaine had no intention of going off by himself, in a world like this (and unworldly as he knew he still was, even after four years; in the company of a Dark Elf) a young man wouldn't last long. *At least, wouldn't last long the way I am*, Gawaine thought gloomily as the horses plodded north. He'd wind up in the company of thieves, or the prey of worse — and there would go all chance of a pure soul and the quest for Truth.

He shifted the harp case a little higher on his back, kneed Thunder forward at a slightly faster pace. Naitachal, who had been sitting with his right leg thrown across the saddle so he could fiddle with the lute, looked up as Star whickered. "Easy, boy! What's the hurry?"

Gawaine reined back and sighed. "Just — to get into Portsmith and away again."

The Bard considered this, then sent his fingers down the strings in a complex minor run. "Ah. I forget; your old Master's holdings are on the outskirts of Portsmith. It's been four years, lad; surely you don't think he holds a grudge, do you?"

"Not the squire," Gawaine replied gloomily. His Master laughed, freed a hand and leaned perilously sideways to clap a hand to his shoulder, hard; Gawaine had to lunge across to catch him and the lute before both fell to the road. Naitachal settled properly into the saddle.

"Well, then! There isn't anything to worry about, is there?" He glanced at the sky, slid the lute around to his back and settled his feet in the stirrups. "All the same, there is no point to spending *two* nights in

Portsmith, if we need not. The good inns are expensive, while the inferior ones are definitely not worth any coin at all." He looked over at his companion and laughed once more. "You look as though you're riding to that execution I saved you from. Don't worry so much! I would not have bothered with the town at all, but we will need things to go on north, there aren't many places above Portsmith where strangers can replenish their supplies. Besides — who knows how far we will wind up riding, or how long it will take?" Gawaine cast his eyes heavenward and did not answer. Naitachal chuckled softly, kneed Star to a trot, and Thunder came after.

*All the same*, Gawaine thought as he tried to relax into Thunder's bone-jarring trot, *there was plenty of bad blood over the horse theft, particularly once Naitachal found the real culprit. A Dark Elf, accusing a squire's son, would have been bad enough; being proven right, though* . . . And it wasn't as though four years had changed either of them enough; his Master, like most elves of either White or Dark persuasion, was so long-lived four years meant nothing to his appearance. *And I've grown considerably, but some things just don't change.* He ran a hand through red curls and sighed heavily.

Their luck turned ill right from the first; Gawaine saw two of the older stablehands in the company of one of the old squire's armsmen, coming out of a shabby tavern — worse, all three saw him. He didn't dare turn to look at them, but the brief glance he had was hardly reassuring: One nudged the second, who exclaimed aloud, and all three stopped cold to stare at the two riding by. It wasn't a nice stare. "Um. Master," the bardling murmured tentatively.

"Hmmm?"

"Those men just now, did you see them?"

The Bard had been staring into space and mumbling to himself. "See — oh. Yes. So?" Gawaine explained. Naitachal considered this in silence for some moments, finally shrugged. "Might have been bad ale. Don't fret it; men who drink at a house as poor as that won't be staying in a good inn, will they?" Gawaine gave him a sidelong, baffled look and shook his head. "Why don't you muffle the beacon," Naitachal continued, a wave of his hand indicating his young companion's hair. "And then even if the squire's let all his stablemen come into town for the day, none of them will recognize you, will they?" The bardling gave him another of those looks, possibly to see if his Master was kidding him; he sighed faintly then and pulled the hood over his hair and right down to his eyebrows.

It was the Bard's turn to sigh: Gawaine looked like a furtive creature with something to hide now. *Well, all right, so he does have something to hide. With all that carroty red hair, one can almost hear him coming.* He'd spoken lightly enough just now, but he had seen those three grim faces and a couple of other men pointing right at them as they crossed a broad square and turned down a side street. *You know, there just might be trouble. I surely do hope not — all I need just now is a brawl.* It wasn't so much that he couldn't take care of himself in a fair fight — fair meaning face to face and without having to resort to bruising up his hands. It was the other thing, the side of himself that he kept even from Gawaine: *He knows I was a Necromancer; he knows I was born a Dark Elf and raised in the loveless, cold environment of such folk.* What the boy didn't know was the sneaking little core of self-knowledge his Master harbored, the dreadful temptation that had come upon him once or twice in past years, since he'd become a full Bard but before he took on this first apprentice: the temptation to use the dark magic he'd known since his earliest days — particularly when he was in a situation heavily loaded in favor of the opposition. Fortunately, there hadn't been any situation yet he hadn't been able to handle without using dark magic, and none so dire he'd even been tempted to turn to necromancy once more — yet. *If things got ugly enough here . . .* Well, he wouldn't let himself think about that. *Think about Gawaine instead, about soothing his nerves; the poor boy's going to make himself ill with all this fretting.*

He leaned over and touched the bardling's knee. Gawaine let out an airless little squeak and he jumped high enough that his body left the saddle. "Ah! Don't — please don't do that!"

"Sorry. Wasn't aware you had gone away."

"Wasn't — hadn't," the bardling gasped. He sucked in air, swallowed, and tried again. "I was thinking."

"Well, stop thinking. We're about to stop, consider how much grain we'll need, and whether you have enough spare coin from last night to help me cover a pack beast."

There wasn't anywhere near so much coin as that, and Naitachal knew it; at least it served to get Gawaine's mind off their present situation.

The sun was nearing the western forest, and they had already made several stops — for feed, for travel wafers and dried meat, fruit and skins of a wine that would survive leagues bouncing around on the back of a horse; for thick woolen shirts, breeches and foot wrappings, and extra blankets — when the Bard turned down yet another side street and then down a very narrow alley between two buildings, and drew up in a tiny courtyard that was mostly smithy. "Weapons-master!" he shouted to his companion; he had to bellow, to be heard over the din. "If we're going into the unknown, we'd better be armed against at least some of the possibilities!" Gawaine, he was pleased to see, was brought out of his funk at once by the mere thought. *More like Kevin than I thought, maybe.*

Unlike most such shops, this one was not run by dwarves, and the new pieces were of human-craft, made by the smith and his help out back. There were plenty of used items, though, from all parts of the land.

Swords, daggers, spears, and ornate halberds ran in ranks down the walls, with a few of the fanciest (and most expensive) at a man's shoulder height, ready to catch the eye and where they could be caught up and tested. Gawaine stopped so short his Master nearly ran him down; he was staring at a gold-hilted, single-edged cavalry sword, the hilt an ornate basket smothered in fine brilliants and rubies, the blade slightly curved and etched. His fingers reached, ran along the cross-grip, and he sighed. His heart was in his eyes.

"Yes, lovely," Naitachal said, and gave him a little shove farther into the room. "If you like, we can spend the next fifty days here earning you enough gold to buy the thing, and then another *nine hundred* and fifty so you can learn how to use it."

"Oh." Gawaine shook himself, cast one last, longing look at the marvelous blade, and let himself be pushed on to the counter.

The man who stood behind it was so short and stocky he might almost have passed for a dwarf — at least, his shadow might have. His face was undeniably human, though, and one of the ugliest human faces Gawaine had ever seen. Even the broad smile when he looked behind the bardling to see the Bard couldn't make such a face even remotely attractive, Gawaine thought. "Hey — I haven't seen you in years! Naitachal, isn't it? Lost track of you — when? — six, eight years ago? More than that, because I heard not long after you went off on some fool's quest for Count Volmar, rescuing his niece on account she was supposedly kidnapped by some of your kind. How'd that turn out?"

Gawaine smothered a groan and turned aside to examine a tray of daggers. At this rate, they would be here for what remained of the daylight hours, and halfway into the night.

To his surprise, Naitachal merely laughed and said, "It's a long story, Fritton; tell you when we come back this way."

"Hah, another ten years from now."

"What's ten years?"

"Ten years to an elf, or to an old man like me?" Fritton demanded. "You didn't come just to say hello to an old fighting pal, though. What can I do for you?" His voice dropped to an unfortunately very carrying whisper. "Say! Isn't that the boy who — ?"

"Just so," the Bard cut him off very firmly indeed. "As to what you can do for us, we're off on a little jaunt into uncharted country, and I thought we should probably go armed."

"You've gotten sensible in your old age," Fritton said. "You still like knives?"

Gawaine turned to stare; his Master was grinning broadly. "I still like them. What do you have — that I can afford?"

What Fritton had was a strap that went from shoulder to hip and held half a dozen wickedly sharp, thin-bladed throwing knives and one pommel-handled double-edged knife no longer than Gawaine's hand, finger to wrist, and nearly as broad where it joined the hilt. Fritton drew it, sliced a piece of thick leather he kept on the counter for such demonstration purposes, and grinned at the bardling. "Make a hole in someone that will *definitely* slow them down, eh?" Gawaine, his mouth suddenly dry, managed to nod. Fritton set the strap aside. "Now then, anything else for yourself, or shall we move on to your companion?"

"I'll do well enough with that," Naitachal said mildly. The weapons dealer cast him a keen, sidelong glance.

"Yes. Probably one would need to be deaf and fool-witted not to know about the Dark Elf who gave it over and became a Bard. I'd not quarrel with any Bard, let alone one who — " He caught himself abruptly, bent below the counter. When he came back up, his face was red. In his right hand were several wooden shafts. "Boar spears," he announced. "You, lad, you're from these parts, aren't you?" Gawaine nodded warily. "Well, then, you'll know how these work, won't you?" The bardling nodded again. "Good. Then let's find one to fit your hand and your muscles." His eyes shifted. "He's riding, isn't he, Naitachal?"

"Riding. Yes."

"How's the horse, then, boy? Placid, or more like — " The weapons-master caught himself again. In spite of himself, Gawaine laughed.

"Nothing like the stallion I was supposed to have stolen, sir." Fritton gave him a sheepish glance, busied himself with spreading the spears across the counter. "He's well behaved — a little excitable, but only when he hasn't been ridden in a day or so."

"Ah. Well, then, what you need . . ." He sorted through the spears, fished two from the stack. "Try this first — no, forget that one, too long — try this instead. Main reason I asked is because of the case; there've been a few horses come through here simply won't have a spear case that rests anywhere near the shoulder."

Gawaine hefted the spear, then another at the man's insistence. He couldn't feel any difference, but Fritton claimed to see one; he set the first aside, bent down and disappeared below the counter for several moments, to reemerge with a worn black leather case and a set of straps and ties to fasten it to the saddle. "Experiment," he urged. "Make certain you find a place where you can free the spear without it catching on anything; your life might depend on it."

Naitachal had been wandering around the room, hands clasped behind his back. As Fritton pulled the rest of the spears together and returned them to the tub behind him, the Master said, "Better set him up for a bow, also. Something I can use, if need be, but primarily for his arm."

They emerged from the rear of the shop just as the last rays of sun were leaving the roof and upper walls behind them. Naitachal had already settled the strap of throwing knives under his outer garments, where he could reach them if necessary but where they wouldn't show; Gawaine carried the bow and the sheathed boar spear loosely in one hand, the quiver containing arrows and two spare strings across his back, where the harp usually sat.

He felt very self-conscious; even though the weapons were used and the cases scratched and stained with age, he had never carried such things before — had never thought to go openly armed. They rode back to the main street in silence, and Gawaine followed as his Master led the way through the center of the market and out most of the way to the northern gate. Fortunately for his peace of mind, it was almost too dark for him to recognize anyone around them, and probably therefore too dark for anyone to recognize him; his hair was circumspectly covered once more — though Naitachal, with a vexed little remark

under his breath, had pulled the hood back off his face
before they left the smithy yard. He finally caught up
with the Bard as they eased the horses through thick
foot traffic near an open-air ale stall. "I didn't know
you had fought with blades, Master. Or that you still
did." His eyes shifted toward the lute hanging across
the Bard's back. Naitachal laughed, and his eyes
gleamed.

"I never really did — I never needed to. And I still
don't. I just like knives."

# Chapter IV

The Sylvan Glade was indeed one of the best public houses in all of Portsmith, which was saying something, since Portsmith, as a large trading center, had plenty of outside custom and therefore needed many inns. Like many of its kind, Gawaine thought as they dismounted and led the horses back to the stables, it had been misnamed to the point of ridiculous: The inn sat, as it always had, right in the midst of a very busy avenue on the north highway, and there wasn't a tree or even a scrawny bush in sight.

It did boast rooms where a customer could sleep the night and not itch for the next twenty nights — and more importantly, be assured of waking at all, whether in the private chambers or the larger and less expensive common sleep room with its thirty pallets. The food was not only clean and edible but excellently prepared; the wines and beers of decent vintage, the large common room comfortable and smelling only of warm bodies, a little wood smoke, an excellently herbed roast and a rack of spiced fowls currently turning on the spit. The cost of a private sleeping room made Gawaine blink, but Naitachal merely paid and gestured the bardling to follow with their bags as he walked behind the innkeeper's young son.

They remained only long enough to wash and shed their cloaks; the smell of food reminded Gawaine how long it had been since he had eaten anything. *Not that*

*I could have kept anything down, earlier.* The look of
the common room had gone a long way toward easing
his nerves, though — it wasn't a place one would asso-
ciate with brawls and barroom fighting. And unless the
squire had increased wages by an impossible amount,
it was well beyond the pocket of any of his stablehands. More importantly, Gawaine hadn't seen any
familiar faces here, and even though the Master had
shoved his hood onto his shoulders when they came
inside, no one had paid any attention to him, other
than the usual looks the hair got.

*It isn't fair. All the tales about the great Druids, the
most holy of the Paladins and the heros — they're all
tall and lean and darkly handsome, every last one. And
maybe that isn't so important, but how far would Rey-
dun the Brave have gotten if he'd looked like a
freckle-faced lad of ten with too much height?*

One of the women who did washing for the squire
had laughingly suggested a rinse concoction, he recalled — something involving walnuts and sage. Back
then, he would never have dared such a thing, knowing the rest of the horseboys would never let him hear
the end of it. He cast a sidelong, thoughtful look at
Naitachal as they settled into a table near the fire. Save
the idea, he thought; Naitachal's sense of humor was
definitely elvish, which made it at least the equal of a
pack of rowdy young boys. Worse: The Bard had a
considerable wit to put behind *his* barbs.

Later, though, when he became Bard, and struck
out on his own . . .

His thoughts were pleasantly interrupted by the
arrival of cups of a fruity red wine, a warm loaf, and a
platter of freshly sliced meat.

The innkeeper came over himself with a jug of wine
as they were finishing the meal, quite some time later.
He cast a would-be casual glance at Gawaine, inclined

his head in Naitachal's direction. "Some of those here tonight bid me ask: Is it possible the Bard would perform for us tonight?"

Naitachal finished chewing, swallowed, and leaned back in his chair. "Perhaps. Not just yet, with so much good food in place." He looked across the table; Gawaine's eyes widened in sudden horror, but the Bard merely grinned. "In a while." The innkeeper nodded, then bent his head again and hurried across the room to replenish other cups. Naitachal leaned on his elbows and laughed quietly. He glanced up, keen eyes meeting those of his apprentice. "You saw his purpose?"

"To make certain of me — that I was who he thought I must be." Gawaine swallowed; his mouth had gone dry and the excellent meal was sitting like a rock in his stomach. "For a moment, I thought — "

"Thought I intended to send you to sing in my stead?" Naitachal's eyes gleamed wickedly, and so did his teeth. "It would be an excellent learning experience for you — but, no. I do not engage in torturing young men, you know that."

*Oh, yes?* Gawaine thought sourly. His heart was still racing.

"I merely wonder whether the innkeeper was assuring himself, since he got a look at you when we first arrived, or if he was examining you for someone else. Don't look at me like that and don't worry so; this is no dockside hole. People who can afford an inn like this tend to behave themselves."

"There are always exceptions to every rule," Gawaine replied pointedly. "As you yourself so often tell me."

Naitachal shrugged and smiled. "Don't worry so," he said again. "And drink your wine. Unless the inn master comes asking again, I intend to be curled up in his nice clean bed before much longer, and asleep long before the late drinkers come through that door." He stifled a yawn neatly against the back of one long-fingered hand. "We should get an early start tomorrow. I would very much like to be beyond the northern gates before the sun warms them."

"With that, I heartily agree," Gawaine said. He shifted his chair so he could watch the rest of the room a little better — without appearing to — and sipped his wine with caution. A sweetish red like this would give him a headache, if he drank too much or too fast. And despite Naitachal's assurances, he didn't feel that confident anywhere within Portsmith or within five leagues of Squire Tombly's horse barns. Better, altogether, if he kept a clear head.

It would certainly make the ride out at such an ungodly hour a lot easier. Thunder's trot, with a hangover . . . He shook his head, set the cup down. Didn't bear thinking about.

He had nearly finished, washing down wine with the last of the now cold bread, when the door slammed open and four young men came in, laughing uproariously and clapping. One of the group bowed, accepting the applause; another, taller than the rest by nearly a head and neatly bearded, elbowed one of the others — an elegantly slim fellow in bright red, his hair so pale as to be nearly white. "Hey!" the tall one shouted. "I know that one! Seven Druids — one to change the lamp-wick and six to share the Truth of it!" Gawaine groaned and let his head fall into his hands; there was scattered laughter but several voices topped the four, bellowing, "*Shut — the — door!*"

"Shut it yourself, peasant!" came the high-pitched retort. Gawaine sat bolt upright, as though he'd been stung and the color left his face so abruptly the Bard leaned over to grab his forearm.

"Are you all right?"

"Uh." Gawaine swallowed, sent his eyes sideways. "Uh. All right. Sure."

"I take it you know them?"

"Uh." He swallowed again; it didn't help much. "Uh. Know them. Sure."

"Wake up, lad," Naitachal hissed, and long fingers dug into his forearm. "Who are they?"

Gawaine winced, and the Bard let go of his arm. "I don't remember names, really; they used to ride with the squire's son. The one with the pale hair and that voice, though; he was right there when the horse was found missing. He was the one who got the squire thinking one of the boys had been responsible."

"Oh." Naitachal considered this in silence. "Oho."

"I don't suppose," Gawaine asked casually, "that we could simply go back to the room now, and get a start on that full night's sleep?"

"Stay put," the Bard said flatly. "See where the innkeeper's settling them?" Gawaine groaned. As large a room as this was, the four had been placed only two tables away from them. "Move, and you'll draw attention to yourself. Sit still; they're too energetic to stay in one place very long." The bardling cast him a dark, disbelieving look. Naitachal shrugged and went back to his wine.

*Of all the low, rotten luck,* Gawaine thought gloomily. *I knew we should never have come this way!* Try and tell his Master that, though! His stomach hurt, and his digestion wasn't at all improved by the thing he'd just remembered: The tall fellow with the neat little point of a beard was called Eldon; Eldon even four years ago had been a master fencer, and before he was seventeen, he had already blooded his blades. Worse still: Eldon and the fellow at his elbow, Waron, had given exhibition fencing matches at the last Harvest Fair Gawaine had attended, and Waron had been at least as good as Eldon. Even worse: He had taken care of both their horses often enough that Waron had known him by name.

His throat was tight and beginning to ache in earnest. He poured himself half a cup of wine and took a deep swallow. Not much help; anything it might have done for him was cancelled when Eldon got halfway to his feet to call for more wine. Firelight glinted off the finely worked metal of the sword-sheath that hung low and efficiently on his hip.

But time wore on, and the four did nothing save drink, laugh loudly and tell more of those awful, groan-making lamp-wick jokes. Gawaine glanced at Naitachal; the Bard shrugged gloomily, as if to say, "I know, puerile humor, but what can you do?" and applied himself to another cup of wine. With Eldon almost facing them and the dandy with the pale hair — Kirland, wasn't it? — staring straight into the flames, Gawaine was nearly afraid to breathe, let alone try and stand unnoticed.

*If Naitachal got up first, and got between me and them, we just might make the room without them seeing me.* Of course, it might all be foolishness on his part; no one had actively threatened him. Then again, these were friends of the young squire, and at the time his friends had been incandescently angry that a mere servant had dared to be proven innocent, that a dirty little horseboy had gotten away scot-free, that what they tried to pass off as "just a silly prank" had resulted in the young squire getting into very hot water indeed.

*I have a swell idea; let's not find out how they feel,* Gawaine told himself, and tried to think himself invisible against the stone and rough board wall behind him while he considered how best to get the Master's attention and make his suggestion about beating a retreat.

*Then again: Dark Elf and Bard — probably the
people glaring at me earlier out there knew full well
who he was, too. It's not exactly a common mix.* And
Dark Elves themselves weren't that common in inns
like this. *Get his attention, do it fast.*

Before he could complete the thought, the innkeeper came by their table with another jug of wine,
and Waron, who had been impatiently waving an
empty cup over his head for all of the space of one
deep breath, jumped up and came stalking over.
"Master Redin, a man could die of thirst in your common room toni—" His voice faded away and his jaw
dropped; his eyes went very wide. The innkeeper,
aware that something was wrong and quite possibly
aware what — but not quite certain how to deal with it
— murmured something no one could quite make
out, shoved the pitcher into the young nobleman's
hands, and practically ran all the way back to the bar.

Waron continued to stare for some moments; the
room had gone quiet as men stared after Redin or in
the direction he'd come running from, to see what had
upset the man so. Only Waron's other three companions seemed not to have noticed anything, but from
the sounds of their voices, they had reached a stage in
their drinking where they wouldn't notice much outside their own party and the bottom of a wine cup;
without some major event to distract them.

"Hey! Waron! Hogging the drink again?" Kirland
shouted. "C'mon, bring it here, share wi' your friends!"
Waron backed away one step, a second, then turned
and hurried back to the table, setting the winejug
down with exaggerated care. He gestured premptorily,
then, bent low and began talking. Gawaine sighed,
exchanged looks with Naitachal, who shrugged.

"They've seen us; we can leave now, right?" the
bardling managed at last.

"We could," the Bard allowed. "Although I am quite frankly loathe to allow myself to be driven from a comfortable seat by the fire and a pleasant cup by four arrogant young sots. And," he shrugged again, "perhaps they'll leave us alone."

"Perhaps," Gawaine replied sarcastically, "Druids can fly."

The Bard's mouth quirked, and his eyes gleamed. "Well, perhaps some can," he replied softly. "If they are sufficiently pure." Gawaine looked at him in patent disbelief and the Bard's mouth quirked once more. "It was a jest. Better than those lamp-wick ones, don't you think?" He pulled the jug across and tilted it, shook his head. "I wonder if the innkeeper plans to come back over here; there's a little left, but not enough for both of us."

"I don't — " Gawaine looked up as a shadow fell across the table. A very large shadow, composed of four very tightly grouped, grim-faced young men.

"Told you it was them," Waron said; his voice held the edge of a whine, and Gawaine suddenly remembered he had whined a good deal before his voice changed. Eldon gave Waron a shove that sent him staggering into the wall, and he pushed forward, stopping only when he was directly over the bardling. *Oh, well,* Gawaine thought, and schooled his face to a complete blank before he looked up. Eldon's brows were drawn together, his lips set in a tight line; unfortunately, he was having a little difficulty standing up straight and his eyes weren't quite tracking. Gawaine bit the inside corners of his mouth, hard; laugh now and Eldon would surely interpret it in a fashion that would go hard on a mere unarmed apprentice Bard.

"What are *you* doing back here?" Eldon demanded rudely.

"Passing through," Gawaine replied.

"Yah. Steal any good horses lately?" The other three found this hilarious; Eldon jumped when they burst into laughter, then squared his shoulders and looked proud of himself. "Send any away — *poof!* — late at night?" He looked around at his companions, who dutifully laughed.

Gawaine waited until the general hilarity had died down. "I was cleared of any part in that incident," he said evenly.

"Incident!" Kirland shrieked. Eldon winced at the shrill sound and gave him a shove. Kirland was a little steadier on his feet than Waron, though; he brushed at his fine shirt and then shoved back. "Keep your hands off the fabric, you clod; I've already told you the stains don't come out." He spun halfway around and planted both hands squarely on the table, shoved his face into Gawaine's. "How dare you call it an incident? Alaine was locked in his rooms with only a cleric and a tutor for company — for a *full year!* And even now his father keeps a close eye on him, and an even tighter rein on his purse! And you call it an incident?"

"Yeah," Waron chimed in, and the fourth of the company wobbled forward to nod vigorously.

"S'if the old man din't — didn't realize it was because Alaine needed money in the first place — "

"Yes, yes, we know all that, Bertin. Keep still, can you?" Eldon demanded. Bertin belched loudly and stepped back. Kirland swore and sent him staggering the other way, into the table.

Gawaine risked a glance at Naitachal, who was showing every sign of enjoying himself. *Beloved gods, I can almost hear him sorting through the rhymes for a new song out of this — yes, call this an incident, too!* He could feel the color warming his cheeks; his very seldom temper was rising. Eldon had turned to look at him and now folded his arms, as though awaiting some further comment. "I was proven to have no part in the *horse theft*," Gawaine said finally; a corner of his mind wondered at how calm he sounded.

"Proven!" Eldon scoffed. "Ask me, it's a question of one magician's word against another's, and what man of sense will trust something like that?"

"Yeah." Bertin was still in the process of cautiously righting himself. "How d'we know it — wasn' your idea all along? N — n — an' maybe you took some a' whatcha got for that horse to buy a magician, say you din' do it, and Alaine did. Huh? How 'bout *that*, Carrots?"

Kirland visibly brightened. "Say! Maybe he *did* hire that Bard, and everyone knows about Bards! He could have done something to the ol' squire, make 'im think Alaine responsible when all along it was — "

"Oh, but," a soft voice cut through his piercing one with dangerous ease, "but then, my very drunk lordling, such a Bard could sway four young fools to perhaps think themselves — say, goats, in a field?" As one, the four turned to stare; they had been so intent upon harassing Gawaine, they had forgotten his companion entirely.

"Hey." Waron blinked finally and licked his lips. "It's that Bard fellow, the dark one."

"Really!" Naitachal applauded silently. "How perspicacious of you, dear lad. And now that we've all introduced ourselves, why don't you go back and drink your wine, and let two tired travelers relax a little?"

For a moment, Gawaine thought it might even work; the Bard's speaking voice could be very persuasive. Two of the four — Bertin and Waron — actually had stepped back from the table and looked ready to turn away. But Eldon and Kirland, perhaps a little less drunk than the other two, or at any rate less influenced by it, didn't move, and Eldon caught his two retreating companions by the arms. His narrowed gaze remained fixed on the Bard; Kirland divided his attention between Bard and bardling.

The room had gone very quiet; so still that Gawaine could hear the fire crackling for the first time all evening.

"How *dare* you order a nobleman around?" Kirland said finally. "We will go where and when we please, and how we please. As for you," he spat in Gawaine's direction, "we are not done with you, *horseboy*. Stand up and come here."

"He is not your property," Naitachal said very softly. "If anyone's, he is mine, and if I were you, I would leave him alone."

*Property.* Gawaine felt his face flame, and he knew it must be as bright as his hair; his hands clenched the edge of the table. The Bard's foot crunched into his shin; he pulled his legs under him and ignored the warning. Waron nudged Eldon and laughed loudly. "Hey. Lookit the horseboy, he din't like what you said."

"Awwww," Bertin chimed in. "Poor li'l thing, is it angry?"

"Awww," Waron replied.

"Enough," Kirland shouted over their laughter. "I said stand up, horseboy. Take what's coming to you."

Gawaine launched himself up and out, fists ready; his hands and nose came into abrupt contact with an unseen barrier. "Damn all, let me at them!" he bellowed.

"Sit down and be still," Naitachal replied. He spoke so quietly, Gawaine should not have been able to hear him, but the words echoed between his ears, rattled his breastbone, and knocked the legs from under him. He fell, a boneless bundle, and only by luck came squarely down on the chair.

Naitachal flowed to his feet; the four youngnoblemen

blinked at him and stepped back as one man, but there seemed to be some barrier behind them as well as before them. The Bard smiled, a seemingly pleasant smile if one were not near enough to see the look in his eyes, and raised his arms. His lips moved, but for some long moments, nothing else and no one else did. And then, with a collective sigh, the four slid suddenly to the floor, four sets of eyes closed.

The barriers dropped away, Naitachal lowered his arms. There was a deep, long silence all throughout the common room, broken by the innkeeper's frightened wail. "Ah, no! What have you done to them?"

The Bard resumed his chair and made himself comfortable before he bothered to look up. "Oh. Nothing much. They'll sleep a few hours, nothing more." As if to prove his words, Bertin began to snore loudly. Naitachal nudged him with a foot, and he stopped. "If you have them taken outside, I doubt they'll even recall the past hour or so." He drew a deep breath and expelled it in a loud sigh. "If I did that spell right, they won't. It isn't something I need very often, though."

"Oh, no, oh, no." Gawaine wondered if the innkeeper had even heard half of that; he was gazing down at the pile of young noblemen and wringing his hands. But he finally knelt, tested all four pulses. He drove both hands through his hair then, and looked up. "I can't toss them out — I wouldn't dare! If they remembered after all! Or if — or if someone on the street robbed them, or did them harm — " *They'd have earned as much*, Gawaine thought spitefully. He shook his head then and forced such tainted thoughts from his mind. The innkeeper drove his hands through his hair again and tugged at it furiously. "But even if they didn't remember, there are thirty or more men in this room who heard everything that was said."

"That's true," Naitachal said thoughtfully. "But there won't be any trouble, because we'll be gone at sunrise."

"Um." The innkeeper blinked rapidly, and Gawaine thought he had never seen such an unhappy man in all his days. "Um, sir, I'm afraid that won't be possible. You and the boy will have to leave at once. Now."

"Oh, dear." The Bard's voice was deceptively mild; his very blue eyes boded no good for the innkeeper, though. "Well, then, you will have to return my coin. *All* of it."

The innkeeper nearly jumped through the ceiling at the very thought. "You — I can't! — "

"All of it," Naitachal said firmly. "Of course, you might let us stay the night. Consider that if I must ride the night, I will need something to keep me awake — composing a set of verses about provincial Portsmith and its so-called finer inns might just serve to do it."

"Oh, lords of light." The innkeeper let his head fall back. "Please, sir, please don't — "

"Consider a man such as yourself, catering to young fools of nobles the way your grandsire must have. Most of us have long since risen above such times, but then, in a backwater such as Portsmith . . ." The innkeeper's jaw was hanging. Naitachal smiled and gently reached over to shut the man's mouth. "Such songs are always in demand, you know: humor, and the chance to look down upon your rustic neighbor. . . ." He paused for effect; the innkeeper groaned and buried his face in his hands. Bertin let loose with another rafter-rattling snore, and half the custom in the still silent room jumped convulsively.

"Master — Bard." The innkeeper's voice came as a mumble between his clenched hands. "Sir, I'm truly sorry, but — what can I do? This *isn't* Silver City. The squire and the local nobles keep a tighter rein on things here than where you're used to."

"I?" the Bard inquired mildly. "I am used to everywhere, innkeeper."

"If you stay the night, and some of their friends come, if they were expecting others, or if someone simply stumbled across them," the man droned on through his hands, "or if someone here has already gone looking for any of their friends in hopes of causing trouble, or if—"

"Yes, yes," Naitachal said hastily. "I get your point, you needn't continue. Oh, do stop, we'll leave! At least," he added sternly as the innkeeper looked up hopefully, "we will leave now, and before any more trouble falls upon you — *with* a full refund, to the last small copper coin I gave you."

"I — yes, all right." Having mentally relinquished his precious profit, suddenly the man nodded so vigorously his hair fell over his eyes. He got to his feet, started to walk away, and stopped as though an idea had just occurred to him. "And you won't — won't write any verses?"

"Dear man, I am a Bard; I write what must be written, when inspiration falls upon me."

"I'll be held to blame—" the innkeeper moaned. Naitachal laughed unpleasantly and waved a dismissive hand in his direction.

"Well, since you cannot win in any event, why don't you fetch my coin? Before I become inspired right here. We shall go retrieve our things and meet you by the door."

"I'll be blamed," the innkeeper repeated unhappily. He cast a glance at the four young nobles sprawled across his floor, turned and fled.

"Poor thing," Gawaine growled. His Master laughed, more cheerfully this time, and reached across to pull him to his feet.

"Yes. You could almost see the cogs meshing,

couldn't you? Trouble now, or trouble later. Perhaps he hopes I will forget the whole thing, and fears they won't." He gave the fallen four one final indifferent look, then turned away and strode from the room, his apprentice right on his heels. As soon as they were out of sight, Gawaine could hear the explosion of relieved conversation behind them.

# Chapter V

Gawaine wasn't able to take a deep breath until they were actually on their horses and out of the inn's courtyard. But once they had ridden past the Sylvan Glade, Naitachal drew Star to a slow walk and turned to his apprentice. "Well. I did get the entire price of the room back. And the meal. We could see if there is another — "

"No," Gawaine broke in, very firmly. The Bard sighed.

"Yes, I suppose you are right. It isn't a good hour, and if those four didn't come looking for us, it would only be because they had gone for the authorities." He sighed again, cast Gawaine a sidelong, appraising look. "I fear we are somewhat noticeable."

"Yes, I fear so," Gawaine replied dryly. It was his turn to sigh. "Well. Now what?"

"Now? If we have bad luck of one kind, the city gates will be shut for the night."

"Otherwise?"

"They won't be," the Bard said gloomily, and kneed Star forward. They rode in silence for some moments, down the broad avenue and past two keen-eyed guards who were keeping massive double gates pressed nearly together. After a mere glance at the two, one of the men shoved the right side open enough to permit the horses through, and pulled it closed again as soon as they had passed. "I truly despise traveling at night," Naitachal said finally, the first thing he had said in a long time. "The only thing worse than travel at night is camping at night — unless you have time to prepare for the worst before the sun sets."

"Yes, I know," Gawaine said. "We have done it before, after all."

"Yes." Naitachal seemed to shake himself, and when he spoke again, he sounded almost cheerful. "Yes, we have — haven't we?" Silence for a distance; the Bard broke it by chuckling. "The look on that young sot's face!" Gawaine, who had grown increasingly tense as they left the lights of Portsmith behind, let himself relax. If Master Naitachal showed no sign of worry, after all . . .

At his side, and just a little ahead, however, Naitachal was — if not truly worried, somewhat concerned. *Things in the night; things that prowl the woods, things that bump across the sky. Things that hunt the night.* There were entirely too many of each, and only two of them to deal with such things. And one of them — despite his previous experiences with camping in a woods — was totally untutored in the possibilities out here. Naitachal, who had only put aside necromancy a bare few years earlier, still retained an active sense of what could be awaiting them out here. *Pray I don't need it. But I am glad I took the lute out of its case and slung it bare across my back.* The strings and the instrument itself might take harm from the damp, but if he needed the thing in a hurry, having to free it up might cost him his life.

Fortunately, his inner sense really hadn't dulled much; he was aware of the banshee before it struck. Enough before to throw up a barrier that probably saved Gawaine's life.

Gawaine had been letting Thunder follow Star,

keeping company with his own gloomy thoughts, when Star stopped abruptly and reared. Thunder danced sideways; Gawaine shouted in surprise and tightened his grip on the reins. His knee and foot slammed into something hard; he could see trees through it. "What — ?"

"Get down and hold the horses!" Naitachal shouted. "And don't meet its eyes!" He waited only until he sensed his apprentice fall out of the saddle, and felt the yank on the reins as Gawaine snatched hold of Star's bridle and pulled at his head, trying to turn both animals away from the threat bearing down on them at terrifying speed. The Dark Elf threw himself to the road, drew the lute against his chest, and waited.

*Fair face, hollow eyes . . . and a voice to drive mad any who listen to it.* He heard the horses, Gawaine's trembling voice as he tried to soothe them. Not very successfully. Without daring to turn from the creature nearly upon him, the Bard said, "Take them back down the road a dozen paces and no more! Wait and do not look on it!" No answer, except the sound of hooves retreating.

He drew his fingers across the strings, experimentally. The banshee threw herself down upon him from a great height, and the sound of that wailing, penetrating voice stood his hair on end and touched something he had not realized still lived, deep within him. "Creature of night," he murmured. "I could take you, mold you to *my* will, if I so chose. The power is in me, thing of piercing beauty, to control you and set you to whatever tasks *I* choose." He could; oh, he could! *A banshee, the power to drive all living creatures mad, all to myself!*

The banshee withdrew a little, perhaps scenting the once-Necromancer's long buried power, perhaps even hearing his words and understanding them. And then, with a howl to break stone, she threw herself against him.

"Master!" Gawaine's voice cracked like a boy's and the horses screamed with terror. Naitachal shook himself and tightened his grip on the fret-board.

"I could — but I no longer wish for such power," he said softly, and then began to sing. The Bardic power smothered temptation, taking everything with it as it always did; his voice gained strength and power as he focused upon what he must do. *Drive the creature away, lest she drive us all mad; drive her hence and leave quickly.* He sang, and his hands drew song from the lute for what seemed hours. The banshee hovered before him, on one side and then the other, above him, but could not find a way past his song. She shrieked, howled, and wailed at him and showed no sign of weakening. *I do not, either,* he reminded himself. *And yet, I can feel the strength draining from me. She cannot hold forever.* She might be able to hold until daylight, though; Naitachal was not at all certain that *he* could. But just as he was beginning to think she could not be routed, with one final, horrid wail, she vanished.

His ears rang and his knees didn't want to stay locked; he shook out his hands, and with a sigh, sank cross-legged to the road.

"Master?" Gawaine's anxious young voice — and Star's cold nose against the back of his neck — brought him back to the moment. He took the bardling's hand, caught hold of the stirrup, and used both to pull himself to his feet. It was dark, but not totally so, and he could see how anxious and drawn Gawaine's face was. "Master Naitachal, it's gone. You'd better rest a little."

The Bard shook his head, clutched two-handed at the stirrup when the world around him wheeled sickeningly.

"As much noise as we made just now? I think not. It isn't a good idea to stay where a banshee was anyway, but there could be —other things as well."

"Other — things." To his credit, Gawaine said nothing else; he made a cup of his hands for the Bard's foot and heaved him into the saddle. Naitachal managed to shove the lute across his back and wrapped both hands around the reins and Star's mane. *I wonder how many hours now, until dawn?* he thought tiredly.

It wasn't very many. They followed the narrow road through forest which began to thin as they climbed a long slope. The road went down to a faint track once they crossed this; the trees were replaced for the most part by rolling meadow. A second hill, a third. The sky was growing light, and the horses whickered, scenting water.

There was a stream running along the base of this last hill, a series of flat stones to cross it, and the trail ran up the far side, vanishing almost immediately in thick, bright green brush. Gawaine looked at his Master. Naitachal sighed, reined Star to a halt, and slid from the saddle. "It's nearly day, there is shade here, and water, and I haven't sensed anything anywhere about us for a goodly distance. And we could use the rest."

"All right." Gawaine, Naitachal noticed with a certain degree of annoyance, didn't look as though *he* needed rest. *Ah, to be twenty, and full of oneself, and to not have battled a banshee,* he thought sourly, and let his apprentice lead the horses down to the stream for a brief drink.

*Some adventure.* He let himself down onto long, soft grass, pulled the lute strap over his head, and laid flat with a little sigh. *I thought a little travel, a little excitement . . . the wrong gods must have been hovering over my shoulder when I thought that.* He was asleep before Gawaine came back with his blankets.

* * *

Gawaine stopped short when he saw his Master flat on the ground, eyes closed, breathing deeply. He cast his own eyes heavenward and sighed. "We could have gone a little farther," he muttered. "Oh, well." He broke out the packet of travel wafers and his cup, walked back over to the stream to get a drink, sat for a time with his back to a tree trunk with his fingers trailing in the water as he munched and drank. The sky brightened, the sun rose. He tended the horses. Naitachal slept.

Gawaine got to his feet, walked up the stream a ways, back the other way. He checked the horses, moved them into shade where there was more grass. Took them back for a deeper drink. Checked their goods. Naitachal still slept. Gawaine sighed, looked back the way they'd come, down and upstream, at the horses, and finally made up his mind. "I'll just go look around while he sleeps. See if there's any better place to camp nearby, or if there are berries ripe. What's on the far side of this hill." He knew the likely answer to that: another hill. But the distant ridge was beckoning to him. He checked his boots, shed his cloak, and practically ran across the stepping stones.

The hill was plenty steep, the air close where brush hugged both sides of the trail. He was moving very slowly and panting by the time the ground under his feet began to level out. But now there were rocks everywhere, a large outcropping of stone and fallen stuff — everything from boulders edging the now winding trail to loose rock in the middle of it, and treacherous piles of scree everywhere. "Have to lead the horses through this," Gawaine muttered to himself. "Especially Star, poor old brute." For all his lean racing lines, Star could be just as stumble-footed as an aged cart-horse. He shook himself, looked back the way he had come, shielded his eyes with one hand to glance at the sky. "Well! Hasn't been nearly as long as I thought, might as well see how far this mess extends — and what's on the far side of it!" He swung his arms, drew a deep breath, and strode on down the trail.

A turn, another turn, and a short, steep ascent, littered with hand-sized stones Gawaine slipped back every third step; he was sweating freely by the time he reached the crest, and the shade of an enormous overhanging ledge of granite. The trail took a couple of sharp bends around more of the same granite, then dropped precipitously.

The sun was nearing mid-morning, and already the day was entirely too hot for Gawaine's taste. "It's these northern lands, the heat comes much too late in the afternoon," he told himself, then jumped and nearly fell as a large red-tailed bird screeched and took flight, almost across his face. He fell back into the ledge, panting, then caught his breath and held it. There had been voices — surely he had just heard voices down there?

Voices in the wilderness could be anyone; Gawaine was nowhere near as experienced as Nattachal, by many a long year, but he had enough wit to realize that whoever spoke down there wasn't necessarily a friend. He dropped to hands and knees and crept forward until he found a place where he could see a large portion of the valley.

Silence, save for the now-distant cry of that hawk. He held his breath. Nothing to see, either. Gawaine edged cautiously up onto his knees, and then got slowly to his feet. Horses — six horses, attached to a cart made up of thick branches — no, of metal bars. His eyes didn't want to accept what they saw, at first. Bars, and clinging to those bars, hands, human and other. And behind the cart . . . He caught his breath. A long line of men sat, heads down, close together. It needed a keen, young eye, like the bardling's, to see the lines of chain that bound the men together. *Coffle.* Men and others, trapped inside a cart. It could only mean . . .

Two Slavers came into his line of vision. Horrid, horrid, ugly — they slid smoothly along the ground beside their sale goods: snakelike lower bodies, human upper bodies, with human arms to hold weapons and human minds to control those they preyed upon. *They said there were no more Slavers!* was Gawaine's first outraged thought. They had been driven from the civilized lands — King Amber had sworn they would be — and now, this! He glared down the hill, a corner of his mind railing furiously at his king, at those who had assured the naive there were no Slavers to haunt the lives of the honest. Fortunately, the rest of his mind was also working, and it assured him that alone — even if he'd brought his bow and boar spear, even if he'd been good with them — he stood no chance of any kind against "only" two Slavers.

But the citizenry of Portsmith and the guards who served there would surely be just as outraged as he was. And there would be enough armed men among them to see justice done here. Gawaine cast one last smoldering glance down the hill and cautiously withdrew. He ran most of the way back to the stream.

Naitachal was awake, sitting with his feet in the stream while he ate. He'd plunged his head in the water, his hair and beard were soaked — and he'd shed his cloak and the heavy overshirt he usually wore. Very dark arms, as deeply near-black as his face, showed almost ebony against the dark gray sleeveless vest. He merely nodded as Gawaine slid down the last of the hill and splashed across the stream without bothering about the stones. "You have news of some kind, I gather."

"News," Gawaine panted. Naitachal chewed his breakfast and waited. "Slavers — there." He stabbed with one hand, then bent over to catch his breath and let his vision clear.

"Slavers," Naitachal said thoughtfully.

"They have — at least thirty — taking them — somewhere. If we go back to Portsmith, get help — "

"Your young friends of last night would like *that*," the Bard said. Gawaine shook his head, flapped a hand.

"Doesn't — doesn't matter! Get some of the guard — Master, this is *important*! We can't let those — those filthy — "

"Yes," Naitachal interposed hastily. "Yes, those filthy — whatevers. All the same. You might consider this, apprentice mine: How near we are, still, to Portsmith. And how distant any other town. And, therefore, where that caravan might be bound?"

Gawaine lost color precipitously; he sat or fell flat onto his backside and stared blankly at his Master. "Oh, no."

"Well, why not? Are all the men in Portsmith any more holy than men elsewhere, or do they put their breeks on a leg at a time, like the rest of us? The city guard should patrol out this far. According to the king's statutes, it quite likely does, to protect those who farm and herd outside the walls but still within the boundaries held by the city masters. That a Slaver caravan dares come so near the city says to me that caravan quite likely has a guardian within the walls." Silence. Naitachal finished his breakfast. Gawaine worked at getting his labored breathing back under control. "How many of them were there?" the Bard asked finally. "Slavers, that is?"

"I saw two."

"Two of them — two of us," the Bard mused. He

grinned broadly. "I would say the odds were very much against them."

"All right," Gawaine replied steadily after a moment. He held up a hand and began enumerating. "My bow, the spear, your knives — " But Naitachal was already shaking his head.

"We won't need weapons against a mere two Slavers." Gawaine stared at him slack-jawed as Naitachal grinned. "We can take them much more easily — and just by playing stupid." He explained; by the time he was finished, the bardling was grinning as broadly as the elf.

# Chapter VI

It took a little time — repacking all the things that Gawaine had taken off the horses to let them rest also, getting them up that steep trail and through most of the stone obstacle course of the flat top of the hill. Finding a place where the horses would have a little grass, and where they could again unsaddle them and cache the supplies and their weapons. Gawaine gazed down longingly at the boar spear in his hand, shook himself and sighed, then set it with the other things in the shelter of an overhanging ledge behind a few stunted bushes. He patted Thunder's warm withers as he passed, and mumbled, "Take it easy, old boy. And keep quiet, all right?" Thunder brought his head up and around, blew hot air over the back of his neck. Gawaine rubbed damp palms down his breeches and looked over at Naitachal, who was waiting for him. *Funny how great this plan sounded just a little while ago*, he thought sourly, but drew a deep breath and followed his Master down the trail.

The wagon and the coffle were still there. At least there was that, Gawaine told himself. *Remember all those sentient beings down there, held captive by those filthy — those foul —* His imagination couldn't conjure up the words at the moment, though he'd certainly heard enough of them back in Squire Tombly's stables. He followed Naitachal when the Bard cut to one side, away from the trail, to slide down a very steep dirt game track. They came out onto the road the Slavers were using a bend behind the caravan. Naitachal touched Gawaine's shoulder to gain his attention, and his eyes held warning. The bardling nodded once shortly. Naitachal smiled, very faintly, and broadly bowed, gesturing to his companion to precede him.

They made it all the way around the bend, and nearly to the last man in the coffle, where the Bard halted with loud exclamations of surprise and horror. The two Slavers came out of brush along the side of the road to grab them. "Nnnnhh! You — do not move, now!" The words were hard to make out, the voice uttering them was so gutteral. "Or — nnnnh! — we shall — hurrrrrt you! Verrry much!" Gawaine gasped as hard humanlike hands bit into muscle; he subsided at once.

Behind him, he heard the Bard's voice soaring into a dramatic falsetto: "Oh, no! Pray do not harm us! Innocent travelers, we — !"

*Shut up!* Gawaine thought desperately. The Slaver holding him turned, and he and his companion barked, in unison, "Silence, slave!"

"P-p-p-please, don't hurt us," Gawaine managed to stutter. "Let us go, we won't — "

"Ooooh, no! We are doomed!" Naitachal hooted, topping him; he rolled his eyes heavenward and waved his arms wildly over his head. The Slaver holding him gestured imperiously.

"Take the youth with the fiery hair to the fore, I shall keep this one at rear of line, where I can watch it. You, slave, hold yourrr — nnnnh! — yourrrr tongue, or I will have it out of your mouth! You, take the youth, go! We leave at once!" Gawaine cast one despairing and frightened look at his Master as he was jerked off his feet and dragged to the head of the coffle; it was not, precisely, acting on his part.

The Slaver prodded and slapped the half-unconscious men at the head of the coffle until he had room for another. He hooked Gawaine into throat and wrist chains, then drew a nasty-looking whip from his belt, holding it under the bardling's nose. "You — nnnnh! — you will walk! As long as I say walk! Orrrr — !" He rolled the last word dramatically and brandished the lash. Gawaine swallowed audibly and widened his eyes as far as they would go.

"Yes, yes, of course, whatever you say!"

"Yes, yes, whateverrrrr — nnnnh! — you say!" the creature mimicked unpleasantly, and slid toward the front of the wagon to get the procession underway. Gawaine cast a cautious glance at the men next to him but at once gave up any idea of forewarning them: all three were overly thin, stoop-shouldered, and bore the expressions of men who had utterly lost hope.

A sense of *something* buzzed at his ear, like an invisible bee. The cart jerked forward, nearly jolting his arms from their sockets and knocking his head backwards. It took a moment for Gawaine to get his feet properly under him, to adjust — not to the idea of being fettered but to the awkward actuality of walking with his hands bound and a strap pressing uncomfortably against his windpipe as the men behind him and those at his side moved with a slightly different pace. He put thought of that, together with the outrage trying to force its way into his mind, all aside. More important things just now: He began to softly hum.

The long line of bound slaves clinked and shuffled along for several moments, then stopped abruptly. Loud voices and extravagant curses filled the air as those inside the wagon fell heavily onto one another. Gawaine bit back an exultant grin as the prison cart tottered under the double burden of all that off-balance weight and the left rear corner that quite suddenly had no support under it. The iron-shod wheel that had been there rolled a few paces away and toppled into the ditch.

Was that really his Master, already working dirty tricks on this dirtiest trick of them all? *Well, no time like the present, is there?* Gawaine took his cue from the man next to him and crouched down as the two Slavers met beside the cart and went into a lot of hissing, snarling and arm waving at each other, reminding the bardling of nothing so much as the squire's breeding master and his horsemaster carrying on over who was responsible for the condition of the breeding pens and the fences enclosing them. He had to lower his head quickly, lest the two catch the amused look on his face and turn on him.

The men and other beings in the cart were still piled atop each other in the corner — those who hadn't been shackled on short chains to the metal bars — and those on the bottom were howling or cursing in pain, while some of those on top were trying to extricate themselves and cursing loudly, while still others cursed all of their companions and tried to get enough of the occupants to move toward the opposite side, and those who had been fastened to short leads hung helplessly and cursed in strangled voices. At last, the two Slavers turned to snarl out, in unison, a nasty enough sounding warning in their own language that even the most hardened-looking occupants of the cart fell abruptly silent.

The Slavers were quiet for a very long moment, also; finally, the senior of the two — the one, at least, who had held onto the Bard and ordered the other around — set thick fists where a man's waist would be and glared at the head of the coffle and then at the occupants of the cart. "You — you, all of you inside! You will — nnnnh! — will move away from the axle!"

It wasn't easy or fast; after all, the occupants of the cart had been *trying* to get out of the corner for some moments. Gawaine could see the patent disbelief and the sense of, "oh *really*?" on the broad clean-shaven face of one of the men. But when the second Slaver came close to the tipped corner and began prodding through the bars with a short-hafted spear, they sorted themselves out right away. Unfortunately, even with everyone who was free to move about the cart in the far corner, the weight shift still wasn't enough to bring the conveyance back to level.

And neither of the Slavers seemed anxious to dirty his hands on a wheel. Another furious consultation; finally the lead Slaver barked out orders. "You in the cart!" He walked around it, pointing to first one and then another of the occupants. "You that I choose will be let out in two groups. The first will hold up the cart, the second will put the wheel where it belongs. You will — you will then return to the cart. Nnnnh! Or we will hurrrt you! Very much!" Gawaine risked a look at the still sloping cart. Most of the occupants were either thoroughly cowed by the Slavers and their whips — or very good at playing the part. *Probably the former,* he thought unhappily. Just this short while chained up had given him a sense of hopelessness that was hard to fight.

On the other hand, there were some rather impressive specimens in there; surely the Slavers hadn't beaten the resistance out of all of them.

He felt that familiar buzzing sensation once more, somewhere between his ear and his mind. He bent his head to hide a smile. "Only" two Slavers. Quite enough to control a coffle of beaten men, a collection of chained and imprisoned creatures, of course. Oooooh, no — to quote Naitachal. These two had left the Bard to his own devices for an awfully long time.

The master Slaver moved back a distance and held his whip prominently; in his other hand, he held a throwing knife that reminded Gawaine of the broad-bladed piece his Master had on that strap of his. Put a hole in someone that wouldn't be easy to close, that ugly friend of the Bard's had said. The bardling shuddered.

The second Slaver already had his whip in hand when he opened the cart and edged back to let ten of the prisoners out. Shoulders slumping, faces averted and heads lowered protectively, those who had been inside lowered themselves to the road, moving carefully as the orders were shouted at them. Seven of them came around to the side of the cart and braced their backs against it so they could lift it when the order was given; two others fetched the wheel, and one of them scrounged around on the road, searching for the pin that would hold it to the axle. The Slavers shouted; the underling sent his whip cracking over heads and his superior yelled at him furiously. "Do not mark that one! I have a buyer for him, but only if the skin is — nnnnh! — undamaged!" He gestured; the prisoners backed against the cart groaned and grunted, and lifted, then jockeyed for position and for better footing as the wheel was rolled into place.

*Now.* He sensed the Bard back there, singing quietly so the Slavers would not hear him; sensed the power of what Naitachal was doing. Gawaine bent his head still lower, and began to hum. Power tugged at him, invaded him and drew on his strength; leaving him briefly giddy and lightheaded; he shut his eyes, set both hands flat on the rock-strewn surface of the road and continued. He could feel movement at his side, sensed the prisoner there turning to stare at him. Well, he must have presented a strange sight, even without the soft hum, even without his lips moving, forming words. "Open, part, fall away, give these two a *very* bad day."

"Clink!"

"Clink, clank!" All the way down the line, he could hear locks snapping open and chains falling from wrists and throats to hit the hard surface of the road. The chief Slaver looked up at the sudden and unexpected — but not unfamiliar — sound, and found himself staring at men who in turn stared blankly at each other or at their unfettered bodies. He yelped as his mind took in what his eyes saw. A moment later, both Slavers bellowed in astonishment as the lock on the cart exploded in a flare of green light and ear-ringing sound. The door slammed aside; several suddenly unshackled and enormous men — and at least one lizardman — threw themselves onto the road with a roar of fury and defiance. Gawaine jumped to his feet, ignoring the blackness that teased his vision, and pitched his voice the way he had to in a large crowded hall: "All of you! Join me, let us see an end to these two!" The men who had been chained together rose as one.

He hadn't misjudged the coffle; most of the men who had been chained together huddled well back from the fighting, but there were still enough to over-whelm the subordinate Slaver — he was still staring in disbelief, jaw hanging, when five men hit him and knocked him flat. He fought his way back up, but an-other ten threw themselves into the fray, and the Slaver went down once more. Someone yanked the whip from his hand and threw it aside; another came up with the short spear and a moment later returned it to him — point first. Gawaine turned hastily away as the attackers backed off, leaving the still-twitching body in the middle of the road. Men looked at each other doubtfully, and then, as if someone had given an unseen signal, they ran — some up the road in the di-rection they had been going, most back the other way.

The occupants of the cart had mostly vanished already; half a dozen or so remained, dealing with the master Slaver, who was apparently more of a foe than his subordinate had been. Though not for very long. In the end there was an empty cart, still listing badly to one corner, a triple line of chain with shackles hooked into it at close intervals, and two very dead creatures that in death bore more resemblance to snakes than they had in life. Gawaine shuddered, then jumped as a hand came down across his shoulders.

"Nicely done, apprentice," Naitachal murmured. "Very nicely done." Gawaine nodded; the Bard's sudden and quiet appearance had taken the breath right out of him. "I do trust none of those we freed went up the slope," he added. "Or that, if they did, they leave anything they find alone. Say, *our* things?"

Gawaine groaned and closed his eyes. "I don't think any of the men in the coffle would have had the strength to take on a path that steep. The ones I could see stuck to the road. But I guess I had better go and —"

"Wait," Naitachal advised. "Catch your breath. Likely you're right. Besides — we have company." He gave his apprentice a sidelong glance and laughed quietly. "Don't look like that! I meant these." He turned Gawaine around and gestured broadly.

Gawaine blinked. Nearly all of the slaves and prisoners had vanished, but a few — a very widely diverse few — remained: a short boy who couldn't have been as old as Gawaine, with an unlined and beardless face under a thatch of poorly cut blue-black hair; a dwarf in what had once been costly black silk; and looming over his shoulder, a lizardman who still wore the painted red-leather crossed straps of a nobleman, though the jewels had been pried out of their fastenings. A brown man, clad in torn Druid's dark green, most of his lower face hidden behind thick brown beard and drooping mustache. Another, broad-shouldered and lean-hipped, with blond hair cut fashionably to turn under at his shoulders and a neat little point of reddish beard, a brief line of ruddy mustache just above his lip. His jerkin had been torn, but otherwise his clothing was impeccable. The last of those who remained was well built also, but less obvious about it. *Probably less taken with himself,* Gawaine thought. *You don't know any of them, don't judge,* he reminded himself. After all, so many did that with him: the hair, the freckles . . .

He became aware he was staring and sent his eyes sideways to look at Naitachal, but the Bard was rubbing his chin thoughtfully and gazing from one to another. "I am the Bard Naitachal," he said finally, "and this is my apprentice, Gawaine."

The muscular fellow took a step forward and bowed extravagantly. "A Bard, is it? Was it your work somehow broke the locks? The God told me it was, just now. Sir, my undying thanks. I am Arturis," he bowed again, "Paladin and hero, and I owe you a very great debt."

"So do we all, if this is so." The lizardman spoke up; his speech was surprisingly unaccented — at least to Gawaine, who had met very few of that race. "I am Tem-Telek, and this" — he turned over a hand, extending a long digit in the dwarf's direction — "is my valet and personal artificer."

"Wulfgar, at your service, oh Bard," the valet said readily.

"Cedric," added the other blond man. He drew on the strap that crossed his chest; an empty quiver rode high on his shoulder, then dropped out of sight as he let go the strap. He smiled ruefully. "Until recently, a champion archer. Just now — well, a man alive, which is something. My thanks to you, sirs. And this, if I recall rightly, is Raven."

The dark man in green bowed his head and

Gawaine sucked in a sharp breath. "You — you're a Druid, aren't you?" he asked in an awed whisper. Naitachal scowled at him and then at the Druid, who nodded. "But, I thought you all lived — "

Naitachal sighed heavily; Raven shrugged. "Most of us live well to the south and east of here, yes. I have spent the past several years in the north, studying the vast wilderness and learning its mysteries. My thanks also, for saving me."

The last of the group stepped forward and bowed rather self-consciously; his cheekbones were red and he alternately smiled and chewed on his lower lip. "Um, well. They call me Ilya in my village. I had come south to sell hides and found that the tales we have are true: This land is full of danger."

"Not so much as all that," the Bard replied mildly. He clapped his hands together and rubbed them briskly. "Well! Now that you are free to go about your business, we two have a long way to go before the sun sets today. So, if you don't mind — "

"But — !" Four of the six spoke at once, stopped to look at each other. Arturis waved his hands for silence and stepped grandly forward.

"Sir, such a debt as I owe you cannot possibly be repaid with mere thanks, and so the God tells me as well. Unfortunately, I had little or no coin in my pouch when these creatures caught me off-guard and put me in that cage, but I do have an undoubted skill with weaponry, and though it is obvious you have great power, could you not do with a sword to guard your back? And the power of the God to aid you?"

*Which of the gods, with so many to choose from?* Naitachal thought dryly. He stopped listening as the Paladin ran on about honor and his God and holy visions. Fortunately, he wasn't the only one irked by the self-styled hero's God-on-my-side, holier-than-all-of-you style (though a quick glance made it unhappily clear to him Gawaine was gazing from Paladin to Druid with the look of the desert-stranded coming suddenly upon water). Before Arturis could get much further with his impromptu combination sermon and sales pitch, Tem-Telek closed the distance between them, looked down his formidable nose at the Paladin and suddenly barked out, "Be still — you make my head ache!" And, while Arturis was gaping at him, too stunned to form a reply, the lizardman turned to the Bard and said, "The man speaks for me, though I would not prattle so. My valet and I do not know this part of the world well, but it seems distant from any cities, or any armed companies of King's guard. There are always dangers upon the road, as Wulfgar and I can surely attest now. All of us can. Might we not travel together for the moment?"

"Whatever the Slavers took from each of us," Raven spoke up diffidently, "will be in the front of the wagon. At least, that was where they stowed my staff. And likely," he turned to look at Cedric, "your bow and arrows."

Cedric turned and ran to the front of the wagon; they could hear the creak of hinges and the slam of something heavy and wooden hitting something ungiving and metal, and then the archer shouted, "I found it! Come and look, all of you — there are enough weapons here to arm a company!" Arturis was already on his way. At a gesture from his Master, Wulfgar went to join them, returning shortly with a sword and a heavy-hafted axe, and a small leather pouch, which he handed to the noble.

Tem-Telek peered inside, smiled and shoved the pouch inside his tunic. "You can put the jewels back on the straps when we stop tonight, Wulfgar."

"Of course, sir," the dwarf replied loftily. "Cannot

have you traveling about like *that*. Very — uncivilized
it looks."

Gawaine spared a look for his Master; Naitachal's
dark face showed nothing, as usual. He himself was
ecstatic: *A holy Paladin and a Druid — and they wish
to company with us! My fate has taken a turn for the
better, all at once!* He had just known it was the right
thing, to go after those Slavers. He just hadn't
expected the reward so soon — or for it to come in
such a form.

Naitachal fought a sigh. *A Druid and a Paladin!
Weren't Slavers bad enough? Well, of course, in good
conscience I could not have turned aside and let the
nasty brutes go on with their wretched cargo. Any
more than I could have let the lad race back to
Portsmith for help — odds are, he'd never had made it
out of the city gates a second time.*

*I wonder which of the nobles of Portsmith was
expecting a shipment of cheap dockside labor? Or
cheap field hands?*

*More importantly, why do none of these show any
distress at my presence? After all, a Dark Elf . . . Gratitude, of course. All the same, not even one sidelong
look, even from our holy Paladin, and such men are as
notoriously narrow of thought as they are broadly
be-visioned.*

*And most important of all, how do I get rid of these
characters — particularly that loud-mouthed wretch
of a so-called pure-minded hero — so the boy and I
can be on our way once again?*

# Chapter VII

With a visible effort, the Bard roused himself from his dark thoughts and turned to his apprentice. "I will consider how best to deal with such thanks as these offer us. While I do that, and while they seek their personal things and arms, why don't you go get our goods and our horses — so we can be about our business?" Gawaine nodded and repressed a sigh. He had been more than half afraid that look on the Master's face earlier meant he didn't want any of this additional company. Including the Druid. *It isn't fair,* he thought rebelliously, but a whole life of obeying orders told — he was already trudging up the road, looking for the head of the regular trail that would lead to the rocky crest. That deer track had been bad enough to slide down — going up it would be next to impossible.

As he slowed, just around the bend, to begin examining the hillside, he heard a tentative call behind him. The big pale-haired fellow now carried a long bow, and the quiver slung over his left shoulder bristled with brightly fletched arrows. "I heard the Bard tell you to fetch your goods, and thought you might welcome help."

Gawaine hesitated, but the archer's smile was broad and infectious. He smiled back and shrugged. "You've let yourself in for a nasty climb," he said and pointed toward the distant rocks. Cedric loudly expelled a deep breath.

"After so long sitting in that cage — or trying to, there wasn't really enough room for above four or five of us to sit at once — I welcome the exercise." To Gawaine's surprise, he made no attempt to lead, simply followed along as the bardling sought and finally found the trail head.

"How long did they have you?" he asked breathlessly as they paused about halfway up. "If — if you don't mind my asking, of course," he added hastily.

"Oh — I don't mind. It's Gawaine, isn't it? Cedric, that's mine — in case you forgot. Well — hard to say, really, but I was injured a while back and had to find other work than archery, until I healed. Man has to eat, you know. Well, I took on with the wrong caravan — and when I realized what and who they were, and tried to leave, they turned me from driver into merchandise."

"Not very pleasant for you," Gawaine said. He turned and set out up the hill again.

"Not very," Cedric agreed cheerfully.

The horses were where he and the Bard had left them, and Thunder was very glad to see him. Star let Cedric saddle him with reasonably good grace, and before long the supplies, weapons and instruments were stowed before and behind the saddles. Gawaine glanced at the sky and sighed; it was already well past midday. They wouldn't get much farther today. He got Thunder turned and out onto the trail. "I would stay back a little, if I were you," he cautioned Cedric. "Let me go first. Star's not as graceful as you might think, looking at him."

"Ah." The archer leaned back to give the black horse a wary look. Star blew at him, shook his head, and suffered himself to be led.

It was almost as bad as Gawaine had feared, getting them down that narrow and steep trail, and he was wringing wet by the time they hit level ground once more. His legs were trembling enough from the exertion, he didn't dare try to mount in front of this stranger, lest he do something embarrassing like slip and crack his chin on the saddle.

There was Naitachal, standing in the middle of the road, face averted so he could stare at his hands. Still sorting things out? Gawaine wondered. As they came up, though, the Bard turned and Gawaine could see what occupied his Master: another strap of knives, only four this time, but fancy enough to have belonged to some noble or other. Naitachal was virtually cooing over a pair of gold-washed and ornately shaped hilts that held very slender, highly polished steel blades.

The Druid was seated on the end of the cart, a long staff in his left hand; off to one side, the boy Ilya was helping Arturis shift the harness on the horses that had pulled the cart, so they could be ridden. Gawaine went over to help; after all, he probably knew more about harness than anyone else here, and it certainly wouldn't hurt if he had a good look at the poor creatures.

To his surprise, they showed no signs of ill treatment or poor feeding. There were even several small, coarse sacks of oats under the seat — sacks no one had bothered to fetch, Gawaine thought tiredly. Of course, if none of these five were horsemen, they might not have realized the stuff was there. More likely, no one had figured on Slavers providing good feed for their horses. But Slavers had excellent reason to take good care of the animals that pulled their merchandise to market. *Those — those filthy — those foul —* Gawaine remembered plenty of words now, but none low enough to apply. He made some suggestions about the rigging of riding straps and the judicious use of blankets to protect both riders' backsides and legs *and* the horses' backs, waited long enough to be certain Ilya understood what he needed to do, and went back over to check the cache box. Two spears rested in the bottom; Gawaine shrugged, took them to put in the leather case with his. Snug fit — but probably a better idea than for the single spear to flop around loose the way it had. He could envision half a dozen circumstances where the thing might catapult out of the case, and every one of those was one where a man would want his weaponry in his hand.

Tem-Telek's valet was hung about with several sword belts, dagger belts, and a spear with a throwing strap halfway up the haft was balanced against his thigh. Just now, he had a double handful of thick-looking fabric. The lizardman had already donned the legging portion of this stuff, and with Wulfgar's help was struggling into the sleeves. A small-looking hood dangled down his back, straps hung loose at the wrists and so did small, lumpy-looking bags. *I wonder what all that is?* Whatever it was — some form of armor, perhaps — the lizardman was certainly in a hurry to don it, and he breathed a loud sigh of relief when the dwarf clipped the last fastenings across his chest. A crossed pair of red-leather weapon-straps — one for a pair of long daggers, the other for a matched sword — went atop the odd suit, the spear into a special case built into the suit that left it high enough on Tem-Telek's back so he could easily reach it.

Arturis practically bristled with blades and a short, thick horn-bow hung from his waist. He had neatened the tear in his jerkin and now wore a helm and body armor — a set of four connecting iron circles that covered his heart and belly — which he was busily polishing. Ilya appeared not to have had any weapons at all on him when he was captured; Wulfgar was pressing a sword on the boy, and when he would not take that, offered him a long dagger instead. Ilya eyed it warily, finally shrugged, and let the dwarf hang it from his belt.

They had all been talking in hushed voices; all at once, all conversation ceased, and the six ex-slaves turned to look expectantly at Naitachal.

The Bard sighed very faintly and let his eyes close for a moment. When he opened them again, he let them move from one to another of the waiting six, back down the line the other way. "I gather you all feel as Tem-Telek does — that traveling together will bring a little safety." He paused and was answered by nods. "Well, then!" He clapped his hands together and rubbed them briskly. "There are six of you, all quite well prepared for the worst, should it strike. There are seven horses and six of you — if you do not object, I think we will take the last horse ourselves as payment, if you like, and also because we may have need of an extra beast where we go."

Silence. The six eyed each other, turned back to look at the Bard expectantly. "And that is — ?" Arturis said finally, when it became clear Naitachal wasn't going to say anything else.

Naitachal shrugged, shook his head. "Well, we do not actually know. We go north, cross-country most of the way, I think. Away from Portsmith, which is that way and away from any town I know, come to that." He waved a hand in a vaguely southerly direction. His voice was a low, slow drone. "Well to the north," he went on after a moment, and his eyes were now slightly glazed.

"Well, yes," Arturis pressed after another silence. "But why that way?"

"Oh, because . . ." The Bard's voice faded. "There may be things up there to give my apprentice something to write about. Or — maybe not. It will be cold, very cold, of course."

Gawaine fought a yawn, and then a grin. He could tell what his Master was doing now — and a very good, subtle job he was making of it. Dissuading them all, making the journey sound so boring that none of them would want to come along. The bardling's amusement faded as he realized those being dissuaded included two who might well hold the key to the Truth. *If at least the Druid came with us,* he thought wistfully. But if Naitachal was dead set against them . . .

Of course, the Master hadn't come out and told them all to ride off; he was simply trying to persuade them to do so.

And he had apparently, this once, met his match in all six. And clearly he hadn't the heart to use his magic to chase off the sad-sack lot of them.

"Oh, well, a little cold weather," Tem-Telek said carelessly. He ran capable hands over the odd suit; his skin stood out very dark green and nonhuman against the pale fabric. "But consider, Master Bard, that already I am far beyond the lands that would be mine — well beyond climes where one such as myself would be comfortable. This was crafted for me by my valet, before we ever left those warmer climes."

"Cold," Naitachal droned on drearily. "Cold like you cannot begin to imagine. . . ."

"My imagination, if not quite the equal of a Bard's, is not so poor a thing as all that," the lizardman broke in coolly. "Nor is the extent of my honor. Will you shame me, leaving me with a debt undischarged?"

The Bard spread his hands wide, finally turned to look at the dwarf. "And you?"

"A little cold is no problem for me," Wulfgar said. "Nor even a great cold. Besides, I too have a sense of honor, and even if I considered my debt to both of you discharged by a simple thank-you, I would certainly never leave my Master. Someone has to make certain his garb is clean and mended — and besides, I have to repair his caste-straps, which will certainly not be accomplished in a single night." Gawaine did not think loyalty required explanations, but did not say so.

"North, do you say?" Cedric mused. "I have heard for most of my days that there are bows in the north so powerful and accurate that they might as well be magical. Think then, what such a weapon would mean to one who earns his coin by shooting at tourneys! No," he added hastily as Naitachal stirred, "do not think of dissuading me, for such a bow — for even the chance that such a weapon exists out there and I might grasp it — I would dare much. And it may be that my skills will be of use to you, Bard though you are. For there are other stories from the north, of evil things and evil men who haunt the roads, of beasts that can tear a strong man asunder — "

"Yes. Well," Naitachal said hastily. "But where we are bound, it is said there are no cities, no towns. Where you expect to find such a bow — "

"Well, I need not stick with you forever, need I?" Cedric demanded reasonably. "But where is this you go, where there are no cities or towns?"

Gawaine opened his mouth to speak, but Arturis got there first. His eyes were wide and he was waving his arms excitedly. "Yes! What the archer says is true, great evils and dire creatures, horrid beasts, and I must go to fight them!"

"Must you?" Naitachal murmured, and he turned his head away to cast his apprentice a broad wink. "But I have never heard of such evils — "

"I am never wrong about such things," Arturis announced confidently. "The God has sent me so many times upon quests against such evils and dread beings, always he grants me a vision, to warn that I

must — must — aaaaaiiigh — !" His voice rose to a
sudden screech and he fell to his knees, swaying and
muttering unintelligible words; his eyes rolled back
and then closed. Gawaine, with a vexed and worried
little exclamation, started forward, but the Bard
caught his arm.

"Now, apprentice," he murmured, "it is a vision; did
you not hear him warn of it?"

"Vision — " Gawaine breathed, and his eyes went
wide with awe. Fortunately, his attention was fixed
upon the Paladin's working face and the sudden tears
running down his cheeks and into his beard from
under mostly closed eyelids, and so he did not see the
exasperated looks Tem-Telek and his valet exchanged,
or the tired expression on Raven's face. Arturis ram-
bled on to himself for a few more moments — or to
his God, if it was not the God using his voice and lips
to convey the message. He finally stirred, opened his
eyes and blinked, looking from one to another of those
around him. "Where — ?" he asked vaguely, then
tossed his head back to throw the long golden hair
over his shoulders and leaped to his feet. "Yes! There
are indeed dread beings and things of no form that
way, Master Bard, and against them you will have no
protection save that of my God and Master, and of my
strong hand! But even if I do not ride with you, that
way I must go, to make a valiant quest against such
things, that I may overcome them for the glory of the
God and for the purity of my soul!"

"Yes, yes," Naitachal said hastily. "Lower your voice,
please, you make *my* head ache now. Come, certainly,
if you must." He looked at the Druid rather thoughtfully. "You say nothing."

"No," Raven agreed, just as quietly. "But I would
say something now. The way you indicate *is* barely
inhabited, and there are few roads. I have lived many

years well to the north of this place, and there is little I do not know of the lands, what can be eaten and what not. I have traveled many of the forests where there are no tracks, and a man might starve before he found his way out again. I can guide you — if you will let me."

The Bard cast another glance at his apprentice; he could almost hear Gawaine's fervent thought: *Oh, yes! Guido mo!* But perhaps he and that Paladin would cancel each other out; and there was no doubting the Druid's services would be useful if he knew half what he said he did.

"Just where is it you go?" Raven asked.

"A valley," Gawaine broke in before Naitachal could say anything. "A valley where summer never comes."

"But I know that valley!" Ilya cried excitedly. "I know it well — it is not a day's ride from my own village!"

"Do you?" The Bard was actually smiling at the young peasant. "Well then!" He glanced upward. "This day is not going to last much longer, and I got little sleep last night. I would greatly prefer some time to prepare a perimeter before the sun sets, and — " he glanced meaningfully at the fallen Slavers and the mess all over the road " — I cannot imagine any reason, including a holy vigil, that would keep anyone *here* for the night." Arturis cast him a sudden, narrow-eyed look. Naitachal looked back at him, smiling blandly, then turned away to mount Star. He looked down at the assembled company, and at Gawaine who now sat on Thunder next to him. "Whichever of you intends to come with us, let us go now."

He was scarcely pleased — but not at all surprised — when all six of those they'd rescued mounted up at once and fell in behind him.

* * *

It was nearly sundown by the time they found a place sheltered from the night winds that Raven said blew mostly from the east around here, where there was water, and where a fire could be built without drawing attention from a long ways away. It was fully dark by the time Cedric and Wulfgar got a fire going, Gawaine got the horses settled, and Naitachal set a proper magical boundary all around the camp, the horses, and right down to the water — a shallow, fast-moving creek that dropped over a stone falls into a pool and vanished into the ground not far below that.

The bardling came back from his tasks to find Raven had already gone through the food packets and had foraged before it got properly dark, and was in the process of fixing some kind of stewlike mess. Without the meat, which was causing a little argument among his fellow ex-slaves. "I can keep you fed and well fed at that," he said flatly. "But not with meat. Not from living creatures."

"This will do very nicely for tonight," Naitachal interposed flatly, before Arturis could invoke his god's views on the place of lesser creatures once more. "I personally do not care if there is meat or not, so long as the food smells as good as this. If you wish roast boar or anything else, Paladin, fetch it yourself." *Or go away and eat whatever you please.* The thought was as clear as if he had spoken it aloud; the Paladin gave him a wary look and subsided.

"Yes. Well, certainly there are times a man does without flesh in order to purify his soul for some greater task." Naitachal sighed loudly, interrupting him once more, then leaned forward and pointed across the fire to where Ilya sat munching a piece of dark, rather stale bread. "Tell us about this valley, why don't you?"

Ilya nodded vigorously, chewed and swallowed.

"Well, in my grandmother's day, she says it was a meadow — grass, flowers, just like in our village and all about it. Wild onions growing on the hillside, a stream and a pond, where geese landed in spring and fall. But there came a winter, a grandfather of all winters, with snow up to the eaves of every roof and wolves and white bears prowling the road, or scratching at the very doors. And in the very midst of this dreadful winter, in the time when there is only so much sun," he indicated with two hands held parallel to the ground, a long finger's-worth apart, "on a long and dreadfully cold night, there was a wind to rattle the chimneys and send soot across the floors, that scoured snow from the road right down to the dirt. Well! People huddled in their houses and awaited yet another storm which would surely crush every hut and shed in the village, and yet, when morning came the village stood as it always had, with only scoured places in the snow to show where the wind had come and fled — and there was a mysterious white wall all about that valley.

"People were curious, of course, and a few went to see what it might be about, a wall where there had been no wall, and all overnight. My grandmama says that there were those who went and touched it, and came back to report that it was real and true, and that it froze the hands of any who touched it. And there were those," his voice dropped to a whisper, "who climbed across it — and never returned."

Silence, save for the snapping of the fire and the soft, plopping bubble of whatever Raven was cooking. "Summer came," Ilya went on finally, and in a much more normal voice, "but the wall remained where it was, and there was ice upon it, still, even in the heat of midsummer. Even now, there is ice, and when I was a foolish boy, I stood upon the shoulders of a friend and gazed across that wall. There is snow and ice, and within there is a tower or a castle, perhaps. Difficult to tell, for it is white and so is all the ground about it. But others have also looked into that valley, and they, too, have seen just what I saw."

"And those who go in there?" Naitachal asked.

Ilya finished the last bite of bread, looked into the fire for some moments, then roused himself and met the Bard's eyes. "I said I would take you there, Master, and so I will. But — to where you can see that wall — only. To my village, and perhaps a little beyond. But no farther. Because those who go beyond the wall do not return, ever again."

# Chapter VIII

The Bard lay open-eyed for some time after the rest of his suddenly greatly expanded company slept. *Magic bows,* he thought sourly. Well, as a lie it was a lot better than that vision Arturis had. *The look on my apprentice's face when he went into that act!* And act it was: Gawaine might be young and unworldly, and utterly mad for mystics, but his Master had been around a lot longer. Naitachal knew a fraud when he saw one.

Perhaps not a fraud; Arturis could be deluding himself, also. The world held as many of that kind as it did charlatans and false prophets. "All the same," the Bard whispered to himself. "All the same, I think I will keep a very close eye on this as-it-were Paladin, to make certain that he does not make off with anything here which is not his — including my coin *and* my apprentice!"

One thing was certain — after that story of Ilya's, there would be no getting rid of any of them; it didn't take a Bard's training to read all those faces and see how intrigued every last one of them was.

Even Gawaine. Naitachal grinned suddenly. *I will wager my lute on it, the lad didn't believe the least in that valley until he heard the peasant's tale!* Well, he certainly believed it now. The Bard shifted, reached down to dislodge a stone from under his hip and tried to get comfortable. Question was — did he believe the tale himself?

Did it matter? It might be merest fable, like the one about the drowned men in the haunted lake — he had personally heard that tale from twenty different men in twenty totally different parts of the land, each one claiming to have known one of the women who had been lured into the water. *That one's so old it's grown a long gray beard.* Could be this was the latest one making the rounds, like those gruesomely awful lamp-wick jokes.

He grinned, settled his shoulders, and closed his eyes. It really didn't matter; his main intent was to get Gawaine away and give him a chance to see something real, to force him to live life instead of just watching it pass. If there wasn't an ice valley — if that had simply been Ilya's way of joining them — well, fine. Besides, if things went on as they had started, it wouldn't matter what was there, just getting there would be more than half the fun.

"*How* many?" The Paladin stared blankly. They had nearly finished the packing before Arturis asked Ilya how many days it had taken him to come south.

The peasant lad shrugged. "I counted my fingers and my toes and then began again, went through, and touched this many" — he held up his right hand with the thumb folded over index and middle fingers — "before I came to that village where I sold my hides — and a woman told me there that if I wished a better price for them, I should go to Portsmith, but it would take me four days more to walk the distance."

It was Gawaine's turn to stare now. "You came within four days of a city that large — after coming all that way south — and you didn't travel on to see it?"

"Why?" Ilya asked. "There were seventeen houses and a tavern where I sold, I counted them, a small market once every five days. What more could this

Portsmith have than that?" He looked from one blank face to another, finally turned to look at Naitachal. The Bard's face was rather grim. "Did I say something wrong?"

"Nothing wrong," Raven patted his shoulder and turned back to the straps he was tightening. "For some of us, there is more than city life — "

Arturis shook himself. "Well, of course there is! Only look at the life I lead, following the ways of my God and taking upon myself the wondrous quests he sets before me — "

"Yes, yes, yes," Naitachal broke in hurriedly. His forbidding expression had nothing to do with Ilya's prattling; he had never much cared for early hours, and having to get up before the sun made him cross. "Why do you not save this wondrous tale for later — *after* we are ready to ride?" *And after I am out of ear-shot,* his narrowed eyes said.

Somewhat to his surprise, Arturis immediately went quiet, except for a chastened, "Of course, sir." The Paladin turned, scooped up a cloth bag, and went to load it onto the spare horse. The Bard stared after him, frowning. He finally shook his head, turned away, and knelt to finish rolling up his blankets.

"Forty days, or a little more." Cedric was thinking aloud, quiver hanging loose and forgotten in his hands. "And with not much food for eight of us — " He blinked, became aware Raven had finished his packing and was watching him.

"There are a good many plants in the northern wilds," the Druid informed him. "Thick tubers and other roots which make good soup, leaves and the like. I myself have lived on the land for a long time and" — he gestured broadly with both hands, indicating his person — "and I do not think I look particularly starved."

"Well, no," Cedric replied doubtfully. "Though

roots and berries are not precisely my idea of a proper meal."

Raven sighed and cast his eyes upward. Naitachal, having given his bags to Gawaine to fasten onto Star's back, sighed in turn, much more loudly. "The bardling and I brought dried meat, and I must say, Raven, that I have no objection to having fresh, if there is someone able and willing to bring down game for us. In fact, I am quite fond of a decent roast, or a few chops now and again, or even a hot stew at the end of a long day."

The two scowled at each other for several long moments and the rest of the group looked at them; even Wulfgar, who had paid no attention to any of them so early in the day, came around his Master's horse to watch. Raven shrugged finally. "As you will. So long as it is not expected that I —"

"You, and anyone else, may eat what — and as — he chooses," the Bard replied, biting off the ends of his words. He looked at each of them in turn. "If that is settled, then? Can we be gone?"

Gawaine settled onto Thunder's back and let the rest of the party precede him; by himself at the rear, he heaved a sigh of relief. He had been utterly certain Naitachal was going to find a way to get rid of the others this morning; he hadn't managed it, though. *A Druid and a Paladin — and at least forty days to learn from both!* His Master turned to see where he was, then reined Star in so they could ride side by side. "*You* look uncommonly pleased with yourself this morning," the Bard grumbled. Gawaine smiled. He knew Naitachal's ways, and why he snapped at everyone — mornings didn't bother him, and he'd long since gotten used to avoiding the Bard until he was properly awake.

"Well — yes. Do you know, I think I am." The Bard

mumbled something under his breath and gave Star a nudge. For some time after, until the sun was well on its way to midday, he rode by himself in the middle of the company, spoke to no one, and was left severely alone.

The land stayed hilly for some days, and despite Arturis's assurances that he knew this area well — and that his God would point the way to the nearest road they never did find anything but a narrow footpath that wound around the bases of the hills. Eventually, these became lower and lower, and full streams less frequent, until by the fourth day they found themselves at the edge of a rolling landscape, dotted with clusters of trees in the midst of tall, bright green grass.

The horses were pleased; the humans, the dwarf, and the lizardman much less so. The trail went straight for as far as they could see, toward a distant, jagged line of something dark. Raven nudged his mount to the fore and waved a hand across the grass. "Sensible folks would cross this in one ride and be beyond it tonight; sensible beings would also stay upon the track. This is not precisely a bog, but the ground is very wet; there are pools in places that you cannot see for the grass grows atop some of them. There can be boggy places, and if I am right about our current location, there may well be places where a man and horse could simply vanish."

"Oh." Tem-Telek shook his head. "I am not worried by a swamp; I know swamps. However, this trail — who makes trails in such a place, and do those who make them wish such as us well?"

Arturis nudged his horse forward and made as if to dismount. "I can lay hands upon the dirt," he announced, "and the God will tell me — "

"Yes, yes," Naitachal and Raven said in chorus. The Bard had already slid from Star's back and was gazing

across the tall grass. "The trail itself seems to me to be
safe; this land may not be if we are caught in it after
dark. There are *things* which inhabit such places, but
are only freed by night."

"Well, but — " Arturis spluttered. Naitachal turned
to smile at him, rather unpleasantly, and his eyes
gleamed.

"Whatever your God tells you of this place," he said
evenly, "I can tell you of Dark Things, and things
which will eat your soul, favored of a god or no. You
know what I am, Paladin."

Gawaine held his breath. The Paladin ducked his
head and stayed put. It was Raven who responded.

"You are a Dark Elf — and were a Necromancer,
and are now a Bard. Even one who has spent long
years in the waste knows who and what you are, Naitachal." The two gazed at each other, and Raven
suddenly smiled. "And were. I see no cause to doubt
your word. But we must pick a way across this place
before the sun has set."

"Of course not," Tem-Telek said calmly. "Even a
hide such as mine is not proof to insects, and let me
tell you, at dawn and dusk, you would not be able to
see anything from here, save clouds of them."

"Yes. Of course." Cedric waved aside insects and
stood in his makeshift stirrups to peer northward. "But
as we can see something now — What is that, Raven
— forest?"

The Druid nodded. "Forest. And again, if we are
where I think we are, that is a very vast wood, and
largely trackless. But I know it well, and will be able to
find my way through it from any side."

"Well, then — " The Bard came back and mounted
Star. "Since this is land you know, you go first." He
gave a subdued Arturis another of those rather malicious smiles. "And since you may wish to commune

with your deity, why do you not bring up the rear?"

Arturis ducked his head again and mumbled, "Sir, certainly." Gawaine gave him a puzzled look as he rode by, but Arturis had closed his eyes and was paying no attention to any of them. Communing already, no doubt. The bardling scowled at his Master's back. Had not Naitachal impressed upon him, often, that it was not polite to make fun of another's beliefs?

Another thing suddenly occurred to him as he pulled Star back into line and away from tempting grass: If Arturis was as deeply devout as a Paladin surely must be — particularly one so frequently smitten with visions — why did he not take offense at the Bard's tone of voice? For that matter, why not call down his god with lightning and fire to fry this disbeliever? After all, an excellent Bard Naitachal might be — but he was just that, a Dark Elf, a Bard, and even if he had been a Necromancer still, he wasn't a god. Nor under the personal protection of one.

So why did Arturis show every sign of being *afraid* of Naitachal?

Gawaine could hear the Paladin just behind him, muttering to himself, and he repressed a sigh. *And if he is as holy as he surely must be to be a Paladin, why do I feel nothing in his presence but a strong desire to strangle him?*

He set his teeth; almost as if he could read thoughts, Arturis had come up close behind him. "Ho, lad, how goes it?"

"Well enough," Gawaine replied neutrally. Silence. He added, rather unwillingly, "And with you?"

Arturis sighed dramatically. "Well enough, though the burdens I bear are enough to bury a lesser man. And once they would have buried me, when I was but an ordinary mortal lad — why, such as yourself, bardling, given to wine and carousing, and —"

"I hardly have the opportunity to carouse," Gawaine broke in. "Before I apprenticed to Naitachal, I was a horseboy in a nobleman's stable, and I worked hard for my bread and four coppers a year."

"Oh, I didn't mean *you*," Arturis replied hastily. "Personally. Though," his voice became rather tearful, and Gawaine turned away, hideously embarrassed by such a show of emotion by a grown man, "once *I* was such a mortal lad, and what dreadful things did I not do? I freely drank red wine, and comported myself at taverns with the most vile of men — and women!" He made a sound that brought Gawaine halfway around, certain the man had swallowed something and was choking. Tears had made streaks down the Paladin's grubby cheeks and were dripping from his beard. Reddened eyes fixed on the bardling's face; Gawaine turned away hastily. "Women," the tearful voice droned on. "I was one of those who sought low women. I sank lower than the lowest, and yet, look upon me now!" Gawaine nodded hastily and hoped he looked busy keeping Star firmly on the trail. "The God found me, in evil company, and he opened my eyes, and sent me upon my first quest to purify my heart, and so I have kept it ever since." He sniffed loudly and nastily. "And so you must think upon yourself, bardling," he went on briskly. "And upon your own life, whether you will keep a pure heart and avoid vile companions, and so come to the Truth."

"Ah — yes, of course," Gawaine stood in his stirrups. The trail widened just a little ways ahead, enough so that three could ride abreast. "Ah, listen, I think I hear my Master calling me. I had better go see what he wants." Star protested as the bardling kneed him; he had almost gotten his teeth in grass and wasn't pleased at having it taken away. Gawaine patted his neck as they left the Paladin behind. "Sorry, old fellow,

I'll see you get some later, I swear it." He sent his eyes sideways, but didn't dare turn to see how far back Arturis was. "But I fear that murder would do very bad things to my purity level, don't you?"

Naitachal hadn't been calling him; he was glad enough to leave off mediating an argument between Cedric and Raven over whether Cedric should try to bag a few of the ducks he'd seen and talk to his apprentice instead. "I don't understand," Naitachal mumbled. "From what Tem-Telek says, those two were quite friendly toward each other in the Slaver's cage, and now listen to them!"

Gawaine did. Raven was glaring at the archer, who stood in his stirrups to gaze out ahead of them and off to the west, where they could hear a large flock of ducks. "You said you were a competitive archer, that you won prizes with your marksmanship — not that you *killed* things!"

"I don't — " Cedric dropped back into the saddle and bared his teeth at the Druid. "I don't simply go around killing things! Don't be so stuffy, and don't act as though you've never been outside your Druid's glen before. You know full well that though you folk don't ordinarily eat meat, others *do*. And I promise you, there have been times when if I hadn't been a meat-eater, I would very probably have starved to death."

"Nonsense," Raven replied warmly. "If you weren't a meat-eater, you would know what plants were good to eat, and you'd harvest them instead of murdering innocent beasts — "

"Well," Cedric growled, "I happen to like the flavor of some beasts, and I don't particularly care if they're innocent or not."

Raven gazed down his long, lean nose at the archer for some moments. "Have you considered," he said finally, "that you might well develop better arm strength and a steadier pull, if you didn't eat meat?"

Cedric gaped at him, completely at a loss for words. Naitachal laughed. "Ah, yes. Pay no heed, archer. I have had Druids tell me my *singing* voice would improve if I didn't eat meat. It's a common flaw in an otherwise pleasant folk. Raven, how much farther do we have to go?" It was a definite and firm change of subject; Raven eyed the Bard sidelong and finally shrugged. "Will we reach forest by nightfall at this rate?"

Raven turned to look out ahead of them. "Can you not see how near the first line of trees is now?"

"You forget, I eat meat and so my eyes are not as sharp as yours," the Bard replied sarcastically. Raven turned to look at him for a long moment, then sighed, and Naitachal flashed him a quick grin. "To answer your question, I am not a woodsman, and I have no way to gauge how trees and woods look in what lighting conditions and from what distances. You, by your own words, have."

"We should reach them well before sunset," Raven said. He cast Cedric one last, sidelong hard look. "That is, if we have no long halts."

"I do not need a full company to shoot a brace of ducks," Cedric said patiently. "And personally, I would rather have no help at all, particularly not the kind of help that glares at me the entire time. I thought you said you were a holy man, Raven. Does not such a man leave his fellows alone?"

"I am a Druid," Raven replied. "And I personally prefer that all living things remain living — even those which others see as convenient to eat, or to kill for gain or profit, or for trophy." His lips tightened. "Even those which enslave others."

There was a momentary, nasty little silence. Cedric, to Gawaine's surprise, broke it by tilting his head back and laughing. "Ah! Well answered! And unlike some who shared that cart with us, and spoke alternately of his god and of how he would murder those Slavers if he had half a chance. Well, never mind. You are definitely a holier man than I, Raven. Go on, all of you. I won't be very far behind, and there will be meat tonight — for those who want it."

# Chapter IX

True to Raven's prediction, they made it out of the wetlands and nearly a league into the woods before the sun went down. Cedric proved as good as his word, also; he caught up with the rest of them just at the edge of the forest, four large ducks dangling from the back of his saddle. Raven pulled his mouth into a disapproving line, but said nothing, for which Gawaine was grateful. He was very impressed by the Druid's knowledge of the land, over and above any hopes he had of learning from Druids in general and this one in particular.

At the same time, he was hungry — and very fond of roast duck.

Wulfgar, who had been largely silent since the journey began, came over to inspect them, and he whistled thoughtfully. "Good shooting, that. Takes skill to skewer a bird so neatly."

Cedric nodded shortly. "I don't like things to suffer; I am a good enough shot that they don't — and I would not shoot anything, if I could not kill it swiftly." He cast Raven a dark look, but the Druid was already riding ahead. The archer sighed faintly. "Any we don't eat won't keep, unfortunately, and there isn't time to smoke meat, so we eat well tonight and finish whatever is left in the morning.

Wulfgar laughed. "Won't hurt my feelings one bit. And my Master quite likes game bird."

They set up camp in a large clearing, flanked on three sides by tall, enormously thick-trunked conifers, and on the fourth by a stream and willows. Naitachal, who had been growing restive as soon as the sun began to near the horizon, breathed a sigh of relief and dropped to the ground at once, letting his apprentice take their horses. He looked around the clearing, nodded briskly. "All right, it's late and I have much to do, to see to the safety of the perimeter. Cedric, you have the meat to manage; Raven, why don't you take young Ilya and gather whatever we need to go with it? And for yourself, of course," he added hastily, to forestall any comment the Druid might have had. Raven merely nodded, gestured for the peasant lad to come with him, and led the way down to the stream. "Just don't go very far," Naitachal raised his voice so he could be heard over the sound of the water, "because I do not want to have to repair the wards once I set them. Tem-Telek." He gave the lizardman his usual nod in lieu of a full bow — a politeness that took into account both the casualness of the present circumstance and that the lizardman was noble. "If you would set up a firepit and stakes for the birds, and let your servant help Gawaine with the horses . . ."

The lizardman bobbed his own head once, politeness itself, and glanced in the dwarf's direction. "You do not mind, Wulfgar?"

The dwarf stretched. "I never mind caring for the horses, Master. Besides, I need to get your cup."

Arturis shifted restlessly from foot to foot. Tem-Telek barely glanced his way as he added, "And if you will fetch firewood, Paladin, that should take care of all for the night."

The Paladin shook his head. "I had intended to spend an hour or so in prayer, before the food was ready — to keep the God's watchful gaze upon us all

this night." He brought his chin up to give Tem-Telek
a down-the-nose stare; the lizardman returned it in
full, and from a greater length of nose. "Besides," the
Paladin added, "there is no need for me to risk splin-
ters to my sword hands when there are two here who
are servants, and — "

Naitachal interrupted him very firmly indeed.
"There are none here, Arturis, who are servants of all
of us. If you would eat and sleep with the rest of us,
you will do your share of the camp chores. Wood. And
should you fetch enough before the rest of us are done
with *our* share of the chores, you may bring water."

"Oh." Arturis stood very still for a long moment,
then sent his eyes sideways, cautiously. "Yes, of course,
sir. At once." Naitachal watched him out of sight
among the trees before settling himself cross-legged
on the ground. *Every single time, every blessed single
time, whatever chore he is offered he objects. Well, fortunately the Paladin hadn't discovered the nerve to
object when I tell him what to do. Yet.* The Bard
shifted around a little until he found a more comfortable seat, and closed his eyes.

Gawaine, who had just come back from the horse-
tether with their instruments, gazed after Arturis; a
frown etched his brow. It really was odd: Very clearly
the Paladin did not like having to do anything for himself, and he argued with everyone about it when he
wasn't simply whining about whatever task he'd been
asked to handle — or taking any watch but the first, so
he could have an unbroken sleep once he was done.
Argued with everyone, that is, except the Bard.
*Maybe,* Gawaine thought, *his god protects him against
anyone except a Dark Elf?* He immediately pushed
the thought aside as improper — certainly more like
the sardonic Naitachal than himself — and went back
to help Wulfgar.

After all, yesterday or the day before, Arturis had spent a very long hour explaining to him how the pure in heart did not ever use sarcasm. "It is a weapon whose sole purpose is to cause the pure and moral man discomfort, and so the God does not smile upon scoffers and the sarcastic." Gawaine sighed. From the sounds of things, Arturis's god was a rather humorless sort, all around.

It was fully dark when they finished eating. Raven had found leaves for a tart but pleasant tea, and had gathered roots earlier in the day, as they rode, for a sour bread while Ilya had located familiar roots along the bank of the stream that he peeled and cooked in the coals. The others ate most of the roast bird; Raven contented himself with tea and bread, and a leathery strip of dried fruit. Naitachal finally set aside his cup and stretched. "Well, Druid. This wood — are we where you thought?"

"I believe so," Raven said cautiously. "In fact, I am nearly certain that I know this stream, though at a point well to the west. Tomorrow will prove it. And if we are, then it will take us four days of steady riding to get through, but there will be safe places the next two nights if I can place us."

"Good." The Bard smothered a yawn and stretched. "It sounds like a long ride, in any event. I suggest we choose the watch and the rest of us get some sleep."

Arturis licked his fingers and spoke up. "I will be glad to take the first — "

"You had the first watch last night," Cedric told him pointedly. "And we all agreed the middle watches would be divided so everyone could have a full night's rest some of the time."

"But — "

Naitachal cleared his throat ominously and scowled

across the small fire; both men went very quiet. "That is better. Cedric, you take the first watch tonight, both as reward for the excellent meal, and because you had the middle last night. Arturis, dear fellow, is it not true that most gods reveal themselves to their beloved children in the small hours, when no one else is awake to see? Or, have you never heard of vigils?" The Paladin opened his mouth, closed it again without saying anything. "I myself will take the last; the rest of you portion out the remaining hours however you will, my stomach is full and my eyes about to fall from my head." He turned away from the fire, wrapped his cloak around him and lay down. "I trust," he added gently, "that you will find a quick — and quiet — means of deciding." Gawaine glanced back at his Master, looked around the fire and shrugged. Raven gave him a very faint smile. Cedric was busy stowing the last of the meat, and Arturis had gotten abruptly to his feet. They could hear him down at the stream, splashing noisily.

Tem-Telek reached into an inner pocket and drew out several thin, brightly colored sticks of various lengths. He chose six, put the rest away. "I doubt any of you will want to gamble on this journey —"

Raven smiled again and shook his head. "I seldom play with tossing sticks, and I do not believe I would gamble — how can I put this politely? Absolutely never with one who carries his own personal set of sticks." The lizardman gave him a very toothy smile in return.

"For an unworldly Druid, you know considerable about worldly things, Raven. And it is true that few who are not of my race ever try to get the best of us at the tossing sticks, and fewer succeed. However, they may serve another purpose." He turned to Ilya, who was cracking a long leg bone with his teeth. "Here, youngling, shortest two sticks take the hours flanking the gallant Paladin, the others can choose from what is left." He drew them sharply back as the young peasant reached for the sticks; his fingers were shiny with bird-fat. "Wait. Better, you name one, and I shall pick it for you."

In the end, Gawaine found himself holding the hours between Arturis and Raven, who would in his turn waken the Bard for the last watch.

It was cool under the trees, and damp; the sound of the stream blended with a constant light wind in the high boughs, just enough so he could never be certain if he heard anything besides trees and water. "The Master set wards, they will hold against anything," he reassured himself. It was only a partially effective thought.

Really, though, with the protection in place all around them, all the watch had to do was keep an eye out for something trying to cross the boundary Naitachal had set — and such an action, the Bard assured them all, would trigger a very bright and unmistakable response. Of course, Gawaine told himself, Thunder and Star would certainly alert him if there was something real out there, trying to get past Naitachal's wards.

He wandered over to run his hands over Star, to check Thunder's legs and feet and lean against him for a moment or so, and finally hurried back to sit next to the coals of the fire, where it was marginally warmer. Arturis had been sitting just here, head sunk on his breast, when Gawaine came awake as and when he had ordered himself to waken. The Paladin had jumped nearly out of his skin when the bardling touched him — communing with the God, making certain they all stayed safe, was what he *said* he had been doing. If it had been anyone else, Gawaine would have been certain the man was sleeping instead.

"Unworthy thought," he told himself firmly. "And unpure. You cannot arrive at the Truth that way, by scoffing. If Master Naitachal does not want to seek out the Truth — well, that is his business, and I suppose he has the right to give the Paladin a difficult time. But I cannot let the Master's attitude influence me against a holy man."

Gawaine glanced around the firepit, taking an automatic count of his companions. Tem-Telek lay closest to the fire, bundled into his warm-suit, an extra blanket covering all of him but a little of his forehead, and the valet slept between him and whatever might come across the wards. Cedric dozed with his head on the empty quiver, his bow and arrows resting on his cloak under his outstretched hand, where he could reach them if there was need. Ilya snored softly a distance apart from all of them, still rather shy, Gawaine thought; after that initial candid burst about the valley, he had lapsed into a disconcerting habit of mumbling and blushing whenever spoken to, and never speaking otherwise.

Raven, he knew, had gone to sleep under the low canopy of a willow, near the creek; the Druid had pointed out his blankets so Gawaine could waken him for his share of watch. Clearly he preferred to sleep a little apart from others; he had said as much the first night. Naitachal, of course, slept as he always did — on his back, hands folded upon his chest like an onyx stone engraving of a dead knight on the lid of a coffin, utterly still, only the slow rise and fall of his breast to show he lived. Arturis lay flat on his stomach, face turned away from the firepit; Gawaine was glad for that, for when the Paladin slept on his back or side, he snored. And not anywhere near as quietly as Ilya.

The bardling sighed, very softly. Four days in this large company, four long days. He had not thought it would be so difficult, traveling with so many. After all, he had heard about Master Naitachal's journey with Count Kevin, all those years ago, and the Master had never said anything then about all this bickering and so many petty misunderstandings.

Including, apparently, his own. He certainly thought he had made it clear to Raven that he was seeking Truth — that he sought not simply answers as so many did, but the Answer, that he wanted to know himself, to raise himself above the mundane, the petty, the everyday. So far, the few times he'd had a chance to really talk to the Druid, he'd learned about edible mushrooms ("assume none of them are, unless you *know*"), how to find ripe tubers, and what grasses were good to eat or for seasoning a tea. How to start a fire with damp wood or in a downpour — but nothing important. So far, the bardling had found himself cautious of his Master's sardonic eye and a little too abashed to simply ask direct and pointed questions about the Meaning of Life. Those few tentative questions he had asked had either gone unanswered, or Raven had talked all around them, leaving him momentarily certain he had a grasp on something vital — only to discover later that he'd learned nothing at all.

Arturis, on the other hand... He'd been wildly eager to convert Gawaine — or anyone else, including Raven, to his own brand of religion and his god. But — "Oh, drat," Gawaine mumbled softly. "He speaks religion and a god and nothing else, except to parade his own previous unworthiness and evil ways and weep over them, and to prate that his god and his way are the only proper ones. If he is right, then what he tells me holds the Answer, his way and his god must be my way to purity and good, and from there to the Truth. And yet — " And yet. The things Arturis said seemed to have nothing to do with anything Gawaine wanted; Arturis and his shameless breast-beating and weeping made him excrutiatingly uncomfortable. And this afternoon, when they first started down that trail into swampy ground, the Paladin had gone right over the edge.

Not that the previous day had been any better; in answer to a simple question about *how* pure was sufficiently pure, Arturis had spent the entire morning telling Gawaine how pure he himself was and repeatedly assuring the bardling that what he really needed was a good role model — Arturis himself. "Pattern your behavior and your thoughts even as I do, lad," he had concluded, "and you, too, can achieve a clean heart and pure thought." After a very long morning of *that*, the only rational thought Gawaine had was, *I would rather die*. He had kept that to himself, though, and Arturis apparently had not noticed how quiet his companion was. Of course, he noticed nothing but himself, once he got on one of his tirades.

The Bard had noticed, Gawaine thought resentfully. He cast his peacefully sleeping Master a very black look indeed. Had noticed and had turned, frequently, to give his bardling an amused glance that clearly said, "If you will ask a fool a simple question — particularly *that* question of this particular fool — look to get the answer you deserve."

It had been midday before Naitachal had finally taken pity on him and had sent Arturis downhill to the stream they all could see to fill their water bottles. Arturis, halted right in the middle of a word, hadn't reacted furiously the way he had when Cedric had ridden by some time earlier and muttered, "Give the poor lad a break, you're wearing his ears to nubs." No, Arturis had ducked his head at once, said, "Of course, at once, sir," and gone off with the string of leather bottles.

At the time Gawaine hadn't felt anything but relief — and just maybe a leftover ringing in his ears. Now it struck him as quite odd, and the question that had occurred to him early on came back: Why should Arturis be so seemingly afraid of another mere mortal, if his purity was a tenth as great as he made it to be, and his god that powerful? Somehow, it didn't seem likely that the Paladin's mother had instilled such nice manners in him

— particularly not when one balanced his behavior toward all the others against his extreme agreeableness whenever the Bard set him a task, or a watch.

All the same . . . Gawaine turned matters over in his mind for a while longer, then brightened. "Maybe he just has difficulty voicing the Truth that has been revealed to him. Maybe he hasn't served his god long enough; when someone argues with him, he isn't able to form a proper response yet." There, now that made better sense. If the Paladin were still searching for the Answer himself, or if he had it but still felt unworthy of the god's attention — well, he might simply be embarrassed to say so. "I will not give up," Gawaine told himself firmly. "A Paladin is a holy man, even I know that much. And — yes! — maybe this is a test! One which he has devised for all of us, to see which has the strength to pursue knowledge, whatever the barriers he raises." Yes, that must be it. He leaned back from the warm stones around the firepit to look into the sky; the stars had moved enough; it was time to rouse the Druid.

He checked the horses on his way down to the stream. Star was stamping his feet restlessly, but Thunder stood phlegmatically and the other horses gave no sign of anything amiss or untoward. It was too bad that a time like this was the only one when he and Raven were alone; with all these sleeping around them, he wouldn't be able to talk to the Druid. Raven seemed rather distant anyway. Gawaine waited until he had splashed cold water on his face and looked reasonably awake, then sought his own cloak and lay down next to his Master.

# Chapter X

The Druid had been more off course than he'd thought, but less than he and Naitachal feared; by late afternoon the next day, he was able to find a trail he recognized that took them to a good place to camp. They rode into the clearing well before dark and the Druid waved an arm that encompassed the area. "There are plenty of roots, and it is still early enough in the season for ground berries. There is water that way" — he indicated a narrow animal trail which went north into thick brush — "and there are cresses, or were the last time I stopped here."

Naitachal dismounted rather cautiously — he had found himself stiff when the Druid woke him early this morning for the final watch, and he hadn't yet been able to ease the discomfort. He cast a dark glance at the back of the bardling's head as Gawaine threw one leg across Thunder's back and dropped neatly to the ground.

"I will tend the horses, unless anyone objects," the bardling offered.

Raven smiled and handed his makeshift reins over. "When you care so well for my poor beast, why should I mind? Unless — Bard, if you have a better suggestion?" Naitachal leaned on Star's back and looked at them both blankly. The Druid repeated his question.

"Eh? Oh, certainly, whatever you like. " As Gawaine turned away, hands full of reins, the Bard caught

Raven's eye and beckoned. "As soon as I have set the wards and eaten I will sleep until my watch. Unless you have a difficulty with this holy man of ours," he added very softly. "If so, then rouse me."

Raven's brow puckered. "Is there any problem? You seem — distracted."

Naitachal managed a faint chuckle and a smile he didn't particularly feel: The Druid had put his finger on the problem all too neatly. "Just a feeling of something about that does not wish us well, nothing more specific than that."

"I see." Raven considered this in silence for some moments, opened his mouth to speak, but closed it again as the lizardman and his valet passed close by. He sent his eyes one way and then the other, made certain they were alone again, and lowered his own voice prudently. "Perhaps there is nothing I can do to aid you, but if there is, please tell me what — and how. Meantime, I will make my own watch. Though," he shrugged, "we are in the midst of a very old forest, one which was old when my many-times great-grandsire was born. And in such a woods, particularly so far north — well, there are always *things* which do not understand the likes of us, and others which actively ill-wish us." He smiled, spread his hands in a shrug. "Still others which might consider us and our mounts a fine meal." Naitachal cast his eyes heavenwards, though in this clearing the treetops were so far overhead and so thick, there was in truth very little sky to be seen. The Druid looked around. "Here comes your apprentice and the peasant lad. I will fetch water and cresses," he said a little more loudly as Gawaine and Ilya came up to unsaddle the remaining horses.

"Are you all right, Master?" Gawaine eyed him curiously. Naitachal nodded sharply.

"Thinking, apprentice," he added pointedly.

Gawaine reddened and hurried away, taking Ilya and the horses with him. They nearly tripped over Arturis, who had gone to his knees right in the center of the clearing and closed his eyes. Naitachal smiled as the two lads tugged at tired horses; Gawaine finally had to hand over two of those he led to Ilya, so he could drag Star well out and around the Paladin. Star could see Thunder tethered not far away and was in no mood to be led away from his companion. The look Gawaine gave the unseeing Arturis as he passed . . . Naitachal grinned broadly and settled down where the Druid had left him, well to the east edge of the clearing, where the ground was thick with dry needles and leaves. He still winced as his backside made contact with the ground.

Maybe it hadn't been such a bad idea to let Arturis travel with them, after all. Gawaine was rapidly losing his glassy-eyed awe of the supposed holy man, and this past afternoon at least had gone well out of his way to avoid another of the Paladin's lectures. *Now that the bardling's seen most of the way through this clod, though — how do I get rid of him?*

Raven wasn't nearly the same problem, and as time went on, Naitachal found himself more and more approving of the Druid. He'd proven useful in finding trails, avoiding soft sand and bogs — providing food, which would have definitely been a problem with so many and only those supplies he and Gawaine had picked up in Portsmith. Raven was soft-spoken and polite, pleasant in a company that included the out-spoken Tem-Telek, the one-sided Wulfgar, the extremely narrow-minded Arturis — and two inno-cents like Gawaine and Ilya, who all too often brought up subjects any experienced grown man would know better than to mention in such mixed company. Raven had even managed to keep a cap on any temper he might have, even when Arturis prated at him. (And so far as Naitachal knew, temper wasn't something the Druids gave over as against their religion, the way some sects did. *His* experience with Druids had certainly been otherwise.)

More importantly, this Druid had had a gift tossed right in his lap — Gawaine's almost puppylike eagerness for Truth — and he hadn't gathered it up. Oh, he was polite enough when Gawaine spoke to him, answered whatever questions the bardling asked, but had never said anything to Gawaine that would even *hint* the Druids had a corner on the Truth market. Naitachal knew: He'd made very certain he was close by whenever the two were together, and he kept an inner sense tuned to his apprentice when he slept.

And unlike Arturis, Raven gave no signs of fearing the Bard. Useful as Naitachal found the Paladin's attitude, he sometimes wanted to strangle the man out of sheer frustration at his timorousness. At the very least, to give him a real cause for fear.

He cast an eye heavenward. It was darker up there, suddenly, and he'd been wasting time — nearly as much of it as Arturis, who hadn't moved an inch from his trance pose. "And pose it is," Naitachal assured himself grimly, "or I'm a Paladin myself!" Well, someone else could deal with the man for the moment; he had a spell to work for the overnight safety of the camp. Not that it would keep out anything determined to get through, of course. But most of the others didn't know that, and so slept better because of it; and anything that *did* manage to cross his lines would find it difficult to simply step over and enter the camp. Besides, the ripples cast by anything even coming close would bring the Bard awake at once. Particularly since he'd bested that banshee, he didn't doubt he could take on anything that might be out there.

"Pleasant thought," he growled. The hairs on his forearms lifted, laid back down as he drew a deep breath and let it slowly drift away, and ordered himself to relax. The spell was time-consuming at best; it was a royal, exhausting pain to work if he was tense.

He wasn't halfway into it when Ilya's distant, terrified shriek brought him to his feet. Gawaine's Bard-pitched yell topped the peasant's cry as easily as his singing voice could rise above a tavern full of loud drunks: "Wolves! There are wolves, across the stream, coming —! Ilya, get up, come on, now!" A crashing in the brush: Both lads pelted straight back to camp, ignoring the trail, and an empty bucket hung forgotten from Ilya's fingers. Moments later, Raven came sprinting up the trail; he spun back around as soon as he reached open ground and raised his hands above his head. Cedric came from the other direction, dropping large chunks of wood possibly in an effort to trip or slow whatever might be behind him; hands now empty, he knelt and dragged the bowcase across his shoulder.

Arturis was climbing slowly to his feet, as though dazed. Tem-Telek nudged him so hard the Paladin staggered and swore a most unholy curse. A moment later, Wulfgar brushed by him, and this time he fell, flat on his back.

Gawaine raced over to where Naitachal sat, to fish out his boar spear and quiver from their pile of belongings, and the Bard snapped, "Next time set them *atop* the rest!"

"S-s-sir," the bardling stuttered.

"Never mind that, get it out and ready — and tell me where I set the lute case!" Naitachal came to his feet as Gawaine wordlessly pointed; the boy yelped and he nearly dropped the case from a height that would be deadly to the instrument. But when he looked up to shout at his apprentice, the words died in his throat. *I surely cried out like that, the first time I saw so many wolves.* The Bard threw the cloth lute-bag aside, swallowed hard, and settled his fingers on the strings. There were at least twenty wolves — large wolves.

Gawaine's knees shook, and so did the hand holding the boar spear, but his voice sounded steady as he shouted for Ilya. "Come over here, by me, we have to guard the Master until he can come up with a spell!"

"Hurry, then!" Tem-Telek shouted over loud voices, terrified horses, and the howling of wolves. The lizard-man ran sideways, caught hold of Ilya's arm and shook him, gave him a shove in the right direction. Gawaine shook his head as the young peasant nearly careened into him; the boy had no weapon of any kind.

"Here!" Gawaine shoved the boar spear into his nerveless fingers and knelt to string his bow. "Can you use that?"

"Use?" Ilya was staring at the spear as though he'd never seen one before; Gawaine rapped his arm with the bow and he nodded. "I have used such a weapon, against wolves, but so many — "

"Then kill them one at a time!" Tem-Telek roared. He and Wulfgar were back to back a short distance away, the lizardman brandished a broad-bladed, double-edged sword while the dwarf held a long-hafted axe and practiced laying about him with vicious half-circle arcs. Arturis had drawn both his swords and stood waving them in the middle of the clearing; he was shouting something, rapid words in an unfamiliar language. Cedric had his bow strung and a dozen arrows stuck in the ground before him, and he knelt to begin firing as the beasts came nearer. Gawaine gave the archer's back a nervous look and hoped he'd manage to put himself at a safe distance

from Tem-Telek's sword and the wild-looking swings
Arturis was taking.

And then, he had no time for further thought; with
a wild howl and a bound, three of the wolves found a
way around the front line and leaped straight for him.

Somehow, Gawaine remembered the object in his
hands was a weapon. He drew back on the bow and
released his arrow; the wolf howled and fell right at his
feet. Ilya fell upon the next nearest with the spear, but
was nearly taken himself when the third attacked as he
was trying to free the point. The wolf he'd pinned
wasn't dead; a massive head that looked to be half
teeth came snapping around after him. Ilya squawked
and leaped back. Fortunately, he'd kept his grip on the
spear, more by accident than intent, and it came with
him. He brought it through in an underhand arc, and
this time the wolf went down and stayed down.
Gawaine's hands were shaking as he fit another arrow
to the string, but before he could loose it, Cedric bellowed, "Down there, you lads!" and his own
red-shafted bolt came streaking across the clearing.
The wolf fell over, twitched and lay still.

Gawaine pulled himself partway up once more,
eyes searching the clearing as his hand felt across the
dirt for the arrow he'd dropped. Ilya knelt next to him,
spear caught between two trembling hands. Behind
him, he could hear the Master, his fingers running
across the strings, his low voice working up some spell
or other. The air crackled with magic; Gawaine was
too shaken to follow what the Bard was doing, though.
Across the clearing, near the path he'd taken to the
stream, he could hear Raven shouting furiously at
Cedric. "You're *killing* them! You do not need to murder them all!"

"Then *do something*," the archer bellowed back.
"Arturis, watch that sword, you nearly had my head!"

The Paladin was still shouting, or chanting, in some alien tongue and apparently heard nothing save himself. Cedric slew another of the wolves and the Druid screamed at him in helpless fury. "I do not intend to die for your beliefs, Druid!" Cedric yelled. A moment later, though, the remaining wolves drew nervously back as Naitachal's voice filled the clearing. A bubble of red formed midway between Cedric and Gawaine, and enlarged to encompass all of them, driving the wolves into the woods. A moment later, the company heard frightened howls and a crashing that faded into distance.

Arturis dropped his swords and fell to his knees, let his head fall back and said something unintelligible. Cedric gazed down at him, a look of disgust on his face. "Our thanks, most blessed God, that heard his humble Paladin and —"

A crash of discordant strings silenced him; Arturis turned partway around, jaw hanging and eyes wide. Naitachal stood and closed the distance between them, lute still cradled in his arms. "I had no idea *your* blessed God went in for Bardry," he said pleasantly, but there was an unpleasant gleam in his eye. "And what was that language you were using, that disrupted my concentration for so dangerously long?"

"Uh — uh, language?" the Paladin asked. He managed a weak smile, but it faded as the Bard continued to look at him. "I — I was not aware I spoke, I — ofttimes the God speaks through my humble instrument, in his own many tongues."

"Ah." Naitachal's teeth gleamed white in the encroaching gloom. "Tongues. Of course. Why did I not realize? Well!" He turned away and started back toward the edge of the woods where he had been seated earlier, stopped as if he had just thought of something, and looked over his shoulder at Arturis.

"All the same, perhaps you would suggest to this God of yours, that the next time we entertain such — guests, if he uses *your* instrument to speak in tongues, I shall use *mine* to give you some other gift. One I do not think you will like at all." And with a final gleam of teeth, he walked off.

Arturis gazed after him in silence for some moments, finally rousing himself and getting to his feet. "He mocks the God," he began in a resentful undertone. Wulfgar tapped his arm, and when the Paladin came around to look down at him, the dwarf shook his head.

"Wouldn't say anything, if I were you," he suggested flatly. "I was distracted myself, and I do not *like* distraction when I am helping my Master protect himself."

"Nor I," Cedric added grimly. He had slung his bow across his shoulder so he could drag dead wolves from the clearing and a distance away from the camp. "If you need something to occupy yourself, Arturis, I could use your aid in removing these. Unless you think they make good companions for the night."

"I — I thought to seek guidance," the Paladin began, but the look in the archer's eye stopped him. "Yes, all right. But it is getting dark out there — "

"Well, then, close your mouth and move your feet," Cedric replied. Arturis cast him a resentful look but said nothing else. Cedric went to another of the dead beasts, pulled his arrow free and dropped it with the rest of his points, then caught hold of the beast's hind legs and dragged it away.

Gawaine looked around and made certain no one was paying any attention to him before he tried to get to his feet. He was shaking so hard, he wasn't certain he'd be able to stay on them once he did get upright. Ilya was a little ways away, helping Wulfgar gather the wood Cedric had scattered earlier, and Tem-Telek was gathering stones to build a firepit.

The bardling started and caught his breath in a gasp as a hand touched his shoulder, but it was only Raven. The Druid nodded in Naitachal's direction — the Bard was sitting cross-legged at the edge of the trees, lute held in still hands, his eyes closed and head bowed, finishing the surround-spell. "Unless he needs you to help him with what he does, why do we not go and fetch water?" Gawaine could feel the blood draining from his face at the very thought of broaching those dark woods, following that narrow path. The Druid patted his shoulder and nodded. "It is all right; I have no magic like your Master has, but I can sense when living things come near to me. And we need water, for ourselves to drink and for the soup. For the horses."

"The horses!" Gawaine said with a pang; he had completely forgotten the horses. But when he hurried over, they were all still where he had tied them — one and all restless, and Star was prancing back and forth as far as the lead would allow him to move.

"They are less frightened than I would have expected." Gawaine ran a hand over Thunder's flanks.

"I did what I could, just now," Raven said, "to soothe them." He caught hold of the bardling's shoulder and led him back over to the head of the trail. "I will help you tend them once we have water."

They had to step aside as Arturis and then Cedric came out of the woods. Raven cast the archer a very black look indeed. "You misled me, back in that Slaver's cart. You said you were a man of gaming skills, not a murderer!"

"Murderer, is it?" Cedric drew himself up to his full height. "And what would you or I have been just now, if I had not had the talent I have, to hit a fast-moving target?"

"Those were not targets, those were living beings!" Raven snapped.

"Oh, yes?" Cedric snapped in turn. "And what am I? Am I not also a living being? Do I not have the right to defend myself against beasts? Beasts which would eat me?"

"You — we might have frightened them away," Raven replied sharply.

"Well," the archer huffed, "you think on that, and sort out a way, and *next* time put your plan into practice before I have to make moral decisions about whether I live or a wolf does! Though I warn you, it will still be me that lives and the wolf that dies, if there *is* a choice!"

The two glared at each other. Gawaine cleared his throat, and when they turned to look at him he said rather timidly, "Uh, Druid — Raven? About the water — ?" Raven muttered something under his breath and turned to lead the way down the trail. Behind him, Gawaine could feel Cedric glaring after them and heard the archer mumbling — too quietly for what he said to be clear, fortunately. Raven's shoulders stiffened, but he kept on going.

# Chapter XI

Gawaine didn't sleep at all well; a part of his mind jibbered away at him, another part jumped at the least noise, and in the few moments of sleep he did catch, his dreams were all wolves and teeth, and wolves' blood everywhere.

The camp reeked of wolves' blood, of course; it was amazing the horses weren't in a heat of panic the entire night, and no surprise his stomach was so queasy. Even more amazing that all the other creatures in the wood which ate meat did not come down on them, with blood so thick on the ground.

They were on their way very early the next day, before the sky was fully light, taking only enough time to saddle the horses and restow their supplies. Raven, who knew these woods at least a little, led them as they marched, on foot and in single file, until the sun rose and they could all see the narrow trail leading north. A short time later, they came to a waterfall and pool, and Naitachal called a halt to allow them to water the horses properly, to make a small fire and brew tea, and to let Wulfgar soak his Master's overshirt from the previous night, for both sleeves were darkly red and stiff with wolves' blood. But the right arm of the silky thing was ripped from cuff to shoulder, and the dwarf mumbled over it vexedly as he scrubbed.

Once the fire was put out and the company ready to move on, the Bard handed around travel wafers, two each, and said, "Conserve these; one at midday, the other some hours later; we will make no stops the rest of this day save briefly for the horses."

"For which you have my blessings," Tem-Telek said shortly. His arm was bound near the wrist, and Gawaine shuddered as he looked at the narrow white band on that dark green, thick-skinned arm, knowing his own would have been sliced from the fingers all the way up, probably right to the bone. Tem-Telek huddled back into his thick cloak, wrapping wool snugly around himself once he was mounted: Wulfgar had immediately stitched the rent in his Master's cold-weather garment, but Tem-Telek had been unable to bear the pressure of the snug cuff against the bandage, and Wulfgar had had to roll up the right sleeve. It was not particularly cold, Gawaine thought, though he himself had left his cloak across his shoulders even when the sun rose to midday, and he gazed at the lizardman in wonder: to have such blood that one's body could not bear even pleasantly cool air. And for the first time, it occurred to him to wonder — why would Tem-Telek bear such discomfort to journey with them? What dire purpose would send him north, when anyone of his kind (and anyone with a sense of self-preservation) should have gone south the moment he'd been freed from that Slaver's cage?

One thing was certain: Neither Tem-Telek nor Wulfgar had given the least hint of their purpose, and it was unlikely a mere bardling would tease it out of either.

He brought himself back to the present moment as Naitachal mounted Star and took the reins from his apprentice's hands. "I agree, no unneeded halts," Raven said flatly as he emptied his tea-making tin onto the ashes of the fire, filled it with water, and poured that all around the edges. He shifted blackened sticks with one toe and turned away to put the tin in his pack. "Let us go. The next camping site is a distance from here, and the sooner we are free of the woods the better. There has been a change in this forest since I was last here, and besides," he added with a resentful glance in Cedric's general direction, "I do not wish any further loss of life *of any kind* upon my conscience." He mounted and rode off. Cedric rolled his eyes but said nothing.

That night, Gawaine was at least as stiff as Naitachal had been the day before and nearly too tired to stay awake for the evening meal — another of the Druid's soups, his own portion topped with a broken-up stick of dried meat. The whole mess was singularly tasteless, but he didn't have the energy to hunt through his pack for the tiny paper of salt.

He didn't sleep much better with a day's ride between him and the last camp; wolves were notoriously fast and tireless runners, and anyway, there were other wolves — and other worse things than wolves — about in these woods.

All day he had dreaded his share of the watches, but once they had eaten, Naitachal spoke up. "We will watch in pairs tonight."

"But that will mean a longer watch at a time — " Arturis began. The Bard turned to look at him, and he subsided.

"In pairs," the lizardman said thoughtfully. "Yes, I think so. A bad night for the guard to fall, I think."

"If you mean to imply that I would sleep on my share, knowing my responsibility to the — " the Paladin began frostily, but Wulfgar merely laughed.

"I am certain your god would never let *you* sleep on the watch," he said sardonically. "But I am merely mortal, and very tired to boot." He glanced at his Master, who was using a sharpening stone on one of his daggers. "I shall watch with you, of course, sir. And you should let me do that sort of work."

"There is a rent in my cloak, besides the one in my sleeve, if you need a task," the lizardman replied. "The edges on my weapons are a matter for my tending which you well know." The dwarf made a rumbling *tch* and fished in his belt pouch for his sewing kit.

"You should tell me these things," he said reproachfully, "rather than going about with your garb in disarray. It reflects badly upon my tending of you, and upon your regard for your own noble rank. Hand the cloak here, move nearer the fire. If no one objects, we will be first pair. Set the rest as you will, Bard."

Gawaine had the middle night hours with a quiet and clearly nervous Ilya, but the largest and loudest thing either saw or heard was an owl, diving on a small rodent that had crept from its hole — lured out perhaps by the smell of the sour flat bread Raven had baked, or by the travel wafers Arturis had left loose in his open bag next to his blankets.

Naitachal came awake at the bardling's first light touch to take the next watch with a silent and self-contained Raven, who vanished into the woods now and again. The Bard was aware of him, though, moving between the trees, stopping to look at the horses, stepping back into deep wood-shadow to commune with some night bird or other, perhaps testing the night air for some message. The Bard stayed near the embers of the fire, for he found the air chill, and he had no need to move about to sense any possible presence. Just now, there were plenty of small, timid beasts out there that wouldn't be within leagues of this camp if there were wolves or other unpleasant things about. Besides, he'd know if there were wolves.

*This time*. If he hadn't been caught in the middle of all that bickering, he'd have sensed them well before they'd attacked the camp. If he'd been left alone to set the wards around the camp. Wretched Arturis; he was proving to be nothing but trouble.

Finally, Raven came back to the fire and Naitachal sent him to his blankets; he went then to waken Cedric and drew him off to one side. "It's been very quiet," he whispered. "And I doubt you'll have any problems. All the same, keep an eye to your watch-mate." Cedric sighed heavily, and went to waken the Paladin.

Another day and night of woods; midmorning the day after, they came out of thick forest and into heavy brush and tall cottonwood. A swift-running river cut across their path, its water the opaque, bone-chilling green that meant it had come straight from a not-too-distant ice field. But Raven said he knew for certain, at last, where they were, and to prove it found a shallow, rocky ford not far upstream. He led them across and up a crumbling bank to a broad track, nearly wide enough for a cart and definitely for two to ride abreast. The trees thinned a little, and changed from cotton-wood to low alder and silver-green bushy things with dark berries the Druid said were good to eat. Gawaine tried them, and found them rather tasteless but filling. They were better than the tart red knobs growing at the ends of thorny rosebushes, but he obediently ate a few of these as well when the Druid insisted. "They keep you from falling prey to the small illnesses that plague the cold regions. They taste better in a tea, of course."

"Of course," Gawaine echoed. "I — Master Raven, why do you spend so much of your time gathering knowledge of this sort? Learning about plants and dumb beasts, when there is — I mean, when you could — I mean — " He faltered to silence as the Druid gazed at him in mild curiosity, and he could feel the heat in his throat and face. *I must be the color of my hair,* he thought miserably, and would have kneed Thunder forward or reined him back. But the Druid touched his leg to get his attention, and when he risked a glance, Raven didn't look at all as though his young companion had asked too personal a question.

"Why do I not spend my time instead seeking the one great Truth, you mean?" Head tipped to one side, Raven studied him; Gawaine, his face still very red, nodded. "Well, I enjoy discovering the things I learn about plants and animals, and how things grow and what purpose they serve in the greater scheme of things. You could look upon that as part of Truth, if you like." Gawaine eyed him, openly sceptical, and the Druid shrugged. "Besides, if I do not keep myself alive and in good health, how will there be any Raven to search for this greater Truth?"

"You are laughing at me," Gawaine protested unhappily. "I deserve it, of course, I know —"

"No," the Druid said. "I do not call you a fool for wanting to know the things you want to know. I merely tell you what is, and if you seek for an answer behind the answer I give you, I fear you will seek in vain."

There was a small silence as they rode on. "Well," the bardling said finally. "Thank you for as much answer as you have given me, Master Raven." A short distance behind them, Naitachal watched his apprentice ride ahead, and he smiled.

Raven, ever sensitive to his surroundings, waited until the bardling struck up a conversation with Cedric, then pulled his horse up to let the Bard catch up with him. They rode in companionable silence for some time. Naitachal stirred, shifted uncomfortably. "I am not half so elderly that a simple ride such as this should wear on my backside. I think I must look out a better saddle when the lad and I return to civilized lands."

Raven smiled. "You can call them civilized if you like."

"Yes. As long as I have spent wandering about them, I should know better." Another silence. Raven broke out his water bottle, drank and proffered it; the Bard took it, drank and handed it back. "My thanks, by the way."

"What — for not attempting to steal the boy? But he is *your* apprentice — and even a mere Druid can see that the gift he bears is suited to your teachings, and not ours."

"Not everyone can see it," Naitachal said. He gestured up the road, where Arturis had turned halfway around on his horse so he could join the conversation behind him. Just now, he was speaking in a voice too low to carry very far — for once — and waving both arms wildly. Gawaine and Cedric, beneficiaries of this one-sided conversation, cast each other a resigned glance; the archer shook his head but Arturis apparently didn't notice. The Druid laughed softly.

"No, not everyone can see it. But the Paladin's blindness is — well, why bother to speak of it, since such speech changes nothing? Though, if I could wish a change in our company, one only, I would send those two — Arturis and that archer elsewhere. Anywhere else."

"Oh, *Cedric* is not so bad," Naitachal said mildly.

"I — oh, well," Raven replied. Gloom seemed to settle on him, all at once. "Perhaps not. All the same, he is entirely too free with those arrows."

"He has not actually killed more game than we would happily eat, you know; and as for the wolves, he stopped shooting once they fled." He glanced at the Druid, but could tell nothing from his face. "Think on that, why don't you?" Naitachal urged. "While I go and rescue my poor 'prentice."

A short while later, with Gawaine at the fore, Ilya — who claimed to recognize the distant line of hills — at his side, and Arturis safely on rear-guard, Naitachal rode for a while by himself and let his mind wander. He was roused by a hard, dark finger poking at his forearm. Tem-Telek's face was grim indeed; the Bard blinked at him and tried to collect his thoughts. "Your pardon, Bard, but I may not have such an opportunity again for who knows how long. I suggest to you, strongly, that we find a way to be rid of that wretched Paladin."

The Bard opened his mouth, but before he could speak, Wulfgar had reined back to his other side and demanded, "Here, you, Bard! Isn't life looking short enough, without the kind of help Arturis is? Why don't we dump him?"

The Bard let his head fall back and began to laugh. "Ah, the minds of the great!" he managed finally. "Never mind, my friends. I was not laughing at you, I promise you that! As to this so-useful Paladin — well, I will speak to him this evening. I cannot think he is comfortable among us. Perhaps he only needs the least of shoves to be pushed upon his way."

But when they finally halted for the night, at the very northern edge of the woods, Arturis was not at all eager to leave them. "No!" he announced loudly, and flung his arms wide, nearly knocking down Ilya who had come up behind him with a load of sticks. "The God has set a higher purpose for me than mere personal comfort, and that is to aid you in this quest! To fail in my bounden duty — "

Doubtless he would have gone on as long as he had breath, and ready tears already edged his voice; Naitachal hastily forestalled him. "Yes, yes, yes, as you say, bounden duty, of course, yes, I understand, it was only a thought for your ease. Well! Yes! If you will have no thought for

yourself, then, why do you not go help fetch the water?"
Arturis opened his mouth, closed it without a word and
went looking for the buckets. The Bard glowered after
him, then turned away mumbling, "Bounden duty.
Bounden duty, my grandmother's feet!"

But the Paladin, for all his wildly dramatic
speeches, did seem to be sincere in his belief, the
Bard thought gloomily. It was enough to make him
feel the least, tiny bit sorry for the poor fellow, and
because of that, when he portioned out the watches,
he gave the first to Arturis.

It was cold out here between the northern edge of the
woods and the undulating, brown scrubby plain that
sloped up and up toward distant snow-tipped mountains.
Gawaine found himself uncomfortably chilled despite the
thickness of his blankets, and he had left on his
foot-wrappings and wrapped his toes in his spare shirt.
More than that, he was restless: always a little stiff from
sleeping on hard, cold ground and riding so many hours at
a time. He tried to remember the last time he had
practiced the mandolin and couldn't, and then wondered
if his hands would even move properly across the strings.
Tried to remember the last time *they* hadn't been so
miserably stiff that it was nearly impossible to make fists of
them the first hour or so he was awake of a morning. His
lower back ached, and there was a cold wind blowing
across his neck.

He rolled to one side and drew up his knees, tugged
at the blanket to get it over his shoulders. The arm
under him was going numb. He sighed, rolled over the
other way, fought the blanket around him again, tried
to recall the lyrics to that war-song he'd sung in the
Moonstone, hoping the exercise might ease him into
sleep. But only fragments came back to him, and now
with his mind scurrying and chattering busily after the
rest of the lines, sleep was gone for good.

A small distance away, he could see Arturis sitting at the fire, which still burned, though it had sunk a ways. The Paladin's shoulders and perfectly combed hair were unmistakable, even in outline; he was apparently staring into the flames or just beyond them, not moving at all.

He didn't move when Thunder and Star nickered softly, or when one of the other horses at the opposite end of the horse line began moving restlessly. Gawaine came silently up onto one elbow, then pulled the blanket snugly around his shoulders and got to his feet. Thunder nickered again, and Star thudded into him, snorting nervously.

Something was wrong, something — Gawaine turned, picked out his Master, and hurried over to grab his shoulder. Naitachal came awake and alert at once. "Something out there," Gawaine whispered. "The horses — that's odd," he added as he turned back. The Paladin still hadn't moved. He did jump convulsively, and yell in what was clearly surprise, when Gawaine shouted out, "Wake up, the camp!" Thunder screamed at nearly the same moment and reared. With a yell of their own, half a dozen men charged the clearing from six different places.

"Bandits!" Raven shouted. "Wake up!" He was on his feet, staff held between his hands at the ready, and the first man to come within striking range caught the end under his chin. He went down in a boneless heap and lay still. Raven leaped over him and went for the man who was trying to break the bardling's horse line and steal the horses, but before he could get there, Thunder reared once more and knocked the would-be robber flat. The man who had caught the Druid's staff on his chin came moaning to his hands and knees and began to crawl away; Tem-Telek, with a horrid oath in his own language, spitted the fellow.

Gawaine stared in brief horror at the limp body, then forced his eyes away as he scooped up his strung bow and fit an arrow to it. Cedric's idea — keep the weapon ready throughout the night — but he'd have done it anyway, after the wolves. His first shot went wild; the second and third sent a dark, short man with wild hair and tangled beard screaming and staggering back into the woods. A moment later he heard him crash to the ground and become blessedly silent.

If there were more than that six, they never showed themselves; after four fell dead, the other two turned and fled.

# Chapter XII

"Well." Naitachal stalked over to the dying fire, where he squatted and concentrated on feeding it small sticks until it caught once more. He came partway up, looked around the clearing, grimaced with obvious distaste. "There is a mess here. Is there no one who will clean it up?"

Cedric cleared his throat; Gawaine jumped and let out an airless little squawk. The archer barely glanced in his direction. "Apologies, lad; didn't mean to startle anyone. Arturis, perhaps you can explain how the mess came to be here in the first place?" Gawaine turned to follow the archer's grim look. Arturis sat hunched over his knees on the far side of the firepit, to all appearances completely spent. Cedric folded his arms across his chest and waited for a reply. The Paladin looked up, his eyes narrowed and his color was high.

"Do you accuse me? You *dare* accuse a holy man of consorting with such — such creatures?"

"Now, Cedric," Raven began mildly, but the archer waved him to silence.

"Of consorting? Not necessarily. But I find it interesting that it was your watch when those men attacked us. In fact, Arturis, more than once I have wakened during your watch — or shared one with you — and you have been so still and so limp, one might think you slept, instead of guarding as you ought."

Arturis gaped at him. Naitachal glanced over at the

Paladin and sent his eyes heavenward. "I — you *dare!*" the Paladin spluttered finally, and he leaped to his feet. "But what else can one expect of such a godless man and such a godless company, that they do not see what is there before them to be seen?"

"I see dead men," Cedric replied grimly. "Four of them. Who were not part of our godless company, but a godless company of their own."

The Bard stirred. "They woke me when they crossed the barrier, but with so much dry brush and," his nose wrinkled fastidiously, "and considering that none of them has bathed in the past year or more, from the message the wind brings me, I do wonder myself that my barrier was the only warning."

There was a nasty little silence. Arturis looked from one grim face to another, and his own showed nothing but bewilderment. "It wasn't — exactly the only warning," Gawaine volunteered. As one, the rest of the company turned to look at him, and he stuttered, "I — I wasn't sleeping very well, and — and, well, I heard Thunder, the — you know, Master, how he gets when there are those about that he doesn't know."

Naitachal nodded once, sharply. "Restless. *And* noisy enough to warn anyone already awake."

Wulfgar was bending over one of the men, peering into his face. "I myself heard the brute, lad; wouldn't ordinarily have wakened me, but I was only dozing just then."

Arturis's eyes were shifting rapidly from one to another of his companions, and now he began shaking his head. "You — you ill-speak me, if you say that I slept through the watches! I was praying, seeking an answer from the God, how far this my quest follows your own secular search. He vouchsafed me a vision, and lo! I was unable to break free of it — "

"Which am I to suppose," Wulfgar broke in testily,

"that your god did not see the peril creeping upon you and your godless companions, or that he did see but did not care to warn you?" He made an uncouth noise and turned to stalk away, but added across his shoulder, "I myself would prefer to worship a god who cares for the welfare of those who pray to him."

"Blasphemer," Arturis hissed. "The God *did* warn me! But before I could declaim his warning, the boy began yelling — and quite shattered my vision," he added, staring at Gawaine in sulky discontent. Gawaine turned away without even trying to come up with a reply, and went over to help Wulfgar drag one of the dead bandits out of the clearing.

Cedric looked around, met Naitachal's level gaze, and both shrugged. Tem-Telek had turned his back on them all, and Raven had vanished from camp somewhere in the past moments. Wulfgar and Gawaine were dealing with one of the bodies; Ilya had another by his feet and was dragging him away from the firepit.

Silence for some time, except for the whispery sound of cloth being dragged over dusty ground, and the horses shifting back and forth on their line as they settled down once more. "Arturis," the Bard said softly, and the Paladin jumped. "Surely you are not happy in our company. We do not worship your deity or — by your lights — respect him. We are all obviously very different folk, but you alone seem to have great difficulties in fitting in with the rest of us. I will not blame you if you choose to leave and find your own way."

But Arturis lifted his chin and gazed at Naitachal, and there was defiance in his eyes. "Will you send me into the night alone, with wolves and men abroad?"

Naitachal sighed heavily. "You must know all of us better than that by now! You fool, of course we will not force you away. I merely said — "

"My God has spoken, and his word is above yours.

Though I would not remain where I was not wanted. But if you will not throw me out to die at the hands of rough men, or by the teeth of demons and wolves, then I will not leave," Arturis said flatly. He got to his feet and stalked off into the darkness. Bard and archer gazed at each other helplessly. And then Cedric grinned broadly, and quite suddenly began to laugh.

"It is *not* amusing," the Bard said.

"Much you know," Cedric replied. He considered this, laughed some more, and came over to the firepit, lowering his voice cautiously. "Obviously we dare not leave the man to hold a watch by himself again; one of us will have to either sit up with him or remain awake at his blankets. But I think I know how to get rid of him during the hours we ride." He glanced cautiously over his shoulder, lowered his voice and spoke rapidly. Naitachal listened in silence, but a wide grin split his face, and then he, too, began to chuckle.

The next morning, the Bard approached Arturis, who eyed him warily across a saddled and partly laden horse. "You know, Paladin, I fear we owe you an apology." Tem-Telek and Wulfgar came upright from their places at the fire and stared. Wulfgar would have spoken, but Cedric reached across to touch his shoulder and when the dwarf looked his way, Cedric shook his head warningly.

"If you say so," the Paladin said shortly, but Naitachal thought he could see pleasure in the man's eyes.

"After all, it is not often a man of your piety and your strength comes along," the Bard went on. "And it is only natural that the rest of us might — well, resent is possibly too strong a word, but you take my meaning, I am certain."

"It is something a man such as myself must live with," Arturis said, and he shook his head sadly.

Gawaine, who was busy checking Thunder's legs, bit the corners of his mouth to keep from laughing aloud, and he could see Cedric bend down, ostensibly to deal with the fire but actually to clap a hand across his mouth. "That I am stronger than most, and — not more holy, of course, but that the God has singled me out for — "

"Yes, yes, quite," Naitachal said quickly. "My concern, you see," he lowered his voice a little, "is that the dangers against us have multiplied in the past few days, and the road north is growing unsafe. And — well, look at us. None of us are so weapon-crafty as you, and some like myself and the bardling, and the peasant lad, we have no real skill in fighting at all. So I wondered how you would feel about riding in the fore, to scout out the dangers for us?" Arturis gazed at him blankly, and Naitachal smiled a deprecating smile, spreading his arms wide. "I would not blame you, of course, if you said you would not. After all, we have not given you an easy time of it recently, and you would be within your rights to say to me nay, and rudely at that."

"Ah." The Paladin shook himself. "But for a godly man, a moral and upright one who serves the God and seeks purity and the True Way — oh, no, Bard, that might be *your* way, but it would never be mine! I will do what you ask," he added grandly.

"Oh, thank you, thank you, thank you," Naitachal murmured fervently. "We will be some moments seeing to the packing still; and of course, it would never do for you to get too far ahead of us — "

"Well, if I am to scout," Arturis began doubtfully, "I should be a fair ways ahead of you."

"But not so far that you cannot call upon us for aid, if you need it," Naitachal added quietly. The Paladin snorted inelegantly.

"Aid! The God is my aid in all things, and so it should be for all who are pure in heart!" He threw the last of his goods onto the horse, and threw himself into the saddle, drawing his sword as he caught up the reins. "I shall ride along the road north, and by all that is right and holy, I shall protect you all with my very life!"

It spoiled the effect a little that he had to wait for Gawaine to come and undo the hobble ropes that bound the horse's front feet. Arturis feigned not to notice anything but a spot some distance away, and when the bardling stepped back, he urged the horse forward at a canter, and shortly vanished down the road. There was a long, deep silence as the hoofbeats died away, followed by the sound of many laughing.

They hadn't lost him entirely, of course; as Naitachal said, it would have been too much to hope for that. Now and again they could hear him in the distance, flushing game, and once bellowing out a warning as he found men waiting at the side of the road. At that, Cedric sighed and drew out his bow and an arrow. "I suppose I really *had* better go and rescue the fellow. Otherwise, he'll probably find a way to come back and haunt us all."

"What a horrid thought," the Bard said, with an affected shudder. "Go, then, but be careful."

"Ho — you should take company to watch your back," Tem-Telek said. "Wulfgar, go and aid him. And call if you need me as well."

"Your wish, my command, Master," the dwarf said easily, and drew his axe as he spurred after the archer.

The rest of the company came up a short while later to find several men dead along both sides of the road where it rose above the rest of the landscape and there were deep ditches. Cedric and Wulfgar waited for them; there was no sign of Arturis. The archer grinned. "Said he had a vision, more trouble ahead, he would go and — "

"Enough," the Bard said firmly. "Bad enough I must listen to *Arturis* talk that way, there is no need for you to quote him."

"Yes." Cedric sighed. "The only difficulty, really, is that he has frightened all the game away from the road."

"And that," Raven said, "is the best reason so far for sending Arturis on ahead." It was the first thing he had said since late the night before — and for the first time Gawaine could remember, the Druid sounded absolutely cheerful.

Arturis came back to join them at sundown, his face flushed and his hair rumpled. He chattered on for a while, and finally was persuaded to go with Ilya, who claimed to know the land hereabouts very well. "There is a stream just a little that way, and in it, very large fish. I can catch a fish for us, if you like, sirs." He gave the Druid a doubtful look from under his thatch of black hair and turned to Naitachal. The Bard nodded.

"I would not mind fish. And perhaps Raven will not mind quite so much if it is fish instead of deer or bird."

"I will not be baited," the Druid said mildly. "But if there is a stream, then there may be cresses, and I might also find root for flour. We could use bread."

"We could use food," Naitachal corrected him. "Of all kinds. Ilya, how much farther to this village of yours?"

The peasant considered this in silence, finally shrugged. "I would need two full days afoot to reach it. With these horses, it may be we can come there by evening tomorrow. I do not promise this. But — yes, it may be."

He led Arturis and Raven around a stand of willow

and off toward the setting sun. The Bard sighed and sank to the ground. "It may be I will strangle him if he does not give me a straight answer."

Cedric looked up from the rock ring he was building for the fire, and he grinned. "I think, Bard, that you have had enough of travel for the moment."

"I think you are not wrong," Naitachal grumbled. He stretched cautiously, mumbling to himself when joints and muscles protested. Finally, he stretched out his legs before him and watched Gawaine, who had unsaddled the horses, hobbled and tethered them, and was now running a curry brush over Star's black flanks. The bardling was coming along, he thought. Still far from ready to strike out on his own, but Naitachal thought he could finally begin to see the Bard in the boy. *Just keep him away from Arturis and his kind.*

Then again — of all the things the Bard had intended to expose Gawaine to on this journey, the Druid and the Paladin would have been the last on his list. The Druid and his influence on the boy were still a question mark; but Naitachal was nearly certain that Gawaine had already begun to question whether Arturis was what he said, whether the man's god and religion were what he said, whether what Arturis offered should be swallowed whole, or taken apart and examined.

Naitachal knew something himself about the quest for truth — not the Paladin's Truth, nor yet the Truth the Druids normally pushed, but the one a Bard sought all his life, through his music, his magic, just from living and experiencing life. With any luck, Gawaine would come to realize that what he sought would be a very long search indeed — and worth every moment of it.

He roused himself as the bardling finished grooming the horses and came over with an armful of their goods, the mandolin case dangling by its strap from one hand. "Where did you wish to sleep tonight, Master?" Naitachal pointed, Gawaine carried the things, set the mandolin carefully aside and dumped the blankets. "Think of it," he said, and fetched a little sigh. "We might have a real bed to sleep in tomorrow."

"Aye, we might." Wonderful thought. "But don't set your hopes too high; consider our friend Ilya. He does not look to me as though he knows what a properly soft, clean bed is."

"Ohhhh." The bardling groaned, knelt to spread out his blanket, and set the mandolin atop it.

"I just warn you," Naitachal said mildly. "So you aren't too disappointed."

"Believe me," Gawaine said, "anything will be better than rocks and tree roots. Anything at all."

The Bard laughed. "I hope those words don't come back to haunt you. Where did you put the other instruments?"

"There. With the food bags." Gawaine pointed.

"Stay, rest a moment. I will fetch them. I want a word with Tem-Telek anyway." *And I hope you didn't call down one of those minor curses on yourself, boy,* he added to himself as he walked away. Anything at all, indeed! Nothing like asking for trouble, was there?

How much trouble, he couldn't have possibly foreseen.

Late the next afternoon, when they rode into Ilya's village, a deep foreboding struck the Bard, though at first he could see no reason for his unease. There were peasants everywhere: abandoning their plows and digging sticks and coming at a run to see who came calling; coming from drafty-looking little huts, and from a pen where a clutch of young pigs were rolling in mud. And then from all directions, calling Ilya's name excitedly.

The Bard looked all around. Odd, there seemed to be no lord's house — no mansion, of course, but there should have been at least a house better made than the rest, larger certainly, where the village master lived. Gawaine, who was riding at his side, leaned over, his brow puckered, and asked in a low voice, "There's nothing here *but* people like Ilya! That isn't right, is it?" Naitachal shook his head, but before he could say anything, they had reached the square    a broad stretch of muddy ground as opposed to the long narrow stretch of muddy ground that was the street. Ilya drew his horse to a halt and threw himself from the saddle; he was surrounded at once by farmers and herders and the muddy boys who had been in the pen with the pigs.

"Oooooh! Oh, Katya, *look*! Look at his lovely red hair!" Gawaine looked down, and his jaw dropped. Naitachal looked all around their horses and closed his eyes. The two of them were surrounded, at least two deep, by young women.

# Chapter XIII

"Oh, *my*," the Bard breathed reverently; there was a gleam in his eye. But Gawaine stared in wide-eyed horror at the sea of apple-cheeked, blond-braided, solidly constructed peasant maidenry surrounding Thunder, and seemed beyond hearing.

Ilya waded back through the mob of young women, caught hold of his knee, and shouted out happily, "Now, my friend, do not be stuffy, I have told my uncles all about you, and you must come down and meet all my lovely cousins!"

"Your — cousins?" Gawaine said weakly.

"Go on," Naitachal urged from his other side, and shoved him off-balance. "Nothing could possibly be worse than sleeping on hard ground, after all — go and be friendly!" Gawaine shot him a nasty look; the Bard smiled blandly and gestured. "You are being stayed for," he said pointedly. Gawaine drew a deep breath, fixed a smile on his lips, and slid from Thunder's back. The concentrated odor of onions nearly dropped him in his tracks, and only a determined effort kept the smile in place as Ilya clapped him on the back and turned him to face the expectant sea of young women. At ground level, they were even more daunting — the smallest of them would make two of him, and they were one and all smiling at him in a most unnerving manner. "My cousins," Ilya announced cheerfully, and he pointed as he rattled off names: "Kayta, and her sister Marya, and the daughters of my uncle Ivan, Marya and Katya . . . " Gawaine blinked at him in astonishment; unless his hearing was going bad, most of the girls were named Marya or Katya — or if there was some subtle variation, it was beyond him. Hard to tell, when he was being eyed like that. "And the daughters of my uncle Ivanya," Ilya finished triumphantly, "Katya, Marya, and Greta!" Twenty or so young women and one boy gazed at him expectantly. Gawaine smiled weakly.

"Ah. Greta! What an — unusual name!"

"Well, they are triplets," Ilya replied at once. "We are not so far removed from civilization as all that, you know — of course they all have different names!"

"Gawaine," Greta cooed, and fluttered pale eyelashes at him. He held his breath, nodded. "Oooh, you do have the most beautiful hair, all the color of carrots and so curly!" One pudgy hand reached out toward the hair that had fallen across his forehead; another slapped hers away. *Onion. I shall never eat another so long as I live. They must use them for perfume!*

"For shame, Greta, he did not give you permission!"

"Now, Katya, he spoke to me," Greta replied in a very injured voice. "And not to you."

"Oh, but he has not had the opportunity to speak to poor little Katya." The slapper pouted and edged neatly between Greta and the bardling. "Ooooh, but his eyes are such a pretty green!"

Ilya beamed. "I knew they would like you, my friend."

"You — you did?"

"Well, even if you had been quite plain, which you are not, of course!" He leaned close and murmured, "After all, it is difficult for the girls here within the village. If a man is not unwedable because he is an uncle, it is because he is a cousin." *Wed?* If Gawaine had not

been held up by so many warm, solid young women,
his knees would have given way. Ilya flung his arms
wide. "Such wealth! Such a splendid choice for any
man, how I could envy you — !"

"Now, cousin," one of the Maryas — or was it a
Katya? — put in with a shrill giggle. "Go away, and let
us set the young man at his ease. You make him
uncomfortable."

"Ooh, yes!" someone well back in the crowd
squealed. "Look, he has gone all red in the face!"

"Oh, like his *hair!*" someone else cried out, and the
whole pack dissolved in shrill giggles. Gawaine looked
about wildly, but Naitachal and Star were no longer at
his side; somehow, in the past few moments, the Bard
had left him and he hadn't even seen him go. *Master!
I'll get you for this!* There — Naitachal had reined
Star in so he could dismount; Gawaine could see him
in earnest conversation with one of the older men. *I'll
get you — if I don't die of onion first!* If he did, he'd
haunt the Bard for the rest of his very long life.

In the meantime, the girls were all trying to talk to
him at the same time — those who weren't whispering
and giggling with each other and eyeing him sidelong.
*I knew what Ilya was — why didn't I think it through,
what his village must be like?* He knew the type, of
course; he'd been country himself, if not small-village
peasant. These should have an overlord somewhere
— obviously not living in *this* village, unless he was
less lord than most, for there was nothing in sight but
pig sheds, tanning sheds, the piled-dirt-slanted-doors
configuration that meant root cellar (probably full to
the brim with onions, Gawaine thought gloomily), and
huts where people must live but that in truth didn't
look much better than those storage and beast sheds
in the middle of the small pig fields. He looked over
the sea of solid, massive, blonde pulchritude, and a

rude old saw of his father's came back to him: "Strong like bull, dumb like ox, hitch to plow when horse dies, good hips for babies . . ."

*Be fair*, he urged himself. They were probably nice people, most such villagers were — share their last loaf with you (or their last onion), give you shelter (and a marriagable daughter). He was breathing a little too fast and despite the cool afternoon breeze could feel sweat breaking out on his brow.

One of the Katyas — a Marya? — slipped her arm through his and patted his cheek. "You aren't paying attention, you silly boy. I asked if you would like to take a walk with me this evening." Several of the other girls began to protest, the rest to giggle and whisper among themselves.

"Walk." He blinked as she leaned close to his ear to whisper; her breath made his eyes water.

"Walk. Or do you not know how, and instead ride that great horse all the time?" More giggles. "There is a very nice *field* I would like to show you, this very *evening*." Someone behind him gasped.

"Katya, how dare you?"

"I asked!" Katya shouted over his shoulder, blowing a gust of onion all over him. Gawaine freed his arm and coughed into cupped hands. Katya and half a dozen others began pounding him on the back with strong, meaty hands. "I have a right to ask, just because I thought of it first, and you did not — oh," she finished in a small voice as he looked up questioningly. She smiled then. *The wolves smiled a lot like that,* Gawaine thought nervously, and now his hands were sweating, too. "What do you say, Gawaine of the lovely red locks?" Her voice had gone all coy again. *Who told these girls that fluttering eyelashes was attractive?* He had never seen anything sillier, and with so many of them, he could almost feel the air swirling around him, the way they were fanning it. "Will you walk with me this evening, across the fields, and tell me of your world?"

They were all waiting. *With baited breath,* Gawaine thought gloomily. Waiting, though, it suddenly and unnervingly occurred to him, like so many cats waiting for a single mouse to poke his head from the hole. . . .

*Trap.*

"Um. Uh. Well." He had never thought faster in his life. "My Master will need his musical instruments readied for this evening, so we may sing and play for you all," he improvised rapidly, "and I must make certain of the strings, or he will beat me."

"Ohhhhh," from a dozen or more throats, and one of the Maryas ran her fingers down his near arm. "Oooh, not beat such lovely, lovely skin? Oh, what a horrid and cruel man he must be, this Master!"

"Um, well, he does not usually — I mean — "

"Oh," the Marya said, and leaned close to his other ear. "If it is that you do not wish to walk with my cousin Katya, I will meet you at sundown. There is a place — "

"Well, ah, I — "

"Marya!" Another of the girls grabbed her arms and pulled her away, but before Gawaine could catch his breath, she had neatly interposed herself in the other girl's place. Closer to him, if anything. "Pay no heed to her; she is a terribly forward girl," this one murmured. "My uncle is a strong man. If you wish to be rid of this Master, he will aid you. Let me take you to him, and while he is dealing with the man, you and I can stroll about the village — there is a field of flowers, just over there, and from it the sunset is so lovely — "

"Ah, yes, I am certain it is." Gawaine bent his head to cough and surreptitiously blotted his brow. "But — but the Master is my own uncle, and I am quite fond of him. Besides, my father who is his brother would be greatly distressed if something befell his brother."

"Oh. A brother. Family. Oh." Girls looked at each other and frowned, as though uncertain how to continue. The only Greta (so far as Gawaine could tell, anyway), giggled then and tugged at his arm. "Why do you not come with me? You must be tired and thirsty, there is my house just yonder, and my mother will give you soup while I fetch fresh milk for you."

"Why, how kind of you to offer. But I am not hungry or thirsty just yet, and —"

"My mother raises the finest pigs in all the village," the Greta topped him, and a discontented murmur ran all around them. "And her pasture backs upon the field of flowers my cousin just spoke of. I am certain I could show you a much finer view than she —"

"Oh, yes, well, how *very* kind." Gawaine could see Ilya a short distance away, talking to one of the grubbiest old men he had ever seen — save for the two even grubbier old men flanking him — and the boy, as though aware of the bardling's gaze, turned and smiled broadly, then spread his arms in a very wide shrug. Gawaine only just managed not to shake his fist in reply. *Think*, he reminded himself hastily. The young women were pressed against him, and he was uncomfortably aware of the presence of more (fortunately clad) female flesh than he had ever felt before in his young life; two of them were fingering his hair again, and now someone was running chubby fingers lightly along the back of his neck. "Well, yes, what a wonderful offer! And I cannot thank you all enough, but my Master has need of me just now."

"I heard no call," one of the Maryas — a Katya? — replied wonderingly.

Gawaine shook his head, winced as several strong fingers caught in snags of his hair. "I instinctively *felt* it," he said.

"Oooh, what a wonderful gift!" a Katya — or possibly a Marya said, clapping her hands together. "How seldom it is we poor girls see a man with such sensitivity!"

"But your hair is so tangled, you must let me comb it," another murmured against his ear. *I thought I had lost my sense of smell for a moment there,* Gawaine thought as onion washed over him in waves.

"Ah — yes — well, no, you cannot do *that*, it is — a — yes, it is an oath I have taken, not to comb my hair until a certain event comes to pass," he improvised rapidly.

"An oath — ah, perhaps," another said, "until you have wed?" The whole group dissolved into shrill giggling and began to whisper to each other. Gawaine gaped at them in open horror, but rapidly composed his face as women turned back to him.

*Remember how the squire used to be rid of men, that voice he used.* "Well," he said, brightly and firmly at once, "I cannot tell you how pleased I am to meet all of you, and I trust we shall have an opportunity to all meet later." *All is the word for it,* he thought fervently. "But I really must go now, so that there is such an opportunity, otherwise my Master will not give me any time to myself." Discontented young women gazed at him; some pouted openly, none of them moved. He added, "Really. But later — "

"Of course!" One of them clapped her hands together and jumped up and down. "It is not as though he will vanish overnight, girls! If you will not go walking with Katya this evening, though, fair Gawaine, then do think of me, and remember that I was the next to ask if you would walk with me."

"I — well." He spread his hands and shrugged helplessly. "It is for my Master to say — "

"Oh, but surely, he does not take up all your time?"

another asked, and batted very round blue eyes at him.

"And if he does . . ." said another, and dissolved into giggles before she could get another word out.

"And if he does, you can always sneak out when he is asleep," two others finished for her, in chorus.

"Well. Well, yes, but that is a greater difficulty, since he sets me a task each evening, and if it is not done when he wakens . . ." He pulled such a very grim face that two of the girls who were still running their fingers through his curls skipped back, squealing. Gawaine took quick advantage of the opening to wade toward Thunder, who stood just out of reach a few short paces — a few very solid bodies — away.

"Oh, how dreadful — !"

" — awful — !"

"Horrid!" one of them finished loudly, then bent her head and clapped both hands across it as the rest shushed her.

A moment later, a gruff male voice shouted out, "And what is this? Do the cattle drop milk in the buckets by themselves, and does the milk turn itself to cheese?" Shrieks and giggles enough to set his ears ringing; Gawaine found himself suddenly able to move and breathe once more as girls scattered in all directions. But as first one and then another passed him, they paused to hiss against one ear or the other: "If I please you, a walk this evening?"

"If my looks gladden your heart, will you walk with me?"

"Remember, I asked you first!"

"Oh, Katya, you lie, I asked him first!"

"No, I did!"

"Let them argue, sweet, while you and I go forth this evening. I know of the loveliest walk — "

The older man cast him a furious glare and

shouldered by without speaking. The smell of him
was nearly enough to knock the poor bardling flat,
even after such a surfeit of onion: He could not
have bathed in months, or even possibly years.
Gawaine mumbled a very uncouth remark under
his breath. *As if I had encouraged them!*

One thing was certain — walks were out, and so
was this field, mere mention of which set them off the
way it did. Any Bard or bardling worth his salt knew at
least a handful of songs about such places and such
walks, after which the parties were as closely bound as
if the words had been spoken over them and the marriage knot firmly tied. *By all the gods, including that
Paladin's, I'd rather die*, Gawaine thought devoutly.

His knees had finally stopped trembling; he gathered up Thunder's reins and set off to join the Bard
and the rest of his companions. A grinning Ilya came
across to clap him on the back once more. "So! How
do you like my village?"

"Um. Ah — very nice."

Ilya chuckled appreciatively, nudged him stealthily
in the ribs. "Very nice, yes! And such lovely, ah —
scenery, don't you agree?" he added meaningfully with
another nudge.

"Oh. Ah — yes. Of course. Very nice."

"We know how a woman should look, hereabouts;
not like those skinny poor creatures to the south. Any
of my cousins is solid enough that when you hug her
you know you have hugged something — and on a
cold winter night, what better than two blankets and
such a wonderful — heh — bolster?" Gawaine backed
off hastily before Ilya could elbow him again. *I wonder
how those girls like being thought of as spare blankets
and bolsters?* he thought in sudden indignation; his
shoulders sagged then. *Probably think they were
being given the greatest compliment possible.* He

blinked; Ilya had been babbling on, but now he looked up expectantly. "I understand," Ilya said, nodding sympathetically. He laid a hand on the bardling's arm. "So much beauty, so unexpectedly, my mind would be in a whirl also. If you need to get away this evening — *you* know" — he winked broadly — "I will do all I can to distract the Bard. If you wish it."

"Oh." Gawaine forced a smile. "Well. I will — ah — *certainly* keep that in mind."

"I am *so* glad you like my village," Ilya went on earnestly. Gawaine began to look around, openly desperate for Naitachal — or anyone who might rescue him. As if in answer to a prayer, Cedric came up.

"Ilya, the man who lives there wants to speak with you, a matter of his hides and the coin you got for them?" Ilya glanced at the door in question and nodded.

"Oh! Then, I must go at once. That is my uncle Ilya and it would not do to keep him waiting. Remember, though," he added meaningfully, and winked at Gawaine once more. Cedric waited until the peasant had vanished through the black opening into the windowless little hut, then chuckled.

"Remember?"

"I have already forgotten," Gawaine said grimly. "Get me away from here."

"Away? How far?"

"Take that silly grin from your face," Gawaine replied, too upset to hold his usual courtesy for the archer's greater years and undeniably greater talent with a bow. "Portsmith would be preferable at the moment — but wherever my Master is will do."

Unfortunately, there were four of the young women in the house with the Bard, two bringing him refreshment while the other two stood against the back wall of the room and giggled behind chubby little hands.

Naitachal merely glanced at the girls and then at his apprentice and remarked under his breath, "Serves you fair for your unthinking remark last night. Next time, watch how your words come out."

Gawaine groaned very softly and held his head in his hands, but all four girls immediately crowded solicitously around him, and a babble of questions — and the accompanying fragrance of onion — smote him. "Bard, is he well?"

"Gawaine, you are not ill, are you?"

"Sister! A great, strong lad such as he, ill?"

"I but asked, sister! Bard, is he — "

"Yes, yes, yes!" Gawaine stayed where he was, this time to hide a smile. Naitachal sounded as harassed as he himself felt, and he sounded much as he did when he was trying to shut Arturis up. "Everything is fine — my apprentice is fine."

The smile faded; there was absolutely nothing funny about the situation. *Wonderful,* Gawaine thought wearily. *He might have at least said I had some dread disease, preferably something that could be spread about, particularly by close contact!* Well, but unless he had greatly misjudged his Master all these years, Naitachal wouldn't actually abandon him to the tender mercies of this bevy of plump beauties. Not that he wouldn't have his fun first. *His idea of fun, anyway.* Gawaine bit back a groan and, greatly daring, brought his head up once more. Four young women were eyeing him closely, but as he looked at them, they squealed and giggled shrilly, and blessedly scattered.

The hut itself was windowless and dark, but still far from airtight. Fortunately. Gawaine wondered how long he could hold his breath. The Bard nudged him in the ribs with a sharp elbow. The girls were gone, though he could hear them outside, and what must be their parents were outside, conversing rapidly just past an unusually broad doorway that led into a small fenced area holding an enormous pig and a number of piglets. Beyond that, there was a slightly larger fenced area where a bony cow and two goats grazed. The two older folks came back toward the house and the reason for the oversized entry became obvious: the wife, at least, could never have made it through an ordinary doorway, and the husband had not much less girth than she. "Think," Naitachal murmured against his ear, "what you would have to look forward to in a few short years. They say many women become their mothers, given time." Gawaine cast him a look of purest horror; the Bard grinned.

A shrill shout from well out in the cow pasture, and the couple turned aside to see what the matter was. "Short?" Gawaine sent his eyes toward the low ceiling. "Short years? Two days in this place will be more than all my previous life!"

"Never mind, we have a moment," the Bard said soothingly. He glanced toward the doorway and patted his apprentice on the shoulder. "That was a bit rough, wasn't it? And unkind of me, I know."

"Yes," Gawaine said grimly.

"The look on your face, though! My poor unworldly apprentice, did you not know what sort of women such a village breeds?"

"And how would I have learned this?"

"A little worldly experience — which," the Bard added cheerfully, "I am seeing that you get. Well, relax a little, Gawaine. I promise I will not leave you alone with any of them, if I can help it. Do avoid being alone with any of them, if you can." Gawaine turned to look at him, and the Bard smiled.

"Alone — with any of them? Are you mad?"

"Yes, well. I see you have already gleaned the

importance of avoiding — compromising situations, shall we say?"

"Yes. Let us say that."

"We will stay here the night, but no longer; Ilya will guide us to the valley tomorrow early. Watch your face when the farmer's brother comes back in."

"How am I to know which is the brother?"

"Or any of the unwed men," Naitachal said patiently. "Many of whom will come for soup tonight, to see the outsiders and to hear music, which I have promised from both of us. Most of these bachelor men do not bathe, or wash their clothing or their bedding until high summer."

"Ah."

"Compose your face, here comes the farmer and one of his daughters! Of course not; a man could die of drafts across damp bedding, you know! At least, they know it, and act accordingly."

"Ahhh — ah, sir." Gawaine managed to pull himself together enough to scramble to his feet and extend both hands for the older man to clasp between rough and chapped ones. "Thank you for your kind hospitality." The man nodded, turned as his wife came in, stepping aside to let one of her daughters pass with a heavy crockery bowl on a painted wooden tray. "And soup — onion soup." Gawaine kept his voice determinedly bright as a by-now familiar fragrance hit him from several directions. "What a surprise! And how very, *very* kind."

# Chapter XIV

Naitachal and Gawaine performed later — or, at least, Naitachal did, and Gawaine attempted to. There was so much whispering and giggling throughout that it quite put him off his stride, and he had to put in extra measures of strumming more than once while he recalled the words, or read the Bard's exaggerated lipping of them across the crowded, torch-lit square. His hands were stiff, as though it had been a year instead of merely days since he had last properly practiced, and after only two songs, his fingertips began to throb from pressing strings to the board. Fortunately, his Master was lenient with him for what had been surely his worst performance in all his four years. Easier than Gawaine could be on himself; he could have crawled from the dusty square into the night, and never come back.

The villagers didn't seem to notice his slips; probably it was the first entertainment they'd had in years, and he was all too unhappily aware that as far as the village maidens were concerned, anything he did simply shone with perfection.

Their traveling companions came with the rest of the village for the concert, and they spoke briefly afterward, before splitting up and going to the individual houses where they would be sheltered for the night. "We leave very early," the Bard said as the square finally began to empty. "So I suggest any of you who might otherwise sit up gossiping and drinking with your hosts forego that pleasure."

"Pleasure," Tem-Telek said fastidiously. "Do you know what they make their liquor from here?"

"Onions?" Gawaine asked in a small voice. The lizardman snorted.

"Worse still — from ugly brown tubers!"

"Yes, but they drop small onions in the cup," Raven put in, "*with* the liquor."

Arturis stirred. "Well, I certainly do not need such a warning, since I do not indulge in such an unwholesome substance as — "

"Yes, yes, we don't doubt it," Naitachal broke in, and under his breath added, "Why does it not surprise me he does not drink?" Aloud, and with a sidelong glance to make certain none of the villagers were within hearing of his very low voice, he added, "And I would avoid the young women, as well. If you would press on tomorrow, that is."

"They are not likely to speak with either of *us*," Tem-Telek said, a wave of his hand taking in himself and his valet.

"I would not wager that, sir — not in *this* place." Cedric grinned, Raven cast up his eyes. Arturis merely looked puzzled.

"Well, but I was asked to take a walk this evening to explain about the God, and the quest he has set before me — why do you laugh?" he demanded. "Bard, your apprentice needs instruction from you on the deference due one such as myself. . . ." His voice died away as he realized the Bard was grinning broadly. And so were Cedric, Tem-Telek, and Wulfgar.

"I would *avoid* the young women." Naitachal wiped his eyes and chuckled.

Arturis gave him a long, dubious look, but finally nodded reluctantly. "Of course, one such as myself —"

"Yes, yes, of course. I believe your host is awaiting you; perhaps he also would learn something of your quest?" Naitachal gestured across the square. Arturis turned and peered into the gloom — with the torches guttering out, it was getting hard to make out individual faces. He finally shrugged and went. Cedric clapped a hand over his mouth.

"For shame, sir Bard! A perfect opportunity, and see how you wasted it!"

Naitachal was still grinning, and his eyes were wickedly bright. "Yes. But at what cost to my own soul to put a man in such peril as that? I could not do it, tempted though I was. Where do you sleep this night?"

"The archer and I have a corner in the house of Ilya's uncle Ilya," Raven answered for them both. He considered this, shook his head doubtfully. "Do they know only seven names in all? I would swear in this entire village there are no more names than that."

"What matter, since they all look the same anyway?" Cedric laughed cheerfully. He clapped the Druid on the back and they set off. Tem-Telek smothered a yawn.

"Wulfgar, have you my knives?"

"Master, of course. And my own." The dwarf glanced at the empty square at the few dim outlines farther up the street, lowered his voice anyway. "Impolite, to distrust offered hospitality. All the same —"

"Polite, impolite —" The Bard shrugged. "Who can say what hospitality means in a place like this, so far from anything any of us know — save, perhaps, Raven?" He cast his apprentice a cheerfully malicious glance. "And when nothing more than a walk across cowpats and mushrooms and damp grass equals betrothal —"

"Don't," Gawaine implored. "Please don't!"

"It was a jest, bardling. Besides, have I not already agreed to let you sleep against the wall, with me between you and whatever — but I see the subject distresses you. Come, they surely rise with the sun in such a place as this; we must be keeping them up long past their usual hour."

Gawaine groaned as he trudged in the Bard's wake. He himself would not sleep the entire night; he was certain of it.

He did sleep, but very poorly indeed, and his few fitful moments were broken by nightmares — most a replay of his arrival in Ilya's village, though there were other horrors, nearly as dreadful. He could only recall one of those the next morning, but in daylight it held no terror, and was now merely a puzzle: something to do with an enormous, white and fanged cloud that swooped low across him and sent him falling into snow.

It had been decidedly odd, sleeping within four walls and under a roof; most unpleasant to share such quarters with constant chill drafts and the by-now nearly unbearable odor of onions: cooked onions, heavily herbed onion soup, raw onions which their host had eaten like apples the whole evening.

Ilya was waiting for them, mounted on the horse he had taken from the Slavers' wagon, when they stumbled into the first rays of a rising sun and a very cool morning. He waited nervously for them to saddle up and stow their goods. A silent crowd of villagers had gathered by the time the company was mounted, including a bevy of tearful young women. "You will come back this way?" one of them asked tentatively, but half a dozen others vigorously shushed her.

"Ill fortune, to speak of such things!" one of them hissed, and the men who stood nearby and had heard the interchange glared all of them into silence.

Naitachal thanked their hosts very prettily, avoided any comment about return trips. For some reason the mere idea of return seemed to cause a disproportionate upset among the older villagers.

The sun climbed the short distance from horizon into thick, gray cloud that now covered most of the sky. "I hope that isn't an omen," Wulfgar growled. Tem-Telek shushed him. They ordered themselves out, then: Ilya at the fore, Raven at his side, the Bard and his apprentice, then Cedric and the Paladin. The lizardman and his valet brought up the rear. With Ilya's horse already cantering, space opened quickly between the pairs of riders.

They rode past the last houses at a near gallop, slowed only a little as they turned onto a deeply rutted cart track. Gawaine was mumbling to himself, "Come back this way? I'll die first."

"Now, apprentice," the Bard murmured, "speak not ill-omened words. Besides with so much open land all about us, why should it be necessary for us to return to this village? Unless you would like to restock there — ?"

"I think," Gawaine said, clipping his words, "that I have enough onion bread and onion pasties and onion pie in my bag to last me for two lifetimes." He cast Naitachal a dark, sidelong look and added, "Master."

"But, bardling, you took none of the onion pudding, or the herbed goat cheese." Cedric had ridden up next to him, unnoticed. Gawaine closed his eyes and shuddered; the archer laughed quietly. "I took a net of the cheese, should you change your mind. It has the most interesting aroma — I think they may have put onions in it." He stood in his stirrups to gaze ahead, and turned to look behind them, to where Arturis was regaling Wulfgar and Tem-Telek with some adventure or other. "It is a wonder to me he does not fall from that horse, the way he flings his arms about," the

archer said thoughtfully. Naitachal turned to look, and
turned back shaking his head.

"More a wonder to me that our scaly friend doesn't
knock him from it."

"Hah," Cedric replied. "He is noble; he would tell
Wulfgar to do it for him. Look — we seem to have run out
of even the cart track." Ilya led them on, across a meadow,
over a rock-strewn slope, and through another meadow
covered in very low, waxy-petaled yellow flowers and a
deep red, ground-hugging plant that looked like rust
rather than vegetation from even a short distance. There
was not so much as a goat trail here. "I think I will go ask
how much farther this valley is." Cedric touched his
horse's flanks and rode on ahead, catching up first to
Raven and then to Ilya, who first shrugged, then shook his
head, and finally nodded and pointed toward a low, brown
hill some distance ahead.

It was nearly midday when they reached the crest
of the hill and rode along a face that sloped gently
toward the north. A short distance on, the face took a
steeper angle down. Ilya halted, let the company catch
up to him. He pointed down the ridge.

"There — can you see where the trail is? You can
see the head of it just there."

"I can," Raven said.

"Good. And that way — " He waved an arm,
snatching it back almost as soon as he'd pointed out
across cool midday air, generally toward the north.
Almost as though he feared something would catch
hold of his extended finger — or bite it off.

They turned as one and looked. At least two leagues
away, in the midst of a brown, rolling land dotted here and
there with patches of grass or the rusty red plant that
covered most of the last meadow, was an enormous blotch
of white. It seemed to be fogged, by distance or perhaps
by the overcast, so that however long they stared, they

could not, quite, make out the shape of what they saw. "A spire, in the middle, I think," Naitachal said finally. "And a great wall about it, perhaps."

"Ah, sirs," Ilya broke in nervously; despite the cool breeze and the lack of sun, there was sweat on his cheeks and his hair clung to his brow. "Sirs, I think you can see your way clear from here, and so I have done what I said, to bring you in sight of that cursed place, in exchange for your company upon the road."

"You have fulfilled your promise," Raven told him, but his eyes were fixed on that distant patch of white.

"Then," Ilya said anxiously, "if I may leave you now? My grandmother Katya has made me a pot of her best onion soup as a welcoming gift, and I would really like to get home to it." With an effort, Naitachal roused himself and turned to clap the boy on the shoulder.

"You have done just as you said, and you are free to go — with my thanks. It may be we will not come back through your village when we are done, and so, this is farewell, I think." The peasant lad gave him a very odd look, but in the end merely turned and rode off. "Yes. Well." The Bard rubbed his hands together and went back to his study of the distant valley.

"Superstitious peasants," Arturis muttered. "A true man of God would never — "

"A true man of *sense* would hold his tongue," Tem-Telek said mildly, but with an unpleasant gleam in his eye, "so that others might think and decide how best to approach this wonder." Arturis scowled at him but closed his mouth with an audible snap.

"Approach — yes, well, why not simply do that?" Naitachal asked. No answer, except for a shrug from Raven, who turned his horse and started down the narrow trail. It was farther than it looked, both the distance to level ground and the distance to the valley. It was midafternoon before they reached it.

A last, low ridge hid their goal; they had to dismount and lead the horses across broken stone and loose rubble. At the top, Cedric, who was leading, stopped short, blocking the way until Wulfgar's growled curse got his attention. He climbed up, started down again, and was abruptly still. The Bard came next — he uttered one mild, very astonished oath. Then Arturis, who stopped mid-track as Cedric had, and had to be pulled aside by the archer.

*What manner of thing* — ? Gawaine thought nervously. But when he reached the crest, he, too, stopped cold and stared. The narrow rut of a trail they had followed led down an incline and across flat ground. It came to a dead end against a wall — a white wall as high as three men standing upon each other's shoulders. And by the feel of the breeze that blew across it and down from the north, the stuff he could see coating that wall and hanging here and there in long, vicious-looking points was indeed ice.

They stared at it in utter silence for a long time. Finally, Naitachal pushed past Cedric and Wulfgar to take the lead; the others followed him, stopping and spreading out as they came up to the base of the wall. "How curious," the Bard murmured, "that the track seems to have been here before the wall — for look how the wall crosses it!"

"And look how *old* this wall appears," Raven said softly.

"And how tall," Cedric said quietly.

"But there is no snow or ice anywhere else in sight — save upon this wall," Arturis protested, but even he spoke in a whisper.

"How very, very odd," Naitachal said.

Gawaine glanced at his Master, at Cedric and Raven standing just beyond him, at Arturis who stood a little apart, past them and nearer the wall, and the other way, where Tem-Telek and Wulfgar stood like pose-matched statues, arms folded, heads tilted, faces very thoughtful. He turned back, took a step forward. "Such a wall," he breathed. "I wonder what does lie beyond it."

"You speak for me, bardling," Cedric said readily.

*Yes!* What was on the other side — a tower? Treasure? And yet, Gawaine thought, what sensible man would want to scale such a dreadful, treacherous surface? *You do,* an inner voice replied readily. But, another voice whispered, *This is not right, not* — normal. *Why should you want to perform such an odd thing as to climb a wall in a place where no wall should be?* "Because it is there," he whispered, and the inner debate was silenced. He took a step, another, laid his hand against cold, white stone.

"I wonder . . ." The Bard rubbed his chin thoughtfully. "There must be a way over this, don't you suppose?"

"We might look further on; it might not be so high in another spot," Raven replied at once.

"But we might not find such a place right away," Cedric put in.

"Very true," Naitachal said. "And I want very much to see what is on the far side of this height, now that we are so near."

"You speak for me." Arturis was running his hands over the wall as far to each side and as far overhead as he could reach. "I would like to climb this now. Surely there is a wondrous adventure awaiting — "

"Or great treasure," Cedric said.

"Or knowledge," Raven said, and took a step forward.

"Or knowledge," Gawaine echoed. He was feeling for handholds, and finding none.

"Or only the top of an ice-laden wall, where none

should be, but even that would be quite wondrous,"
Naitachal said. He strode down to the wall. "Yes, I
think I must see what is there."

"There was a tower — I thought," Raven corrected
himself carefully, "that I saw the tall spire of a tower.
Or a palace. If there is indeed such a tower, I would
look upon it, and if it was a trick of distance and my
eyes, I would still look, to see what I mistook for a palace where none should be."

"You speak for me. After all," Cedric put in, "it is
still daylight, and the wall is not *that* high."

"High enough," Naitachal said, and Gawaine held
his breath, afraid the Master would change his mind,
but just then Tem-Telek spoke up for the first time.

"Wulfgar, have you those metal points? If you could
put those together with some of the spare leather
straps, we could bind them to our feet and hands — "

"I can make climbing spikes," Wulgar replied readily.

Cedric came back. "Here, I will aid you."

"And I," Arturis volunteered. Everyone stared at
him.

The dwarf hauled down his bags, the two men
came to join him, and all three squatted over the pile
of straps and clinking metal pieces. Tem-Telek
remained where he was, a little apart from the others,
gazing at the wall with a curious half-smile on his face;
Gawaine saw both that and the puzzled look on Master Naitachal's face as he gazed at the lizardman. He
forgot both then, as the wall claimed all his attention.

A short while later, a jingling of metal roused him.
Cedric tapped him on the shoulder and held out a set
of straps studded at intervals by solid-looking metal
spikes. "Put one on each of your feet; I will help you
with the hand ones, if you like." He had to —
Gawaine's fingers were so cold from running them
across the icy wall, it was a wonder he had enough

feeling left in them to grip anything. Cedric gave him a boost up and held him in place until the bardling found a hold for his feet and hands, then sat down to attach his own straps.

Gawaine looked back only once; it made him feel dizzy, looking down from even a short man's height off the ground, for some reason. Besides, he couldn't climb like that. He tilted his head back, banging it against the mandolin in its heavy cloth bag. The wall loomed steeply, but fortunately not quite straight up and down. He could see gray sky above it, and when he brought his eyes down to the surface in front of his face and a little above it, he could see fine cracks — and others not quite so fine that might take the spikes. They did; he moved his feet cautiously, but after a moment or so discovered that they seemed to have eyes of their own — at least, they quickly sought out cracks, and in no time, his hands were curled over the top of the wall.

He hauled himself up, hooked a knee over the smooth edge and only then looked back. The Bard was to his right and nearly to the top, Cedric was only just behind him, and as he looked the other way, Arturis grunted and pulled himself over the top and onto his belly. Raven had one hand upon the top of the wall now, and Wulfgar was on his feet, turning back as he stripped off one of the sets of spikes so he could extend a hand to his Master, who was the farthest back of them all. Gawaine brought the other knee up, stood cautiously, and gazed northward.

A truly amazing sight met his eyes, and his jaw dropped. "It's — there's another wall, look, and it goes on — "

"Taller," Naitachal said, and he sounded nearly as surprised.

"But look, between!" Arturis shouted. "Look down

there — a passage, and it fades into a point either way. It must go on for twenty leagues in both directions — why, *surely* this is a most wondrous quest — !" He fell silent. All of them stood in that silence, looking toward the newly revealed wall or up and down the corridor that lay between them.

"There is snow down there," Raven said thoughtfully.

"Or ice," Cedric said.

"Or both," Wulfgar added rather impatiently. "Well, now what do we do?"

Arturis turned to stare at him rather blankly. "Do? Why, we go on, of course! Into that alleyway, to find what there is to be found — "

"Well, certainly," the Bard broke in impatiently. "But — "

"Well, then, let us go!" Arturis shouted joyfully, and practically threw himself down the wall. He slipped and skidded and went flat on his face at its base, but picked himself up a moment later, apparently unhurt. Gawaine was not far behind him, the Bard right on his heels. The rest followed. "I say we go that way," Arturis began importantly, and pointed to his left.

"Why?" Cedric got between the Paladin and the way he wanted to go before he could simply take off. He pointed the other way. "Why not *that* way? It looks flatter to me — "

"How can you possibly tell?" Gawaine demanded.

"It *looks* flatter," Cedric replied stubbornly.

"But I am sworn to fight in the honor of the God, and left is the direction of all evil things!" Arturis shouted.

"All the more reason to go the other way," Naitachal said. "Since I have less interest in evil things than in discovering what else may be here." He looked around. "Tem-Telek, what do you think?"

The lizardman shrugged and drew the hood of his suit closer over his brow. "Whichever direction the rest of you think. I hardly care."

"I go with you," Wulfgar said immediately. "Of course."

Tem-Telek smiled very briefly. "Of course."

"And Raven — ?" the Bard went on. The Druid shrugged, rolled his eyes heavenward. "Well, then, I say we go —"

Gawaine sighed as Cedric and Arturis shouted him down — less shouting at the Bard, he thought, and more at each other. But now Naitachal had taken offense and was shouting impartially at both of them. Raven sighed heavily, stepped aside, and folded his arms. Gawaine was reminded of the old squire's horsemaster, coming upon a pack of squabbling boys. "We might be here forever at this rate," he muttered resentfully. He looked around, avoiding Raven's overly patient eye and the lizardman's amused one. His eye lit on the far wall. *Why bother with left or right, when there is forward?* he decided, and without further thought crossed the corridor and began climbing. Halfway up, he glanced down at his companions: The archer, Arturis, and his Master were now nose to nose, each waving his arms and trying to shout the other two down; Wulfgar had joined in and was jumping up and down, trying to be heard, and Tem-Telek was trying to get his servant's attention, without success. Raven remained where he had been, a little apart, except now there was a sardonic smile on his lips.

The ground seemed to shift and blur; Gawaine hastily turned his attention back to the wall before him, and a few short moments later, he was atop it. "Master," he called down. "Hey — Master!" Naitachal turned all around, and finally looked up. The others fell silent and gazed at the bardling expectantly.

"What's on the far side?" the Bard demanded. But Gawaine had come up onto his knees, and in turning to get to his feet had caught movement out westward; he was staring wide-eyed along the corridor.

He pointed. "Um. Better ask what's out there, to your left." As one, Naitachal and the others turned to look. At some distance, but nearer them than the farthest point they could see — uncomfortably nearer — the space between the two walls was filled with enormous, ugly men in black leather and heavy armor, and every one of them held a drawn sword.

"There must be fifty of them," Cedric whispered. "Where did they come from?"

"Unimportant," Naitachal snapped. "Where we go, *that's* what's important right now. Up and over the wall, everyone!"

But he reckoned without Arturis. The Paladin gave a great and convoluted cry in his "tongues," then shouted, "For honor, and the greater glory of God!" and, drawing his sword and a long knife, ran straight for them.

"They will kill him!" Raven cried out.

"They had better, or I will kill him myself," Naitachal said grimly. "There won't be time for all of us to clamber up either wall before they're on us."

"No," Cedric said calmly.

"And no sense in dying for no cause," Naitachal added.

"No." The archer had reached for his bowcase, but he let go of the strap and his hands fell to his side.

"Not when we do not know what their intentions are," the Bard finished. He glanced briefly up, met Gawaine's frightened eyes as several of the armed men surrounded Arturis and the Paladin went blessedly silent; the rest were coming toward them across ice, snow, and faded brown grass at a ground-eating trot.

"Boy, drop down to the other side, out of sight — don't you argue with me, just you do it!"

"Sir!" Gawaine was suddenly trembling so hard he had to crawl across the top of the wall. He sat on the far edge, scrabbled with his feet for a toehold, then turned and began letting himself down as carefully as he could. A yell from the other side startled him; his hands skidded off thick ice, and before he could stop himself, he was sliding at high speed down the wall. And then falling. He never remembered hitting the ground.

# Chapter XV

The Bard heard a slithering, scraping sound, muted by the wall to his right. He winced as Gawaine's startled shout faded rapidly and was abruptly cut off. *Hope he's all right*, he thought worriedly. There wasn't time for anything else; they were surrounded and two of the black-clad guards grabbed him.

"Rope!" one of them shouted hoarsely. A coil of it was passed over. *Come, that's a heartening thought*, Naitachal decided. Men armed like these didn't carry rope unless they intended to capture, rather than kill. A short distance away, he could see Arturis, who was trussed like a game bird, gagged, and thrown across a massive shoulder. The Bard held his arms wide, hands extended so their captors could see he held no weapon — just in case — and let one of them go through his clothing without comment. The man ran his hands across both straps of knives, touched the short sword Naitachal had appropriated from the Slavers' cart, felt down his leg and brushed the boot dagger. But he took none of them. He also left the lute where it was, across his back, then bound the Bard's hands together before him and left a length as a lead.

Naitachal glanced at the inner wall and sighed as he was tugged to a brisk walk. *Hope the boy's all right.* Anyone's guess what was across *that* wall; probably another, the way things looked. He gazed thoughtfully at the outer wall then, watching it slide past. *I can't think why it was I wanted to cross that in the first place. Odd. Extremely odd.* As though something had invaded all their minds — his included (*and I should be proof against such a thing*), and made it irresistable.

It certainly wasn't irresistible anymore; Naitachal felt as though he'd just ridden out of a thick fog, and the wall on both sides of him was all at once nothing more than a puzzle. Interesting, certainly; mysterious, to be where it was, with no explanation. Not worth dropping their guard, leaving their horses and food, and crawling over it. Or standing and yelling at each other, clear targets for anyone who wanted to take them.

He glanced ahead, and then to his right. One of the guards still carried Arturis, who was struggling feebly. Raven walked just before him, with Cedric at his elbow. The bowcase still bounced on his shoulder. *They did not take any of our weapons. They carry weapons of their own, so they know what the things are. This is not good, if they do not fear what we might do.* Perhaps they simply had no specific orders to deal with weapons, and would not act on their own. But that was as foolish as — well, as foolish as leaving strangers armed whom you clearly regarded as enemy. More likely, these men had no cause to fear their small company, armed or not. Depressing thought, that. Naitachal forced his mind elsewhere.

Wulfgar trotted along next to him, and at his side, the lizardman, who was positively smothered in coils of rope. As if aware of the Bard's contemplative gaze, Tem-Telek turned his head, managed a faint smile and the least of shrugs, then turned back to watch his footing.

*Not a bad idea,* Naitachal thought; there were small stones here, half-buried in frozen ground, making footing suddenly hazardous. He applied his eyes to the path before him, but his thoughts were still with Tem-Telek. Of all the curious events of this day, this had to rank high

among them: He himself had been caught off-guard from
the first, but the lizardman did not seem at all surprised.
*And what is he up to? I wonder. . . .* What about that
cold-weather suit Wulfgar had constructed for him, or his
refusal to part company with them.

Oh, most folk thought of lizardmen as having
expressionless faces — it was why most humans would
not play games of chance with any of Tem-Telek's kin-
dred. But Naitachal knew better than that: He had
spent the better part of a year in one of their villages,
gathering magic and songs, and he knew the great
Tu-Turo well. Tem-Telek wasn't keeping a gambler's
face on a startling situation; he simply wasn't startled.

*He expected this — or something like it.* Well, if
there was any opportunity at all, Naitachal thought
grimly, he would find out what it was that Tem-Telek
had expected. *He might have warned us — warned
me!* He hadn't — and Gawaine was back there. Somewhere. In who knew what condition, provided the boy
was still alive. The Bard sighed faintly. *He is young for
his years, and naive; I must not forget he was also self-
sufficient at a very young age, and can physically take
care of himself as well as anyone.* It wasn't as comforting a thought as it might have been.

The guards slowed, then stopped. Naitachal stirred
and would have asked a question, but the guard who
had the other end of his rope turned such a fierce face
in his direction that he prudently closed his mouth and
waited. After a moment, they began moving once
more, up a low slope and then through a broad opening in the right-hand wall. There was a thick fog here,
as though it had been trapped under the heavy arch —
or as though someone or something wanted to keep
some secret from the prisoners. When he blinked the
last of the fog from his eyes, Naitachal saw they were
in the middle of an enormous, bare stone courtyard.

In the distance, all around the perimeter wall, stood statues: men, beasts, and there, surely, a lizardman. No grass, no tree, no bush grew here, and the air was winter-cold. Tem-Telek shuddered and rubbed one side of his face and then the other against his shoulders, as though to warm it.

"The Great One will see them, at once." Unnoticed, another of the guards had come toward them. He wore a tunic over his black leathers that bore a curious device: a large and intricately faceted crystal that gave off glints of light as the pale, wintery sunlight touched it, and surrounding this, a white coiling shape, something like a snake and yet — not quite. Before Naitachal could get a better look at it, they were hustled across the courtyard toward a broad, low set of steps, up these and through a massive set of doors. And then a second; down a long, white marble corridor lined with statues, and through a third set of doors into an enormous chamber. The doors struck the walls with a brassy clang that bounced, echoing, off the distant ceiling.

"Great One!" a deep voice intoned formally. "I bring you guests!"

"Bring them." The voice that answered was deeply resonant and set an overhead chandelier of a thousand faceted crystals to shivering. Fully a hundred candles were set into the chandelier, and in the four which were spaced evenly and hung low from that great, distant overhead vault. Naitachal gazed upward into light, and rainbows of light, to a distant, exquisitely painted and gilted ceiling.

He staggered as the man leading him tugged, brought his eyes down to the floor, which was a parquet of gold-veined marble, upon which had been scattered priceless rugs. Here and there, in seemingly no special arrangement at all, stood tables and shelves,

the surfaces of which were buried under fringed
silken cloths and delicately carven boxes, golden bas-
kets and wondrously glazed vases, crystal bottles and
enameled wicker boxes woven with thread of gold
from which depended brilliants and faceted stones of
blue, red, and smoke, or enormous beads of amber.
The guard tugged again to get his attention; in the
very midst of the marble floor stood a huge fountain,
with ebony figures of mythic beasts to hold up the
bowl, a pillar entwined with gilt snakes and vines, all
supporting a smaller bowl of pure, clear amethyst.
Through that palest lavendar, Naitachal could see the
filial: a diamond the size of his fist.

There was no running water. It had frozen into
streamers that rose high above the amethyst bowl and
spilled down to the gilt one below. The larger bowl
was encrusted with pearls and rubies.

Beyond it, more tables, sideboards, high shelves
and low, smothered in precious items, and everywhere, scattered among the priceless goods, wondrous
statues — of plain, pale stone, these, marble or something similar, but eerily lifelike, to the very expressions
on their faces. Some held boxes from which dangled
strings of jewels, while others held ornate and
begemmed candelabras, or single golden candlesticks,
and yet others garments across outstretched hands —
garments of the finest silks and cloth of gold, into
which had been set rubies and emeralds, or scores of
tiny brilliants, or thousands of tiny round, gold-veined
mirrors. Two other statues held matching oval mirrors
with intricately carved and gilt frames, reflecting each
into the other, an endless procession of guards and
Bards fading into unguessable distance. Naitachal
glanced at it, looked away at once; he was familiar with
the phenomenon, and it invariably made him dizzy.
Besides, there were more rugs and carpets here, and

goods strewn across the glassily smooth marble floor, making footing trickier than ever.

Heaped boxes and carved wooden chests blocked their view of the far end of the chamber: boxes from which spilled more exquisite jewelry, more fine cloth, more priceless goods. The Bard wrinkled his nose. Any of these objects, taken by itself, would have been a pure joy to look upon, to touch — possibly to wear or simply to place upon a wall or a floor and behold. Taken all together, though — it was the worst excess of appallingly poor taste he had ever seen in his life, and for the first time, he found himself wondering what manner of being surrounded himself with such an excess of material possessions.

They skirted the boxes, threaded their way two at a time along a narrow passageway toward a wall hung with a single panel of tapestry — stiff with gold thread and jewels, of course — and finally came into a small square of open space before a low dais.

It was hung about with cloths, surrounded by more of the beautifully made statues, and strewn with palest silvery blue carpets worked with a pattern of what might be real platinum. The finest of these led up four shallow steps, stopping at the base of a massive throne that looked to be carved from a single piece of flawless rock-crystal. The back rose to great height; Naitachal frowned and peered more closely. Near the very top, where the crystal had been carved into a complex pattern, a plain silvery box was suspended within the stone itself.

Just beneath the box, however . . . The Bard caught his breath in surprise; so still had the creature been, he had not noticed his presence until this moment.

It might have been a lizardman, with all color washed from his limbs and body — but, then again, not quite. For one thing, it was larger than Tem-Telek by at least half: Its arms and legs were longer, and they tapered to exquisitely small, long-fingered hands and very tiny feet shod in silver slippers. The whole body gleamed like a polished pearl; the eyes were so pale a blue as to be colorless. As he met those eyes, the creature stretched its mouth in what might have been meant for a smile, revealing many long and very sharp teeth.

There was a long silence. Finally, the enthroned creature waved a hand, and rumbled, "Release them. And go away."

*Not good,* Naitachal thought as the guard undid the knots that held his hands together, then stepped back and vanished the way he had just come. *He must know he can best all of us, readily.* He let his eyes move cautiously to one side, then the other. They were all there — save, of course, the poor bardling. Cedric and Raven stood shoulder to shoulder, quietly and warily watching the throne and its occupant; Arturis had been deposited on his backside, and still sat where he'd found himself, staring at the dais as though stunned. Wulfgar was fussing with his Master's cloak; Tem-Telek stood very still, arms folded across his chest. If anything, he looked merely thoughtful. Still, the Bard was certain, not surprised. *We must talk, we two*, he thought grimly, and then wondered if they would have any chance for conversation, any time eyond the next few moments for anything at all.

Arturis interrupted his gloomy thoughts by springing to his feet and drawing his sword — nearly beheading Cedric, who jumped back with an angry oath. "I demand to know why you have brought us here!" he shouted. The creature turned that unnervingly pointed smile on him and said nothing. Raven caught hold of the Paladin's sword arm and murmured something in his ear, but Arturis shook him off. "You are no one to imprison us, and you have no right to lay black hands upon the servant of the true God!" The creature stirred at this, but only to hold out his very small and pale hands and fix a thoughtful eye upon them. He looked up as Arturis began spluttering once more. "Against the one God, the legions of Evil are helpless, and right shall prevail!" His voice set the crystal chandelier far overhead to tinkling. The creature glanced up, then settled his shoulders more comfortably against his crystal throne and fixed a very interested gaze upon the Paladin.

Arturis went on at some length, finally faltering to a dry-voiced halt. The enthroned creature crossed one leg neatly over the other and folded his hands upon his knee.

"Yes. Are you done?" Arturis gazed at him, wide-eyed. Before he could reply, if he indeed intended to, the creature went on. "I am Voyvodan, and this land — all the land within these great walls and all that sits upon them, and all the goods within — it is all mine. And so, I suppose my question is, where have you come from? And why do you dare to trespass here?"

"Trespass?" Arturis shouted. "We — trespass?"

"You are nothing I had brought here," Voyvodan replied calmly. "But, then, I do bring in a great many things, so it is possible — I will ascertain. You are in no great rush, are you?"

Arturis gaped at him, and Raven spoke up. "None, sir. None at all."

"Polite. It is good to know you are not all going to be so hard upon my crystal." He raised his own voice just a little. "Come!"

A rustling behind the throne, footsteps clicking on marble, mounting the steps back there — and then a familiar head, a very familiar thatch of ill-cut black hair, and under it, Ilya's sheepish grin.

"Ah." Naitachal spoke up for the first time. There didn't seem to be any advantage in keeping quiet, anyway; this Voyvodan knew quite well he was here. He met the pale eyes with a level gaze of his own. "And now many things are revealed. I do not think, all the same, that *that*," he jabbed a finger in Ilya's direction, "is your property."

"No?" Voyvodan returned his level stare for a long moment, glanced at the red-faced Ilya, and shrugged. "But if I recall the rule correctly, possession is nine-tenths of the law, is it not?"

"The law," Arturis mumbled. "The *law*? You dare — unholy, dread creature, you dare to flout the King's law? You dare speak in such careless disregard of the God's law? I shall show you law, I shall — " His voice rose to a shout once again, and he brought up the sword, evaded both Raven's and Cedric's snatching hands, and threw himself forward. Voyvodan merely leaned forward, smiled and, as Arturis leaped up the last two steps and raised the sword above his head, he made a curious, deft little gesture. Arturis froze; a fog or a mist enveloped him for the least of moments, and when it cleared there was a heroic stone statue upon the top step, stone sword upraised and a look of purest fury upon its face.

"Ah." Voyvodan edged a little further forward to inspect his new statute, ran a hand down the counterbalancing arm, then leaned back. "As I believe I was saying? Possession is nine-tenths of the law. The other tenth is scattered about my courtyard or in here, holding the prettiest of my favorite goods." He turned to look over his shoulder, past Ilya, and raised his voice once more. "Come!" Three guards hastened around the dais and then onto it, lifted the statue that had been a Paladin, and bore it a short distance away to a square pillar. One of them took the sword from its fingers, while another went into the main part of the room and came back with a dreadful ornate candelabra, which he held up inquiringly. Voyvodan nodded energetically. The candelabra was placed in the upraised hand, the candles lit.

Voyvodan frowned. "Turn it a little this way — no, too far, back. Perhaps if you drew it out back from the carpet — better, but now it is too far turned away from my throne." Naitachal tuned him out; this could go on forever, and he wanted some answers while he still had a chance to hear them. He folded his arms and fixed Ilya with a black eye.

The boy glanced at Voyvodan, then back, nervously, at his former companions. The Bard cleared his throat ominously. "You lured us here."

"I — ah — well," Ilya temporized tremulously.

"Lured us here, and then put Voyvodan's *geas* upon us, so we would climb that wall and then argue among ourselves long enough for those men to capture us. Didn't you?"

Ilya swallowed, looked right and left. Shrugged. "It's better than being a candlestick," he said simply.

"I — well, possibly," Naitachal admitted.

"You were coming here anyway," Ilya pointed out reasonably. "If you hadn't been down between the walls, arguing, there wouldn't have been any capture like this. Just — a whole new bunch of statues." He was looking from one to the other of them, visibly puzzled, and the Bard's heart sank. *He knows there is one of us missing* — Or maybe not. As Ilya peered at them, the Bard moved casually, as though blocking the lad's view of something or someone.

A moment later, Voyvodan claimed his attention. "You may go now, peasant," he said indifferently. "But hold yourself ready, should I ask your services at another time."

"Master, I shall." Ilya immediately prostrated himself on the top step of the dais, scrambled to his feet as the creature began tapping one foot impatiently, and hurried back down the steps behind the throne. Naitachal heard a rustle of draperies, saw the long tapestry move, and allowed himself a faint sigh of relief. Whatever Ilya suspected or thought, he was gone, and to all appearances, out of Voyvodan's thoughts entirely.

Voyvodan was indeed concentrating upon the company before him. Finally, he extended a long, attenuated arm and pointed at Wulfgar. "You. Dwarf. Can you make things of beauty?"

Wulfgar drew himself up proudly. "Certainly I can."

Tem-Telek edged forward. "And I am his assistant," he piped up eagerly. The Bard's eyebrows went up; Tem-Telek positively gushed. Most unlike him.

Voyvodan merely nodded and said, "Then you must stay with him, of course. I shall come back to you two later. You," he went on, and this time pointed at Cedric. "You wear a bowcase that is worn but well tended, and a bow which bespeaks itself as a well-used item. Is this a weapon with which you are skilled?"

"Skilled beyond any man in your service," Cedric replied with a sweeping bow. "I have won great tournaments, and supported myself by my winnings for many a year. There is no target so small, and none so craftily hidden or magicked, that I cannot strike its very heart."

"Ah." Voyvodan smiled and sprawled back on his crystal throne. "Then we, too, shall speak at a later time, for I am very fond of tourneys and contests of skill. And you, Druid. What skills have you that may be of interest to one such as myself?"

Raven spread his hands in a broad shrug. "Whether they will hold interest for you, I cannot say. I am a student, and a lore-keeper."

"A student — ah, yes, I see!" Voyvodan chuckled deeply, setting faceted crystal all over the chamber to chiming. "You Druids are ever given to soft speech concerning yourselves. By your words, I shall assume that you have indeed vast knowledge and a great source of lore at your fingertips. We shall discuss this in the near future, you and I. You," he went on, and his eyes met Naitachal's. "Just set that hood back upon your shoulders, if you will." The Bard let it fall, and the two gazed at each other in silence for some moments. "You bear an instrument, I think, in that case upon your back."

"I carry with me a fine lute," Naitachal said softly.

"Are you then a Bard?"

"I am."

"What — no further word to tell me how great your skills and talents?" Naitachal smiled very faintly and shrugged. Voyvodan laughed. "Yes, well! Only a very great Bard would behave so, I think. And — a Dark Elf, and at one and the same time a Bard! How truly fascinating! We must talk, you and I, about how such a blend is possible — "

"I am counted as a Master," Naitachal broke in, finally stung to words. The creature folded his oddly small hands together and the faint smile became a smirk. It faded as he looked from one to another of his prisoners, and then he waved a hand and sat upright.

"Well! Each of you fascinates me — how truly pleasant a change of affairs. I will consider your fates. For now — go."

Cedric looked blankly at Raven, who turned to gaze at the Bard, but a moment later, guards came and surrounded them, and led them down the long throne room and out into the hall.

# Chapter XVI

This time the guards merely escorted them, rather as though they were honored guests instead of prisoners. *But since none of us know the way outside from here, and since we are many times outnumbered,* Naitachal thought gloomily, *it scarcely matters whether they bear weapons openly against us or not.*

He fully expected a cell at the end of this narrow corridor, and only himself to occupy it, and it was with great surprise that he found himself ushered into a vast, high-ceilinged chamber hung with beautiful tapestries and lit with fine lamps and — even better — a great fire upon the enormous hearth. Even more surprising, the rest of the company was ushered in after him, and only then was the door closed. All the same, his keen ears caught the snick of a key turning in a heavy metal lock.

There were thick, cushioned chairs flanking the fire, and a table in the center of the room which held bread and fruit in golden bowls — and an enormous covered dish which sat over a flame and from which a very pleasant steam issued. Tem-Telek murmured something under his breath and hurried over to the hearth, where he stood for some moments, hands extended, soaking up warmth. Wulfgar busied himself with locating the supply of sticks and logs, and built the fire even higher, while Cedric wandered over to the table and lifted the cover of the pot. The fragrance of a hearty soup filled the chamber; Raven went over at once to join him.

"We must talk, you and I." Naitachal came up to stand beside the lizardman, though the fire was nearly too hot for him. Tem-Telek gazed at him appraisingly.

The dwarf shoved a last log into the flames with his foot, looked from lizardman to Dark Elf and back again. "Master. You will have soup?"

"I certainly shall," Tem-Telek replied vigorously. "My innards are nearly frozen solid!" He let Wulfgar bring a chair and settle him close to the flames. Naitachal took another and drew it not quite so close, then waited patiently until the valet brought a board with two plates of soup, fresh warm bread, and sliced meat and cheese which he set on a small table between them, let him fuss over the lizardman for a few moments, then gently cleared his throat.

The dwarf eyed him narrowly, gave the least of shrugs, and tucked a snowy white cloth in the throat of Tem-Telek's cold-weather suit. "If you need anything else, Master, you or the Bard, I shall stay near," Wulfgar murmured, and left them.

Tem-Telek sniffed carefully, then dipped a spoon into the thick broth. "Quite well prepared."

Naitachal dipped bread in the soup, tucked a large bite in his cheek and said abruptly, "Yes. However, I did not come over here to be warmed and tended to and fed soup."

"No, of course not." Tem-Telek took another sip of broth, nodded, swallowed. "You saw beyond my facade of common traveler with a debt of honor to discharge, and you want to know what my intentions are."

The Bard waved that aside. "I little care about your intentions. I am much more curious as to what that thing is, how it has come by such a disgusting ostentation of wealth, and why it is that you alone were not surprised by its presence here."

Tem-Telek looked at him for some moments, then went back to his soup. "You did not know?"

"If I did, would I be asking you?" the Bard demanded testily.

"Voyvodan is a Snow Dragon," the lizardman said. "And as to the rest of your question — I was surprised, but not so much as you apparently were. I knew there must be such a creature here, though not its name."

"Snow Dragon — impossible," the Bard snorted.

"Not impossible," Tem-Telek said mildly. "Eat your soup before it turns cold, it is really too excellent to waste like that." He waited until Naitachal took several spoonfuls, and ate some of his bread, then went on. "He is a Snow Dragon, a creature of the lands far to the north, and he has all the powers of that clime at his disposal: snow, ice, cold, and storm. So much I knew. I suspected he might also have other powers, as he showed us with that poor Paladin." Tem-Telek sipped more soup; he did not sound particularly sorry for Arturis. "Given that he is as long-lived as any Red Dragon, he has doubtless had many years to acquire such powers and skills, along with his undeniable wealth." The lizardman considered this last comment thoughtfully, swallowed bread, and corrected himself. "Undeniably atrociously arranged wealth."

"Arranged," Naitachal snorted. "He has simply thrown it down as it has come to him, nothing more."

"By that alone, you should have known him to be a dragon."

"Dragon — lizardman, in all my very long years, I have never heard tell of *or* seen any such beast which was not red and a dweller in hot dry climes! Nor have I ever heard tell of any which resembled no dragon but rather a bleached, skinny-limbed version of — well, of yourself," he finished more mildly. Tem-Telek merely turned up the corners of his mouth briefly and indicated the Bard's neglected soup with a small gesture.

"I admit, Bard, they are not common, nor commonly spoken or sung of. All the same — like a Red Dragon, he collects beautiful things; not merely treasure, but other things of beauty. Unlike a Red Dragon, a Snow Dragon has three forms, of which you have seen one — the humanoid. He also has an intermediate form, of which I know little. In his dragonoid shape, he is vast — as long as ten men laid end to end."

"But how —"

"How did I know he was here? As I already told you, Bard, I did not know that this particular Snow Dragon was about, merely that there was one. And that was a simple matter: Wherever a Snow Dragon makes his lair, summer never comes." He made a small shrug, smiled, and picked up his soup plate to drink the last drops. "I am glad that his collection of fine things extends to the supplies in his kitchens, and to his cook." He shrugged again, held out the plate, and waited until Wulfgar came to collect it, refill it, and bring it back. "But I really had not intended to be taken."

"Yes," the Bard replied dryly. "Nor had I, by whatever might have been here. The creature has strong magic indeed, though. I had no more idea I was under his compulsion than — well, I had no notion of it."

"Of course not. Voyvodan is quite old, and has therefore had many, many years to hone his abilities. Older than any elf, White or Dark," he added, with a sharp glance at his companion. "He is a dilettante, of course, like most of his kind — easily amused but also easily bored."

"And he collects costly things," Naitachal said as he

wiped up the last of his soup with the last of his bread.
"And beautiful ones."

"Yes. But beauty to him does not mean quite what it
does to you or to me, Bard. Or even to a Red Dragon.
In his case, it means quality of any kind — like intelligence, or skills such as Cedric's or Wulfgar's. Or yours,
of course."

"Of course," the Bard replied. He heaved a gloomy
sigh. "He may simply turn us all into statues tomorrow."

"Possible," the lizardman replied judiciously. "But
unlikely. I think it more likely by far that he will set us
problems to solve, according to the skills he perceives
in each of us, or those we have claimed. Which is
good, because if you can hold his interest, or pique his
curiosity, he will keep you alive."

"What if he loses interest?" Cedric had come up
behind them, unnoticed by either.

Tem-Telek shrugged. "I would not let him do that,
if I were you. If you can no longer hold his interest by
your talents, then you will do so by his own methods
— much as a cat entertains himself with a mouse."

"Oh." Cedric considered this. "I do see your point."

"Of course, the mouse can either allow itself to be
batted around," the lizardman went on thoughtfully,
"or he can surprise the cat, and extend the period of
play. For a very long time, with any good luck at all.
Please," he urged as Raven and the dwarf came over
to join them, "I do suggest you keep that in mind.
Because remember, if he loses interest in you — well,
he *is* a dragon."

"Ah." Raven and Cedric spoke together.

"I have no desire to become anyone's — or any
*thing's* lunch," Cedric added firmly. "I came to tell you
there are two adjoining chambers with warm fires and
soft beds. Quite as fine as the best inn I have ever
stayed at, and at less damage to my purse."

"You may find the cost higher than mere coin," Raven reminded him.

"Quite likely will, unless we can find a way from this place," Cedric replied with a shrug. "And I will not give up hope of that, until it becomes clear I must."

Wulfgar gave a short bark of laughter. "What — until you are that near the creature's teeth?"

"If need be," Cedric replied soberly. He turned to the Bard. "Gawaine — what became of him, have you any notion?"

Naitachal shook his head. "I heard him fall — or, rather, slide down the far side of that wall. I *think* if Voyvodan had taken him, he would have put him with the rest of us. If he is still alive."

"If he slid down the wall, he may well be alive," Tem-Telek replied. "Particularly since his blood is nothing like my own. And remember, as powerful as a Snow Dragon is, it is not *all* powerful. He cannot read your thoughts, and he cannot see into every corner of his realm from where he sits. It is quite possible that so small a thing as a mere bardling may escape him."

"You reassure me," the Bard said sarcastically.

Gawaine groaned and patted the ground gingerly with both hands, then felt his arms cautiously. He ached all over, and he was half frozen from lying on the dirt and ice. Opening his eyes wasn't much help: As far as he could see in the direction his body was pointed was a corridor much like the previous one. He groaned again and managed to sit up by clinging to the wall and then leaning against it. The other direction was no better: Two tall walls ran far into the distance, converging finally in a point.

At length he sighed and pushed slowly and cautiously to his feet. There was a constant frigid breeze blowing here, his backside had long since gone numb, and his feet were going to sleep. There was no sound anywhere, save the faint shrill sound of wind hissing across the wall high above him, or whispering through long-dead grass. "Well, then, if anyone is to save me, I guess it must be myself." At least the climbing spikes were still firmly attached to his hands and boots. "A wonder I did not impale myself on them when I fell," he grumbled. His ear stung, and when he touched it his fingers came away with flecks of frozen, dried blood clinging to them; apparently he had scraped it on the way down, but fortunately couldn't have bled very much. "The blood is half frozen in my veins, anyway, by the feel of it. Ah, well. Forward or back?"

But the wall he had slid down was nearly straight up and down here, and he could see no cracks anywhere. No wonder he had slipped. The inner wall, then. He staggered over to it, caught himself on the palms of both hands against the spikes, and leaned against the wall for a moment, eyes closed, to catch his breath. Better. "Well — not really better, but not so bad as it could be, I suppose." He opened his eyes and studied the wall. A long crack ran diagonally past his nose, and another crossed it not far above his head. "As though it were meant for me — now there's a truly unpleasant thought!" But he could see nothing else for it. He drew a deep breath, let it out in a gust. Felt over his shoulder to discover the mandolin had apparently come through the fall intact. "Small wonder, with my entire body to cushion it. But Master Naitachal would have my ears if I broke it." Well, he would if he was still alive.

He shook himself, which set his head to pounding, leaned against the wall until it subsided. "If you cannot think a single pleasant thought, then move!" he ordered himself, and reached up to fit the spikes into the crack.

It was a slow climb, even though the wall was nowhere near as high as the last one, and it sloped so he might almost have made it without his spikes — at least, if he'd been less chilled and stiff. He finally rested on the top, eyes closed, and stayed there until his breathing slowed. The breeze was much stiffer here, though. He sat up, flung a leg over to the other side of the narrow wall, and found himself looking down into a little box of a courtyard. There was no ice or snow down there, which he found immediately heartening.

Instead, there was a plot of well-tended spring-green grass, and in the very midst of that an apple tree, and among its dusty green leaves a gleam of red. *Apples*. The tree drew him. He dropped down from the wall and hurried over to it, laid a hand against rough bark. He had never in his life, he thought in awe, felt anything so wonderful, so *real* — as though every other apple tree he had ever touched in his life had been a fraud, this one the only true. "I wonder what the apples are like," he murmured, but as he looked up into the branches in search of a ripe piece of fruit, movement caught his eyes.

Something on the far side, well up in the branches; something large, something bright, struggling. He stepped away from the trunk and shielded his eyes. A snare — someone, he realized indignantly, had set a snare and caught a bird. "Who would dare to set a trap in such a tree as this?" But that was unimportant at the moment; the bird was flapping its bright wings frantically, and would surely do itself harm if he could not free it at once.

But what kind of bird was so enormous, and had flame-bright wings such as this one?

"Bird? It's — no, it's a — a woman?" He was gaping openly now. Bird — woman — he couldn't decide.

But his low words had drawn the creature's eye, and

it was a woman's voice that cried out, "For your own love of life, fair youth, free me!"

"I shall!" he cried, and ran back to the trunk where he shed the climbing spikes and the mandolin case. It was only the work of a moment for him to swarm up into the branches, but it took him a little more care to edge out onto the high branch where the snare was set, and he had to balance himself carefully to free the knife from his belt and hack at the net until the bird could fly free.

He sighed, edged cautiously backward and down the trunk, put the spiked straps in his bag, and picked up the mandolin to sling it across his back once more. But when he stepped out from under the canopy of the apple tree, the bird flew down and sat upon the grass, plainly awaiting him. She extended her wings as he went onto one knee before her, and said in a clear woman's voice, "Do not bow, youth. Sit instead, and speak with me a little."

"Lady, I shall." He might have been in one of his own songs. He sat cross-legged upon the grass and the bird — nearly as tall as he when he sat — stood upon the grass before him, so near he might have touched her flame-feathered breast, had he dared. "I am Gawaine, bardling to the Master Bard Naitachal. How are you called?"

"I am Fenix."

Gawaine looked around him, at the walls enclosing the tiny garden. "What — what is this place, and how do you come to be in it? And — there were others with me, my Master and three men, a lizardman and a dwarf."

"A wondrously mixed company," Fenix said gravely. "But this place — this is the castle of the Snow Dragon Voyvodan, and the walls and spires are his. As are your companions, I fear, for Voyvodan takes as prisoner all who venture within his domain. This garden and the tree are mine, as this valley once was, before the Snow Dragon came and set his spell of never-ending winter upon it. He set that snare for me, knowing I must come back to my tree when the apples were ripe."

"Why? Are they — are they magic apples?"

Fenix made a small, tinkling sound that must be laughter, and he felt himself blush. "Do not be embarrassed," she said at once. "It is a fair question, since you do not know. They are not magic. They are apples." He looked at her in confusion, shook his head, and Fenix said, "Go, and take one, and bring it back." He got to his feet and walked under the canopy; the heady scent of apple surrounded him. He searched among the lower branches until he found a good-sized and bright red fruit, pulled it from its branch and went back to sit before the bird, apple in his outstretched hand. "Eat it," Fenix urged.

He eyed it nervously, but the odor was making him terribly hungry. He bit into it; juice ran down his chin and his eyes went wide. "Apple," he breathed in awe.

"Just so," the bird responded. "It is perfect, no one who bit into such an apple could ever resist them again. So the Snow Dragon knew, and so he planned the one trap which I could not evade."

"Perfect apples." Gawaine gazed at it, then took another bite. Something Raven had said, about truth in the least of things — ? He couldn't recall. But if there was such a thing, there was surely the truth of apples in this fruit. He finished it, licked his fingers, set the core to one side. "What will you do, Fenix?" he asked finally.

"I do not know." She sighed, and he thought he had never heard such a sad sound in all his life. "This was my valley, as I told you, and this tree mine, and even though the Dragon is a dread threat, I cannot leave them. But more — there is also here a scroll, and set within it, Absolute Truth. The gods themselves put that scroll within a platinum box and sealed it inside a great crystal chair, and they gave to me the task of guarding both chair and scroll. Now," she sighed again, "Voyvodan sits upon the chair, and fills his palace with gaudy and costly things, and riches of all kind, and yet the greatest wealth of all hangs just above his head, suspended in the crystal, and he has no notion that it is there."

Gawaine considered this in stunned silence. Before he could ask anything else, Fenix uttered one final sigh and flew away.

He sat where she left him. "She might have been a little more helpful," he mumbled. "After all, I did rescue her." Oh, well. Master Naitachal had told him enough of his own experiences — enough so he that knew one couldn't really count on magical creatures. He fumbled through his bag and pulled out the spikes, looked at them, and sighed himself. "Well, she *did* tell me what to look for. I suppose it is up to me to find the others and rescue them." Easier said than done, he was certain, but he had to do something. At least, *attempt* to do something.

It was hard work, getting the leather straps snug around his hands without anyone else's help, but he finally managed it. He got to his feet then, and turned slowly in place, studying the walls each in turn. "That one, I think. Goodness only knows which direction that is — or which one of those I came down."

He had lost all sense of direction, but when he reached the top of his chosen wall, he discovered direction didn't really matter. For as far as he could see in all directions, a hundred or more walls stretched, and turned, and bent back on themselves and each other, and went on, as near as not, forever.

# Chapter XVII

In later years, he never could recall that time very clearly: It seemed forever that he climbed walls, scrambled over walls, and stood upon walls to look across a myriad of other walls. There was nothing else: The sky and its thick blanket of uniform gray cloud did not change, the wind was a constant, chill presence, the walls all alike — a bland white, the only differences being whether they were coated with ice or not, their tops draped in snow or not, whether he skidded down into a corridor, a box, a rectangle. Now and again, he thought, he slept. A few times he paused to eat sparingly of the few supplies he had left, or to take a swallow of very cold but rather stale water. It must have been days — many of them, the way it felt — or maybe time was stretched oddly, like the corridors that seemed to go on forever, for there had been no night that he could recall.

Once he found a small six-sided area, but like the rest of the maze, it was surrounded by steep-sided white walls, barren within and without. There was no other place like Fenix's courtyard, with its grass and growing tree, and he began to regret that he had not thought to take at least one more apple.

Another upsetting thought struck him. *Poor Thunder. I wonder how he is?* Had the Snow Dragon found the horses? Had his men? *I hope the latter; that someone has found them and unsaddled them, taken them somewhere out of the chill and fed them, and cared for them.* He didn't have much hope of that, really. Thinking of his horse took his mind off his own troubles, though. A little.

He had no idea any longer which way the outermost wall of the maze might lie, where the spire they had seen so long before from that high ridge was, or how long he had been searching. *Days? Hours?* Who could tell? The heroic purpose that had moved him, under Fenix's tree, that had sent him climbing the nearest wall in hopes of rescuing his Master and the others — and just possibly destroying Voyvodan — now seemed very foolish indeed. "I am no hero," he mumbled gloomily. "And cannot even recue myself." He could not even make use of what small magic he *did* have, for his hands were so stiff and frozen he could not have touched the mandolin strings, even if he had been able to croak out song — even if the cold air all around him would not have snapped the strings at once, and quite probably damaged the instrument for all time.

He was so weary, he scarcely remembered the mandolin hanging at his back, save that he remembered to climb and descend in such a fashion as not to cause it more harm than the cold was surely causing it.

He *was* weary enough that nothing of a song even came to his mind now — there was nothing anywhere, had never been anything but this maze. Would never be anything else, evermore. He struggled on.

Some short while later, he stumbled upon yet another small box of a courtyard and discovered this one to be occupied: A dozen or so little brown mice had somehow gotten into this barren hole and become trapped. Gawaine stood upon the wall and looked down at them; the mice stood upon their hind legs and gazed up at him, and their whiskers and noses twitched. "Oh, poor creatures," Gawaine said softly. "You will starve here." He moved along the edge of the wall and the mice followed him, so that at length he finally had to turn and catch hold of the wall, and let himself down, hoping they would move aside when he let go. And then, once he was within the little box courtyard, he wondered how he would catch such wild creatures, but the mice simply crouched down by his feet and gazed at him. "Poor creatures," he said once more, and crouched down himself, extending a hand. The mice sniffed at it, and showed no fear of the fingers. "Here," he said. "It must surely be time for some meal or another; let us share what is left of my bread, and then I will free you from this place — at least, from this box of a courtyard, if not from the maze entirely." He broke up the bread, which had gone hard, and scattered it before him, and scraped a little hole into which he poured a spoonful of his water. The mice ate the bread and drank the water, while he ate a travel wafer and drank a scant swallow from his bottle.

When he was done, the mice suffered themselves to be picked up without so much as a squeak; he settled them securely in the bag at his waist that had held bread, then climbed out and released them in yet another of the seemingly endless corridors. "Good luck to you," he said as he let the last of them go "and I hope you fare better than I, and that you do not trap yourselves again, for next time there may be no one to save you." One of the mice stood upon his hind legs and caught hold of the bardling's boot, then they all turned and scurried off.

Gawaine watched them go and laughed ruefully. "I must be going mad, talking to mice as though they could understand what I said!"

He walked a ways along the corridor, but after a little time, climbed one of the walls again. He had already discovered that he could walk as far as he chose, in any direction, along one of these narrow lanes, and it would neither bend nor end — and they were colder by far than any of the little box areas, or even than the tops of walls.

There were more of the corridors, though, paralleling this one, or going off at their own strange angles — and more courtyards, and more again. In some of these, he could just see rare and wondrous things, and now and again he stumbled into courtyards which held such treasures: a tree whose leaves were green stones, and the berries upon it rubies; a winged horse so real to the eye, but which felt like cold stone when he laid a hand against it; a vine with leaves as large as himself that reached up into the sky — and yet, he could only see it when he stood beneath it, not when he was upon the wall, and he could not touch it at all, though he was certain he could hear harp music, high above him. A round glass ball, taller than he, and within it water, and a golden fish which swam up and down, and looked at him with bulging eyes. Statues of three odd little men with enormous ears and short pants, each holding a flat, round object on a stick, and at the feet of one, a tiny, incredibly ugly stone dog. Another statue, this of a panther, hung about the throat with strands of gold and pearl, and in another place, one of a wolf or an enormous dog, this hung with chains of silver and ice-blue faceted sapphires. A ring of iron holding up a filigree ball, and a creaking mechanical clockwork beast, which lumbered up and down a long, narrow courtyard with a deep path worn in its midst.

So many and varied were these wonders, so rich or simply curious, that at first he had stared in awe or astonishment or pure amazement at such carelessly strewn wealth and beauty. After a while, he took little note of them, and passed by the most costly of them with a mere glance.

There were other living things, too: a stallion so enormous, and so wild of eye and stance, that he dared not attempt to approach it but left it where it was; a panther which paced up and down a long passage that fortunately for him was one of the very few that was crossed by a bridge, a high-arced, foot-narrow silver passageway — and that beast, too, he let be. But not far beyond the panther, in another square walled space, he came across a small wire cage and found within it small birds — linnets. "Poor sweet things, what harm have you done any?" The cage might have been made for mice, he thought; perhaps the birds had strayed into it, drawn by corn, though mostly they ate flaxseed. Poor, hungry, prettily bright little linnets, no more magical than the mice had been — no more than he was himself. He fed them a little crumbled travel wafer — all he had left now, and watched as they flew into the gray sky, red and yellow against the gray.

It heartened him, somehow, watching something escape this maze. But when he climbed onto the wall, moments later, he could see the spire in the center for the first time in a very long time.

"That is the way I must go, then," he whispered. The air seemed suddenly much colder than it had. He cast the tower another glance and dropped down into the next corridor.

The sky remained steadfastly gray, and once again he lost track of time, and of the number of walls he had scaled. But now and again, he could see the dragon's fortress, and it looked to him as though — just maybe — he was coming closer to it.

He edged across one very thick wall, down into another of those endless corridors, and debated

resting a moment or so, but he had scarcely sat down
when he heard voices. Men's voices, many of them —
harsh, deep voices. Panicked, he leaped to his feet,
looked both ways wildly. He couldn't tell where the
voices were coming from, but they were surely louder
than they had been a moment before. *Hide.* He
scrambled up the next wall and threw himself over it
just as twenty men came marching by twos down the
lane he had just left. *Hide, this is no time to go weak-
kneed!* he ordered himself furiously, and threw
himself down the other side of the wall, up and over
the next one and down it, before he even dared stop
moving. Reaction buckled his knees, then, and he slid
down the wall, rough stone catching at his shirt and at
the mandolin case. He let his eyes sag shut. The in-
sides of his lids retained a curious vision, a
man-turreted and spired palace of white stone that
shone and glittered, but was no larger than a decent-
sized cottage or inn. Grass and a hedge — and bright
color, perhaps flowers?

Possibly more beasts. But he had knocked the
breath from himself in falling, and he'd gone utterly
limp at escaping those guards; he could no more move
than open his eyes for the moment. Whatever was
here, even a panther or a wolf — even his death — it
would have to wait.

The sweet scent of roses and spice brushed against
his nostrils; he heard the soft whisper of fine cloth, and
then a low, sweetly resonant woman's voice: "Sir. Sir,
are you capable of movement?"

Sheer surprise opened his eyes, and his jaw
dropped: Surrounding him where he sat with his back
against the highest wall he had yet come down were
women — at least twenty of them, one as different
from the next as rubies from sapphires, emeralds from

diamonds, or roses from peach blossoms. And each was the most wondrously beautiful girl he had ever seen — in his life. "Like the apples," he said softly.

One of them — a girl who could not have been as old as he, with gloriously dark red hair and the greenest eyes he had ever seen — turned to another, possibly even younger, who was gazing at him through enormous china-blue eyes, from under a fall of white-gold hair. "Ariana, did he call us apples?"

"Small wonder he is delirious," Ariana murmured gently, "if he has come all the way from the outside world to this our prison." At that moment, another pressed the two aside and knelt before him. Black, straight hair fell from under a sky-blue and gold sheer veil; the stuff brushed against his hand as she leaned toward him and fixed him with blue-black eyes that held a worried expression.

"I am Lyrana, and your life is in danger. The guards who just went by will surely come here in a moment, and if they do, and if they find you . . . Will you put yourself in our hands and trust us?" He looked from one to another of the three nearest him and nodded at once. "Good, I am glad to see you are sensible. Ariana, Edorra, we three are the strongest — let us aid him to his feet. Miritas and Dulcena, go and spread the cloth carefully over the small table in the gazebo, quickly!" With a flurry of many-colored skirts and a heady scent, young women scattered, while Lyrana and the other two tugged and finally got the bardling to his feet. "You are worn, lean upon my arm," Lyrana directed, and led him across open garden and soft grass to a small pavilion wound with flowering vines. Up two steps, and now he could hear men a distance away, roughly demanding entry, but Lyrana calmly helped him up the last step, across the pavilion, and she thrust him under a low, long table. She caught at his arm as he scuttled under. "Keep up your courage. If it is possible to save you, we will. Keep utterly still, and if you feel a foot press against you, then move, as quietly as possible, to the other end of the table. Go!"

He did, settled onto an extravagantly thick rug, warm for the first time in ever so long, and got his breathing under control as loud, harsh voices came near, and then heavy footsteps clomped across the pavilion. "Yes, Captain?" Lyrana's voice, he thought, polite but cool. "Does the Master come, or perhaps wish to see one of us?" He heard a chair scrape back, and then another, saw first a daintily small blue-slippered foot peek under the long cloth, and then another — slender, this one, but not improbably tiny, and the shoe itself looked almost practical. As he looked at it, it swung forward and nudged against his shoulder; he glanced down and through his legs, began edging cautiously back.

The man's voice lost most of its edge and became almost deferential. *Ah, but who could be rude to such beauty?* Gawaine thought. "Your pardon, miss, I'm sure, but — well, one of m'lads saw a man, or thought he did, coming across the walls, and of course, we had to check — "

"A man!" Another voice, one he hadn't heard before.

"A man!" Several other voices, and the first one chimed in, "Not an armed man! Oh, Captain, how fortunate you were nearby! He could — why, he could be anywhere!"

"Um, yes, well, you'd not miss him, if my man saw rightly, for he had the reddest hair you can imagine."

Yet another girl uttered a small shriek. "Red hair — ah, lud, there was a man with fire-red hair in my village, once; he murdered five women before they caught him! A devil, they said, and I believe it!"

"A devil!" Another girl exclaimed.

"This is terrifying," Lyrana said; it was her foot, Gawaine decided, that had nudged him down to this end of the table. "You must search carefully, Captain. We do not all want to be murdered in our beds!

"Yes!" Ariana chimed in quickly. "We have been at tea this past hour out here. Who knows what manner of thing might have invaded the bedchambers?"

"Or the kitchens," another cried out, and Gawaine suddenly grinned. They were doing an excellent job of acting, but an act it surely was; a girl half as clever as Ariana had looked would not have been carrying on so. *She sounds more like all those Maryas and Katyas*, and he had to bend down and bite the side of his hand to keep from laughing aloud. He froze in place as Lyrana spoke.

"Why, he might even be under the very table, Captain — you had better look!"

The captain laughed, and his voice relaxed, became downright avuncular. "Why, Miss Lyrana, you girls all said you had been at tea this past hour. How would a man with flame-red hair have sneaked past you to hide under the table?"

"Oh, you will think me foolish, Captain," Lyrana said, and she sounded terribly embarrassed, "but the very thought of a man, here — besides yourself, of course, for we know how well Lord Voyvodan cares for us."

"Um — yes, well." Gawaine could just see the captain's enormous scuffed leather boots shifting beyond the cloth. "Well, tell you what, miss — ladies — we'll just check the house itself, make certain there's no one about. If you should see a man with very red hair, though —"

"Why, if I see him, I shall scream!" the girl who'd spoken of redheaded mass murderers announced firmly. "Like — like this!" She illustrated; Gawaine caught his breath sharply, but fortunately the girl's noise — and the resulting babble from the rest of the girls and the guardsmen — covered him.

"Well — well, yes, miss," the captain replied, "you do just that, and wherever we are within the Master's walls, I am *quite* certain we shall hear you."

"So long as you come to our rescue in time," Lyrana replied coolly. "Can you not leave us a guardsman in the house, for protection?"

"Well — miss — um. You know how the Master feels about men here. Any men, even mine. I can set a pair of guards outside the gate for you, though. That way you'll be certain to have protection. Just in case."

"I understand." Gawaine watched as Lyrana withdrew her feet from under the table, and her voice faded a little. "We do truly appreciate it, Captain. You understand — the Master does care for us quite well, but so often we are alone for such a long time, and it is worrying to most of us."

"We'll care for you," the captain said. "Of course, you know we will. The Master would not care to see any of you distressed."

There was, perhaps, a question in his last remark, and Lyrana replied, "We know you do your best, Captain. I shall certainly say as much to the Master, if the matter ever is brought up. Shall I walk you to the house?"

"I can manage, miss. You finish your tea, and try not to worry, all of you." Enormous boots clomped away.

A low, female voice murmured, "He is not yet gone, nor those who serve under him. Stay quite still." A little while later, the same voice said, "They have gone through the gate and barred it. Wait to a count of ten, and then come out."

He did, to find young women scattered casually

about the grass, walking arm in arm and chatting nearby. Four of them were still seated around the table inside the pavilion. And Lyrana, standing at the end of the little table, gazing toward the gates.

She had the most wonderful hair he had ever seen: blue-black, heavy and straight, it hung nearly to her knees. Her face was the clear white of finest cream, her eyes enormous, very slightly tip-tilted at the outside corners, and the darkest midnight blue he had ever seen in eyes. "Now," she said briskly, resuming her seat and waving him to the one next to her, "if you will wait for just one more moment, while we make certain there are no guards about save the two at the gate, we will have some explanations — on both sides, poor man," she added with a smile, "for you must have as many questions as we."

# Chapter XVIII

Ariana came striding across the grass, brushing her hands briskly. "Well, they've left. And those two boys the captain put on guard are such blushing babes, they will never dare enter — unless we scream for them." She looked at Gawaine. "And there is a trick of the air here, or these walls. They cannot hear us beyond them, unless we do scream."

"Thank you for telling me," Gawaine said simply.

Lyrana had been studying his face, and he could feel the color spreading out from his cheekbones. "Questions, I think, can wait," she said at last. "You look utterly exhausted, poor man. When did you last eat a proper meal?"

"Proper?" He laughed faintly. *Is this to count that stuff in Ilya's village?* "If you accept onion soup and onion bread as food, well then —"

Lyrana smiled and shook her head. "Ariana, see if there is something for this poor man to eat, will you? Or," she added quickly as the girl frowned the least bit, "if you would rather stay here, find Irene — she knows the kitchen better anyway." The smile widened as Ariana practically ran across the grass and spoke to another of the girls, who at once vanished through a finely carved door, into the small palace. Ariana returned at once and claimed a chair — not at his elbow as he might have expected, but across the table from him, so he could see both young women without shifting. *And I would swear, she knows it would make me uncomfortable to have two such lovelies so close as that — any unwed women, after that village — and she is being polite.* Ariana smiled at him as she sat down, but the smile was just friendly, and even a suspicious male could have read nothing in it. *No walks in onion fields at sunset here,* he thought, drew a deep breath, and relaxed against the cushions of his chair for the first time. "You must not be uncomfortable among us," Lyrana said. "We do not mean ill when we stare, you know, and really, we do not mean to stare, but it is that — well, it has been some time since any of us has seen a man, unless you count Voyvodan, in his prime form, and even at that there is little human about him." She shuddered a little, but waved a hand when he would have surged to his feet with a confused thought of protecting her, comforting her — perhaps both. *Touching her, at the very least,* he thought in even more confusion, and now his ears were hot. "As to your question," Lyrana went on calmly, "the people in the village where I came from consider onions palatable. I ate them, of course; a village girl in my end of the kingdom learns early to eat what there is, and not to fuss over what she would rather have." She tipped her head a little to the side as he stirred and looked surprised. "What?"

"I — I am sorry, I — " Gawaine swallowed, drew a deep breath, and said in a rush, "I thought you all noble — "

He stopped. Lyrana let her head fall back and she laughed, but somehow, because of it, he felt more at ease with her — the laughter, he felt certain, was not *at* him. "Fine clothing, and so on, yes! Well, one or two of us are noble, or at least gentry. And others before us have been." The smile left her face, but before either of them could say anything else, a pair of young women approached, each bearing a laden tray. "Irene, and her twin sister, Iris," Lyrana said as the two came into the pavilion and began laying out plates, cups, and food and drink before him. "Though you would never know them twins to look, would you?"

"Ladies." Gawaine slid back from the table and sketched them a seated bow. Iris looked at Irene and Irene back, and they laughed cheerfully, then gave him matching bob-courtesies in return. He wouldn't even have thought them sisters, except by the hair: wonderful stuff, the same shade of brown each with strands of red in it, so that lantern light made it coppery. Iris wore hers loose, and it rippled down her back to her waist. Irene had hers in a thick plait that hung so long she could surely sit upon it, and it was worked with pale blue ribbons to match her gown. Her face was smoothly round and wonderfully cheerful; her light brown eyes had greenish flecks and a very shrewd depth to them. Iris had a longer face with a dusting of faint freckles across a slender nose and prominent cheekbones, a wide, cheerful mouth, very dark brown eyes that gave her a thoughtful look, even with that delightful smile. Both girls plied him with food — a cold green soup, a platter of hot sliced bird slathered in gravy, a bowl of some kind of green and red pickle that was chilled but hot on the tongue, and one of the finest white loaves he had ever tasted.

He hadn't realized he was so hungry until the food came; he ate, and ate more, and none of the women spoke to him, or asked him any questions save, "More of that?" or "Another cup of wine?" until he was full. He was profoundly grateful; he couldn't have replied without putting aside his fork or his bread, and they could see that, despite what must be a near overwhelming curiosity about him — and gave him the courtesy of allowing him to simply eat, unlike the

Katyas and Maryas and that Greta. He sighed happily.
There was certainly more to beauty than mere looks
— say, intelligence?

Once he was finished, he made a bare-bones story
of his arrival here, and of his separation from the rest
of his company, with only a bare mention of Fenix and
her apple tree. "I cannot think where the others might
have been put," he said finally. "I have looked and
looked, and found nothing but walls and corridors and
courtyards and dreadful cold — well," he added with
an abashed smile for the women surrounding him,
"that is, until just now. Thank you for the food. But I
had better leave, before I am found here and get you
into terrible trouble."

"Oh, I think we can deal with that," Lyrana said quietly. "We are given hours of warning before Voyvodan
comes, of course — he would be very displeased to
find any of us in less than perfect state, but even he
realizes that it is not *quite* possible to hold oneself in
court-perfect readiness at all times. And the guards do
not come in here without a knock of warning and an
invitation from one of us. Voyvodan, you might well
imagine, would be less than pleased to have his fair
possessions mistreated by so much as an unsoft word
or rude deed, and the guard seems to believe we go
about in here not always clad to receive them."

"Oh, Lyrana!" Iris gasped, and then laughed cheerfully. "Is that how you managed that poor guard?"

"And does he really think we walk about unclad in
here?" Irene asked. "But what a clever idea!"

Lyrana shrugged and grinned at the twins. "Clever
only because it worked." She looked at Gawaine and
actually winked. "So, there would be time to hide you,
if there is need."

"Do stay a little," Ariana said, and Irene added,
"Please do. It is so nice, having someone new to talk

to. Of course, there are always new girls, but — " She stopped in confusion, and her sister patted her shoulder.

"I am certain the Bard understands what you mean, dear."

"I am glad to give you my company for a little while," Gawaine said with another smile all around. "And I fear it is bardling, not yet Bard. Unfortunately, I do not dare play my mandolin for you, lest the guards or the Snow Dragon hear me, and for that I am sorry, for often I do sing for my supper." All at once, he felt quite comfortable in the middle of so many fair ones, not at all his stumble-tongued and easily abashed self. *It is this place, and food after so long on short commons, nothing more,* he told himself. It must be; he certainly did not *feel* the least like his normal self. "But tell me something of yourselves. Why have you come here?"

Momentary silence, as young women looked at each other and then at him. "Well!" Ariana said. "I was second daughter to a count, and about to be forced into a marriage I did not want, and so one afternoon I took my horse and rode out to a hilltop to decide whether I should do as my father ordered and make the best of a bad bargain, run away by myself, or if I should trust my tutor, who claimed to care for me enough to run away with me." She shrugged. "There was a flash of light, a blast of terrible cold, and my horse threw me. I remember nothing else until I awoke here."

"We," Irene said, "are a farmer's daughters, and we experienced the same flash of light and chill upon the road to market with two of Father's goats."

"And I was tenth child of a poor herder," said another girl, a ravishing white-blonde with skin so pale the blue veins showed over her temples. "And I had taken the geese to the stream when I saw the water was frozen solid, in the very midst of summer. And an odd man stood upon the far side, a very white man, and he offered me a place here, instead of what I had." She shrugged. "Well, think of it: In exchange for a hard life, little food and a barren cottage that was stiflingly hot and smelly in summer, cold and drafty in winter, he offered me silks and jewels, a woman to dress my hair and care for my clothing, servants to feed me choice dainties. What girl of sense would not accept? I did     and found myself here, with no memory of how I came to be here." She sighed. "It was truly wondrous at first, having nothing to do but remove the wear of years upon my hands, make friends, and play games or embroider. Now, even with so many friends and so many things to hold my attention, I am bored."

"Bored?" Gawaine blinked at her.

"Certainly," Lyrana said. "There is nothing to do save play at noblewomen's games and hobbies. There are no books, though I have asked for them myself. He will not permit us a tutor, though many of us are lettered and have done their best to teach the rest of us. Though I think even with books and reading, one would become bored after a while, for worst thing of all, once a girl wakens in this courtyard, there is no going out again." Several of the young women stirred and Lyrana added, "Well — not to leave this palace, or these walls, we are certain of that." Gawaine's brow puckered, and Lyrana added gently, "After all — he *is* a dragon, you know."

"Oh — ah, *no*," Gawaine whispered. With a groan, he let his eyes close and lowered his head down onto his hands. Lyrana's voice went on above him.

"I am eldest of us here, and have been here longest — though I am but twenty. There are five of us who came not long after I did — and there were fourteen here before me, who no longer are. Voyvodan sent for them, you see, and they never returned."

"And you think — " He could not finish the sentence.

"Each of them was older than Lyrana is now," Irene said simply.

"Yes. And no longer a beautiful, fresh-faced girl of that age and dewiness that makes older men become foolish over them," Iris added shrewdly.

"He is a dragon, and therefore collects things of beauty, and perfect things," Lyrana said after a moment. "But once those things loose that bloom of perfection — well, he has also had the roses dug up twice and replaced since I have been here. And there was nothing amiss with them but that the flowers were no longer quite so huge as they had been, and there were tiny brown spots upon the leaves." She considered this quietly, and many of the girls sighed. But before Gawaine could say anything — or even think of anything to say (*somehow, "I'm sorry" doesn't seem to cover being eaten by a dragon because you reached the ancient age of twenty-one*, he thought unhappily) — Lyrana stirred and looked around, and then smiled at Gawaine, who smiled back and went very slowly bright red. Out of the corner of his eye, he could see Iris and Irene exchange knowing glances, Ariana cast her eyes upward, and several sets of fair, and fairly clad, shoulders sagged. "I think," Lyrana went on, "that perhaps *I* should show him about, while there is still a little light. Unless anyone objects?"

Irene shook her head and Iris laughed. "We both have eyes, my dear. And you are senior here, after all. Go."

"Thank you. Gawaine?" Lyrana rose gracefully and held out an arm as neatly as any countess, which he took as deftly as any count. She led him out of the pavilion, across the neatly tended grass. But as they came up to the little palace, she turned to the right and led him along a graveled path, all the way around to the back. "There is a grate, just here," she murmured, keeping her voice low and a glance to their right reminding Gawaine that the wall was very near here. "And it leads to a tunnel — but you will see."

He watched in great surprise as Lyrana gathered her hair back and wrapped a ribbon around it, tucked her skirts in the sash at her waist to keep them from trailing, and then bent to tug at a ring which lay in the middle of a grate. She pulled her gown close before her, raised her eyebrows and smiled at him, then turned and rapidly descended. Gawaine followed, catching hold of the grate at her instruction from the dark below, and pulling it back into place. He went the rest of the way down slowly, for the steps were oddly constructed and not at a height his feet and legs recognized, but finally he reached ground once more, and a hand touched his shoulder. Lyrana, he knew at once, even in the dark. Her scent, which was spicy and fruity at once, brought a *sense* of her. She brought forth a tiny light from somewhere, a candle flame caught in a glass ball, and held it aloft. It was just enough to guide their feet.

After a little while, they came into dim light; several of the little balls had been set into curiously shaped wrought iron holders — tiny dragons with their hands spaced to hold one, or birds which held one between them, and others just intricately wrought with no real form to them. All about were stacked boxes and crates. Lyrana indicated these with a wave of her hand as they passed by. "It is one of Voyvodan's storage rooms for things he no longer wants immediately to hand or eye. Come, this way."

Left to himself, he would have been even more lost here than he had been above, but Lyrana walked quickly and tirelessly, leading him through a maze of corridors. She paused at a plain door and said, "We will come back here, shortly, for this is a safe place for you to sleep the night."

*We?* He liked the sound of that very much, and by the look she gave him, he didn't think he had misunderstood her meaning. All the same, this was no tavern girl to love and leave. *She has learned to take each day and live as much as she can in it. But, if I could somehow save her from Voyvodan* . . . That unfortunately reminded him: There were a few others who needed saving from the Snow Dragon — like his Master. And what if the dragon came visiting that courtyard and could tell that one of his bevy of maidens was no longer — ah, exactly . . . Gawaine sighed very quietly, and followed Lyrana along the corridor.

She didn't take him much farther — just into a little, square room, with grates set in the low cciling on opposite sides, and two doors leading away on the other wall. "Here," she murmured very quietly, "is how we see what is going on, here and in other parts of Voyvodan's maze. That is his throne room, so you must be very quiet until I am certain he is not there." She peered upward for a time, finally nodded and beckoned.

Gawaine rested his weight on both hands, and with his nose practically against the heavy grate, looked across the floor of the Snow Dragon's throne room. High above, he could see a beautifully painted and gold-trimmed ceiling that rose and fell in vaults, and below that, long windows clad in the richest velvet and gold drapes he had ever seen. Below that, spread across the floor, chests, boxes, crates, epergnes, statues, jewels, gems, cloth — the most dreadful welter of costly and rare things he could ever have imagined. "How does he *find* anything in all that?" he whispered.

For answer, Lyrana touched his arm and indicated the way they had come with a nod of her head. She led him back down the corridor and stopped at the plain door. Within, there was a small windowless room that held only a bed covered in thick furs and pillows, a little table, and under the table a small and unfigured wooden chest. Gawaine breathed a sigh of relief. This was better than Voyvodan's throne room, by far. This was — familiar. Comfortable. What he knew.

Lyrana might almost have read his mind. "I like this little room, it reminds me of home. Better, from your perspective, it is quite safe," she added as she closed the door behind them, "for the dragon cannot come down here, and his men almost never do, and then only to bring some object he desires and has left fallow for a time. They make a great noise then, and hurry along the tunnels and return at once — they are said to be haunted, I am told." She pushed him onto the bed and knelt before the chest. "I have a few medicines in here, and I most certainly heard you strike your head when you fell. Set aside your bags and lie back."

He stood the mandolin upright against the wall, set his pack, his cloak and the belt bag, and then his weapons before it, then sat back. It made him nervous, all at once, sitting in this very strange place; more nervous when Lyrana came over with a bottle and strips of white cloth and leaned very close to him while she examined his head. "What wonderful hair you have," she said suddenly. "So unlike the men I knew in my village — red as a flame and so thickly curled. You must have a dreadful time keeping the girls out of it." She didn't wait for a response — which was just as well, Gawaine thought — but went on at once, "You have a bump, just here — does that hurt?" He inhaled spice-and-fruit and clean warmth, and rather dizzily shook his head. "Well, that is good, I think," Lyrana said doubtfully. "But I will clean it all the same, and then you must lie back and rest."

"Mmmm. Yes — ouch! — yes, I think so. I am — awfully tired all at once."

"Tired!" She pulled back from him a little, and he realized with a start that he had put his arms around her — *to keep from falling over*, he told himself hastily. He started to move them, but she freed one of her own hands, placed his together at the back of her waist once more, and went back to her task. "I should think you are tired, with all you have done of late," she said after a comfortable silence.

"I shall kill that dragon for you," Gawaine mumbled. But at that, Lyrana leaned back once more, bottle in one hand and damp pad of cloth in the other, and her eyes were very wide.

"Now, you must absolutely give over *that* idea at once," she said flatly. "Here, wait, let me finish, and then I can give my whole mind to the subject. And you can lie down, before you fall." She patted at the back of his head with the cloth; the stuff stung, but not too badly, and when she was finished, she freed herself from his grasp and gave him a shove so he fell over onto the bed. She returned the medicine to the box, wrinkled her nose at the used bandage and stuffed it into the box, too, then came over and sat on the edge of the bed. Gawaine slid over to make room for her. She edged farther onto the covers and slid pillows under his head. "Are you awake enough to listen?"

"Fine," he insisted — not very truthfully. "Why not kill that dragon? Solve everyone's problem, right?"

"If you could, perhaps. But you can't. No one can." That brought him a little more awake. "Why not?"

"Because he doesn't keep his heart in his body." She gave him a very wary look, then, as though daring him to laugh. What she saw apparently satisfied her, for she went on at once. "Because he does not keep his heart in his body, he cannot be killed by any weapon that strikes him."

"But if one used the weapon against his heart," Gawaine began, and Lyrana laughed and shook her head.

"Oh, yes! If one did! But it is well hidden, somewhere in the palace. Most likely somewhere within his throne room, since he works magic there, and he must have it near for that." She sat back and looked at him. Gawaine frowned, concentrating as hard as he ever had in his life.

"Well then, it would only need someone to find it, and if it is in the throne room . . ." His voice died away; that throne room. There was enough — *stuff* — in that throne room to fill five palaces, and with no order to any of it.

Lyrana nodded and her fair face had gone grim. "Exactly. And anyone who comes near enough to do him damage — well, if he does not eat them, or step on them, he turns them into statues."

"Statues?"

"Later. I must leave before much longer. All the same, it was clever of you to figure out that killing the heart might kill the dragon. So, why don't you use some of that cleverness and help all of us find a way to escape this place? Your companions, and mine — and you and I?"

He would have argued with her, but there was something about her eyes, about her face, and with a sudden pang he remembered that she might be numbering her days before Voyvodan came to take her away. "Oh. Lyrana, I swear I will."

"Good." Her face smoothed out and she became all briskly business. "I have spent a long time here, you know. Perhaps I will be able to help you. Once you have slept a little, we will find your Master and the others — will that ease your rest?"

"Yes, thank you. And after all, my Master *is* a Bard. And a Dark Elf. He may have some ideas of his own." He could have bitten his tongue; ordinarily, this was not a good thing to inform anyone right away. But Lyrana merely nodded.

"Yes — they are as long-lived as any elf, are they not?" She considered this, smiled. "All the same, what an unusual combination; they do say most Dark Elves turn to necromancy if they choose magic. Did you say something?"

"I? No. Um. Dry throat, I guess. I think I set my water bottle on the floor — thank you." He drank warm, leathery water from the bottle she handed to him, conscious of her warm, searching gaze on his face, then lay back down and settled his shoulders against the furs and cushions. Lyrana set the bottle where it had been and leaned forward to lay a hand over his forehead. He sighed happily and closed his eyes. "Sleep," she said softly. "I will try to be here when you waken, but if I am not, stay here and I will not be long. Promise me."

"I — mmm — promise," he murmured, already half asleep. He thought he felt her lips brush against his forehead, but that might have been wishful thinking, or a dream.

# Chapter XIX

Naitachal came slowly awake from dreams that left him with a strange, mixed sensation: pleasure and impending doom, in equal parts. For several moments, he lay as he found himself, eyes closed. There was a mattress under him instead of tree roots and stones, soft warm blankets over him instead of those inadequate things he and Gawaine had bought in Portsmith, and his own inadequate cloak.

*Gawaine*. He sat bolt upright, blinking furiously as a brilliant light like winter sun on snow hit him from all sides. The room slowly came into view: ice-blue walls, pale velvet drapes, ice-blue carpets scattered about a highly polished wooden floor of intricate parquet-work — what he could see of it from this bed, he thought gloomily. Probably the rest of it was inlaid with semi-precious stones, or he would look down to see the lost Golden Calendar Medallion of the Horoniqas under his feet when he put them over the side. In such a place as this, nothing seemed too fantastic.

Gawaine. "Ah, poor lad, I forgot all about him and slept like a lamb while he probably lies frozen out there — somewhere."

"You had better worry about yourself just now, Bard." Raven came quickly into the room. "This Voyvodan has sent servants with food and clothing for all of us — and a politely disguised order to eat quickly so he can speak with us."

"Ah. Yes." Naitachal was almost disappointed to find the floor where slippers had been placed for him was a plain length of carpet. He stretched, got to his feet and followed the Druid into the main room, where Wulfgar or someone had already built up the fires. He would have to put Gawaine from his mind for now, the Bard decided; Raven was right. Get all of them somehow out of this predicament and then he could devote his energy to finding his lost bardling.

It was always possible Gawaine had won free of the maze anyway, gotten to the horses and escaped. The thought cheered him most of the way through an excellent breakfast.

Somewhat to his surprise, the usually deferential Wulfgar was not waiting upon Tem-Telek, and with the lizardman's cloak tossed over the chair back, Naitachal could plainly see the noble had removed what gems he could, and both his red leather straps. He remembered then: Wulfgar was to be the Master here, the lizardman his apprentice. To his amusement, Wulfgar appeared to be enjoying himself, and he put on a rather bossy voice whenever the servants came within hearing.

"Now, just you don't embarrass me," he said gruffly. "I know how you are, and it can't be helped, more's the pity, but just the same, you don't talk around this big feller unless I say. Or he does, a'course." Tem-Telek bowed his head deferentially, but the Bard saw a wicked gleam in his eye, as though he, too, was getting a certain amount of fun out of the deception. *If they can pull it off, that is*.

The clothing was a pleasant surprise — well-made and good quality, practical clothing rather than the fancy silks the Bard had half feared.

The throne room caught him as much by surprise as it had the previous day. The Snow Dragon was sprawled in his throne, waiting for them. "I shall set you tasks," he said abruptly, before they could all finish bowing. "According to what you have told me of yourselves." He smiled toothily at each of them in turn. "Please me, and finish the things I ask of you, and perhaps I shall let you go. You, dwarf. You and your servant, come forward." His eyes narrowed as they swept over the pair, and for one awful moment, Naitachal feared all was up, but Voyvodan merely smirked and waved an arm. Four servants came forward, two carrying a clockwork man of polished brass and steel, the other two a huge and heavy box full of cogs, pins, hooks, fasteners — and most curiously of all, a large chessboard of alternating brass and steel squares. The Bard, standing on tiptoe, would have sworn he could see an exquisitely detailed brass king, and a steel knight mounted on a polished black stone horse. "I — ah — I acquired this a time ago," the Snow Dragon said carelessly. "And it broke. It is a goliwak, an automaton which plays chess. Fix it for me — if you can."

Wulfgar was already peering into the box and poking at the clockworks. He shrugged. "Certainly. A mere nothing, it should be. But I cannot work here."

Voyvodan nodded. "Certainly not! The servants will take you to a workroom. When you are finished with this — mere nothing, you can rejoin the others." Wulfgar inclined his head and poked Tem-Telek as though reminding a gawky apprentice to bow, then took hold of the dark shirt the lizardman was wearing over his cold-suit and pulled him from the chamber in the wake of the four servants and the goliwak. Voyvodan watched until they vanished behind the fountain, then leaned back and stroked his chin. "Ah," he said finally, got to his feet and strode across the dais, shouldered past Cedric, and clapped his hands together. The sound rang crystal chandeliers all up and down the room and echoed against the high ceiling.

And Arturis, suddenly again a very human Paladin atop his stone pedestal, finished his massive swing — with the now guttered-out candelabra. He stared at it blankly, then at his surroundings, and blinked as the Snow Dragon began to laugh. The Paladin's face went a deep unlovely red and he gripped the fancy thing, leaped down from the pedestal, and began to stalk forward. Voyvodan at once stepped back. "Ooooh, noooo, it frightens me!" he lisped in a high, shrill voice that reminded Naitachal of one of Ilya's cousins — or all of them. "Oooh, don't *hurt* me, I am so afraid of candle-wax!" Arturis stopped and gazed at him, now as much bewildered as angry.

"Why do you mock me?" he asked. But there was knowledge in his eyes, and anger again, and when he spoke again he sounded like himself once more. *Unfortunately*, Naitachal thought, and cast his eyes tiredly ceilingward. But why would the beast free him at all? "How dare you mock me, godless creature?" Arturis shouted.

"Ah — well, let me think," Voyvodan replied earnestly. "Because I lack amusement, or because there is no point to a Paladin who is not active and about to act heroic — or to slay *dragons*?" he added slyly. "Or perhaps I did not want a heroic statue where you were — or perhaps you are not a hero at all," he added pointedly.

"I — not — I not a — ?" Arturis spluttered.

"Be careful, you are spitting all over yourself and my floor," Voyvodan pointed out.

"Be damned to your floor *and* to you!" Arturis shouted. "The God knows me for an unholy man and yet he protects me, for one day I shall find his holy light —"

"Ah, stow it," the Snow Dragon growled, and the floor rumbled. Arturis, as startled as anyone else in the throne room, fell momentarily silent. "Well, then. Unholy, is it? And a Paladin, and servant of a god, and such a servant that this god bespeaks him regularly. Does he send you notes, or whisper into your ear, or perhaps bathe you in pink light and then send you — *dragons* to slay?" A flash of many pointed teeth; Arturis swallowed and abruptly lost his high, mottled coloring. "Well, Paladin, this hall has excellent acoustics and I am certain your god is nearby. Tell you what, you call upon him to aid you, and then — well, then, I shall try you myself, and if he has protected you I shall not be able to eat you, shall I?"

"Eat — you eat — I, you, eat?" Arturis babbled in a high, breathy voice. The Snow Dragon snorted; pale blue smoke wreathed the Paladin, who suddenly looked as though he might fall down.

"Eat," Voyvodan said cheerfully. "You know — you yourself do this to meat, don't you? And if you are not the chosen protected Paladin of this god, why, then what are you to me but meat?" Arturis gaped at him. "I usually," the Snow Dragon went on thoughtfully, "begin with the feet. Are yours clean? Nothing quite so unpleasant as unbathed feet — perhaps we had better have a servant in here to deal with them now. Just in case, you know." He paused, tilted his head to one side as though expecting a response. "I could begin at the other end," he went on after it became clear Arturis was momentarily beyond speech, "but that is so dull! They only scream once when you bite the head off first, you know. But — should you not be kneeling, and waving your arms, and calling upon your god? I haven't all day, you know; plenty to do, and there are still these others to deal with."

"Ohhhhhh. Oh, no. Oh, no." Arturis closed his eyes

and began to sway. The dragon let him go on for a while, but finally sighed loudly and tapped him on the shoulder, at which the Paladin screamed and leaped backwards. Voyvodan gave him a little silent applause.

"Sanctimonious prig," a voice whispered against the Bard's ear; he started and cast Cedric a reproachful look. "Well?" the archer demanded softly. "He's a phony, a fake. No more Paladin than — than Voyvodan is. I can handle much in this world, but not a hypocrite!"

"It may be he's as deluded as anyone else," Raven put in quietly from Cedric's other side. "Look." Voyvodan was walking all around Arturis, studying him thoughtfully. Arturis had fallen to his knees, his hands over his head, and had gone into a by-now familiar line of babble, his so-called "tongues" interspersed with real words, and Naitachal, who disliked the man as much as anyone, had to admit Arturis seemed to believe in what he was doing.

The Snow Dragon was keeping up a running commentary, a basso counterpart to the Paladin's tenor melody: "Bah. This god of yours couldn't turn cream into butter, and you yourself wouldn't *know* butter if it bit you. If this is a true trance, I am a Paladin myself. Well, where is this god of yours? Look, you started when I touched you — I can still touch you, Paladin. Well, now, why are you looking at me? I have always heard that in a true trance, a pure man — so sorry, you are not pure, you said so and at length — but a god's pet Paladin should be oblivious to anything else. Your trances are fake, Paladin."

"The God will strike you dead," Arturis began angrily. Voyvodan began to laugh.

"He has a large enough target, why does he not simply do so?"

"You deny the God, you evil — you evil — !"

"I deny no gods, Paladin," Voyvodan replied easily.
"I am well aware of many gods. I have seen a few in
my day, and it may be your personal god was one of
them. One loses track, after a while, you know."
Arturis blinked at him, stunned into momentary silence. "No, I merely deny that any deity would have
anything to do with a bombast such as yourself."

"You — I — "

A very testy snort silenced him. "Oh, do be still! I
wager when I eat you, I will find you taste of meat and
wine, and fine foods, that your flesh is soft as a Paladin's and a hero's should never be. Because I wager,
little man, that you have taken the easy way: lip service
to a higher way of life and no substance behind it. You
want men to call you Paladin and hero, and women to
swoon at your coming, but I doubt if these companions of yours could tell me of one heroic thing you
have done in any of their presences." Naitachal looked
from the corner of his eye at Raven and Cedric, who
were gazing at each other in open surprise.

"That is a vicious lie, not true at all," Arturis whim-
pered, and the all-too-easy tears began to run down
his cheeks. "It is a test, set to me by the God, to find if
I am strong. And I am strong, and I will not fear this
evil, nor give in to any temptation, and I will greet my
death as a moral and upright servant of the God — "
His voice was gaining strength as he went on, repeat-
ing familiar words and phrases, and no doubt he
would have continued for hours, but Voyvodan began
to laugh.

"Why, this is most amusing, quite the best fun I
have had in a very long time! I do quite enjoy the mar-
tyr's speech — do you know it well? Will you be able
to recite it again, if I ask? Say, tomorrow, when I dine?
Give me again the bit about moral and upright, that is
particularly funny."

*What is he doing?* the Bard wondered uneasily. The dragon had stalked partway around Arturis once again, and the Paladin was pivoting to keep an eye on him; his color was alarmingly high and his hands clenched into fists. "Funny?" he shouted suddenly. "I will show you funny! *This* is funny!" And, snatching up a spear from a nearby open box, he threw it at the dragon. At that distance, he could not possibly have missed.

"Oh, good shot!" Voyvodan applauded. The others stood gaping: The spear had gone halfway into his chest and the haft was still quivering. He wrapped one of his long, white hands around it and tugged; the point came free. No blood, anywhere. "I like this game even better. My turn, I think?" Arturis turned as white as Voyvodan was normally, and he stumbled back a pace. Voyvodan brought up the spear, cocked his arm and, the Bard noticed, made a curious gesture with his other hand. Arturis was once again a statue, this time with his arms out in a futile effort to ward off the spear, and a look of utter horror on his face. The Snow Dragon dropped the spear and rubbed his hands together. "I simply *love* it when they freeze that way. Look at his face, isn't it wonderful?"

"Um, yes. Wonderful." Naitachal cleared his throat and slipped the lute free of its case. He had never thought so fast in all his life. *Sing, entertain — amuse the creature. See how long you can keep him sidetracked.* "I wonder, have you ever heard the tale of Beatrice and the Manticore?"

"Beatrice — I don't believe so. Do you know this?"

*All four thousand, seven hundred twenty-four verses of it, sonny boy,* the Bard thought grimly, but he kept his face pleasant and merely bowed as the Snow Dragon resumed his throne, straightened up and began to sing one of the silliest, most convoluted songs that had ever come to his attention.

For a while, he almost dared think it was going to work. But somewhere around verse three hundred seventy, Voyvodan waved a hand, and Naitachal discovered he could move his lips all he liked, but no sound would come. "We can come back to this later. Perhaps," he added meaningfully, and beckoned to Cedric and Raven. "You both look to me like men who would like puzzles."

"Puzzles?" Cedric asked. Raven nudged him in the ribs and nodded.

"Any Druid worth his grove enjoys puzzles, sir."

"Well, then! We know you will enjoy them, and of course, you cannot go without company, that would never do. Solve the puzzles you find in my maze, and you may go free."

"If not?" Cedric asked.

"Oh." The Snow Dragon smiled unpleasantly. "I think the puzzles themselves will take care of that little difficulty." He gestured, and several guards came up to bustle the two of them away. Naitachal sighed and watched them go. When he turned back, Voyvodan was sprawled back in his throne, watching him. After a moment, he waved his hand and leaned forward. "Well, Bard?"

"Well?" He could talk again. "About the rest of this song, now," he said rather firmly, but Voyvodan interrupted him.

"Stuff silly Beatrice. I am heartily bored with Beatrice. Know any funny songs about Paladins?"

# Chapter XX

Gawaine lay very still when he woke, and gazed wide-eyed into near-darkness. There was one of those small globes with a candle flame locked in it, set on the floor near the door.

Unlike his Master, he recalled at once where he was, and why. He smiled at the little glass ball — as clear an "I'll be back" as any written message might have been, and stretched, hard. Lyrana. Beautiful, clever — *and she likes me*. Or what she thought he was, maybe; but before he could follow this line of thought and become thoroughly depressed, there was a tap at the door and Lyrana slipped into the room. "I hope I didn't wake you, you certainly needed rest," she began. "But I thought you would like to see what is happening in Voyvodan's throne room."

Gawaine leaped to his feet. "He's there?"

"He is. And some men, and I *think* a dwarf and what must be your Bard. Hurry, if you can," Lyrana added, "because it is always hard to say how long Voyvodan will keep at anything."

Gawaine ran his fingers through his hair. "I am ready now." In the hallway was another black-haired young woman whom he had seen the previous day. "This is Rianne," Lyrana said hurriedly. "The twins and Ariana are at the grate. Come, let us hurry."

Iris and Irene were watching the throne room through the grate, Ariana peering over their shoulders. As Gawaine came up, they stood aside and let him look for a moment. Gawaine looked up on the figures of his Master, the Druid, and the archer — and a curiously white lizardman-like creature, who was walking in a circle, clearly baiting Arturis, who had gone into one of his trances — or something similar. Irene was watching over his shoulder, and she turned to her sister and wrinkled her nose. Lyrana got his attention then and whispered against his ear, "There is a better place, where we can talk if we are careful, and all of us can watch. Come."

She led the way at a very quick walk, Gawaine right on her heels, the other girls bringing up the rear. They went out the left-hand door, up a precipitous — and fortunately well lit — flight of stairs, along a narrow corridor, and came out opposite a high, clear wall. Gawaine stopped so dead one of the girls crashed into his back. Lyrana leaned close to his ear again. "This is the back wall of the throne room, or a part of it; from the other side, this room cannot be seen, and there is no way in but the one we came. They cannot hear us out there, either, though we can hear them."

Gawaine nodded; he was intent upon Arturis and the Snow Dragon for some moments, but his eye was caught by the throne — and something high up, embedded in crystal. *The box. The box which holds the scroll of Ultimate Truth. Fenix did not lie to me.* His fingers itched. Oh, for a way into that chamber, to somehow lay hands upon that box! He came to his senses abruptly as Voyvodan changed Arturis into stone — the first time Gawaine had seen this done. Lyrana laid a hand on his arm, and her face was sympathetic.

"What a fool, sister," Irene murmured.

"Who — that Paladin? I said as much yesterday, when Voyvodan first made him a statue. But oh, do look at the tall blond fellow, is he not handsome and brave?"

"Well, all right, yes," Irene said rather grudgingly. "But his companion, such wonderful dark eyes, and a Druid to boot. I do so admire a man of learning." A moment later, she added, "Oh, no! He is sending them into the maze — I feared it."

"So did I." Iris sighed and realized Gawaine was looking at her. "He always sends the bravest ones into the maze," she said sadly.

Irene squared her shoulders and brought her chin up. "Well, sister, this time it will not go all his way. After all, what can he do to us? Make us statues? Have us for — "

"Hush," her twin said vigorously. "Enough of that! You are right; let us go and see what we can do to aid them." The two hurried off. Ariana and Rianne gave each other a very resigned look, and Rianne leaned close to Lyrana's ear to murmur something; moments later, they, too, were gone. Gawaine frowned, turned to see what was wrong, but Lyrana gave him a conspiratorial grin, and he smiled back and took her hand.

His Master was singing, the dragon listening with every sign of interest. Gawaine began studying the chamber as best he could, but after a while he had to give it up; there was absolutely no way anyone could find a dragon's heart in all that. It could be anywhere. But — "There is a way," he whispered, "to find the dragon's heart. If the dragon himself were to show us — "

"Show us — ?" Lyrana caught on at once. "Of course. Trick him, or find another way to expose its hiding place!"

The Master finished his second song, and the dragon chuckled and applauded, but when Naitachal asked, "And now, if I might finish the song I started — ?"

"Bother Beatrice," Voyvodan said rudely. "And go

away, I am tired of music. Back to your rooms. I will send for you when I want you." He gestured and guards came to escort the Bard away. Gawaine watched him go and sighed heavily; his Master looked small and rather defenseless between those two hulking, black-leather-clad brutes.

Lyrana tugged at his hand. "Come, I know where he is. I found them this morning quite early. I will take you there."

"You can't, it isn't safe," Gawaine began, but Lyrana laughed and tugged again.

"Not into the room, through another grate, silly! Come on."

They reached the grate only moments after Naitachal was put back into the room; Gawaine could hear the click of the lock and the retreating tramp of heavy boots. He looked around as best he could through the grate; it seemed to be built into a hearth, next to and partly behind a stack of sticks and logs for the fire. There were bits of bark and sawdust everywhere, drifting down through the bars. He waited until Naitachal came over to warm his fingers at the fire, then hissed urgently. "Ssst! Master! Here, behind the wood!"

Naitachal stood very still for a long moment, then a slow grin spread across his face. "By all my buttons, and every spare string I possess, I think it must be Gawaine."

"So it is."

"You can't think how glad I am to hear your voice, lad. How are you?"

"Well —" Gawaine gave him an even briefer summary of events than he had the young women, then listened in turn to Naitachal's tale. "I did see the last of it, in the throne room. Listen, though — this — um, this is Lyrana, one of the girls I found in that little palace."

Naitachal's eyes gleamed so that Gawaine feared some embarrassing remark from his Master — the kind of remark Naitachal would ordinarily make if he found his apprentice with a pretty girl — but this time he merely smiled and inclined his head politely. "I am very pleased to meet you, my dear Lyrana. And my thanks for taking such good care of Gawaine. Where are you two, by the way, and how did you get there?"

"Yes, well, Master Naitachal, that could be a long story, but it's all tunnels down here, under everything, and Lyrana knows many of them. Including about the throne room. And listen — " He went on for some moments, and Naitachal finally interrupted him.

"Yes, yes, I know all about dragons' hearts; it would not have surprised me to learn he hid his elsewhere, even before I saw that poor fool Arturis try to murder him and fail so shockingly. And do you know its whereabouts, my dear girl?" he added politely, as though just recalling that it would not do to alienate this young woman.

"Well, that's what I was about to tell you — listen," Gawaine said, and explained. When he had finished, Naitachal sighed very deeply and shook his head.

"I should have expected something of the sort. Ah, well. That would seem to be my problem, wouldn't it? A way to get him to reveal where he hides it — why not? How simple? No, never mind me, lad and girl, I'm muttering to myself. Why don't you leave me to that little matter, and go see what you can do for Wulfgar and his new apprentice, Tem-Telek — if you can find him? Voyvodan set them a truly dreadful task, and I don't know if even a dwarf is the equal of such a mess."

"I saw that myself, before Gawaine awoke," Lyrana said calmly. "Very much a mess, I agree, but we shall do what we can. Good thinking to you, Master Bard."

"Thank you, dear girl," Naitachal said. He clasped

his hands behind his back and began pacing the floor
as they withdrew from the grate. Lyrana considered
for a moment, then nodded and took Gawaine's hand
to lead him down yet another corridor.

Farther than the throne room, this, but better lit
and wide enough they could walk side by side the
entire way. When Lyrana halted beside one of the now
familiar grates, Gawaine grinned. There was no mis-
taking Wulfgar's voice, even if the tone of bossiness
was as unfamiliar as the ingratiating, "Yes, Master,"
that Tem-Telek tossed into each pause.

"Just hand me that driver — no, not that, the other!
No — well, yes, that one will do, if you find me two
more cogs just like this one in the box. And a pair of
screws like this."

"Yes, Master. I'm sorry, Master."

"Here, it isn't your fault, it's just how you are. You can't
help not being a dwarf and having such great clumsy
fingers — are they still out there, sir?" Wulfgar added in a
much more normal — and much softer — voice.

Tem-Telek's was also very prudently lowered. "I
haven't seen a guard anywhere. All the same, there
may be sound ducts directly to the throne room. This
grate, for instance —"

"Well, then," Wulfgar said softly, then raised his
voice once more. "Have you found those bits yet? Just
you keep looking, and I'll — yike!" he squawked, as he
peered down into the grill and came face to face with
Gawaine. "Where did you come from?" he hissed.
"And was it necessary to scare me half silly?"

"There are no speaking devices," Lyrana began.

"Who are you?" Wulfgar interrupted in a fierce
whisper, and then, as her words sank in, he glanced
over his shoulder and bent down to murmur, "Shhh.
Don't tell 'im. He's enjoying 'isself, and so'm I."

"Good," Gawaine whispered. Tem-Telek came over

to see what was going on, and the bardling gave him a thumbs up. The lizardman grinned, looked toward the door and wandered away. They could hear him sorting through the box of parts. Wulfgar's face fell.

"Just as well it's come to a game right now; it's a game we'll lose soon enough. There's a bit gone missing from the box, and I think that nasty critchur took it a'purpose. Though I suppose with so much junk up there, he could have simply lost it. Either way, doesn't matter. We'll never get this goliwak working without it, and if we don't — well, he didn't look so hungry to me, but they say looks can deceive, don't they?"

Gawaine opened his mouth and closed it again; he couldn't think of anything to say. But Lyrana tugged at his hand and put her own face up to the grate. "We'll be back. We'll think of something."

Wulfgar merely nodded, too sunk in his own gloom to show any surprise at the bardling's companion. "Yes, you do that. We'll work on what else we can." He squared his shoulders deliberately and turned to shake a finger at the lizardman. "Now, then! Haven't you found those cogs yet? I know, you're none too bright and all I could afford for an apprentice, but you just apply yourself, d'ye hear?"

"Oh, yes, Master," Tem-Telek responded fawningly. Gawaine and Lyrana tiptoed away. He was fighting laughter; the lizardman must have studied acting under the same Master that Naitachal had, because just now he reminded the bardling powerfully of Naitachal's act with the Slavers. Well, it had fooled them; it would probably fool a Snow Dragon, too.

Lyrana led him up a flight of steps and into the open. They were in a small garden, grass surrounded by intricately patterned beds of flowers, and a wrought iron frame that held two climbing roses, a red and a white. Lyrana settled into the shade of this and patted the grass next to her, but before Gawaine could sit, his ears caught the sound of wings.

Could it be — ? It was. Lyrana caught her breath and clapped her hands softly together as the wonderful, flame-colored bird landed upon the grass. Gawaine went onto one knee and explained about the goliwak, the two working to reassemble it, the missing part. Then held his breath. Fenix flapped her wings, and for one heart-stopping moment he thought she would simply fly off and leave him, but she furled them and said, "Ask the mice." And then she did go, vanishing immediately beyond the walls.

"Ask the mice," Gawaine echoed. "Oh, wonderful."

"Well," Lyrana asked reasonably. "Why *not* ask the mice?"

"For the first thing —" Gawaine began as he turned around, but he never completed the sentence, for there at his feet were two mice. He cautiously edged himself down cross-legged, and one of them stood on its hind legs and caught at his boot, looking into his eyes, he would have sworn, while he explained the problem once again. "Can you help us?" he asked simply when he was done.

He almost expected them to answer, and was vaguely disappointed when they simply turned and scurried away. He shifted around so he also sat in shade, next to Lyrana, and she took his hand again.

"I feel so silly," he said finally.

"Why don't you wait a little, and see if they come back?" Lyrana asked. "I think that — oh, look!" She pointed. The mice were back, dragging a little cloth bag between them, and this they brought over to lay at Gawaine's feet. He took it up, turned it over, and finally poured the contents into his hand. Lyrana looked over his shoulder, and they both gazed at a complex brass and steel cog.

He recalled himself with a shake. Not ordinary mice, these. He bowed as well as he could, seated, and said, "Thank you, my friends."

"Yes, thank you," Lyrana added gravely. She got to her feet. "We had better take this at once, before the dragon sends to find out how they are doing."

The tunnels seemed dark and airless after that little garden, and Gawaine was getting very tired of them, but the look on Wulfgar's face when he handed the cog through the grate was truly gratifying. He turned to look at his companion. "Should you go back? Or is there time to check on Cedric and Raven?"

"Your maze-solvers?" Lyrana nodded. "Time enough. And they may need us." She looked up and down the corridor, finally leading him back the way they had come earlier. Gawaine, by now thoroughly turned around, held onto her warm fingers and allowed himself to be led.

Cedric and Raven weren't in the first place she expected them to be, nor the second, and he thought she looked a little worried, but as they came up to the third grate, Gawaine saw figures huddled there — Irene and her sister, gazing nervously up and into the passageway. Iris tapped her twin on the shoulder to get her attention, pulled her a little aside so Gawaine and Lyrana could look, and Lyrana's brow puckered. "Oh, dear, this isn't very good."

"No, I know," Irene said.

Gawaine looked. The two men were surrounded by a veritable legion of roughly armored, huge-muscled brutes who looked like they belonged in arenas, fighting each other for coin and fame. *Probably all lost their jobs when King Amber came into power*, he decided. The king had definitely been against gladiatorial contests. Cedric had the bow and arrows he had taken from the Slavers' wagon, but Raven only his long staff; they were not only outnumbered, but it seemed even Cedric couldn't do much against such a monstrous mob.

Someone tugged at his sleeve; Irene was trying to get his attention. "There's a place, a little on, not very far, I think. A kind of a hole in the wall and rough steps onto it. It isn't very high at that point. If — if he could get above them, would it make a difference?"

Gawaine nodded at once. "Now, if I can only get his attention!" Cedric proved impossible, but Raven finally glanced toward the grate, and more by accident than chance, Gawaine caught his eye. There was a lull in the fighting; the gladiators had drawn back a little and were discussing some kind of strategy — and tending to a couple of wounded men Cedric had hit during this last sortie. Raven whispered something against Cedric's ear; Cedric nodded once and the Druid moved casually away from him, stopping with his feet just short of the grate, then kneeling down as if to tighten his sandal. Gawaine whispered instructions as quickly as he could; Raven finally got up and walked away, and the bardling watched him anxiously, uncertain if he'd taken it all in. Knowing the man wouldn't have dared speak or even nod didn't help much just now. But a moment later, Raven spoke softly against Cedric's ear once more.

Cedric loosed five arrows in quick order at the clutch of men, and then three all at once. The gladiators bellowed in rage, but their immediate forward progress was slowed by the three fallen men who writhed on the ground at their feet. By the time enough of them could clear the wounded, Cedric and Raven were well ahead of them, and then lost around a bend in the corridor.

Irene and Iris ran ahead, pacing them down the tunnel, and Gawaine came pounding right after, Lyrana's hand secure in his. At length, Iris stopped and pointed at a grate, and Gawaine ran over to it, stood as tall as he could and thrust his hand up through the bars. "Straight across from here," Iris hissed at his left ear. "Point it out to them, quickly; I hear the others coming!"

Anyone could have heard them coming. Gawaine withdrew his hand hastily as pounding feet came near. The pack of enemy stopped cold as an arrow struck the ground in front of their feet, fired from above. Gawaine looked: Raven crouched on the wall looking first one way and then another, but Cedric stood behind him, another arrow fitted to the string. "You had better go away now," he said mildly, though he had to nearly shout to be heard. "Or I will kill you all. At such a distance as this, I could not possibly miss a sparrow, let alone such enormous men as yourselves. Still, I bear you no ill will — "

"No?" one of them snarled furiously. "Well, we see it different like! Come down from there and we'll kill you quick, both of you!"

"Don't think so," Cedric said calmly. He drew back on the bow and loosed another arrow, and another was fitted to the string before the man he had shot, squarely in the chest, realized he was dead and fell over.

"Don't look," Gawaine whispered.

"I must," Iris said, and Irene nodded her head. "I cannot desert such a valiant hero. Why — look," she added in sudden wonder. "Little birds — bright little birds! What are they doing out there?"

"Linnets," Lyrana said as she leaned against Gawaine's back for a better look. "But — oh, look what they are doing! They are distracting those men, so the archer can shoot them!"

They were. *My linnets,* Gawaine thought proudly. His friends, at least. Cedric's and Raven's friends, undoubtedly, for they were swooping wildly at men's heads, diving at their eyes, and Cedric's arrows were going true. Finally, when there were as many men dead on the ground as standing, one of the remaining gladiators drew the rest off, and without a word they turned and left.

Cedric climbed down and looked at the men he'd slain, then came across to the grate. "Feared you might be dead, lad. I'm very glad to see you are not. Hello!" he added softly. "And in fair company as well!"

"It's because of them I am here at all," Gawaine said. "This is Lyrana behind me, and these Iris and Irene. They knew about the wall and got me here just in time."

"Then I must thank you, ladies." He turned a little. "Ho, Raven!" he said. But the Druid was intent upon something across the wall. Cedric turned back with a shrug. "I'll get him down to give you his thanks also. But — is this a safe place for you to be? I would find it distressing if any harm came to you on my account."

Irene gave him a smile so dazzling it broke his concentration, and whatever speech he had intended to make went unsaid. "Do not fear for us, brave archer, for we know this maze well. Consider us a weapon, instead — for I think it is often the unexpected weapon that wins a battle, is it not?"

"Oh, well spoken indeed, my lady," Cedric said softly, and his color was very high indeed. He glanced over his shoulder. "Raven! Hssst, Raven! Come here!" The Druid was already down from the wall, however, and coming toward them quickly. "What," Cedric asked anxiously, "are there more of those men coming back?"

"There is a tiger in a courtyard," Raven said. "A great handsome beast, bound in chains and muzzled as well. If we do not free it, I think it may well die."

Cedric gazed at him for some moments, and finally said, "A tiger? Free it? Are you mad?"

"I can control it," Raven replied calmly. "I think I can." He shook himself and looked down at the grate. "Gawaine, is that you? I was quite surprised to hear your voice. Pleasantly surprised. I fear we all thought you dead. Does Naitachal know?"

"Yes. Listen," Gawaine said hurriedly. "This is Iris, she is a captive here like her sister Irene and many other girls, including Lyrana here. They are willing to help us, if you will let them." He quickly gave Raven the explanation he had given Cedric. The Druid merely nodded.

"I will not lecture anyone who is captive of that Snow Dragon on safety, or living long; we must free ourselves, certainly. All of us. I will be very glad of your help, fair one." He put his fingers through the grate, and Iris gave them a squeeze of her own. He stood then and turned back to the wall. "Speak of freeing things," he added firmly, and strode across the corridor and began climbing the wall. Cedric sighed and shook his head.

"He will get us both killed. Surely even a Druid cannot control a half-starved tiger! Well, I suppose I must do what I can to back him up." But as he stood up, Raven dropped out of sight. There was a roar moments later, and then Raven came back across the wall, scarcely hurrying at all. He climbed down, and as he reached the ground, a huge, golden furry object hurdled across the wall in a single bound. Cedric caught his breath and took a step back; Raven stood where he was.

The tiger inclined its huge head and in a deep voice said, "My undying gratitude to you. I would have slowly died in that place, but now I am free. Your servant, sirs."

"You talk!" Cedric whispered. The tiger gave him a sidelong look.

"Anything can talk, if it chooses," it replied, and turned to Raven. "Set me a task, that I may prove my gratitude."

"Easily chosen," Raven said readily. "It nears nightfall, and it seems we two must stay within this maze until we overcome it — or it kills us. If you would consent to guard us this night, while we sleep . . ."

"Easily granted," the tiger replied.

Irene spoke up then. "And we know of a place, not far from here, where you can at least sleep free of drafts. It is the way you were going — come, we'll guide you."

"Come," Lyrana said softly against Gawaine's ear. "Your friends will be well cared for this night. Let us go and tell your Master what has happened, and see if he thought of anything." Gawaine nodded and let himself be led away. Iris and Irene, he thought with amusement, scarcely heard them say goodbye. Then again, neither had Raven and Cedric.

# Chapter XXI

Naitachal had not thought of anything, however, and he was extremely cross because of it. Gawaine passed on messages from the rest of the company and drew Lyrana away quickly, before the Bard could forget his manners.

It was very pleasant to be back in the gazebo, rather like coming home. He and Lyrana ate, and then Lyrana explained what they had done during the day, with a few words from Gawaine, here and there, and then some of the girls who had remained in the courtyard the day talked, though they had very little news of interest. Still, what news they had was all good: The guard had been pulled from their gate, and no message had come from the Snow Dragon.

Later on, just as the moon rose, Ariana came from the small palace with a harp, which she held out to him. "None of us can play it very well, though I think it is a very good one. If you were to play for us and not sing, any passing guards might not hear, and even if they did, they would only think it one of us."

Gawaine settled it on his knee and ran his fingers experimentally across the strings. His jaw dropped. "Oh, great Master of us all."

"It is a good one, then?" Ariana asked anxiously. Gawaine began to quietly laugh, and shook his head helplessly.

"I think he means yes, very much so," Lyrana said softly. Gawaine managed to nod, finally sat up straight once more and drew his hand across the strings. Sweet, sad song filled the courtyard. He only put the harp aside much, much later, when his fingertips were beginning to hurt in earnest, and reluctantly put the instrument into Ariana's hands.

"You should keep this," she said, and tried to hand it back, but she shook her head then. "No, of course, I was not thinking. It is safer by far here, indoors and in its case, and if Voyvodan should come looking for it . . ."

"Just so," he said, and stifled a yawn against the back of his hand. Lyrana stood and tugged him to his feet. "I think I had better go now," he mumbled sleepily.

She nodded. "Yes. Come, I will guide you." He knew the way to that small sleeping chamber by now, but at the moment, it seemed terribly rude to say so. Lyrana took his hand and led him across the grass, walking slowly at first so each of her companions could wish the bardling a good night, then more quickly as they stepped onto the gravel path. He was practically asleep on his feet by the time she opened the door to the little room, and later he could not have said if he found the bed by himself, or if she had tucked him into it. She was gone when he woke.

In later years, he could not say how many days passed while the company was spread about trying to accomplish impossible tasks for the dragon, or trying to bring about his downfall — or lying sprawled across the floor on his stone backside, hands clasped imploringly over his head, for Voyvodan had unfrozen Arturis once more and teased him until the ersatz Paladin had begun to retreat from him in terror, had finally tripped on a spill of silk and lay waiting to become a midday snack. Gawaine slept in the little chamber and ate the breakfast that Lyrana brought him, or walked the corridors at her side while she tirelessly moved from the back of the throne room, to the little room where Wulfgar and Tem-Telek were putting the chess-playing goliwak together, to the vast chamber Naitachal occupied alone most of the time.

Or to the corridors where Cedric and Raven fought gladiators and mercenaries, wolves and dreadful beasts who looked like nothing any of them had ever seen before, snakes and great flying things like bats. Each of these enemies promptly vanished at sundown, though; food and bottles of water were tossed over the wall to them, and they were left alone until sunrise.

Left to it alone, even two such determined men as Cedric and Raven might have been lost long since, but the tiger came faithfully back to guard them each night, and Iris and Irene always found a nearby grate where they could talk for long hours before the two men must get a little sleep. Always, one of the twins at least remained close by, to give what aid she could — suggesting a place ahead where it might be easier to hold off a horde of men, or an overhang where massive bats could not swoop upon them. But neither girl left the men unless it was to scout out a place ahead, or to fetch more and better food than the pittance the dragon had tossed to them.

It was, all the same, terribly wearying — particularly when there was no end in sight but one which would prove ill for Druid and archer.

It was curious, Raven thought, that in all his days of seeking knowledge it should come to this: battling and killing men and other things, to stay alive. There had been many times in his life — even on this journey — where he would not have defended himself so fiercely, and killing anything would have been unthinkable. But now and again, he could catch a glimpse of Iris's pale, anxious face against one grate or another, and he would grow truly fierce in his determination to break free of this maze and somehow rescue her from her own fate.

Cedric, of course, had no such compunctions about slaying enemies as the Druid did; but he was growing weary of this wholesale slaughter, and often only thoughts of his companion — who would fare badly without a skilled archer at his side — and of Irene, who worried so terribly for his safety, kept him going.

He and Raven spoke about it, now and again — mostly in lulls in the fighting. "This grows boring," Cedric said once.

"Yes." Raven sighed. "I think back to the grove where I was first taught — "

" — my first Master," Cedric said longingly.

"And then the northern woods, and I think, how peaceful. But how lonely — "

"Lonely," Cedric agreed quietly. "A man should have company."

"Company, yes. A fair, clever lady — one with wit and beauty both, and a cottage — "

"A vine-covered cottage."

"With roses all about, and an herb garden," Raven went on thoughtfully.

"A shooting range," Cedric said dreamily.

"No onions," Raven said suddenly. Cedric turned to grin at him and both men laughed, suddenly cheered.

"No onions. But — think of it, no more wandering, no more living from day to day, hand to mouth — "

"Sleeping under the trees," Raven put in.

"Just a house, and a fair partner — children, of course. One or two."

"Or so," Raven agreed. "Perhaps start a small grove of our own — is that something coming?" he added sharply. Cedric stiffened, listened for some moments, shook his head finally.

"Not yet." He sighed.

"Small grove." Raven picked up the thought where he'd left it.

"Archery school," Cedric sighed again, "with Irene to help me teach the youngest pupils.

"Iris," Raven murmured. They sighed in unison, and Cedric peered out along the corridor, held up a hand and said, "Hold that thought." Half a dozen creatures — manlike except for the snakiest necks either had ever seen — came thundering along the corridor, waving spears and shouting. Cedric laughed grimly and set an arrow to his string. "Lovely targets, those — long as my forearm, three times as thick and not even armored!" And in fact, it took but one arrow each, as quickly as he could shoot them, before the corridor was again free of all life save their own.

In the throne room, Voyvodan sat at the edge of his crystal throne and gazed eagerly at the walking goliwak that came toward him, flanked by Wulfgar and Tem-Telek. He tapped long nails against the armrest while Wulfgar explained the row of buttons on the thing's back, waited for a guard to bring it a table and chair, then pressed the buttons that would cause the automaton to sit, put the chessboard down, place the pieces in correct order along both sides and move one forward. "King's pawn to King-Four," Wulfgar explained. "First level of skill, but of course you can set it for however good you are."

Voyvodan eyed him in clear astonishment. "I do not play chess, dwarf!"

"Well, no. But in that case," Wulfgar pushed another button, "the blue button will cause it to play itself, game after game, until you press it again."

"Ah." All three of them watched for a while as the goliwak made a move with the steel pieces, then turned the board around, gazed at it a while and finally moved a brass piece. Turned the board again. Voyvodan sighed happily; Wulfgar and Tem-Telek eyed each other sidelong. The Snow Dragon turned his head and called out, "Come!" Servants came from behind the dais with another half-assembled goliwak, this of steel and bright copper, with pink slippers on its feet, a stiff skirt about its waist, and another huge wooden box of cogs, bits, pieces, screws, ends, and fittings. "It came apart a while back," he said with a helpless little shrug. "Fix it, and we shall see what we shall see." Wulfgar merely bowed, then tugged at a suddenly very indignant lizardman's elbow to remind him who and what he was supposed to be and get him moving. The servants followed, carrying the dancer and the box of parts.

Voyvodan watched the chess player for a while, finally got up and walked around behind it, and pressed the blue button. The goliwak fell over, face first, into the board, scattering pieces everywhere. The Snow Dragon gestured to one of the servants to pick up the mess and looked around thoughtfully. Finally, he sent one of the other servants for a guard. "Have you been throwing food and drink to the fearless maze hunters?" he asked. The guard nodded. "Not quite enough to keep them going at full speed?" The guard nodded again. "Well?" the dragon asked.

"Well, sir, they're still fighting. Quite hard. They just took out a brace of your snakemen. Sir."

"Ah." Voyvodan drew himself up to full height; the guard cringed, but the dragon merely said, "Well! How amusing! Let us go and see, shall we?"

Behind the throne room, Lyrana squeezed Gawaine's hand and nodded toward the stairs. They took them, two at a time, and raced down the corridors, coming up behind Irene and Iris at one of the grates just as the dragon came striding along the corridor to confront Raven and Cedric. "Oho!"

"Sir," Raven said quietly. Cedric wiped the last of his arrows against a little dried grass next to the wall, shoved it into the quiver, and got to his feet. The dragon ignored both of them; he was walking around the dead snakemen, eyeing the bodies thoughtfully and making little vexed noises with his tongue and teeth. Iris, who was nearest the grate, stepped back to let Gawaine forward, and buried her face against her sister's shoulder.

"I do wonder at such talent as yours, archer," the dragon said finally, and very pale eyes met level blue ones. "Are you so skilled always, or were these a fluke?"

Raven touched his companion's arm, and behind Gawaine, he heard Iris or Irene murmur, "Oh, no! Don't answer that!" But Cedric drew himself up to full height and said, rather grandly, "I told you I was skilled. Is this not proof enough? Why do you not let us go?"

"Hah." Voyvodan let his head fall back and he laughed. Gawaine blanched and Lyrana's hand clutched his tightly. "Well, then! A true test of such — talent! You, Druid! You will go stand against that wall — do you see, there is a wooden gate, just there? You will stand there, and this archer will outline your body in arrows." Cedric gasped and the color left his face. "You will do this," the dragon said meaningfully. "Or else —"

"We shall do it," Raven said quietly before Cedric could find his breath once more. "If I may speak to my friend a moment, however?"

Voyvodan gave him a very toothy grin. "Why, certainly. After so much time together here, I am certain you will wish to bid each other a fond farewell!"

Raven drew the archer aside and patted his cheek hard. When that had no effect, he pinched the other's earlobe. "Raven! Raven, I cannot! I can't do that — if I misshot by only the least hair, if you flinched, or if there was a breeze when I released — I cannot — !"

"You can," the Druid said flatly. "Do not, and we are both dead, do you doubt it? Do it — why, I myself will sing your praises about the land when we win free of this place!" He leaned back to look at Cedric, who gazed at him in agony. "Please, do not worry so much, my friend. You have missed nothing in all the days I have known you. Truly you are as good as you say. And I will not move, not so much as a hair's worth, I promise you that. Come, he is waiting. Courage!" Cedric merely shook his head. His eyes were dark with misery, but Raven patted his shoulder encouragingly and walked steadily to the wooden gate, turned and set his back against it, folded his arms across his chest and waited.

If he felt the least fear, there was no sign of it in his stance or his eyes, and somehow, this gave the archer back a little of his nerve. He took out an arrow, set it to the string, sighted — and shot. It went just where he had intended it to go, a finger's worth from Raven's right ear. The Druid gave him a faint smile and a wink, and did not move.

Cedric set his teeth in a mirthless grin, returned the wink and pulled out another arrow. He was terribly aware of the dragon, watching eagerly for the shot that would skewer Raven to the gate. And he was aware of Iris and Irene at that grate. He put the twins from his mind with a terrible effort; this was not the time to dwell on what they would think if he failed. The dragon cleared his throat ominously. Cedric sighted, and shot.

He gained a little nerve as he went on, and Raven stood quite still, arms folded, grave eyes fixed on his face, and finally he reached for an arrow and found the quiver empty.

"Hhhmph!" the dragon snorted, and he looked as uneasy as he did angry. Raven stepped steadily away from the gate and turned to look at it. Cedric came across to begin pulling arrows from the wood and

Raven helped. By the time they were done, the dragon had quite vanished. Cedric stuffed the last arrow into his quiver and staggered; the Druid caught him before he fell over and helped him over to the wall where the last rays of a late afternoon sun still shone next to the grate. Raven touched his companion's arm and nodded significantly; a capable little hand had reached through the grate, as far as it could. Cedric sighed, closed his eyes wearily, and caught hold of the fingertips — all he could touch through the narrow bars. Raven came around to the other side and leaned down to ask, "Are you both all right?"

"I think so," Iris said softly. "That was so bravely done of you, to simply stand as you did. I doubt I could have."

"It wasn't so awful," Raven said with a faint smile. He took the fingers Iris reached to him, and settled down on one elbow so he could put his face as near the grate as possible. "I had something else to think of, and keep before my eyes, than arrows. And I knew he would not miss."

"More than I did," Cedric said faintly. His eyes were still haunted. "I thought when we first came here that I was invulnerable to anything that creature might do. Now — " His fingers closed around Irene's.

"He does not know of us, at least," Irene said in a vigorous whisper. "And shall not."

"No," Iris added.

"No," Cedric said. "But the threat that hangs over you — "

"Was there before you came," Irene broke in. "And is it not better to have been in such peril as this and found — well, what we have found, my sister and I? — than to have simply remained in our old life and grown old knowing nothing of such matters?" Cedric looked down at her and thought her face flushed, but she was smiling up at him with a look that made his heart turn over. "When we are old, you and I, we shall look back on this," she said very softly, "and think, how wonderful and how strange, that we should have been so afraid."

He smiled in turn, and tried to put fear from him so she should not see it in his eyes. "So we shall."

"We had better go and find food for you," Iris said. "We will not be gone for long, though." Fingers were withdrawn from the grate and the two hurried off. The smile slipped from Cedric's face and he held out a hand to Raven, who clasped it over the grating.

"I have slain many a beast and many a man in my day," Cedric said softly. "But the fear this day, that I should miss the mark and kill my friend — "

Raven shook his head. "But I knew my friend would use such great care that my life would be in no real danger at all. Look," he added, "they are tossing our usual banquet across the wall, and the tiger is coming to guard us for the night."

Gawaine and Lyrana had slipped away silently once they were certain Raven had not come to harm. Gawaine finally drew his companion to a halt and leaned against the wall. Lyrana smiled faintly and came into his arms. They stood there for some moments, and finally the bardling stirred and said, "Thank you."

"Yes," Lyrana said softly. "I needed just to hold someone, too. I am glad it was you. Come," she added as he let her go, "I fear the dwarf and his companion may need help again."

"No doubt of it," Gawaine said grimly.

"One thing good of all this," Lyrana said with a smile. "Voyvodan is so very busy running from one to another of your people, that he has had no time for *us*."

*I would she had not reminded me of that,* Gawaine thought, with a sudden sinking sensation in his stomach.

But then he, too, had had no chance to think of it — quite possibly Lyrana had not either, and that was something to be grateful for.

"The twins seem quite happy, don't you think?" Lyrana said after a while. "And those two — Raven and Cedric — "

"Awfully nice fellows," Gawaine said as she hesitated. "You could not ask for nicer fellows."

"I thought so," Lyrana said, but turned to flash him a grin. "With a certain exception, of course."

Wulfgar and Tem-Telek were in trouble once more — but trouble of a different sort, as Tem-Telek explained while Wulfgar stomped about the workshop and swore in half a dozen colorful languages. "The thing was intact, apparently, and the whole box of parts and so on a mere sidelight, the dragon's sense of humor, if you will." He snorted inelegantly. "But there is something inside which is frozen, and the clockworks of this piece are so delicate even my artificer fears to take it apart."

Lyrana and Gawaine looked at each other, at Tem-Telek's drawn face, back at each other, and as one, said, "Mice." Before Gawaine could turn away to head back up to that small garden, though, he felt a now familiar tugging at his breeches and looked down to see three mice. He knelt, explained the problem — feeling extremely silly, still, the whole time. But the sense of foolishness vanished at once when he held down his hands and the mice scrambled onto his palm, let him lift them to the grate and through it. He heard Wulfgar's startled, "Huh?" and Tem-Telek's low murmur, but by the time he got to his feet, there was not much to see — a dancer held against the wall by wires, a table full of tools next to it, and before it Wulfgar, hands on hips, glaring at the thing's middle, just above the fluffy skirt.

A moment later, there was movement about where the belly button should be on a human dancer, and a small brown shape came scurrying out with something in its teeth. Wulfgar, who looked rather stunned, took it, turned it over in his fingers, then reached out blindly and touched the button in the dancing goliwak's shoulder. Arms and feet began to move. Tem-Telek hastily pulled it down from the wire framework, and the steel and copper figure began twirling its way across the little room. With a mighty oath, Wulfgar stumbled out of its way, then ran to get the door. "Hey, apprentice!" he bellowed over his shoulder. "Get up here, and help me catch this wretched thing!"

Gawaine looked up at the grate to meet three sets of very bright shoe-button eyes. "Thank you, little friends," he said gravely, and held up his hands so the mice could climb onto them.

Lyrana was laughing helplessly. "Oh, my," she said finally, and wiped her eyes. "Oh, my. We had better go check on your Master, and find something to eat ourselves, don't you think?" Gawaine, by now fairly familiar with this part of the underground maze, took her hand and led the way back to the grate under the firewood.

Naitachal was not there. A moment later, when they stopped at the grate overlooking the throne room, though, they found him; he was playing the lute and singing a very persuasive sounding song about the simple life, the pleasures of the pastoral, the purity and joy of open spaces. Gawaine grinned, and led Lyrana on.

# Chapter XXII

Voyvodan was not nearly so pleased with the dancer as he perhaps should have been, though he spent some time watching it spin and leap about the crowded throne room while Wulfgar and Tem-Telek waited nervously, and Naitachal stood by concealing impatience as best he could by tuning his lute. Finally the Snow Dragon sighed heavily and lowered his chin into his long-fingered white hands, and gazed narrowly at the artificer. "Come," he said loudly.

A servant came from behind the dais, a silver tray in his hands, and upon the tray a clear glass bottle. He set it on the table where the goliwak chess player still sat, head bowed over his board. Wulfgar looked at the bottle, then at Tem-Telek, and bit back a sigh of his own. Within the bottle was an extremely delicate model of a ship — any part of which would be well beyond the grasp of his stubby fingers or the lizardman's either, even if either could get such a digit into the bottle. Voyvodan confirmed the dwarf's worst fears: "The rigging is supposed to go up and down and the rudder to work, but it does not. Someone apparently loosed the thread which is supposed to hang outside the bottle. Fix this, why don't you?"

"And then come back?" Wulfgar asked rather waspishly. The dragon's eyes narrowed to mere slits.

"Why — would you rather not?"

"Oh, oh, well," the lizardman interposed before the

irritated Wulfgar could form a reply that would serve both of them ill, "well, do you know, I have never enjoyed myself so much, so many wonderful things to do, so much I am learning." He chattered on brightly for some moments, falling silent only when the dragon cleared his throat ominously. Wulfgar gathered up the tray, bowed neatly if not very deeply, and turned to stalk from the throne room, Tem-Telek right at his heels. Voyvodan watched them go, then turned to look at Naitachal.

"I fear they do not like me, Bard. And you — how do you feel?"

The Bard shrugged and gestured broadly, taking in the lute he held. "You give me this wondrous instrument to replace my old battered one, and you think I will not sing your praises forever?"

"Mmmm, yes. Or rather," the dragon added hastily as Naitachal nodded and struck a chord, "do not do *that*. Not just yet. Sing me something, ease my boredom. I am *bored*, Dark Elf."

"Oh. Well, this," Naitachal struck another chord, "was quite the rage when I left Silver City, perhaps you will like it." He ran a complicated run up and down the strings and began, "Oh! The life of a lord is no longer for me, I shall shed my possessions, my soul shall be free, where the deer and the turtledove run, so shall I, and sleep with a shepherdess under the sky."

The dragon snorted; Naitachal risked a glance in his direction, then looked at him in surprise. Voyvodan was snickering, holding his sides. "Do go on, why do you stop? This is the funniest thing I have *ever* heard!"

Naitachal smiled deprecatingly, played the introductory notes again, and sang, "I shall cast off my jewels and take up a crook, and set aside riches to sleep in a nook. With the possum I shall become friends, and the mole, for material things are such — a drag on my soul."

He went on in the same vein for quite a while. The

dragon was still laughing helplessly when he dismissed him a very long time later. Back in his chamber, the Bard blotted a damp forehead and collapsed into a chair. "Gracious!" he muttered. "I must come up with some more verses to that. I was nudging at him with enough Bardic power to knock over a barn, and he never even noticed!"

Perhaps because it wasn't working — well, he wouldn't think about *that*.

He stared gloomily into the fire for some time, and at length was roused by a hissing among the sticks and logs: Gawaine, and the lovely young woman who had become his shadow — and vice versa, of course, Naitachal thought, and realized with a pang that he might well lose his apprentice before the bardling ever had a chance to become a Bard. *Not if I can help it, though,* he told himself grimly, and bent over the grate to hiss urgently, "Hey, Gawaine! You can't think how glad I am to see you! How about making up some verses to 'The Shepherd, the Shepherdess and Lord Emerald' for me? I am running out of ideas — fast!"

A distance away, Wulfgar and Tem-Telek stood on opposite sides of their table and gazed gloomily at the bottle. "You know, we need another of Gawaine's mice," the lizardman said finally. "Where is that lad when you need him?

"Who," Wulfgar replied softly, "is to say we do?" He pointed; his Master stared. Two fat brown mice stood on their hind feet, tugging at the dwarf's sleeve, and between them, one of the smallest baby mice either had ever seen. "I feel like an idiot." Wulfgar looked around the chamber. "However. Sir and madam, if such you are, and young master or mistress, whichever you are — as if anyone but a mouse cared," he added from the side of his mouth to his Master, who grinned in reply. "This wondrous toy is said to have a thread within that makes the sails go up and down, and by such action to keep us alive. If we do live, I shall see that the best of my bread is yours, this very afternoon." He stared; the two large mice dropped to all fours and seemed to be talking to the baby, which — with a little prodding — crawled into the narrow neck of the bottle. One of the adults poked its nose in after the baby, all of it that would fit. Wulfgar and Tem-Telek watched breathlessly as the little one slid and fell all around the ship, finally caught hold of a bit of near-invisible thread with its teeth, and slipped and slid back to the neck. Wulfgar had to tip the bottle so the little creature could get back out, but when it came tumbling to the table, it still held the thread.

The dwarf took it and bowed generously to all three mice. Tem-Telek was patting his pockets, and he brought out a chunk of bread and a twisted paper of raisins, both of which he set on the table. "Our thanks," he said very formally. The mice began to chew on the bread. The lizardman looked at his artificer, who looked somberly back.

"Thanks, yes," he said softly. "But I wonder how that dragon will feel about it?"

"I have an idea," the lizardman said after an uncomfortable little silence. "Let us not go in search of him with this repaired wonder just yet. In fact, let us not go at all, until he sends for us, and needs must."

Raven and Cedric were very thirsty; the previous night's food had been tossed over the wall to them, but there had been only half as much water as usual, and the grates here were of a tightly meshed wire, through which the girls could pass them nothing save comforting words. By midday, they were very thirsty indeed, and not a little hungry.

Also more than a little surprised: after nearly non-stop fighting for days, there had been no one to battle at all — merely a large wall of metal and spikes that had pushed them along the corridor and left them. Raven glanced around and sighed faintly. The grates here were no better than those they had left behind — there would be no extra drink or food through them. He smiled then; Iris and Irene had pressed their hands against the grate so they could be seen, and he thought he could see Iris's beloved, grave face down there in the dimly lit tunnel.

Cedric touched his shoulder. "Look," he said softly. Raven felt the hackles come up on the back of his neck. He turned and saw Voyvodan, sitting where the metal wall had been. "It just — went," Cedric said even more softly. "And he was there instead." Both men gazed at the Snow Dragon. Voyvodan smiled broadly and gestured, beckoning them as he summoned a table, covered in the finest white damask, and upon it three begemmed golden cups with matching saucers, and a truly hideous teapot, tall as a man's arm and wrapped in little fat winged figures, vines, roses, trumpet flowers, tiny birds dining on the nectar of those flowers, and stylized bees.

Raven looked at Cedric and Cedric at Raven; the two finally shrugged and approached the table, sitting as Voyvodan summoned delicate little silk-striped chairs and a quartet of silk-clad men, who played upon viols and flutes behind him. He gestured; the three cups were filled with a clear, fragrant tea. Raven's mouth watered: rose hip and citrus grass, he thought; one of his favorites. But he was thirsty anyway.

Cedric swallowed dryly: orange and spice, how had the dragon known what he liked best? And his mouth was so dry. . . .

Voyvodan chuckled softly. "Three cups, two of you — and only one of them safe."

"Safe?" Raven asked, as softly.

"The other two — well, I wonder," the dragon asked of no one, rather thoughtfully, "how long a man might writhe in pain from a truly dreadful poison, before a *friend* saw him from his agony?" Raven went so white, Cedric thought he might faint dead away. But the Druid squared his shoulders and said, "Why, no time at all. Did you not know the truest test of friendship?" Cedric closed his eyes; he would have wept, but there wasn't enough moisture in him for tears. "I will test the liquid," Raven added firmly. Cedric's eyes flew wide in alarm, and he would have denied the Druid, but Raven met his eyes, warning in them. "I am, after all, a Druid. If I cannot tell base liquid from good, why then, all my learning has been for naught, and I will be glad to die." The dragon glared at him, then shrugged and sat back. "How long have I to choose?" Raven asked, and he sounded quite calm.

"As long as you like — so long," Voyvodan added thoughtfully, "as I do not become bored waiting for your choice, of course."

"Of course," Raven echoed, and bent over the cups.

*Scent.* There were plenty of substances which held no scent and others that did, any of which could readily kill a man. He smelled nothing. That meant nothing. Color, then: but that was not as much help as it could have been, for each of the cups was not — quite — the color of the others. He glanced up, then sideways. Voyvodan was gazing into the sky, at the walls on each side, slewed to look at the musicians behind him. Cedric looked very, very tired.

Perhaps there was nothing for it but to set the cup and the liquid to his lips, and see if any of them numbed skin or had an odd taste. But some noise down the corridor was distracting the dragon, and Raven stared as a brown bird no longer than his thumb fluttered swiftly between him and Cedric, lit upon the center cup and took a drink from it. The bird sat back up, a bright eye met the Druid's with what he was suddenly sure was intelligence and meaning, and then it hopped once and flew quickly away.

*I stake my life upon what I have sought to learn all my days, and what a Druid is supposed to know — the ways of beasts and birds,* Raven thought rather grimly. As Voyvodan turned back and began to tap his nails against the tablecloth, Raven picked up the middle cup, inhaled warm steam, and took a sip. "Ahhh." He set it down again and smiled. "How very nice of you, sir. That is my favorite flavor, how did you know?" *No reaction at all,* he thought in sudden relief. His tongue and throat told him the same story, as did his stomach: there was nothing in the cup but water, heated and steeped in leaves, rose hips, and the tart grass that he loved so. He smiled and pushed the cup into Cedric's fingers. "Here, have some. It is wonderfully soothing." Cedric gazed at him anxiously. Raven nodded once, and the archer closed his eyes and drained the cup.

It was Raven's turn to watch closely now, but Cedric sighed happily, smiled and said, "How pleasant, the very best tea I know, spices and orange!" When he opened his eyes, and Raven turned to look, the dragon was gone. So were two of the cups and the entire quartet. The ugly teapot remained, now on a bare, rickety table, but when Raven stood to pour another cup of tea from it, there was only cold water within.

"Water is just as good," Cedric assured him. "Listen, though. Do you hear anything?"

"Hssst!" It was Gawaine, down in the tunnel with Lyrana and the twins; he was trying urgently to get their attention. "How did you know that was safe, Raven?" he asked

"Oh." *That bird might have been delirium, or my own imagination.* He wasn't going to bring it up unless someone else did; the last thing Cedric needed just now was to think his stout left shoulder was going mad. "Well — I did my best, with the knowledge all Druids have, of course. But — well. If I had guessed wrong, Cedric would have at least known one cup was the wrong one."

He flushed then, deeply touched as Cedric wrapped his arms around him. "My friend, I cannot repay you, ever."

"Nonsense," Raven said gruffly, and gave the archer a hard enough embrace to drive the air from him. "You have saved my life more than once, already. I but repaid a little of the favor." He leaned back; he could feel moisture in his eyes, and Cedric's were suspiciously wet. "All right?"

The archer nodded. "All right." He knelt to lay his fingers against the grate. Irene held hers against the other side of the wire, but it was so finely wrought neither could touch the other. "Gawaine, has the Bard made any progress?"

"Beyond what we know about the dragon's heart?"

"Toward finding it," Raven corrected him gently. His eyes were fixed on Iris's, and though it was hard to tell through so much mesh, he thought she was smiling.

"Not that I know of," Gawaine said. "We will let you know if he does."

"Yes, well," Cedric said with a deep sigh. "Tell him, if there is any way he can hasten things along a little — my friend and I here would greatly appreciate that."

"Well." Gawaine shifted from foot to foot uncomfortably. What could he possibly say to these two, situated as they were? Particularly with the twins on either side of him, both with their hearts in their eyes?

"We shall tell him," Lyrana said calmly. "And do all we can to help him and you, of course." She squeezed the bardling's fingers to get his attention and indicated the corridor with a jerk of her head. Gawaine followed her, leaving the twins in the tunnel and the two fighting men above. He glanced back only once; the whole situation threatened to break his heart and freeze his thoughts in a sea of misery — he would be no use to anyone if he could not *think*. "Though," he whispered so quietly even Lyrana could not hear him, "even if I could think, who is to say it will help?"

There was no sign of the Bard, either in the throne room or in the chamber with the fireplace.

Naitachal lay at full length on his back on one of the beds in the next room, eyes fixed unseeing on the distant ceiling, and he thought furiously. "So far as I can tell, the songs are not working," he mumbled to himself. "Though it is too early to be certain. But it is such a roundabout method for conquering the creature, and time grows so short, and all seems to depend upon what I do here. . . ." He sighed, let his eyes close. *I could yoke him to my will. In my old life, I knew a myriad of spells which would control a mere dragon, even one of vast size. I could take hold of him, force him to release those hapless young women, my bardling, all the others. I could . . .*

He sighed again and tried to think of something else. Anything else. It wasn't working. "It is a good thing the boy isn't here," he muttered, "to see how near the surface the old way still is. If it causes me dismay, what would it do to an innocent like Gawaine?"

He gazed up at the ceiling for a very long time. Finally, he sat up. "Yes, I could do it. I *think* I could do it. Provided I could come up with a certain salve, another certain paste. a bottle of — yes, well, that is the whole rub, isn't it?" *A dead body, or several dead bodies — or one which the Necromancer kills himself — to create the bottle of liquid, to seal the spell.* "Whom should I kill, then? Even in the old days, when I saw no other way of life for myself, I never did *that*." It might even have been the one thing that let him break free from a life ordained to him by his people since birth. "And once I begin, well, where would it end? Besides — " He considered for a while, turning down fingers one at a time, and finally laughed sourly. "Not even that wretched Paladin! Worthless as I find him, he finds worth in himself. How could I do it?"

*Keep at the songs,* he told himself firmly. *And — hurry it up.* He grinned suddenly. "Yes. And the next impossible thing before breakfast?" That reminded him: He hadn't touched the excellent breakfast the dragon's men had brought him. The bread was probably stale, but there had been a wonderfully ripe peach.

# Chapter XXIII

Gawaine didn't sleep very well that night — the room seemed too stuffy, the mattress lumpy. He knew that was nothing to keep a man awake, though, not after as much distance as he'd covered up and down those tunnels and all about the Snow Dragon's maze these past days. He was deeply worried: about Lyrana, about Cedric and Raven, and about the twins, who were becoming increasingly attached to both men. *But there is so much danger in that maze, how can it possibly be they will live long enough for Master Naitachal to save them?* Save all of them. He was not worried for himself, of all of them the only safe one. But Wulfgar and Tem-Telek . . . All of the young women, Lyrana's companions, who had done nothing to warrant their present placing.

At first light, Lyrana brought him tea and cakes as she always did — and a message. "Wulfgar and Tem-Telek finally had to deliver the ship bottle very late last night. Voyvodan was *not* pleased. And he has set them another task, one in which I fear the mice will be no aid." Gawaine stuffed a cake in his mouth, swallowed a little tea to wash it down, and staggered to his feet.

"We had better go, then," he said. Lyrana gazed at him anxiously.

"You are becoming worn, did you sleep at all?"

He might have said the same thing of her, he thought uncomfortably. Lyrana looked wan and edgy, compared to when he fell over her wall. Then, she was nowhere near as drawn-appearing as the twins. He was not certain either of *them* had slept in days. But he could not send Lyrana away; even if he had wanted her to go, she would not leave. *It is my life, too*, she had said vigorously, and thereafter refused to discuss the matter at all. Irene and Iris very much felt the same, and would not be moved for considerations of their own safety. "If we do one small thing in all this time to save either of those poor brave men," Irene had added, "then it is worth all."

"I will not leave Raven in any event," Iris had said.

Gawaine shook his head to clear all such gloomy thoughts, and ran fingers through his hair. Lyrana gave him one more worried look, then shrugged and led the way.

She took another branch just before they got to the workroom where the dwarf and lizardman had toiled so many days. "They were moved to another chamber, one the dragon could reach himself, for near the main gates and large courtyard, the corridors are large enough for him to walk in his man shape."

She halted at a grate; Gawaine came to look. This set of bars was set a little above floor level. Both his companions were up to their ankles in glittering saw-dust that filled the entire room, and even the corridor was fragrant with the smell of cedar chips. He could see Tem-Telek, who looked upset enough for it to clearly show on his normally expressionless face. "The mice cannot help us, Gawaine cannot help us — what shall we do? Uh — Master," the lizardman added hastily. "Separate this stuff from the gold, or we die, and I doubt that creature will give us very long!"

He stared then. Wulfgar had let his head fall back, and he was laughing heartily. "Oh, come, now! Master, I could free us from a trap like this with both eyes closed — yes, and asleep, too! Here," he added, with a return to his Master personna, "just you leave off wringing those great grubby hands of yours and find me a board, long enough to block that entry. Here, now, quit that fussing! I know, I know, you can't 'elp it, it's how you are, but all the same, you find that board, and set it across the doorway to block it. 'Ere, let me see. No, that's all right, the floor dips a bit just there, it's all we need. Go on, go on. And Gawaine," he raised his voice a little sharply, "if there should be any such being about, should quit the camp, as they say, and make certain he is nowhere that *water* might collect."

"Water?" Lyrana asked. Gawaine thought for a moment, nodded and tugged at her arm.

"Water. He is going to flood the chamber floor, I think. I have seen it done, when one of my old squire's men found garnet in the quarry: Pour water across two separate kinds of thing, and the heavy one will settle, the other float away."

"Ah! Of course!" She clapped her hands together once. "Sawdust is much lighter than gold, of course, but how clever of him to think of it, and under such pressure, too!" She peered doubtfully all around them, finally led the way down another tunnel and out into the open, where Irene and Iris sat huddled together rather miserably.

"There is another corridor just across there," Iris said, "where they are. But there are no more tunnels under here, only one small hole in the wall a little farther on, and the best we could do last night was to talk to them a little." She sighed and rested her head against her sister's shoulder. Irene patted her hair absently and finally tugged at her arm to get her attention. Iris sighed once more. "I know, we must go back a while to freshen up, and get some food and water, in case there is a chance to throw it over."

"You certainly had better freshen up," Lyrana said, eyeing both of them critically. "If Voyvodan saw either of you now, you would be no use at all to your men. He would have you washed and eat you at once," she added flatly, and Gawaine winced. But the brutal approach worked: Iris scrambled to her feet, helped her sister up, and with only the least longing look at the wall, they hurried away.

Lyrana and Gawaine stood listening: sounds of battle, men shouting angrily or in pain, an occasional shrill scream, but over all, Cedric's strong, calm voice and now and again, Raven's equally relaxed reply. Neither of the listeners could make out anything the two men actually were saying to each other, or to those they fought, and Gawaine finally shook his head and let Lyrana lead him over to the crack in the wall the twins had mentioned. Fortunately, she knew this area better than he, even if not very well. He might have been an hour or more locating the space. If he pressed against it and stood a little off-side, though, he could see a very narrow edge of the fighting on the other side.

Cedric looked particularly haggard as he turned now and again to fire an arrow into their pursuers; Raven's face was expressionless, but there seemed to be little he could do just now with his own talents to aid them. He had a belt of throwing knives and a bow of his own, shorter than Cedric's, with a pack of gleaned and wildly mismatched arrows. He was not very good with any of them at any distance; only so-so when one of the pack broke free to come close. Just the fact of his having weapons helped keep the enemy from blindsiding Cedric, though.

Gawaine moved a little, went on tiptoe and then down into a squat at the crack, until he had a sense of the terraine in there. *Dear lords of light, they will never win free of that!* Voyvodan had set them a course like nothing he had ever seen: pipes to run through, inclines to run up, ropes to swing across or go over hand over hand, rope ladders to climb . . . and behind them, well ahead of the pack, four hulking brutes who were astonishingly nimble for the size of them.

By the cheerful-sounding chatter Cedric was tossing one way and Raven the other, he gathered Voyvodan had intended that one leave the other behind as brute-bait. But the two men were taking care of each other, cooperating in getting one other over the awful barriers or watching each other's backs and flanks. As the bardling watched anxiously, Cedric clambered deftly to the top of a flat, narrow wall that ran taller than he and side to side across the tunnel, kept a drawn bow and a keen eye on the four brutes until Raven managed to pull himself up by the rope that hung down the middle of the wall. Raven caught his breath, pulled the rope loose, and dumped it down the back side of the wall. He grinned at Cedric, who grinned back and gave the muscle-bound quartet a very gallant bow before he and the Druid jumped down from the wall and vanished.

Gawaine drew a deep breath, leaned briefly against the gap, and finally shook himself. "Well, they made it out of that section."

"The dragon will not be pleased," Lyrana said unhappily.

"No." *Not at all pleased*, Gawaine knew. The two were still alive, but Voyvodan was certainly going to step up the odds once more. "Come, we'd better get you back."

When they returned to the grate leading into the gold and sawdust room, there were puddles and pools of water everywhere on the tunnel floor, and water dripped from the metal bars; inside, Wulfgar was rubbing his hands together and chuckling, while his so-called apprentice used a scoop to gather up the gold. "All so simple," the dwarf said, "if one knows that gold is heavier than nearly anything else. I merely dammed the doorway, appropriated some piping from the hallway, and used it to flood the chamber. Sawdust floats, gold sinks — and so it goes, eh?"

"Yes, Master," Tem-Telek said, broadly fawning as always, but Gawaine thought there was respect in the words this time.

They stopped to check on *his* Master. Naitachal was pacing before the hearth, mumbling to himself, sorting out rhymes for yet more verses, and it was an indication of his mental state that he welcomed the interruption to the creative process. He didn't look very good, either; the bardling had never seen him so thin, gray-faced and harassed. But he dredged up a genuine smile as Lyrana hissed a greeting. "Ah, well, what news for me, Gawaine? And good morning to you, Miss Lyrana." He listened, sighed when Gawaine finished telling him about the gladiators, grinned briefly over Wulfgar's success, frowned a little at the bardling's description of the twins. "Not good. They had better take a while for some rest, or they will be less than no use to Cedric and Raven."

"They know," Lyrana sounded resigned. "I told them."

"Yes. Well, remind them that if they join irreversibly with that Snow Dragon, flesh to flesh as it were, it will probably be the end of their beloved men, because they'll both give up."

"I hadn't thought of that," Lyrana said, and nodded once. "Yes, that should convince them to hold back for an afternoon."

"Sleep," Naitachal urged softly. "Or at least rest; decent food, a glass of wine, some time before the mirror, clean clothing and re-dressed hair. Certainly their young men will appreciate the effort also, won't they?"

"If they come again to a place where they can *see* the twins," Gawaine put in doubtfully.

"Oh, bother that, they will hear the difference in the girls' voices. I might suggest," Naitachal added mildly, "that you yourself could use a little such care, my dear Lyrana. I think my apprentice would be a trifle displeased if something untoward happened to you. Such as winding up a Snow Dragon's — "

"Yes," Lyrana said quickly. "I do see your point, Sir Bard."

"Good. Do not forget it once you leave me, please. However" — he shook himself — "have you thought of any more verses for this wretched song?"

"We came up with another lot last night. Here." Gawaine pushed a thinly rolled strip of paper through the grate. Naitachal unfurled it, letting the end drag on the floor as he read the first lines. He chuckled, shook his head, read a little further and laughed some more. "He hasn't tired of it yet?" Gawaine asked, and he sounded more than a little astonished.

The Bard snorted. "Do you realize 'The Shepherd, The Shepherdess and Count Emerald' now has nearly twice as many verses as 'Beatrice and the Manticore'?"

"Good lord and great Powers," Gawaine replied devoutly.

"Well may you say," Naitachal replied testily. "It is working, the throne room is only half as full of *things* and *stuff* as it was, but it is still such a welter of material possessions as to make a devout priest with vows of impoverishment out of the most hardened. I have to work as hard at keeping my temper these days as I do at creating more song."

"Yes, sir. But there is one other good thing: The

dragon is enough under your spell that he no longer becomes bored and sends you away — and he hasn't put you under a silence spell since that first time, has he?"

"No. I almost wish he would," Naitachal said gloomily. "I know, I know, wouldn't do, would it? We're running out of time, apprentice. If you have any time to spare from writing verses, you might think of a god to pray to. Besides Arturis's."

"I — ah, yes. Well. You know, I think Fenix is the one helping us — you know, the mice and the linnets, all that. Maybe she can do more, maybe she — "

"Talk to her, if you can, Gawaine. Though I do fear it's less a matter that she doesn't want to help more, or that ordinarily she could not. The dragon has her power blocked by his own, some spell of his own. And the only way to break such a spell . . ." He paused expectantly. Gawaine sighed and the two finished, in chorus, ". . . is by killing the dragon."

"I'll talk to her anyway, Master."

"Do that. I had better ready myself; Voyvodan ordinarily sends for me about now. You take that young woman back to her courtyard and see she gets something to eat. There is no point in having her so thin she could slip through these bars, is there?"

"No point," Lyrana said before Gawaine could think of anything to say. "We'll return, later."

"Yes." Naitachal sighed and turned his eyes back to the long strip of paper. "You do that. You know where I will be." As they turned away, they could hear him chuckling at something else one of them had written.

But when he heard the last sounds of their footsteps, Naitachal turned away from the grate, let the sheet drop to the table, and his face went very grim. "There are spells," he whispered to himself. "Spells to cause disease, any of which just might eliminate

Voyvodan. Or perhaps those which set deadly accidents in the path of an enemy, and it may be one of *those* would at least distract a Snow Dragon long enough for me to free that Fenix. And any of five separate spells I can think of, just off the top of my head, right now — any of those might kill him and free the Fenix. And us."

Yes. Oh, yes. He sipped a cup of now cold soup gloomily. Just kill someone else. Someone he knew. *And whom shall I choose? Gawaine? His beloved? One of those poor girls who follow Raven and Cedric and have worried themselves to threads over the two? Wulfgar? Or Tem-Telek, who is after all "only" a lizardman?*

As well decide to somehow reconstitute Arturis and use *him*; there was no "only" to Tem-Telek, whose sense of humor was so like his own. Or Wulfgar, who was clever as a cageful of monkeys and who was as much a pleasure in company as Raven — or as skilled in his own way as Cedric. Naitachal groaned and let his head fall into his hands. *Keep at it. At least, you have not yet run out of notions for verses to that horrid song; and Gawaine is truly coming into his own at last, now that lives depend upon what he does. Who would have thought of such a thing to focus his attention? And the dragon is still interested. . . .*

He brought his head up as someone tapped at the door. A servant stood there. "Master Bard, the Great One would see you. He wishes to know if you have remembered more of your wonderfully funny song — and if you will sing it to him."

The Bard brought up a smile from somewhere, got to his feet and gathered up his lute. "Sing — why, what would give me greater pleasure?"

When he arrived in the throne room, he blinked and stopped dead in his tracks. He could now see all the way from the double doors to the throne, and there was clear floor all the way to the windows, most of the way from doors to throne; on the right side, he could see a goodly stretch of open flooring. The dreadful fountain was nowhere in sight.

There was still enough costly and rare stuff in here to pay the salaries of all the King's troops for the next thousand years. Naitachal sighed, squared his shoulders, and walked down the long — now very plain — carpet to the throne.

## Chapter XXIV

Gawaine would have left Lyrana right at the end of the gravel path, but she would not let him go, instead leading him over to the pavilion where he had first hidden. "Ariana, I must go freshen up. Has Voyvodan sent any message?"

The girl shook her head. "You know he has not, you were here last night. It is nearly time for tea and sandwiches, Gawaine, surely you will stay and eat with us? It seems quite a long time since *most* of us have seen you."

He hadn't eaten much the night before, and the very thought of food reminded him how little of his breakfast he had: two deep swallows of tea, one very small iced cake. Besides — it really wasn't fair to the rest of these poor bored young women to only spend his time with one, however much that one meant to him above and beyond the rest. He nodded. Lyrana squeezed his fingers and left him, returning a short while later with most of the other girls and the twins — who bore trays of sandwiches, more of the small cakes, a basket of ripe fruit and a plain, large silver pot and cups. Lyrana set a plate in front of Gawaine and began pointing out the variety of sandwiches, while Iris, who had changed from a dark blue to a very pale pink gown, and who had redone her hair in a high crown of plaits, began to pour tea into the row of cups.

Irene, who was passing the cups out, froze. The

fragile porcelain struck the step and shattered. "Oh, no!" she whispered in horror. "Oh — oh, look!" Ariana gazed over her shoulder and when Gawaine would have gotten up, she vigorously gestured him down again.

"It is Voyvodan! What shall we do?"

"Go on pouring tea," Lyrana said steadily, though she was even paler than normal and her eyes were huge. "Here, those of you sitting around, stand up, go and look. Create a barrier, for goodness sake!" A flurry of skirts. Gawaine sat alone at the table, gazing dumbly at the plain wooden surface — today, no one had brought a cloth, no place under there to hide. A tug at his hand roused him. "Up!" Lyrana hissed, and pointed. Above the table, in the very midst of the pavilion, was a trap door. "Hurry — no wait, let me, first!" She clambered onto a chair at the far end of the table, giving herself a clear view over the other girls' heads and also blocking any view into the middle of the little open-sided building. "Here he comes!" she added anxiously, but behind her she heard the extremely faint whisper of wood sliding against wood. She glanced quickly behind her — no sign of Gawaine then scrambled down as the Snow Dragon came across the lawn.

Gawaine, by putting his face against a gap in the latticework just under the roof, could see quite clearly and without much danger since one of the climbing roses was sprawled all over this side of the pavilion. He fought a sneeze, finally pinched his nose hard and breathed through his mouth. The floor of this little garret was thick with dust and pollen, and the rose was a very strong-scented one. He settled down cautiously, avoiding the scattered heaps of cups, teapots and plates, cloths, several balls, and a stack of badly warped racquets.

Voyvodan topped even Lyrana by two heads' worth, but he would have stood out anyway as the young women clustered around him and called out cheerful-sounding greetings. "Ah, well," he purred, turning to look at each of them, "it struck me all at once how long since I had seen you. Probably would not have thought of you at all for several more days, my dears, but my new Bard — wonderful man, I must send him to you sometime — well, he has been singing to me lately, quite a lot, and today he mentioned beautiful ladies, and do you know, it reminded me how I had been neglecting you." Gawaine stifled a groan and closed his eyes. That had been one of *his* verses, designed to start the dragon of thinking about divesting himself of his collection of girls. Mistake. "Let me see," Voyvodan went on. "How are you all doing? Stand still so I may look at you — here, spread out a little, can you not? I grow dizzy the way you all move about."

Girls stepped back a little and stood quite still as Voyvodan walked around each of them in turn, gazing earnestly into one fair face or another, muttering to himself now and again. At length he came to the twins and Lyrana, who stood together nearest the pavilion steps, and he frowned, then beckoned and put his face quite close to theirs. "How curious. It cannot be so long as that since I last saw you; surely you twins were fresh-faced babes the last time I came to visit and you, with all that lovely black hair — Lyrana, isn't it? — why, my dear, is that a *line* between your brows?"

The twins looked at each other in clear panic, but Lyrana cleared her throat, folded her hands behind her back and said softly, "It is just possible, sir. Though, really, it has not been terribly long since you were here last. There has just lately been — oh, I am not quite certain how to say — " She hesitated, and

Voyvodan tipped his head to one side. Lyrana shrugged rather helplessly.

"I see. You perhaps do not feel well? Or are you unhappy? Is the food not good, or the variety not as you would like it? The wine, perhaps?" He let his voice trail away.

"How kind of you," Lyrana exclaimed. "And how clearly you see things. In truth, we have not felt particularly well lately — at least, at first, I did not, and then the twins nursed me and I fear that they now feel worse than I did at first."

"Not sneezing? Fevered?"

"Oh, no, sir, nothing so dreadful as that. It is just — well, food has no taste to speak of, and wine gives me a horrid headache; my stomach is not taking food very well, and so I find I have not much appetite."

"Sleeping at all well? Too much?"

"Oh, no, sir. That is — I sleep very little, it seems, and when I do, I have such awful dreams! When I waken from them, I scarcely care to try to sleep once again."

"And you both have this same — difficulty?" Voyvodan asked the twins, who nodded in unison.

Iris nodded. "It is difficult for me to keep whatever I eat in place, even plain bread. My stomach is just upset all the time."

"My poor little ones," the Snow Dragon said, and patted first one and then the other on the back, quite gently. "How terrible. You should have sent at once to let me know you were unwell."

"But it seemed such a small thing, nothing to worry you about," Lyrana objected. "After all, we know full well how busy you must be, managing your affairs in order to keep us all in such fine estate."

"Ah, but," Voyvodan said smoothly, "I am not keeping *you* in fine estate, my dearest, if you are unwell.

Here, I shall order special delicacies sent to you from my own kitchen: sweet bread and candied violets, frosted grapes and a very finely prepared white fish, with even the tiniest bones already taken out for you. Will that help?"

Lyrana shrugged; the twins, Gawaine thought, were beyond speech. "We can but hope. It certainly does sound tasty — but," she waved a hand to take in the tea table and the sandwiches and cakes there, "so did that meal, and I find myself scarcely able to eat any of it."

The Snow Dragon mounted the two steps, bent over the table to examine the food and the teapot. "Well. This all looks fine, but you should have different teas, you three. I will have my physician prescribe healing teas which soothe distressed stomachs and others which let one sleep and keep nightmares at bay. And here," he added as he stepped back outside and cast a glance upward. Gawaine froze, closed his eyes tightly and waited for discovery and the end, but after a moment opened them again to find Voyvodan was peering into the distance and waving his hand. For the first time in as many days as the bardling could recall, the sun came out and cast hard-edged shadows from the pavilion to the grass. "You shall have sunlight and blue sky for the next several days, does that suit you?"

"Oh, yes, sir," all three girls answered in chorus.

"Good. Then I shall take my leave, there is much work to be seen to this day. But all of you, take care that you do not also become ill, and if anyone else does, send at once so that I may have you cared for. And you — twins and you, Lyrana — eat and drink the things I send, walk about in the sunlight and take very good care of yourselves. You must," he added meaningfully, "preserve your beauty."

"Of course, sir," Lyrana said respectfully. Voyvodan

walked all along the line of girls, giving each a close look. Then he turned and went back across the lawn and out the gates. The guards closed them tightly behind themselves.

"Oh, my. I think I really *will* be ill," Irene said quietly. Iris, who had buried her face in her sister's shoulder, seemed incapable of responding. Lyrana smiled faintly.

"Please don't be ill, we've come through for the moment." She glanced up at the top of the gazebo and nodded once. Gawaine was already on his way across the dusty floor and fumbling with the trap.

"I thought we were all three dead," Iris mumbled against Irene's shoulder. Irene patted her hair absently.

"So did I, sister. Fortunately, *one* of us was capable of thinking. Lyrana, how did you do that?"

"*Why* did you?" Gawaine asked as he came down the steps, brushing at his clothes.

"Well, if he had simply thought us, let us say, getting *old*," Lyrana said with a twist of her lips, "he might have decided to fetch replacements and — well, anyway. However, if he thinks us only a little unwell, and possibly contagious, he would be more likely to do what he did: try to get us well once more. He certainly isn't likely to eat us if we're sick." She spread her hands wide. "He really is quite lazy, you know. It is bound to be simpler for him to heal sick girls than go looking for new ones."

"You terrify me," Gawaine said simply. "I feared the worst."

"Well, so did I. It clarifies one's thinking to an amazing degree, though, staring death right in the face." Lyrana gave him a broad smile and took his hands. "It also gives one a fierce appetite. Let us go and see about those sandwiches."

Some hours later, she overrode Gawaine's objections and went back with him to look into the throne room. The Bard was just being escorted out, Voyvodan sat on his crystal throne, and servants were working furiously to shift goods from the chamber. Bardling and girl stared at each other in amazement; there was nothing left but bare walls, a few unfigured carpets, two stacks of chests, and one truly hideous carved sideboard holding a silver tea service in an extremely ornate pattern. "By my gruesome hair, it's working!" Gawaine breathed. Lyrana simply grinned and gestured toward the stairs with her head. They took them two at a time.

Naitachal was pacing the hearth, stopping now and again to gaze anxiously at the woodpile; his shoulders sagged when he heard the now familiar hiss. "We're very nearly there, apprentice."

"Fortunately," Gawaine replied grimly. He explained. Naitachal fetched a deep sigh.

"Yes. Time is running out, for all of us. But he asked that I return shortly. I got his leave to come back for a dish of soup and some bread. Get your mandolin, get yourselves to that grate, and hold yourself ready."

"Sir? What are you going to do?"

"Who knows?" the Bard replied gloomily. "But," he added and pushed aside his cloak; Gawaine could see the glint of metal there — one of the straps of knives, "whatever it comes out to be that I do, I will be ready for it." Gawaine nodded and the two ran off. Naitachal sighed again and added, very softly, "I hope." He thought back on what he'd just said to them and shook his head. "I have spent entirely too much time around that creature; my sentences don't scan any better than his anymore."

Gawaine stopped by moments later, rather out of breath, and in his hands he held a wonderful harp. "I brought this instead. Lyrana's waiting for the twins. She'll be a moment or so, and when she comes I want to go with her and warn Cedric and Raven what we are doing, if I can." Brief silence. "Um, Master? What are we doing?"

"Do you know your own words to this — dratted epic?" Naitachal asked. "All the ones you and that sweet black-haired child wrote? And — can you sing that with full Bardic power?" Gawaine shifted, and his face had gone so pale the freckles stood out clearly, even through the grate. Naitachal held up a hand. "Wait. Think instead. As though my life, and yours — and that of your young woman — depended upon it?" Gawaine gazed at him for a moment longer, finally nodded.

"I — I — they will. That's what you're saying, isn't it?"

"That they *may*. But anything less than what you are capable of, Gawaine — no. It will not do this time."

"Then — then I can." The bardling glanced behind him and added hurriedly, "They're here. I'll be back as quickly as I can, Master."

"Go, then." He spoke to thin air; Gawaine was already gone.

Raven and Cedric sat in the middle of a corridor, upon bare ground, serving as each other's rear-guard and as a prop. "My friend?" Raven said finally.

"My brother?" Cedric replied.

Raven smiled, though there was no one to see it. "Yes. My brother." The smile faded. "Time is running out for us."

"I know it." Cedric sighed. "At least we have had sleep, all thanks to you for freeing that tiger. I would never have done it."

"No. But I could not have protected us from those snakemen."

"And I would never have known which cup was the safe one to drink from."

Raven nodded. "Yes. But between us . . ."

"Yes. Between us. All the same, you are right, my brother. Time is running out rapidly."

"And not only for us," Raven said gravely. "The twins — they near twenty, you know."

"I know." Cedric sighed again. "Likely we will be dead long before they, all the same."

"Or perhaps we will all win free of this place," Raven said. "Do not discount the Bard, or that boy Gawaine."

"I forget them," Cedric replied simply. "It seems sometimes there never was a life when I was a master archer and won prizes and acclaim — "

"To think," Raven said softly when the archer's voice faded away, "that I once thought you a boaster, and one who wanted nothing but things to kill." He turned partway, and Cedric slewed partway around to look at him. "But it is often in this world that a man misunderstands his brother, as I did you."

They turned back to watch up and down the corridor. Cedric broke a long, tired silence. "Do you know what I will do when we all get out of here? I will take Irene, and together we will go in search of one of those wondrous northern bows the tales spoke of. Not magical, of course; what man would want such an unfair advantage?"

"Or need it, if he is you?" Raven murmured.

"Thank you, my brother. And when I find that bow, I will wed Irene, and win as much money as I can, as quickly as possible, so that we may found a school of archery — just a small one, but exclusive, so that the sons of counts and kings and earls will come, and I can afford such costly things as she deserves."

"Yes." Another long, exhausted silence. "Do you see anything that way?"

"No. Do you?"

"No. Have you any water?"

"A little — enough. Here." Cedric passed the bottle. He tensed then. "Did you hear something?"

Raven came partway around, listened intently, finally nodded. "It is Gawaine. Hist, lad! How goes it?"

"Dare I talk?" Gawaine asked, and when Raven reassured him, he passed on all his messages and added, "I think you are nearly free of this place, for I just found a small courtyard I have not seen since that first day across the walls."

"You are sure of this?" Cedric asked.

"Utterly certain," Gawaine replied. "Or I would never have said. You are within two corridors of the outermost wall, and freedom."

*Or whatever the Snow Dragon will throw at us there, if we get so far,* Raven thought, but he said only, "Good work, lad. And — Iris, how is she?"

"She and Irene are coming, as soon as they can get away with food and water. They both send their love, and Iris said to tell you that she knows you will find a way out very soon." A small silence, and when Gawaine spoke again, he sounded rather anxious. "You both seem so worn down. Are you going to be all right?"

"Of course," Cedric said.

"I am sorry, that was a fool's question."

"No, I took your meaning. We're still holding strong."

"And with the news you just brought us," Raven said, "I feel much better than I did."

"Well — good. I have to go. Good luck to both of you, and hold on as best you can."

Raven leaned against the wall and gazed at Cedric, who was leaning into one shoulder, gazing back at him. They listened to the bardling's receding footsteps.

Cedric finally straightened up, took back his water bottle and pointed. "We had better move on, I suppose. You know how Voyvodan is."

"Tosses *really* horrid things our way when we decide to rest," Raven agreed. "How he knows, every time, though . . ." He started forward. Cedric came up beside him, and they walked down the corridor together.

Somehow there was a bend ahead of them, where there had not been one before. Cedric hesitated, but Raven nodded him on. "I think I hear someone behind us, anyway; let us see if we can't set a trap for them."

"Let's," Cedric said. But as they rounded the corner, it became immediately clear the trap had already been set; and not by them.

Bodies littered the ground along both walls and lay thick everywhere between. Behind them, they could definitely hear something — lots of men or others — running toward the corner. "Go on, quickly!" Raven hissed. "This is no place for us!"

Too late. As Cedric ran light-footed between dead men, he slammed into an invisible barrier and fell flat, all the wind knocked from him. A resonant laugh rang from wall to wall. Raven, who had come to help his companion back to his feet, turned. Behind them were men — little men, fully a hundred of them, filling all the space between the walls, armored so nothing of them showed save the shape in leather and black metal, each armed to the teeth. Behind them, the Snow Dragon, who bared his teeth and laughed again. "You have entertained me well, for a goodly time," he said. "But you will never pass the barriers on this place — not on your feet," he added meaningfully, and vanished.

Cedric scrambled to his knees and jammed all the

arrows he could fit a hand around into the dirt before him, pulled out another and fit it to the string. "I fear he means it, Raven."

"I fear he does," the Druid said steadily. He was standing, bow strung and an arrow at the ready. He freed one hand to set it briefly on Cedric's shoulder. "It has been a very great pleasure to know you."

"Ah. And will continue to be," Cedric said. He laughed quietly. "Here, or in another place. If you survive this day, and I do not, give Irene my love."

"And the same for me. But I think we will live or die together."

"Quite likely. Here they come!" Cedric shouted, and loosed three arrows in quick succession. The three men at the fore fell, but others skirted them and came on. More died, and then more. Cedric laughed as their enemy paused. "All those bodies impede their progress!"

"More important, to my mind, they shoot no better than they do," Raven said.

"And so few are armed with bows," Cedric agreed. "To stretch the drama, no doubt    look out, here they come!"

Another fierce fight; the remaining small men withdrew, but could go no farther than the turn in the corridor. Another of Voyvodan's invisible barriers, no doubt. Cedric came up onto one knee and a foot, shot again; a man staggered away and fell, vanishing beyond the barrier. "Odd," Raven said. He was still standing and could see farther. "He went through."

"Dead or unconscious — perhaps that makes the difference," Cedric said. "Can you hold them a moment or so? I need more arrows, and I see at least one dead from here who has a quiver."

"Go," Raven said. He brought his string back, stood ready while the archer felt his way across the nearby bodies. He came up with three quivers, plenty of arrows from all around them, and then he gasped. "What is it?" Raven asked. "I dare not look."

"No, don't, I'm coming back." Cedric came running back, eyes wide and a bow held out before him. "Oh, you beauty," he whispered, and ran his hands over the smooth horn and wood surface. "You perfect, perfect beauty. If your string is only good — wait." He turned one of the quivers upside down, spilling arrows everywhere, felt in a pocket that covered the base, and brought out a coiled string. "I knew a northern man who kept his spares just there." He bent down to string the weapon, held it up again. Raven risked a glance: It seemed to him just another bow, much like the other Cedric had, save this was half again as long. But the archer's heart was in his eyes, and his color very high. "With this in my hand, I surely cannot lose the day. With this to rout the foe, my brother, we shall win free of this dread hole and the walls entirely."

Raven drew a ragged breath and spoke past a suddenly very tight throat. "So we shall. 'Ware, brother, they are coming once more!"

"So they are," Cedric replied calmly. "What is that? Oh, no, Raven, look!" He pointed. The Druid took his eyes from the approaching men to stare at the little bare patch of dirt Cedric indicated. A voice just touched his ear, "My brother, I am so sorry." And then, Cedric's hand came down across the back of his neck and he fell, stunned and, very briefly, unconscious. When he came to himself, the enemy was still working its way toward them through the piled bodies and discarded weapons.

Cedric knelt, back to him, bow up and arrow to the string. Raven staggered to his feet, dizzily fell forward. Into the barrier. It suddenly became horribly clear: Cedric had knocked him out to roll him past it. "No! Cedric, no!"

The archer turned to give him a quick, rueful smile before he went back to his watch. "One of us will live, my brother."

"No!" Raven cried. "How long do you think I will survive if you are not there to help me?"

"Long enough," Cedric replied softly. "I will not see my brother die. And it may be I can hold them off long enough for the Bard to do his work. If not — well, then, remember me, Raven." Raven swore and cried and beat on the barrier with his fists, but Cedric turned and smiled at him once more, and said, very softly, "Be still, you will distract me. Give Irene my love."

Raven beat on the barrier with his bow and, when that broke, with his bare fists. The enemy gave a great roar and suddenly leaped forward. A moment later, Cedric was surrounded, and then down.

# Chapter XXV

When the tap came on the door, Naitachal caught up his lute and said, "Come in, please," fully expecting Voyvodan's servants on the other side. His jaw dropped when it opened and Gawaine came in, followed by Lyrana. "Get out! At once!" the Bard hissed urgently. "If you are found here — !"

"If we are, so what?" Gawaine said flatly, and Naitachal stared at him, startled into silence. "We are all dead, is that it? But we are all dead anyway, why play at it, and draw it out as poor Cedric and Raven do? Have you seen Iris and Irene lately, Master? Voyvodan nearly had them for *lunch!*"

"I know it is bad," Naitachal began uncertainly, but he fell silent again as the bardling chopped a hand.

"It *is* bad. But what you intend — oh, Master, I saw what you carry, but you already know you cannot kill him. Not by manmade weaponry."

"I know that."

"Whatever you do — all right, say you find a way to get him to reveal his heart, and you throw one of those dreadful blades right through it and he dies of *that!*" Gawaine said. "What then?"

"Then he is dead," the Dark Elf said steadily, but his eyes fell before his apprentice's did.

"Yes," Gawaine said very softly. "And you, who are a Dark Elf and were a Necromancer, and who spent all these years in becoming a Bard and then wielding that

magic, in training me so I could in turn become a Bard
— you will chance falling back into that dark study and
that foul, dead and undead magic once more."

"And if I said that any cost to me was worth killing
Voyvodan?" Naitachal asked. Gawaine shook his head,
but Lyrana answered for them both.

"No. Because those like Gawaine who love you and
who live on to recall your memory daily — as those
who love you must — they will know what cost you
paid, and they will regret it every day that is left to
them. Because whatever cost you think to trade for
your own life is too great for them to bear. Can you not
understand that?"

Silence. The Bard looked from one to another of
them. They gazed levelly back. "No," he said finally,
and sighed. "But I will give over my plan, and perhaps
I will live long enough to learn the meaning of your
words. Will that satisfy you?"

"Well enough," Lyrana said. "Gawaine, tell him
what we decided."

A little more reluctantly, Gawaine spoke, but as
Naitachal's face cleared and he began to show enthusi-
asm for the plan, the bardling took heart. "If you will
at least let us try, sir," he finished.

Naitachal gazed at him for a long moment, finally
nodded, and closed the distance between them to
clasp his apprentice's arm. "Yes. All right."

"After all, sir," Gawaine added with a rather
abashed grin, "you will still have your knives, if I fail."

"Yes." Naitachal actually winked at him, rather
gravely. There was a tap at the door, and he squared
his shoulders and said, "Yes?" A servant stood in the
widely open doorway. Naitachal ignored the two pairs
of feet just behind the slab of carven oak and repeated
himself: "Yes?"

"Sir, Voyvodan would see you now, if you are pleased."

"Pleased. I think," Naitachal said thoughtfully, "that he has never chosen his words better. Lead on, my man. I will follow." The servant led the way down the corridor. The Bard came on behind him, conscious of light footsteps behind them both.

The man would have held the door for him and waited outside, but Naitachal bowed him in. "Please. Here, carry my harp, my shoes are so smooth-soled these days, and the floors so slippery between here and the throne, if I drop that, we are probably both dead." The servant blanched, took the proffered instrument, and led the way down the now rugless marble floor, past windows where no draperies now hung. Past a circle on the floor where the fountain had been, and then past the hideous sideboard, which had been cleared of its display of atrocious silver service but which was too heavy for any less than ten servants and a hand-cart to shift. Naitachal stopped and clapped his hands together, as though in astonished amazement and praise of the newly barren chamber — in reality to both search for any remaining items in the throne room (besides anything that might be hidden inside that dreadful teak cabinet, which would be Gawaine's and Lyrana's problem, not his) and to give those two a chance to sneak up behind him and take shelter behind that sideboard. *Providence*, he thought fervently, *what a lovely provider of small miracles, to clear an entire room of a world's wealth and leave behind one small barrier.*

He had no more time for thought. Voyvodan sat at the very edge of his chair, nails of both hands tapping the crystal. The Bard glanced at the box suspended in clear stone above the Snow Dragon's head. *And I once thought that was his heart. Little chance, caught in stone as it is. I simply hope Gawaine has no designs on it. The gods would not take it well, that a green boy*

*chose to bypass a life's experience and simply steal the
one great Answer.* He turned his eyes away from that,
then, as well. No point in letting Voyvodan know the
thing was there, if he had forgotten it.

"How wonderful this is, sir," he breathed softly.
"And how fair!"

"Yes," Voyvodan agreed, rather smugly. "Soon I shall go
in search of a shepherd's crook, and many sheep to keep
here with me." *Oops,* Naitachal thought. "Meantime,
have you anything else to sing for me?"

"Well, if you really do not want any more of the last
song?" Naitachal asked, rather suggestively, and held
his breath. He wasn't certain he could recall any of
those new verses, and he'd left the sheet behind in his
astonishment at the change in Gawaine. To his relief,
Voyvodan shook his head.

"Oh, no. I think we have had enough of *that*, don't
you? Something else, to celebrate this new simplicity.
You choose, my Dark Elf Bard, and if I do not like
what I hear — why, I shall ask you to sing another," he
finished with a broad, toothy smile.

"Ah. Good. I am so glad to hear that," Naitachal
said, and ran his fingers across his lute. "This is a
rather simple song, even for Your Greatness's new
style of life, perhaps — however!" he added hastily as
the Snow Dragon glared him down, and began to sing
the lullaby Gawaine had used to close his performance
at the Moonstone what seemed a lifetime ago.

After two verses, Voyvodan's eyelids began to flutter,
and after a third, he stifled a truly terrifying yawn against
the inadequate back of his hand. After a fourth, Gawaine
began to sing with his Master, and at the fifth, Naitachal
stepped back to let the bardling come up behind him with
the harp. Voyvodan's eyes fluttered again, and closed. His
chin sank to his breast, and with one deep, shuddering
breath, he seemed to sleep.

"What now, apprentice?" Naitachal demanded in an urgent whisper. Gawaine shook his head, glanced meaningfully at the throne where the Snow Dragon was stirring once more.

"Help me sing this child to rest," he warbled, and Naitachal dutifully picked up his lute and sang on.

It was no good; they could put him deeply to sleep — but not for very long. They could keep him snoring on that throne only so long as both were able to sing and play. No longer. Naitachal glanced at his bardling, cast his eyes upward, and then froze and nudged him, hard. Gawaine scowled, but looked where Naitachal was looking: High above them, in the space which had been a vault between two truly gruesomely ornate candelabras, there hung a brilliantly decorated, gilt egg. The bardling never missed a note, to his credit, but he looked a question at the other. Naitachal nodded energetically, then shrugged as much as to say, *All right, what's next?*

Gawaine ran an extra line of riff, and then a second, and then, with one wary eye to the throne, a very long and complicated run. Voyvodan slumbered on. Suddenly, he broke into song again, and this time, the words were some Naitachal had never heard from the boy before — and there was full, hair-hackling, power-strong Bardic strength behind them. "Oh Bird of Fire, upon the wind, who flies to her home, and aids her friend, who brings to the world the warmth of flame, and melts the frost, and ends the game." He paused once more, then sang other words, but Naitachal could not evermore recall what they were, for through one of the tall windows came an enormous, flame-colored bird, and as the bardling strummed and sang, she flew about the chamber three times and then directly to the gilt egg suspended from the ceiling.

Naitachal roused himself and began to play; at least

he could provide counterpart for the lad's magic, he thought, but with one elbow he managed to shove his cloak aside, freeing the strap of daggers — just in case.

Fenix had the egg, a series of yellow strings caught in her beak, and now she was trying to use those powerful, long wings to slow her descent, but she could clearly not decide which way to go. The Bard nudged his apprentice. Gawaine nodded vigorously, but after a moment's strumming shook his head and shrugged.

Just long enough, Naitachal thought happily, and he took up the lullaby: "The bird of flame brings dreams and alone, she sets a pillow beneath the throne." *It wasn't going to work*, he thought anxiously, but Fenix fluttered down to the floor, tugged mightily, and finally managed to slide the egg beneath the footstool at the Snow Dragon's very feet. "The bird of flame," Naitachal sang quickly, "flies far away, but holds close, lest she alone may save the day."

"Doesn't scan," Gawaine mumbled under his breath.

"Doesn't matter, if it works," Naitachal sang softly, and watched as Fenix flew up to the ceiling, where she circled. He added in song, "The sky falls," and finished the line with a truly horrid crash of strings.

Voyvodan shook himself; he had, perhaps unfortunately, let his head fall back so the first thing he saw was a barren ceiling, with only three golden threads swaying in the breeze wrought by a flame-colored bird. He let out a roar and leaped to his feet. Naitachal turned and fled straight down the room, hoping the young people would have the sense to hide behind the sideboard. *At least I can draw the dragon off,* he told himself. But there was such a horrid crash, the Bard spun around and gaped.

The dragon stared at the pile of kindling that had been a footstool and at the silvery fog coming from under it. "Ah, no," he said, very softly, and fell over, dead.

"The scroll!" Gawaine shouted, but Lyrana had his arm and was tugging furiously.

"Leave it or you will die!" she shouted in turn, "and so will your Master and so shall I, for I refuse to leave you!" That caught him. With a groan and then a low curse, Gawaine turned from the throne and pulled Lyrana toward the doors. Windows shattered; he let go of Lyrana to grab Naitachal's right arm, and she somehow caught hold of his left in both hers. Between them, they hauled him outside as the ceiling groaned and fell, and the walls began to collapse inwards. Somehow, moments later, they stood out in the court-yard, shivering a little in the bleak sunlight, and stared blankly as the spire simply melted, the walls of the pal-ace vanished into a fog, and the white walls all around them began to melt and fade. A little while later, there was nothing around them but a barren meadow of sere grass dotted here and there with stone statues, a very few low white brick walls and the little palace that belonged to the girls.

Gawaine picked his way through the rubble, Lyrana right behind him, in what he prayed was the proper direction. Too late. He slowed uncertainly, then stepped over the brow of a very low hill to find Raven seated upon the ground, head bowed, and resting against his breast Cedric, pierced by many arrows and bleeding from many wounds. "We won," Cedric whispered.

"Of course we did," Raven said, and there were tears in his voice. "Did you ever doubt we would?"

"Give — Irene my love," Cedric whispered and coughed harshly.

"She is coming, I see her now," Lyrana murmured. But Cedric coughed one last time, just a little, and quietly died. Raven bent his head low and wept.

Gawaine stood and motioned the twins on — they would know eventually, better they know now, he thought, but he turned away from them before he must speak, knowing he could not. Lyrana gripped his hand and let it go, and stayed to comfort her friends.

Back in the courtyard, Naitachal sat cross-legged now, talking to a slender woman with astonishing hair the color of a bonfire, and eyes of the deepest, purest green. "I fear I can give you no other thanks," she was saying as Gawaine came near, "than to give you the power to free these who were caught by the dragon's power, and now need not be so." She bent to take his shoulders between long-fingered pale hands and spoke against his ear. "That is — that's all?" the Bard asked in wonder.

"Do not the most arduous spells sometimes prove to be the most simple?" the Fenix asked him, and without further comment she bent her knees a little, sprang into the sky, and was transformed once more into bird shape. "Farewell, for this time!" she cried out. "But not forever, my friends!"

"Farewell, fairest creature," Naitachal murmured in wonder, then shook himself as Gawaine knelt before him. "Here, hold out your hand," he ordered. Gawaine did; the Bard took it, let it go. Gawaine gazed at it blankly, for he had felt nothing, but Naitachal said, "I have just given you *her* power, to change any of these who are stone back to living. Touch them, it is done."

Somewhere along the line, Wulfgar and Tem-Telek wandered out of the rubble. Naitachal clasped hands with both of them and sent them out to transform stone to living beings, for there were many, many of these scattered all about the space that had been the dragon's courtyards and maze. At some point, Gawaine could not precisely recall, Raven joined them, the dead

Cedric borne in his arms, Iris at his side, and a distraught Irene following. But Raven, when he found out what they were about, set his friend and companion down and insisted for his part in the retrieval. "Cedric would not be angry that I saved other living beings, though I could not save him."

"Because he would not let you," Irene sobbed. She fell on her knees at the archer's side and began to compose his body, and Iris turned to aid and comfort her as best she could.

At length, they all stood in the very middle of what had been a great courtyard and only one statue remained: Arturis, frozen once more in heroic stance, this time with a newly bloomed daisy clutched in his upraised fist. "And what," Naitachal demanded softly, "shall we do with this?"

"If you say take it back with us," Wulfgar said, "I shall kick you all the way from here to Ilya's village."

"You speak for me, Wulfgar," Tem-Telek said.

"I cannot think what sort of fool you take me for," Naitachal began vigorously, but he was stopped midword by a hail. They turned as one to see a number of men, peasant-clad, coming down the steep trail and across the meadow, leading the horses that had been left outside the walls what seemed a lifetime before. Star snorted and Thunder whinnied a welcome. Naitachal folded his arms, stepped back and waited.

Ilya, his color very high indeed, gave him a faint smile and said, "How glad we all are to see you again! And will you be pleased to rest in our village for a while?"

"I had rather die," Gawaine said flatly before Naitachal could think of anything to say. The boy gaped at him. Gawaine gave him a scorching look and went back to rubbing Thunder's heavy gray neck.

"Me also," Wulfgar said.

"Do you know," Naitachal added softly, "what you

have done? All of you? Who not only let us go unwarned into this place but actually *brought* us here?"

Ilya lost his high coloring precipitously. "But we had no choice but to bring him people! He would have eaten me, and all my uncles and cousins — !"

"Yes. You could have warned folks that it was not — precisely — a safe place to go." Naitachal folded his arms and glared down at the boy, and then at the uncles flanking him when the men would have protested. Silence, except for the sound of one young woman weeping. "I shall tell you, though. I am willing to spare all your lives. If!" He held up a hand, and the boy and the uncles who were about to swarm him with back-slaps and praises fell silent once more, and gazed at him nervously. "If, you take a gift from us. In fact," he added rather mildly, "there is bound to be a young woman among you who will think him *quite* a gift." He gestured grandly. "Arturis."

"He is stone," Ilya said reprovingly. "Very much stone."

"He will not be when you get him," the Bard replied sternly. "And he is yours for life."

"But — such a great Paladin, he will not wish to remain with the likes of us!"

"Oh," Naitachal grinned, "do you know, I believe he will?" Silence again. The uncles and Ilya looked at each other very warily indeed, but finally nodded. "I trust you will keep in mind that you are about to be discovered by the outside world. Most of those who were here as statues are already gone — back to the south, or wherever they came from."

*Except that poor boy,* Gawaine thought, with a glance at the twins, and the boy who had come from their village after they had simply vanished. "She won't remember me, I don't think, sir," he had told the Bard.

"Not after so long, and so much grand living, and wealth and fine things. But — well, Irene's mother was so worried for her, and for Iris of course, but Irene's mother knew I had always meant to speak for her." He had gazed at the distant, weeping girl and sighed for her pain, and shaken his head then — a fine, handsome head, Gawaine thought judiciously, and not just a pretty one, but a sensible brain within it. "Poor sweet, how terribly she has suffered. But I shall see she is escorted safely to her mother — and the hero's body as well, if she would bury it in our grave-yard. And if Iris and the Druid her intended choose to stay a while with us, well, it is long indeed since we have had anyone to teach the children." *Perhaps*, Gawaine thought, and felt as though he saw everyone and everything with new eyes. There was something new in his breast, a core of power that bubbled all around his heart, that could surge out through his fingers when and if he chose, that could spill into the words he used to shape songs. *How very odd, after so many years of seeking, to suddenly find it, and not at all the one thing I thought I would find.* Truth: Truth was a thing of many parts, each coming at different moments to catch a man off-guard, he decided. Warm fingers squeezed his. *Case in point.* He sighed, deeply contented, and turned to Lyrana, who wrapped her arms around him. Her eyes were still red with weep-ing. But that was only right. Poor Cedric. More properly, he realized, pity those who still live and cared for him. Raven. Irene. Himself, though he had known the man for such a short time. *But I won't for-get him,* he told himself. He could already feel the words joining themselves, one to another. By the time he was finished, no one who heard his song would ever forget the beloved, great archer who was also a true friend.

He came back to the present once more. Naitachal had sent the villagers a distance away and was walking all around Arturis's statue, frowning at it and stroking his chin. Gawaine went to join him. "Master. What do you intend next?"

"Next?" The Bard shook himself. "Why — a return to civilized and warm lands, where onion is used *very* sparingly indeed in an occasional jar of pickle, where a Bard's fingers do not freeze upon the strings and the fret-board, and where there are White Elves in taverns such as the Moonstone to give a difficult time. But, you should no longer call me Master, you know."

"Oh, I know," Gawaine said calmly. "All the same, there are things you know I have not had time to learn, and if you have no objections, I would remain in your company a while to find them out — and to oversee your choice of a new apprentice."

"Ah." Naitachal laughed quietly. "And your very fine young woman?"

"Oh," Lyrana said easily. "Well, from all Gawaine has told me, you two have not lived a particularly ordinary life so far, nor have either of you been terribly good at practical matters. Now, I am certainly glad he has the sense to stay with you and learn the rest of what a Bard must know before he goes out to seek our fortune. And so long as he does remain with you, Bard, I think you will be quite glad of my company, for if ever there was a practical person, that person is Lyrana."

"Ah. Well, with such an offer before me, how can I refuse either of you — for now, at least?" Naitachal asked, suddenly quite cheerful. He turned back to glare at the statue, but Tem-Telek was now walking all around it, gazing thoughtfully at the stone Paladin. Finally he nodded and gestured to Wulfgar.

"I like your idea, my friend. Implement it, so please you."

They all turned to look as Wulfgar bent down and opened a very plain metal chest, set within it the largest boulder he could carry or fit within, closed the lid once more, and fastened it about with as many chains and locks as it would possibly carry. He stood and nodded. Tem-Telek reached out, lightly lifted the daisy from Arturis's fingers, and touched him.

The Paladin shook himself, shook his head, gazed around blankly. "You have done it, oh servant of the one God," Wulfgar said blandly. "The dragon is slain, the palace and all the maze destroyed — you have saved us all."

Arturis blinked at him for a very long moment and finally smiled. "Yes. Well, of course, I knew that I would conquer him eventually. Because, just listen, I will tell you in full how the God — "

"Yes, yes," Naitachal said hastily. "Well, it is not *entirely* over, for when you and your deity slew him, there was left over one small thing."

"Yes?" Arturis came down off his pedestal and frowned at the trunk.

"It is the Snow Dragon's power. Even the most powerful god cannot destroy it, and if any should realize what is in there, and seek to use it . . ." Naitachal gazed at the Paladin, mock horror widening his eyes. Gawaine closed his. *He acts no better than he did for those Slavers.* But Arturis was no more discerning an audience. He nodded vigorously.

"Why, we dare never let this anywhere near the southern lands!" He exclaimed. "And — why, yes, it is all coming clear. I see my task: I must stay here and guard it, and these ruins, and I must never fail in my vigil."

"No one but you could do it," Tem-Telek murmured.

"Yes, that is so," Arturis broke in, and doubtless he would have gone on for some time, but there was a tap on his shoulder. He turned to find Ilya looking at him anxiously.

"Sir, the Bard warns of people coming to raid these lands now Voyvodan is dead. Will you not stay and protect us with your great strength?" Arturis gazed at him, then at the trunk between his feet, and finally turned to nod. Ilya smiled and sighed with relief. "I am so very glad to hear it, and so will everyone be! There is a place for you and that chest, already prepared," he chattered on, and two of the uncles came to pick up the trunk and bear it before the bemused Paladin. "But just now, I think you must be hungry after so great a quest. We would all be so glad to hear of your adventures over dinner. My cousin Katya makes the best onion soup. . . ." The voices faded into the distance. Gawaine watched them onto their horses, onto mules and into wagons, watched them drive and ride away. He turned back to find Tem-Telek and Naitachal clinging to each other, laughing helplessly.

"Yes," he said firmly. "I am glad we are not done with each other yet, Master. Because there is something to be said about your sense of humor. . . ."

"Ah, stuff my sense of humor," Naitachal said and wiped his eyes. "Let us gather everyone together who is going with us, and begone. I think, Gawaine, there is surely some adventure or other awaiting us well to the south of *this* place."

"Adventure," Gawaine groaned, but he wrapped his fingers around Lyrana's, and they smiled at each other.